THE BEST EARLY STORIES OF F. SCOTT FITZGERALD

THE BEST EARLY STORIES OF F. SCOTT FITZGERALD

Edited and with an Introduction
by Bryant Mangum

Foreword by Roxana Robinson

THE MODERN LIBRARY
NEW YORK

2005 Modern Library Paperback Edition

Published in the United States by Modern Library, an imprint of The Random House Publishing Group, a division of Random House, Inc., New York.

LIBRARY OF CONGRESS CATALOGING-IN-PUBLICATION DATA
Fitzgerald, F. Scott (Francis Scott), 1896–1940.
[Short stories. Selections.]
The best early stories of F. Scott Fitzgerald/edited and with an introduction by Bryant Mangum.
p. cm.
Includes bibliographical references.
ISBN 0-8129-7477-8 (trade paper)
1. United States—Social life and customs—Fiction. I. Mangum, Bryant II. Title.

PS3511.I9A6 2005b
813'.52—dc22—2005043859

Printed in the United States of America

www.modernlibrary.com

4 6 8 9 7 5 3

F. Scott Fitzgerald

Francis Scott Key Fitzgerald was born on September 24, 1896, in St. Paul, Minnesota. Though both his parents were Irish Catholics they came from very different social backgrounds. His father, Edward, was descended from a long line of cultivated if impoverished Maryland gentry. His mother, née Mollie McQuillan, was the offspring of self-made immigrants who had prospered in the wholesale grocery business. When the child was two the family moved to upstate New York, where Edward Fitzgerald worked as a salesman for Procter and Gamble. In 1908 the Fitzgeralds returned to St. Paul, and twelve-year-old Scott enrolled in St. Paul Academy; later he attended the Newman School, a Catholic prep school in Hackensack, New Jersey. Handsome and ambitious, Fitzgerald was a precocious and self-centered youth who proved unpopular with his peers. "I didn't know till fifteen that there was anyone in the world except me, and it cost me *plenty,*" he recalled.

In 1913 Fitzgerald entered Princeton University. Although he never graduated, his college years were crucial to Fitzgerald's development as a writer. He formed friendships with classmates such as John Peale Bishop, an early literary mentor, and Edmund Wilson, who became his "intellectual conscience." He wrote lyrics for musical revues produced by the school's famous Triangle Club and contributed plays and short stories to *The Nassau Literary Magazine.*

In 1917 Fitzgerald left Princeton and joined the army, receiving an infantry commission as a second lieutenant. In 1918, while stationed near Montgomery, Alabama, he met a capricious Southern belle named Zelda Sayre at a country-club dance, and the two began a stormy courtship. All the while Fitzgerald worked feverishly on a first novel called *The Romantic Egotist,* subsequently retitled *This Side of Paradise.* "I know I'll wake some morning and find that the debutantes have made me famous overnight," he said in a letter to Edmund Wilson, adding, "I really believe that no one else could have written so searchingly the story of the youth of our generation."

Indeed, the appearance of *This Side of Paradise* in 1920 brought Fitzgerald instant success. The book established him as the prophet and golden boy of the newly dawned Jazz Age. *Flappers and Philosophers* (1920), a collection of short stories, immediately solidified his reputation. The same year he wed Zelda Sayre, who gave birth to a daughter, Scottie, eighteen months later. In 1922 Fitzgerald brought out another novel, *The Beautiful and Damned,* and a second volume of stories, *Tales of the Jazz Age.* The couple settled for a time on Long Island, and in 1924 they journeyed to France, where Fitzgerald wrote *The Great Gatsby* (1925). The Fitzgeralds quickly made friends with a number of expatriate Americans, including a then unknown writer named Ernest Hemingway, who became Fitzgerald's "artistic conscience." Though he published a third collection of stories, *All the Sad Young Men* (1926), the author's heavy drinking and destructive marriage took an increasing toll on his writing.

By 1930, when Zelda suffered a complete mental breakdown, the couple's extravagantly led life read like scenes from Fitzgerald's fiction. "Sometimes I don't know whether Zelda and I are real or whether we are characters in one of my novels," he confessed. Struggling against a mountain of debt, he wrote *Tender Is the Night* (1934) as well as scores of short stories, some of which were included in his final collection, *Taps at Reveille* (1935), before announcing his own "emotional bankruptcy" in a series of confessional essays, beginning with "The Crack-Up," which appeared in *Esquire* magazine. In 1937 Fitzgerald resettled in Los Angeles, where he had worked periodically as a screenwriter. He died there suddenly of a heart attack on December 21, 1940. *The Last Tycoon,* an unfinished novel about Hollywood, came out in 1941. Several works drawn from his unpublished papers appeared posthumously, notably *The Letters of F. Scott Fitzgerald* (1963), *Dear Scott/Dear Max* (1963), *As Ever, Scott Fitz—* (1972), *The Notebooks of F. Scott Fitzgerald* (1978), and *Correspondence of F. Scott Fitzgerald* (1980). Zelda died in a hospital fire on March 10, 1948.

"Fitzgerald lived in his great moments, and lived in them again when he reproduced their drama," observed critic Malcolm Cowley, "but he also stood apart from them and coldly reckoned their causes and consequences. That is his irony, and it is one of his distinguishing marks as a writer. He took part in the ritual orgies of his time, but he kept a secretly detached position.... Always he cultivated a double vision. In his novels and stories he was trying to intensify the glitter of life in the Princeton eating clubs, on the north shore of Long Island, in Hollywood, and on the Riviera; he surrounded his characters with a mist of admiration, and at the same time he kept driving the mist away.... It was as if all his fiction described a big dance to which he had taken, as he once wrote, the prettiest girl... and as if he stood at the same time outside the ballroom, a little Midwestern boy with his nose to the glass, wondering how much the tickets cost and who paid for the music."

Contents

THE BEST EARLY STORIES OF F. SCOTT FITZGERALD

Foreword

Roxana Robinson

What is more beautiful than the landscape of loss? What is more heartbreaking, more haunting, more romantic?

F. Scott Fitzgerald saw the world as a place of unbearable beauty and unlimited glamour. He saw it as illuminated by the glory of the natural landscape, by the glitter of the people, and by the perilous, irresistible pull of love. He was a romantic, and the greatest of his writing is charged with feeling and haunted by a longing for something irretrievable.

In these stories, written between 1919 and 1923, when he was in his early twenties, we see him setting out on the mountain of his experience, choosing the veins of ore he would begin to mine. We know—as he does not—which ones will peter out and vanish, and which will deepen to become the mother lodes of his work. He writes, of course, about his generation, and about their experience, and of his own. He writes of their rebellion; he writes about a beautiful and impetuous young woman who seems the soul of this rebellion. He writes about wealth; he writes about religion; he writes about class; he writes about the great divide between the North and South. Some of these themes will be part of the great work that lies ahead, and some are part of the great work in this collection. All of them are set against that wide, murmuring landscape of loss.

The rebellion of Fitzgerald's generation is shown through various means, and religion and the young woman both play a part in it. The young woman appears in almost all of these stories, and is, in her earliest incarnation, "The Flapper." Frivolous, saucy, and impetuous, she was an innovation, and utterly unlike her literary contemporaries. Ellen Olenska from *The Age of Innocence*, published in 1920, was also beautiful and high-spirited, but she was deeply respectful of society's rules, and suffered when these rules were broken. The Flapper flouted rules with impunity. She scorned chaperones, curfews, long skirts, maidenly virtue, and seemly behavior. Suddenly it was hard to tell a nice girl from the other kind.

Fast cars, rowdy drinking, wild dancing, and the bobbing of hair were all part of the roil of social revolution. It's hard now to imagine how shocking bobbed hair was, but at that time, a woman's hair was never cut. A young girl wore her hair down in braids until she was old enough to put it up. The heavy, majestic burden, pinned discreetly aloft, was a declaration of womanhood, holding the promise of hidden sexuality. A woman's hair was her crowning glory, and a source of pride. (When my great-grandmother had scarlet fever, the doctor ordered her to cut off her ankle-length locks. She refused, instead coiling her hair on the floor beneath her bed. Death, apparently, was preferable to shearing, though she survived.)

The wild women of the 1920s cared for none of this. They wore their hair short and swingy, with thick bangs and saucy spit curls, and they ignored the shock waves rippling through the ranks of stolid matrons. "Bernice Bobs Her Hair" is about many things—women's friendship, and social conventions, and ways in which a young woman might present herself to the world—but it's also about the social risk and private daring entailed in "bobbing."

Some of the Flappers are northern and some southern: the differences between the cultures were significant to Fitzgerald, whose father was from an old Maryland family. Fitzgerald was stationed in Alabama during the War, where he fell in love with the famously wild Zelda Sayre, of Montgomery. Zelda's incandescent personality illuminates many of Fitzgerald's women, though another important model for them was Ginevra King, a northerner, who was the object of an earlier, unrequited love. The North and South were potent presences in his work, and at times they nearly dominated the narrative.

Beautiful and hallucinatory, "The Ice Palace" tells of the southern girl Sally Carrol, who comes from a "languid paradise of dreamy skies and firefly evenings . . . [one of the] soft-voiced girls, who were brought up on memories instead of money." When she visits Harry, her fiancé, in Minnesota, Sally Carrol encounters a new world—a bleak frozen landscape dotted with isolated farmhouses and blanketed in snow.

Describing the South, Fitzgerald's tone is ironic and patronizing; he both articulates and disparages its easy charms. But when he turns to the North his tone becomes earnest, acquiring richness and authority: this may be the first emergence of Fitzgerald's mature voice. Powerful, dark, and intense, it is superb writing.

> There was no sky—only a dark, ominous tent that draped in the tops of the streets and was in reality a vast approaching army of snowflakes—while over it all, chilling away the comfort from the brown-and-green glow of lighted windows and muffling the steady trot of the horse pulling their sleigh, interminably washed the north wind. . . . She thought again of those isolated country houses that her train had passed, and of the life there the long winter through—the ceaseless glare through the windows, the crust forming on the soft drifts of snow, finally the slow, cheerless melting, and the harsh spring . . .

Visiting the Ice Palace, Sally Carrol becomes separated from Harry, and wanders alone through the black and chilling halls. In the deep silence she stumbles finally to a halt, overtaken by ecstatic terror. This is her introduction to the true nature of the North, which, she now understands, is beyond her—endless, ancient, and implacable. After her rescue, Sally Carrol flees to the easy life of the South, where the moment of fear and transcendence will never be repeated, and where such demands are not made upon the soul. The South is a pleasant place, but the North, Fitzgerald tells us, is one of dark magnificence. It is this sense of brooding nobility—as well as Fitzgerald's passionate, incantatory voice—that overshadows the human characters and dominates this story.

For all her unconventional ways, Zelda refused Fitzgerald, at first, on very conventional grounds: financial ones. The beautiful young women in Fitzgerald's work are often wealthy, or aspirants to wealth. Money held a deep and ambivalent fascination for the author, who had grown up poorer than his neighbors. In St. Paul, his family lived modestly among the very rich, and Fitzgerald went to school and college with their sons. He had seen the rich from very close, but always from below. Money played a powerful part in his world and in his writing, and its influence was something he explored, in ways increasingly subtle and complex.

In the light and frothy entertainment "The Offshore Pirate" wealth is seen as benign. The very rich are very benevolent here, and the consequences of wealth are happiness. The saucy Flapper, who stamps her foot and will not do as she's told, meets her match in a dashing young Lochinvar, and by the happy ending everyone is rich and in love. The counterpart to this romantic diversion is the dazzling satiric fantasy "The Diamond as Big as the Ritz." In this moral fable Fitzgerald both revels in the notion of great wealth and excoriates those who possess it. Here the rich are outrageously corrupt, stupefyingly wealthy, and utterly lacking in humanity. Everyone, including the narrator, is consumed by avarice: it is an extravaganza of dreadfulness. The height of depravity occurs when the host, in a moment of apocalyptic hubris, offers God a bribe. The ending is happy in that the monstrously swollen, overblown fantasy has exploded. Everything has been destroyed, everyone reduced to human proportions, flawed and struggling. This is a playful but savage attack on the influence of affluence, something which would continue to be the subject of Fitzgerald's scrutiny. He would use it as a kind of awful magnifier to focus on mankind's basest instincts.

Religion is at the core of the stories that bracket this collection, "Benediction" and "Absolution." Fitzgerald was raised a Catholic, and the Church was initially important in his work—a worldly Jesuit plays a significant part in *This Side of Paradise*—but the religious presence would fade. A powerful sense of its diminishment prevails in the masterly "Absolution."

Rudolph, a young boy from the working class, begins to neglect his religious obligations. His father discovers this and punishes him. The details of the beating, of the house, the narrow hallway, the timid mother, are all rendered with heart-stopping precision, but this is more than an intimate familial struggle. It is set against the larger backdrop of the mysteries of religious experience, with its combination of stricture and sensuality, ecstasy and abstraction. When Rudolph visits the priest at home to discuss his sins, little help is offered by this servant of the Church. The priest's mind is giving way. He can no longer withstand the insistence of the beautiful, irresistible world—of the body, of the senses, of another kind of ecstasy.

> Outside the window the blue sirocco trembled over the wheat, and girls with yellow hair walked sensuously along roads that bounded the fields, calling innocent, exciting things to the young men who were working in the lines between the grain. . . . For five hours now hot fertile life had burned in the afternoon. It would be night in three hours, and all along the land there would be these blonde Northern girls and the tall young men from the farms lying outside beside the wheat, under the moon.

This paean to the sensual, physical world could hardly be more vivid or heartfelt, nor could it offer a more absolute antithesis to the incoherent thicket of philosophical abstractions surrounding Rudolph. Religion seems here to lose its centrality and purpose, yielding to something more immediate, more tangible and more real.

But perhaps the most powerful and familiar aspect of the work represented in this collection is neither a character nor a subject but a state of mind. In the beautiful "Winter Dreams," Fitzgerald creates an elegiac realm which he will establish as his own: this is the landscape of loss.

Dexter, the protagonist, lies on a raft, in a lake, at night.

> There was a fish jumping and a star shining and the lights around the lake were gleaming. Over on a dark peninsula a piano was playing the songs of last summer . . . and because the sound of a piano over a stretch of water had always seemed beautiful to Dexter he lay perfectly quiet and listened.
>
> The tune the piano was playing at that moment had been gay and new five years before when Dexter was a sophomore at college. They had played it at a prom once and because he could not afford the luxury of proms in those days he had stood outside the gymnasium and listened. The sound of the tune and the splash of the fish jumping precipitated in him a sort of ecstasy and it was with that ecstasy he viewed what happened to him now. The ecstasy was a gorgeous appreciation. It was his sense that, for once, he was magnificently atune to life and that everything about him was radiating a brightness and a glamor he might never know again.

When Fitzgerald wrote this he was twenty-six, married to his adored Zelda and the father of a ten-month-old daughter. His first novel had received critical acclaim and commercial success. He was rich, beloved, and successful. Didn't the world lie easily within his grasp? Didn't he have every cause for jubilation?

Perhaps. But instead of jubilation, Fitzgerald's twenty-six-year-old voice is full of longing. The gorgeous moment, even as he celebrates it, is permeated by the sense that this ecstasy may be the last he will ever savor. The sense of loss, its mysterious potency and its presence, deep within the heart, provides a dark and steady undertow within Fitzgerald's work. His gaze was directed backward. It was as though he sat in a carriage watching life unrolling steadily behind him, receding, in all its beauty and complexity, into the blue distance; held up, as it was vanishing, to his musing scrutiny. His task was not to chronicle the splendor of what was to come, but to record the loveliness of what was gone.

Maybe all great fiction is about loss. Maybe the purpose of great fiction is to reveal the chasm that lies between ourselves and the exquisite vanished world that—we realize now—we so cherished. Certainly that is what the great fiction of F. Scott Fitzgerald does, and it does so with such elegance, such strength and tenderness and intimacy, that it seems as though each moment he creates is one that we have lived through. Each one strikes deep into us, reverberant and powerful and sobering, like the sound of a gong, recalling to us something we once knew.

—

ROXANA ROBINSON has written three story collections, *A Glimpse of Scarlet, Asking for Love,* and, most recently, *A Perfect Stranger.* She is also the author of three novels, *Summer Light, This Is My Daughter,* and *Sweetwater,* and a biography of Georgia O'Keeffe. She has received fellowships from the Guggenheim Foundation, the National Endowment for the Arts, and the MacDowell Colony. Robinson's fiction has appeared in *Best American Short Stories, The Atlantic, The New Yorker, Harper's, Daedalus,* and *Vogue.* She lives in New York City and Maine.

Introduction

Bryant Mangum

The stories in this collection come from a brief moment that F. Scott Fitzgerald would recall as the most thrilling and enchanted time of his life. In a retrospective essay, "Early Success," he describes an episode at the height of the Jazz Age—a time near the publication of *The Great Gatsby*—when he drove through the twilight on the French Riviera looking at the sea below and was, for an instant, reunited with a younger version of himself at the very beginning of his career. He went "back into the mind of the young man with cardboard soles who had walked the streets of New York" and relived those dreams from that earlier time "when the fulfilled future and the wistful past were mingled in a single gorgeous moment—when life was literally a dream."[1] That moment had begun in September 1919 when Maxwell Perkins, then a new editor at Charles Scribner's Sons, had written to tell Fitzgerald that his novel *This Side of Paradise* had been accepted for publication, news that was followed quickly in November by a letter from Harold Ober, assigned to market Fitzgerald's stories at the Paul Revere Reynolds agency, reporting that *The Saturday Evening Post* had bought his story "Head and Shoulders" for $400. In February 1920 the *Post* would publish "Head and Shoulders," and *This Side of Paradise* would appear on March 26. A few days later, on April 3, he would marry Zelda Sayre of Montgomery, Alabama, whom he had met in July 1918 and who had agreed to become his wife, at least partly on the strength of the promise of his now seemingly assured "early success." In the six-month period preceding the publication of *This Side of Paradise,* Fitzgerald wrote and sold eight stories, five of which appear in this volume; in its afterglow—those four years leading up to *The Great Gatsby*—he wrote and sold not only his second novel, *The Beautiful and Damned,* but eighteen more stories, four of which appear in this volume and all of which derive energy from Fitzgerald's wistful backward glance toward what he called the "all too short period"[2] when he and the young man roaming the streets of New York with cardboard soles were one. These ten stories, inspired by that time when life for Fitzgerald was literally a dream, are, as it turns out, not only the best early Fitzgerald stories; they are among the very best of the nearly 170 stories that he wrote during his entire professional career, 1920–40.

Seen through the lens of those dizzying events of the fall of 1919, Fitzgerald's entry into the profession of authorship seems effortless and painless, which of course it was not. After the Armistice Fitzgerald had returned to New York from Montgomery, where he had been stationed during the war, and took a job with the Barron Collier advertising agency, doing work that he later admitted detesting. In his spare time he continued to revise and submit the novel that would eventually become *This Side of Paradise,* as well as revising old undergraduate stories, but his submissions resulted in a disheartening stream of rejection slips. His one success, the sale of "Babes in the Woods" in 1919 to *The Smart Set,* depressed him because it brought only $30 and because it was an old undergraduate piece written two years earlier, a fact which, he said, made him feel that he "was on the down-grade at twenty-two."[3] In the midst of these personal crises and also during a time in America when events leading up to and away from the May Day riots had left his generation, as he said, "cynical rather than revolutionary,"[4] Zelda broke their engagement, and when Fitzgerald's frantic and unsuccessful trips from New York to Montgomery in the spring of 1919 failed to persuade her to change her mind, he concluded that he was "in love with a whirlwind and I must spin a net big enough to catch it out of my head."[5] When Zelda threw him over, he "went home [to St. Paul] and finished my novel."[6] Perkins's letter accepting *This Side of Paradise* arrived in mid-September 1919. Then, in just under six months, came a letter from Zelda that began, "Darling Heart, our fairy tale is almost ended, and we're going to marry and live happily ever afterward"[7]—the first two parts of which were in fact soon to come true.

Perkins's letter and finally Zelda's acceptance of Fitzgerald's proposal became bookends for the formative and most important period in Fitzgerald's development as a professional writer. In *F. Scott Fitzgerald's Ledger,* which contains a detailed diary and auto-bibliography that Fitzgerald kept religiously for most of his professional life, he wrote these words at the top of the page for 1919, his twenty-second year: "The most important year of life. Every emotion and my life work decided. Miserable and ecstatic but a great success."[8] Looking back from the vantage point of 1937, he would characterize the months leading up to September 1919 in more pragmatic terms: "While I waited for the novel to appear, the metamorphosis of amateur into professional began to take place—a sort of stitching together of your whole life into a pattern of work, so that the end of one job is automatically the beginning of another."[9] The earliest phase of his professional life, that two-year period from which the stories in this volume emerge, was a time when life, for Fitzgerald, was literally a dream; and the beauty of the stories comes from the conviction—not altogether different from Jay Gatsby's conviction just before he kissed Daisy and "wed his unutterable visions to her perishable breath"[10]—that, in the forty-one-year-old Fitzgerald's words about the twenty-two-year-old dreamer, "life is a romantic matter."[11]

It was on the solid rock or butterfly's wing, depending upon one's perspective, of this view that life is a romantic matter that Fitzgerald entered the profession of authorship in late September 1919. The first two stories he wrote after the acceptance of his novel, "Benediction" and "Head and Shoulders," show him confronting the central dilemma of professional authorship—the problem of how one who is a serious literary artist manages to earn his living through his writing. After the numerous rejection slips that he had received during the demoralizing spring and summer of 1919, one can imagine Fitzgerald's quandary as he pondered the direction to take in his story writing after the acceptance of his novel. In the end he followed an understandable impulse to return to his already published undergraduate fiction in search of a salvageable narrative, and he found it in "The Ordeal" (*The Nassau Literary Magazine,* 1915), a fictionalized version of a visit he had paid to his cousin Tom Delihant at the Jesuit monastery in Woodstock,

Maryland, during the Easter season of 1912. In the revision of this story into "Benediction," Fitzgerald transferred the moral conflict of the male protagonist in "The Ordeal" onto a female character, Lois, who is of the generation that Amory Blaine in the already-written-but-yet-to-be-published *This Side of Paradise* characterized as one "grown up to find all Gods dead, all wars fought, all faiths in man shaken."[12] Set free in the moral minefield of the dawning Jazz Age, Lois demonstrates as convincingly as any previous Fitzgerald character how a member of her generation begins to form a code for living in such a time; and her code, grounded in freedom and independence from traditional beliefs, will wind itself through these early stories, finally coming into its most lyrical expression in "Absolution"—the last story in this collection. With "Benediction," Fitzgerald seems literally to have discovered the principle of artistic detachment or aesthetic distance, a discovery that will lead in his most mature work to that often-cited quality that Malcolm Cowley labeled "double vision"—simply defined, the ability to participate emotionally in experience while, at the same time, retaining the ability to stand back and view it objectively. And while all good literary artists possess this kind of vision to a greater or lesser degree, great writers like Fitzgerald couple it with a lyrical quality that creates magic. Nowhere is this magic quite so evident as it is in *The Great Gatsby,* where it is expressed in the construction of the rational, if poetic, Nick Carraway, who observes and chronicles Jay Gatsby's romantic quest for Daisy Buchanan. Those looking for something approaching the earliest expression of Fitzgerald's double vision will find it in "Benediction."

As an ironic monument of sorts to his portrait of Lois, his earliest credible representation of the emerging new woman of the Roaring Twenties, *The Smart Set* paid $40 for "Benediction," prompting Fitzgerald from this moment forward to approach professional authorship from a different angle: he began, on the one hand, paying greater attention to the literary marketplace, specifically considering the kinds of stories slick magazines would be more likely to buy; and, on the other, he turned the marketing of his stories over to a literary agent, Paul Revere Reynolds, who quickly assigned the handling of Fitzgerald's work to Ober. The first manuscript that Fitzgerald sent the Reynolds agency was "Head and Shoulders," and the *Post* bought it for $400. Fitzgerald's letters to Ober in those weeks and months after his first sale of a story to a commercial magazine indicate Fitzgerald's awareness of the fact that he was now writing stories with an eye on what he hoped would become their eventual market—most often the *Post,* which had a circulation in the 1920s of 2,750,000.

The delightfully ingenious "Head and Shoulders" is Fitzgerald's first concerted effort to write for what he perceived to be the slick magazine audience, and though it is in some ways over the top and a dramatic departure from the seriousness of "Benediction," it contains the beautiful lyricism that lifts all of Fitzgerald's fiction above the level of the merely popular. There are also complexities beneath the surface of Marcia Meadow's charming into a marriage the stodgy and scholarly Horace Tarbox, complexities that draw power from Scott's projected anxieties about the potential danger of actually catching the whirlwind Zelda, with whom he was in love. In the course of writing "Head and Shoulders" with the popular magazine audience in mind, Fitzgerald managed to do something, the repercussions of which he could not possibly have envisioned: with Marcia Meadow—whose philosophy is caught in her line "'At's all life is. Just going round kissing people"—he introduced the large American magazine-reading public to the Fitzgerald flapper; and from the moment that *The Saturday Evening Post* arrived on newsstands and in mailboxes a week after St. Valentine's Day 1920, he became the creator of the flapper in fiction. American audiences and magazine editors began from that moment to ask for Fitzgerald's flapper stories by name. In the end, counting "Head and Shoulders," his first true flapper story, and his last, "Rags Martin-Jones and the Pr-nce of W-les" (*McCall's,* July 1924), Fitzgerald would write only ten of these stories—twelve if the boundaries of the genre are loosened slightly; and thirteen if one includes his resurrection of the Southern belle variation of the flapper-grown-older in his 1929 story "The Last of the Belles." It is largely on the strength of the dozen true flapper stories, and the ongoing commentary on the flapper as a figure in popular culture supplied by both Scott and Zelda in magazines and newspapers of the early 1920s, that the Fitzgerald flapper came to occupy a prominent—and seemingly permanent—space in the American psyche.

As Fitzgerald would later comment, "The Jazz Age had a wild youth and a heady middle age,"[13] and there is perhaps no better exhibit of its wild youth than the American flapper. Her outward flamboyance—her bobbed hair, her flapping galoshes, her rouged face, her short skirts—made her perhaps the most visible outward representation of the revolution in manners and morals of a postwar generation whose inward spirit was less festive, a spirit echoed in the phrase "lost generation." Fitzgerald, of course, did not invent the flapper, but he did invent the flapper in fiction, bringing her for the first time to the attention of the more than two and a half million readers of the middle-American mouthpiece, *The Saturday Evening Post.* The stories in this volume provide perhaps the best record that exists of the flapper in her first blush: "Benediction," "Head and Shoulders," "The Ice Palace," "Bernice Bobs Her Hair," "The Offshore Pirate," and "The Jelly-Bean."

At first Fitzgerald was taken aback by the enthusiastic response to his fictional depiction of the American flapper, recalling that when he received hundreds and hundreds of letters after the appearance of "Bernice Bobs Her Hair" he had thought it "rather absurd."[14] But in fact he made it a point to become an authority on this new cultural phenomenon, having his brightest and most exemplary flappers spell out the flapper creed, as Ardita Farnam does in "The Offshore Pirate": "I began to see that in all my idols in the past some manifestation of courage had unconsciously been the thing that attracted me.... My courage is faith—faith in the eternal resilience of me...." Then in popular magazine pieces during the early twenties, examples of which are included in Commentary and Illustrations (page 269), he and Zelda did as much as anyone to keep the flapper alive in the public consciousness. In interviews, Fitzgerald delighted in categorizing various types of flappers. In one of these, subtitled "Novelist Says Southern Type of Flapper Best," Fitzgerald "classifies American flappers according to their locality."[15] Accompanying the article is a quarter-page map of the United States containing cartoon renditions of flappers from every geographical area and depicting Fitzgerald with a pointer singling out the Southern flapper. Given Fitzgerald's relationship with the quintessential flapper–Southern belle Zelda, few will be shocked to learn that Fitzgerald liked the "Southern Type of Flapper Best," nor is it surprising that one of his greatest stories, "The Ice Palace," was inspired by trips that he had taken to see Zelda in Montgomery in the months preceding the composition of the story, trips he had made to urge her to resume their engagement. The other two stories inspired by his connection to Montgomery are "The Jelly-Bean" and "The Last of the Belles" (*Post,* March

2, 1929). In these stories, known now as the Tarleton Trilogy, Fitzgerald creates a hybrid of the flapper and the Southern belle, another original Fitzgerald creation and one whose philosophy and outlook are a product of both her Southern heritage and of the movement toward social liberation of women in America during the 1920s.

Of the flapper-belles in the Tarleton Trilogy, Sally Carrol Happer from "The Ice Palace," with her two sides—"the sleepy old side you love" and the side that "makes me do wild things"—comes closest to embodying the originality and complexity that distinguishes all of Fitzgerald's flappers, whatever their type. Nancy Lamar in "The Jelly-Bean," on the other hand, has no apparent loyalty to the chivalric tradition and seems surely headed toward an unhappier end than Sally Carrol: "I'm a wild part of the world, Jelly-bean," she tells Jim Powell before her wild side leads her to marry her suitor from Savannah during a drunken evening. The growing darkness of mood in the Tarleton stories foreshadows the approaching end of Fitzgerald's flapper stories. When an interviewer reminded him in 1921 that he had brought the customs of the flapper to the attention of the older generation, Fitzgerald responded that "My new novel will, I hope, be more mature. It will be the story of two young married folk and it will show their gradual disintegration—broadly speaking, how they go to the devil."[16]

In those dreamy months during the winter of 1919 and spring of 1920 during which Fitzgerald was creating his early flappers and securing his reputation as the flapper's historian, he was having difficulty making progress toward a novel that would follow *This Side of Paradise.* It is likely that "May Day," written in March 1920, was originally the beginning of what he thought would become that novel, though he eventually compressed its three episodes and brought them together as a long short story in "May Day," which he sold to *The Smart Set* for $200. In these episodes he captures the feeling of those days around the May Day riots of 1919 that grew out of a nationwide postwar sentiment against socialists and other dissidents and were fueled by anarchist bombings. The riots took place all over the country, most notably in Boston and New York, and Fitzgerald continued throughout his life to maintain they had "inaugurated the Jazz Age."[17] The story shows Fitzgerald at a pivotal moment when he began to draw from recent personal experience, to communicate its poignancy and residual pain, and yet to distance himself from it by juxtaposing it against historical events that place individual conflict—Gordon Sterrett's in the case of "May Day"—in a social context. As it happens, it also shows him in the grips of a brief flirtation with the philosophy of determinism that he could not finally embrace fully because it so depreciated the role of the romantic vision. When Fitzgerald's experimentation with naturalism reached its dead end in *The Beautiful and Damned* he began shaping the aesthetic and philosophical underpinnings of what would become his most powerful affirmation of the romantic vision in *The Great Gatsby,* and he did so in stages evident in three stories featured in this collection: "The Diamond as Big as the Ritz," "Winter Dreams," and "Absolution."

In *The Great Gatsby,* Fitzgerald enshrines Gatsby's "gift for romantic readiness," which causes him, in spite of his tragic death, to turn out "all right in the end,"[18] according to Nick—an assertion that Nick can make because Gatsby never wavered in the pursuit of his dream that originated in a mind that romped "like the mind of God."[19] It was, in the end, "the foul dust that floated in the wake of his dreams,"[20] the corrosive materialism of the American Dream gone bad and embodied in the immorality of the very rich of East Egg, most obviously in Daisy and Tom Buchanan, that finally betrayed him, not his enormous capacity to imagine and to dream. "The Diamond as Big as the Ritz" is Fitzgerald's first major step toward *The Great Gatsby*'s indictment of wealth and of its effect on the romantic imagination, and the *Post* predictably declined the story because of its anticapitalistic message. Ultimately it was sold for $300 to *The Smart Set,* whose readers would immediately have gotten its message and appreciated it, though Fitzgerald maintained that he had not written the story as an indictment of materialism. Later he would look back on the months of his early poverty as he walked the streets of New York, and then his sudden reversal of fortune with the acceptance of his first novel, as having heightened his mistrust of the wealthy: "The man with the jingle of money in his pocket who married the girl a year later would always cherish an abiding distrust, an animosity toward the leisure class—not the conviction of a revolutionist but the smouldering hatred of a peasant."[21] One could argue that in "The Diamond as Big as the Ritz" this smouldering hatred came close to the surface in the form of a fantasy which damns those like Percy Washington and his sisters, Kismine and Jasmine, who would bring friends home knowing full well that the price of their momentary pleasure would be the death of their friends.

It is likely because of Fitzgerald's determination to avoid open blasphemy against the money god and his desire to remain in the good graces of the popular magazine audience that we have "Winter Dreams." This story was written immediately after "The Diamond as Big as the Ritz," while the Fitzgeralds were living at the White Bear Yacht Club in St. Paul, the thinly disguised setting for Dexter Green's meeting of Judy Jones, and it is unquestionably the most important forerunner of *The Great Gatsby.* Like Jay Gatsby, Dexter Green in "Winter Dreams" invented a kind of self that he thought would make him acceptable to the "nice girl," Judy Jones, who like Daisy Fay in the novel is "nice" primarily in the sense that she is rich and respectable. And Dexter, whose father owns "the second best grocery store" in town, sets out to make a fortune with the primary goal of being able to enter the world of Judy Jones, much as Gatsby sets out to make the money that he believes will win him access to the world of Daisy. The parallels between story and novel are as striking as one would expect in a story that Fitzgerald later described as "[a] sort of 1st draft of the Gatsby idea."[22] In the end, "Winter Dreams" is, of course, a hauntingly sad love story that is, beneath its surface, a study of the power of a spoiled rich girl to determine the course of a poor, young romantic's winter dreams of a better life than his father's. With Ober's difficulty in selling "The Diamond as Big as the Ritz" Fitzgerald had come to understand that in order to use the popular magazines as a workshop for what he professed to consider his "serious" work—his novels—he could not openly attack values that were sacred to middle-American magazine audiences.

In September 1922, after sending "Winter Dreams" to Ober, the Fitzgeralds moved to New York, settling in Great Neck, Long Island, and remaining there until they sailed for Europe in April 1924. Their time in Great Neck is important not only because Long Island would ultimately provide the models for East Egg and West Egg in *The Great Gatsby,* but also because it was here that Fitzgerald began an early draft of the novel, a draft from which only "Absolution" survives. In letters, Fitzgerald alluded to "Absolution" as being closely related to *The Great Gatsby,* in one case referring to it as "a picture of [Gatsby's] early life,"[23] and his comments have provoked speculation and debate about the relationship of the story to the novel. The most reasonable explanation regarding the connection between the two is this: At least as early as April 1924 Fitzgerald had been at work on a novel that had a strong

Catholic element and included a protagonist who would evolve from a character like Rudolph Miller in "Absolution"; he eventually put this novel aside, apparently scrapping it altogether after salvaging what was probably its prologue, which he sent to *The American Mercury.* Then when he returned to the novel during the summer and fall of 1924 he began anew on what would become *The Great Gatsby,* perhaps bringing his earlier conception of Rudolph Miller to bear on his ideas about Jay Gatsby's past.

What we know for certain is that Rudolph Miller and Jay Gatsby share much in common. Like the young Jimmy Gatz, Rudolph Miller has a need to create an alter ego in order to thrive in a higher class of society than the one into which he was born. Both Miller and Gatsby have fathers who worship at the altar of American materialism, as is clear from Mr. Miller's adulation of the empire builder James J. Hill and from Mr. Henry Gatz's reverence for his son's success, which, if Gatsby had lived, would have made him, according to his father, "[a] man like James J. Hill."[24] In the case of Rudolph's father, the tension in his life passed down to his son comes from being pulled between his faith in the Roman Catholic Church and his "mystical worship" of Hill. Rudolph's stunning revelation after his exchange with the deranged priest—the realization that "There was something ineffably gorgeous somewhere that had nothing to do with God"—is a denunciation of at least one of his father's sacred beliefs. As Fitzgerald put it in a letter, "the priest gives the boy a form of Absolution (not of course sacramental), by showing him that he (the priest) is in an even worse state of horror + despair."[25] Rudolph's absolution lands him squarely at the doorstep of the modern world where old beliefs no longer prevail—in short, at the doorstep of the Roaring Twenties.

Fitzgerald's best early short stories, from "Benediction" to "Absolution," arc elegantly over the Jazz Age, and there is such thrill in their telling that it is perhaps easy to overlook the truth that they are, in the end, cautionary tales. In "Early Success" Fitzgerald said this, in retrospect, about his stories and novels of the early twenties: "All the stories that came into my head had a touch of disaster in them—the lovely young creatures in my novels went to ruin, the diamond mountains of my short stories blew up, my millionaires were as beautiful and damned as Thomas Hardy's peasants."[26] Indeed, the stories in this collection paint pictures filled with despair as well as euphoria. In them the American flapper is born, she comes of age in a burst of momentary liberation, and she heads toward matrimony. The Southern belle merges with the flapper and explores the world only to move back South to live out her days under a blanket of the chivalric code—in a worst case, marrying a razor manufacturer after a drunken evening and presumably living unhappily ever after. The intellectuals and artists of the stories are driven at best to frustration and irony and at worst to cynicism and suicide from lack of appreciation of their work, while the social climbers find themselves lured into the traps of the very rich, who would toy with them before condemning them to death or prison deep within a diamond as big as the Ritz. And then there are the romantic dreamers, particularly the men: their plight, especially if they happen to be caught in the spell of an enchantress, is youthful disillusionment and finally middle age, during which they can ponder "the gray beauty of steel that withstands all time."

In the trailing light of these early stories and of *The Great Gatsby* soon to come, Fitzgerald would spend years, in his words, "seeking the eternal Carnival by the Sea." By 1931—far too soon, he believed, to write about the Jazz Age with perspective—he was looking back on it nostalgically and from a distant third-person point of view that he hoped would provide objectivity: "It bore him up," he remembers in "Echoes of the Jazz Age"; it "flattered him and gave him more money than he had dreamed of, simply for telling people that he felt as they did, that something had to be done with all the nervous energy stored up and unexpended in the War."[27] In just a half dozen years more, when the wistful past had become barely a memory to him and the fulfilled future was now itself the wistful past, he would require twilight on the French Riviera to recover the time that had seemed "so rosy and romantic to those that were young then."[28]

NOTES

1. F. Scott Fitzgerald, "Early Success," *The Crack-Up,* ed. Edmund Wilson (New York: New Directions, 1945), p. 90.
2. "Early Success," p. 90.
3. "Early Success," p. 86.
4. "Echoes of the Jazz Age," *The Crack-Up,* p. 14.
5. "Early Success," p. 86.
6. "Early Success," p. 86.

7. Matthew J. Bruccoli and Margaret M. Duggan, ed. *Correspondence of F. Scott Fitzgerald* (New York: Random House, 1980), p. 51.
8. *F. Scott Fitzgerald's Ledger* (Washington: Bruccoli Clark/NCR, 1972), p. 173.
9. "Early Success," p. 86.
10. *The Great Gatsby* (New York: Scribners, 1925), p. 134.
11. "Early Success," p. 89.
12. *This Side of Paradise* (New York: Scribners, 1920), p. 304.
13. "Echoes of the Jazz Age," p. 21.
14. "Early Success," pp. 87–8.
15. *The Romantic Egoists: A Pictorial Autobiography from the Scrapbooks and Albums of F. Scott and Zelda Fitzgerald,* ed. Matthew J. Bruccoli, Scottie Fitzgerald Smith, and Joan P. Kerr (New York: Scribners, 1974), p. 97.
16. *Romantic Egoists,* p. 79.
17. *Tales of the Jazz Age* (New York: Scribners, 1922), p. viii.
18. *The Great Gatsby,* pp. 2–3.
19. *The Great Gatsby,* p. 134.
20. *The Great Gatsby,* p. 3.
21. "Pasting It Together," *The Crack-Up,* p. 77.
22. *Dear Scott/Dear Max: The Fitzgerald-Perkins Correspondence,* ed. John Kuehl and Jackson R. Bryer (New York: Scribners, 1971), p. 112.
23. *The Letters of F. Scott Fitzgerald,* ed. Andrew Turnbull (New York: Scribners, 1963), p. 509.
24. *The Great Gatsby,* p. 202.
25. Bruccoli and Duggan, *Correspondence of F. Scott Fitzgerald,* p. 212.
26. "Early Success," p. 87.
27. "Echoes of the Jazz Age," p. 13.
28. "Echoes of the Jazz Age," p. 22.

A Note on the Text

Nine of the stories in this volume have been reprinted from original first printings of the volumes in which they were first collected: *Flappers and Philosophers* (New York: Charles Scribner's Sons, 1920), *Tales of the Jazz Age* (New York: Charles Scribner's Sons, 1922), and *All the Sad Young Men* (New York: Charles Scribner's Sons, 1926). Only minor typographical corrections have been made, three of them silent punctuation changes. In "May Day" one proper name has been changed and one word has been deleted. Both of these are noted within the text. For the sake of consistency the Roman numeral I has been removed from the beginning of "The Diamond as Big as the Ritz." The text of "Winter Dreams" was reprinted from *Metropolitan Magazine*, December 1922. The stories are arranged chronologically by date of composition.

THE BEST EARLY STORIES OF F. SCOTT FITZGERALD

Benediction

The Baltimore Station was hot and crowded, so Lois was forced to stand by the telegraph desk for interminable, sticky seconds while a clerk with big front teeth counted and recounted a large lady's day message, to determine whether it contained the innocuous forty-nine words or the fatal fifty-one.

Lois, waiting, decided she wasn't quite sure of the address, so she took the letter out of her bag and ran over it again.

"Darling": *it began*—"I understand and I'm happier than life ever meant me to be. If I could give you the things you've always been in tune with—but I can't, Lois; we can't marry and we can't lose each other and let all this glorious love end in nothing.

"Until your letter came, dear, I'd been sitting here in the half dark thinking and thinking where I could go and ever forget you; abroad, perhaps, to drift through Italy or Spain and dream away the pain of having lost you where the crumbling ruins of older, mellower civilizations would mirror only the desolation of my heart—and then your letter came.

"Sweetest, bravest girl, if you'll wire me I'll meet you in Wilmington—till then I'll be here just waiting and hoping for every long dream of you to come true.

"Howard."

She had read the letter so many times that she knew it word by word, yet it still startled her. In it she found many faint reflections of the man who wrote it—the mingled sweetness and sadness in his dark eyes, the furtive, restless excitement she felt sometimes when he talked to her, his dreamy sensuousness that lulled her mind to sleep. Lois was nineteen and very romantic and curious and courageous.

The large lady and the clerk having compromised on fifty words, Lois took a blank and wrote her telegram. And there were no overtones to the finality of her decision.

It's just destiny—she thought—it's just the way things work out in this damn world. If cowardice is all that's been holding me back there won't be any more holding back. So we'll just let things take their course, and never be sorry.

The clerk scanned her telegram:

"Arrived Baltimore today spend day with my brother meet me Wilmington three P.M. Wednesday Love

"LOIS."

"Fifty-four cents," said the clerk admiringly.

And never be sorry—thought Lois—and never be sorry——

II

Trees filtering light onto dappled grass. Trees like tall, languid ladies with feather fans coquetting airily with the ugly roof of the monastery. Trees like butlers, bending courteously over placid walks and paths. Trees, trees over the hills on either side and scattering out in clumps and lines and woods all through eastern Maryland, delicate lace on the hems of many yellow fields, dark opaque backgrounds for flowered bushes or wild climbing gardens.

Some of the trees were very gay and young, but the monastery trees were older than the monastery which, by true monastic standards, wasn't very old at all. And, as a matter of fact, it wasn't technically called a monastery, but only a seminary; nevertheless it shall be a monastery here despite its Victorian architecture or its Edward VII additions, or even its Woodrow Wilsonian, patented, last-a-century roofing.

Out behind was the farm where half a dozen lay brothers were sweating lustily as they moved with deadly efficiency around the vegetable-gardens. To the left, behind a row of elms, was an informal baseball diamond where three novices were being batted out by a fourth, amid great chasings and puffings and blowings. And in front as a great mellow bell boomed the half-hour a swarm of black, human leaves were blown over the checker-board of paths under the courteous trees.

Some of these black leaves were very old with cheeks furrowed like the first ripples of a splashed pool. Then there was a scattering of middle-aged leaves whose forms when viewed in profile in their revealing gowns were beginning to be faintly unsymmetrical. These carried thick volumes of Thomas Aquinas and Henry James and Cardinal Mercier and Immanuel Kant[1] and many bulging note-books filled with lecture data.

But most numerous were the young leaves; blond boys of nineteen with very stern, conscientious expressions; men in the late twenties with a keen self-assurance from having taught out in the world for five years—several hundreds of them, from city and town and country in Maryland and Pennsylvania and Virginia and West Virginia and Delaware.

There were many Americans and some Irish and some tough Irish and a few French, and several Italians and Poles, and they walked informally arm in arm with each other in twos and threes or in long rows, almost universally distinguished by the straight mouth and the considerable chin—for this was the Society of Jesus, founded in Spain five hundred years before by a tough-minded soldier[2] who trained men to hold a breach or a salon, preach a sermon or write a treaty, and do it and not argue...

Lois got out of a bus into the sunshine down by the outer gate. She was nineteen with yellow hair and eyes that people were tactful enough not to call green. When men of talent saw her in a street-car they often furtively produced little stub-pencils and backs of envelopes and tried to sum up that profile or the thing that the eyebrows did to her eyes. Later they looked at their results and usually tore them up with wondering sighs.

Though Lois was very jauntily attired in an expensively appropriate travelling affair, she did not linger to pat out the dust which covered her clothes, but started up the central walk with curious glances at either side. Her face was very eager and expectant, yet she hadn't at all that glorified expression that girls wear when they arrive for a Senior Prom at Princeton or New Haven; still, as there were no senior proms here, perhaps it didn't matter.

She was wondering what he would look like, whether she'd possibly know him from his picture. In the picture, which hung over her mother's bureau at home, he seemed very young and hollow-cheeked and rather pitiful, with only a well-developed mouth and an ill-fitting probationer's gown to show that he had already made a momentous decision about his life. Of course he had been only nineteen then and now he was thirty-six—didn't look like that at all; in recent snap-shots he was much broader and his hair had grown a little thin—but the impression of her brother she had always retained was that of the big picture. And so she had always been a little sorry for him. What a life for a man! Seventeen years of preparation and he wasn't even a priest yet—wouldn't be for another year.

Lois had an idea that this was all going to be rather solemn if she let it be. But she was going to give her very best imitation of undiluted sunshine, the imitation she could give even when her head was splitting or when her mother had a nervous breakdown or when she was particularly romantic and curious and courageous. This brother of hers undoubtedly needed cheering up, and he was going to be cheered up, whether he liked it or not.

As she drew near the great, homely front door she saw a man break suddenly away from a group and, pulling up the skirts of his gown, run toward her. He was smiling, she noticed, and he looked very big and—and reliable. She stopped and waited, knew that her heart was beating unusually fast.

"Lois!" he cried, and in a second she was in his arms. She was suddenly trembling.

"Lois!" he cried again, "why, this is wonderful! I can't tell you, Lois, how *much* I've looked forward to this. Why, Lois, you're beautiful!"

Lois gasped.

His voice, though restrained, was vibrant with energy and that odd sort of enveloping personality she had thought that she only of the family possessed.

"I'm mighty glad, too—Kieth."

She flushed, but not unhappily, at this first use of his name.

"Lois—Lois—Lois," he repeated in wonder. "Child, we'll go in here a minute, because I want you to meet the rector, and then we'll walk around. I have a thousand things to talk to you about."

His voice became graver. "How's mother?"

She looked at him for a moment and then said something that she had not intended to say at all, the very sort of thing she had resolved to avoid.

"Oh, Kieth—she's—she's getting worse all the time, every way."

He nodded slowly as if he understood.

"Nervous, well—you can tell me about that later. Now——"

She was in a small study with a large desk, saying something to a little, jovial, white-haired priest who retained her hand for some seconds.

"So this is Lois!"

He said it as if he had heard of her for years.

He entreated her to sit down.

Two other priests arrived enthusiastically and shook hands with her and addressed her as "Kieth's little sister," which she found she didn't mind a bit.

How assured they seemed; she had expected a certain shyness, reserve at least. There were several jokes unintelligible to her, which seemed to delight every one, and the little Father Rector referred to the trio of them as "dim old monks," which she appreciated, because of course they weren't monks at all. She had a lightning impression that they were especially fond of Kieth—the Father Rector had called him "Kieth" and one of the others had kept a hand on his shoulder all through the conversation. Then she was shaking hands again and promising to come back a little later for some ice-cream, and smiling and smiling and being rather absurdly happy... she told herself that it was because Kieth was so delighted in showing her off.

Then she and Kieth were strolling along a path, arm in arm, and he was informing her what an absolute jewel the Father Rector was.

"Lois," he broke off suddenly, "I want to tell you before we go any farther how much it means to me to have you come up here. I think it was—mighty sweet of you. I know what a gay time you've been having."

Lois gasped. She was not prepared for this. At first when she had conceived the plan of taking the hot journey down to Baltimore, staying the night with a friend and then coming out to see her brother, she had felt rather consciously virtuous, hoped he wouldn't be priggish or resentful about her not having come before—but walking here with him under the trees seemed such a little thing, and surprisingly a happy thing.

"Why, Kieth," she said quickly, "you know I couldn't have waited a day longer. I saw you when I was five, but of course I didn't remember, and how could I have gone on without practically ever having seen my only brother?"

"It was mighty sweet of you, Lois," he repeated.

Lois blushed—he *did* have personality.

"I want you to tell me all about yourself," he said after a pause. "Of course I have a general idea what you and mother did in Europe those fourteen years, and then we were all so worried, Lois, when you had pneumonia and couldn't come down with mother—let's see, that was two years ago—and then, well, I've seen your name in the papers, but it's all been so unsatisfactory. I haven't known you, Lois."

She found herself analyzing his personality as she analyzed the personality of every man she met. She wondered if the effect of—of intimacy that he gave was bred by his constant repetition of her name. He said it as if he loved the word, as if it had an inherent meaning to him.

"Then you were at school," he continued.

"Yes, at Farmington.[3] Mother wanted me to go to a convent—but I didn't want to."

She cast a side glance at him to see if he would resent this.

But he only nodded slowly.

"Had enough convents abroad, eh?"

"Yes—and Kieth, convents are different there anyway. Here even in the nicest ones there are so many *common* girls."

He nodded again.

"Yes," he agreed, "I suppose there are, and I know how you feel about it. It grated on me here, at first, Lois, though I wouldn't say that to any one but you; we're rather sensitive, you and I, to things like this."

"You mean the men here?"

"Yes, some of them of course were fine, the sort of men I'd always been thrown with, but there were others; a man named Regan, for instance—I hated the fellow, and now he's about the best friend I have.

A wonderful character, Lois; you'll meet him later. Sort of man you'd like to have with you in a fight."

Lois was thinking that Kieth was the sort of man she'd like to have with *her* in a fight.

"How did you—how did you first happen to do it?" she asked, rather shyly, "to come here, I mean. Of course mother told me the story about the Pullman car."

"Oh, that—" He looked rather annoyed.

"Tell me that. I'd like to hear you tell it."

"Oh, it's nothing, except what you probably know. It was evening and I'd been riding all day and thinking about—about a hundred things, Lois, and then suddenly I had a sense that some one was sitting across from me, felt that he'd been there for some time, and had a vague idea that he was another traveller. All at once he leaned over toward me and I heard a voice say: 'I want you to be a priest, that's what I want.' Well, I jumped up and cried out, 'Oh, my God, not that!'—made an idiot of myself before about twenty people; you see there wasn't any one sitting there at all. A week after that I went to the Jesuit College in Philadelphia[4] and crawled up the last flight of stairs to the rector's office on my hands and knees."

There was another silence and Lois saw that her brother's eyes wore a far-away look, that he was staring unseeingly out over the sunny fields. She was stirred by the modulations of his voice and the sudden silence that seemed to flow about him when he finished speaking.

She noticed now that his eyes were of the same fibre as hers, with the green left out, and that his mouth was much gentler, really, than in the picture—or was it that the face had grown up to it lately? He was getting a little bald just on top of his head. She wondered if that was from wearing a hat so much. It seemed awful for a man to grow bald and no one to care about it.

"Were you—pious when you were young, Kieth?" she asked. "You know what I mean. Were you religious? If you don't mind these personal questions."

"Yes," he said with his eyes still far away—and she felt that his intense abstraction was as much a part of his personality as his attention. "Yes, I suppose I was, when I was—sober."

Lois thrilled slightly.

"Did you drink?"

He nodded.

"I was on the way to making a bad hash of things." He smiled and, turning his gray eyes on her, changed the subject.

"Child, tell me about mother. I know it's been awfully hard for you there, lately. I know you've had to sacrifice a lot and put up with a great deal, and I want you to know how fine of you I think it is. I feel, Lois, that you're sort of taking the place of both of us there."

Lois thought quickly how little she had sacrificed; how lately she had constantly avoided her nervous, half-invalid mother.

"Youth shouldn't be sacrificed to age, Kieth," she said steadily.

"I know," he sighed, "and you oughtn't to have the weight on your shoulders, child. I wish I were there to help you."

She saw how quickly he had turned her remark and instantly she knew what this quality was that he gave off. He was *sweet*. Her thoughts went off on a side-track and then she broke the silence with an odd remark.

"Sweetness is hard," she said suddenly.

"What?"

"Nothing," she denied in confusion. "I didn't mean to speak aloud. I was thinking of something—of a conversation with a man named Freddy Kebble."

"Maury Kebble's brother?"

"Yes," she said, rather surprised to think of him having known Maury Kebble. Still there was nothing strange about it. "Well, he and I were talking about sweetness a few weeks ago. Oh, I don't know—I said that a man named Howard—that a man I knew was sweet, and he didn't agree with me, and we began talking about what sweetness in a man was. He kept telling me I meant a sort of soppy softness, but I knew I didn't—yet I didn't know exactly how to put it. I see now. I meant just the opposite. I suppose real sweetness is a sort of hardness—and strength."

Kieth nodded.

"I see what you mean. I've known old priests who had it."

"I'm talking about young men," she said, rather defiantly.

"Oh!"

They had reached the now deserted baseball diamond and, pointing her to a wooden bench, he sprawled full length on the grass.

"Are these *young* men happy here, Kieth?"

"Don't they look happy, Lois?"

"I suppose so, but those *young* ones, those two we just passed—have they—are they——"

"Are they signed up?" he laughed. "No, but they will be next month."

"Permanently?"

"Yes—unless they break down mentally or physically. Of course in a discipline like ours a lot drop out."

"But those *boys*. Are they giving up fine chances outside—like you did?"

He nodded.

"Some of them."

"But, Kieth, they don't know what they're doing. They haven't had any experience of what they're missing."

"No, I suppose not."

"It doesn't seem fair. Life has just sort of scared them at first. Do they all come in so *young?*"

"No, some of them have knocked around, led pretty wild lives—Regan, for instance."

"I should think that sort would be better," she said meditatively, "men that had *seen* life."

"No," said Kieth earnestly, "I'm not sure that knocking about gives a man the sort of experience he can communicate to others. Some of the broadest men I've known have been absolutely rigid about themselves. And reformed libertines are a notoriously intolerant class. Don't you think so, Lois?"

She nodded, still meditative, and he continued:

"It seems to me that when one weak person goes to another, it isn't help they want; it's a sort of companionship in guilt, Lois. After you were born, when mother began to get nervous she used to go and weep with a certain Mrs. Comstock. Lord, it used to make me shiver. She said it comforted her, poor old mother. No, I don't think that to help others you've got to show yourself at all. Real help comes from a stronger person whom you respect. And their sympathy is all the bigger because it's impersonal."

"But people want human sympathy," objected Lois. "They want to feel the other person's been tempted."

"Lois, in their hearts they want to feel that the other person's been weak. That's what they mean by human.

"Here in this old monkery, Lois," he continued with a smile, "they try to get all that self-pity and pride in our own wills out of us right at the first. They put us to scrubbing floors—and other things. It's like that idea of saving your life by losing it. You see we sort of feel that the less human a man is, in your sense of human, the better servant he can be to humanity. We carry it out to the end, too. When one of us dies his family can't even have him then. He's buried here under a plain wooden cross with a thousand others."

His tone changed suddenly and he looked at her with a great brightness in his gray eyes.

"But way back in a man's heart there are some things he can't get rid of—and one of them is that I'm awfully in love with my little sister."

With a sudden impulse she knelt beside him in the grass and, leaning over, kissed his forehead.

"You're hard, Kieth," she said, "and I love you for it—and you're sweet."

III

Back in the reception-room Lois met a half-dozen more of Kieth's particular friends; there was a young man named Jarvis, rather pale and delicate-looking, who, she knew, must be a grandson of old Mrs. Jarvis at home, and she mentally compared this ascetic with a brace of his riotous uncles.

And there was Regan with a scarred face and piercing intent eyes that followed her about the room and often rested on Kieth with something very like worship. She knew then what Kieth had meant about "a good man to have with you in a fight."

He's the missionary type—she thought vaguely—China or something.

"I want Kieth's sister to show us what the shimmy is," demanded one young man with a broad grin.

Lois laughed.

"I'm afraid the Father Rector would send me shimmying out the gate. Besides, I'm not an expert."

"I'm sure it wouldn't be best for Jimmy's soul anyway," said Kieth solemnly. "He's inclined to brood about things like shimmys. They were just starting to do the—maxixe,[5] wasn't it, Jimmy?—when he became a monk, and it haunted him his whole first year. You'd see him when he was peeling potatoes, putting his arm around the bucket and making irreligious motions with his feet."

There was a general laugh in which Lois joined.

"An old lady who comes here to Mass sent Kieth this ice-cream," whispered Jarvis under cover of the laugh, "because she'd heard you were coming. It's pretty good, isn't it?"

There were tears trembling in Lois' eyes.

IV

Then half an hour later over in the chapel things suddenly went all wrong. It was several years since Lois had been at Benediction[6] and at first she was thrilled by the gleaming monstrance with its central spot of white, the air rich and heavy with incense, and the sun shining through the stained-glass window of St. Francis Xavier[7] overhead and falling in warm red tracery on the cassock of the man in front of her, but at the first notes of the *"O Salutaris Hostia"* a heavy weight seemed to descend upon her soul. Kieth was on her right and young Jarvis on her left, and she stole uneasy glances at both of them.

What's the matter with me? she thought impatiently.

She looked again. Was there a certain coldness in both their profiles, that she had not noticed before—a pallor about the mouth and a curious set expression in their eyes? She shivered slightly: they were like dead men.

She felt her soul recede suddenly from Kieth's. This was her brother—this, this unnatural person. She caught herself in the act of a little laugh.

"What is the matter with me?"

She passed her hand over her eyes and the weight increased. The incense sickened her and a stray, ragged note from one of the tenors in the choir grated on her ear like the shriek of a slate-pencil. She fidgeted, and raising her hand to her hair touched her forehead, found moisture on it.

"It's hot in here, hot as the deuce."

Again she repressed a faint laugh, and then in an instant the weight upon her heart suddenly diffused into cold fear.... It was that candle on the altar. It was all wrong—wrong. Why didn't somebody see it?

There was something *in* it. There was something coming out of it, taking form and shape above it.

She tried to fight down her rising panic, told herself it was the wick. If the wick wasn't straight, candles did something—but they didn't do this! With incalculable rapidity a force was gathering within her, a tremendous, assimilative force, drawing from every sense, every corner of her brain, and as it surged up inside her she felt an enormous, terrified repulsion. She drew her arms in close to her side, away from Kieth and Jarvis.

Something in that candle... she was leaning forward—in another moment she felt she would go forward toward it—didn't any one see it?... anyone?

"Ugh!"

She felt a space beside her and something told her that Jarvis had gasped and sat down very suddenly... then she was kneeling and as the flaming monstrance slowly left the altar in the hands of the priest, she heard a great rushing noise in her ears—the crash of the bells was like hammer-blows... and then in a moment that seemed eternal a great torrent rolled over her heart—there was a shouting there and a lashing as of waves...

... She was calling, felt herself calling for Kieth, her lips mouthing the words that would not come:

"Kieth! Oh, my God! *Kieth!*"

Suddenly she became aware of a new presence, something external, in front of her, consummated and expressed in warm red tracery. Then she knew. It was the window of St. Francis Xavier. Her mind gripped at it, clung to it finally, and she felt herself calling again endlessly, impotently—Kieth—Kieth!

Then out of a great stillness came a voice:

"Blessed be God."

With a gradual rumble sounded the response rolling heavily through the chapel:

"Blessed be God."

The words sang instantly in her heart; the incense lay mystically and sweetly peaceful upon the air, and *the candle on the altar went out.*

"Blessed be His Holy Name."

"Blessed be His Holy Name."

Everything blurred into a swinging mist. With a sound half-gasp, half-cry she rocked on her feet and reeled backward into Kieth's suddenly outstretched arms.

V

"Lie still, child."

She closed her eyes again. She was on the grass outside, pillowed on Kieth's arm, and Regan was dabbing her head with a cold towel.

"I'm all right," she said quietly.

"I know, but just lie still a minute longer. It was too hot in there. Jarvis felt it, too."

She laughed as Regan again touched her gingerly with the towel.

"I'm all right," she repeated.

But though a warm peace was filling her mind and heart she felt oddly broken and chastened, as if some one had held her stripped soul up and laughed.

VI

Half an hour later she walked leaning on Kieth's arm down the long central path toward the gate.

"It's been such a short afternoon," he sighed, "and I'm so sorry you were sick, Lois."

"Kieth, I'm feeling fine now, really; I wish you wouldn't worry."

"Poor old child. I didn't realize that Benediction'd be a long service for you after your hot trip out here and all."

She laughed cheerfully.

"I guess the truth is I'm not much used to Benediction. Mass is the limit of my religious exertions."

She paused and then continued quickly:

"I don't want to shock you, Kieth, but I can't tell you how—how *inconvenient* being a Catholic is. It really doesn't seem to apply any more. As far as morals go, some of the wildest boys I know are Catholics. And the brightest boys—I mean the ones who think and read a lot, don't seem to believe in much of anything any more."

"Tell me about it. The bus won't be here for another half-hour."

They sat down on a bench by the path.

"For instance, Gerald Carter, he's published a novel. He absolutely roars when people mention immortality. And then Howa—well, another man I've known well, lately, who was Phi Beta Kappa at Harvard, says that no intelligent person can believe in Supernatural Christianity. He says Christ was a great socialist, though. Am I shocking you?"

She broke off suddenly.

Kieth smiled.

"You can't shock a monk. He's a professional shock-absorber."

"Well," she continued, "that's about all. It seems so—so *narrow.* Church schools, for instance. There's more freedom about things that Catholic people can't see—like birth control."

Kieth winced, almost imperceptibly, but Lois saw it.

"Oh," she said quickly, "everybody talks about everything now."

"It's probably better that way."

"Oh, yes, much better. Well, that's all, Kieth. I just wanted to tell you why I'm a little—lukewarm, at present."

"I'm not shocked, Lois. I understand better than you think. We all go through those times. But I know it'll come out all right, child. There's that gift of faith that we have, you and I, that'll carry us past the bad spots."

He rose as he spoke and they started again down the path.

"I want you to pray for me sometimes, Lois. I think your prayers would be about what I need. Because we've come very close in these few hours, I think."

Her eyes were suddenly shining.

"Oh, we have, we have!" she cried. "I feel closer to you now than to any one in the world."

He stopped suddenly and indicated the side of the path.

"We might—just a minute——"

It was a pietà, a life-size statue of the Blessed Virgin set within a semicircle of rocks.[8]

Feeling a little self-conscious she dropped on her knees beside him and made an unsuccessful attempt at prayer.

She was only half through when he rose. He took her arm again.

"I wanted to thank Her for letting us have this day together," he said simply.

Lois felt a sudden lump in her throat and she wanted to say something that would tell him how much it had meant to her, too. But she found no words.

"I'll always remember this," he continued, his voice trembling a little—"this summer day with you. It's been just what I expected. You're just what I expected, Lois."

"I'm awfully glad, Kieth."

"You see, when you were little they kept sending me snap-shots of you, first as a baby and then as a child in socks playing on the beach with a pail and shovel, and then suddenly as a wistful little girl with wondering, pure eyes—and I used to build dreams about you. A man has to have something living to cling to. I think, Lois, it was your little white soul I tried to keep near me—even when life was at its loudest and every intellectual idea of God seemed the sheerest mockery, and desire and love and a million things came up to me and said: 'Look here at me! See, I'm Life. You're turning your back on it!' All the way through that shadow, Lois, I could always see your baby soul flitting on ahead of me, very frail and clear and wonderful."

Lois was crying softly. They had reached the gate and she rested her elbow on it and dabbed furiously at her eyes.

"And then later, child, when you were sick I knelt all one night and asked God to spare you for me—for I knew then that I wanted more; He had taught me to want more. I wanted to know you moved and breathed in the same world with me. I saw you growing up, that white innocence of yours changing to a flame and burning to give light to other weaker souls. And then I wanted some day to take your children on my knee and hear them call the crabbed old monk Uncle Kieth."

He seemed to be laughing now as he talked.

"Oh, Lois, Lois, I was asking God for more then. I wanted the letters you'd write me and the place I'd have at your table. I wanted an awful lot, Lois, dear."

"You've got me, Kieth," she sobbed, "you know it, say you know it. Oh, I'm acting like a baby but I didn't think you'd be this way, and I—oh, Kieth—Kieth——"

He took her hand and patted it softly.

"Here's the bus. You'll come again, won't you?"

She put her hands on his cheeks, and drawing his head down, pressed her tear-wet face against his.

"Oh, Kieth, brother, some day I'll tell you something——"

He helped her in, saw her take down her handkerchief and smile bravely at him, as the driver flicked his whip and the bus rolled off. Then a thick cloud of dust rose around it and she was gone.

For a few minutes he stood there on the road, his hand on the gate-post, his lips half parted in a smile.

"Lois," he said aloud in a sort of wonder, "Lois, Lois."

Later, some probationers passing noticed him kneeling before the pietà, and coming back after a time found him still there. And he was there until twilight came down and the courteous trees grew garrulous overhead and the crickets took up their burden of song in the dusky grass.

VII

The first clerk in the telegraph booth in the Baltimore Station whistled through his buck teeth at the second clerk:

"S'matter?"

"See that girl—no, the pretty one with the big black dots on her veil. Too late—she's gone. You missed somep'n."

"What about her?"

"Nothing. 'Cept she's damn good-looking. Came in here yesterday and sent a wire to some guy to meet her somewhere. Then a minute ago she came in with a telegram all written out and was standin' there goin' to give it to me when she changed her mind or somep'n and all of a sudden tore it up."

"Hm."

The first clerk came around the counter and picking up the two pieces of paper from the floor put them together idly. The second clerk read them over his shoulder and subconsciously counted the words as he read. There were just thirteen.

"This is in the way of a permanent goodbye. I should suggest Italy.

"Lois."

"Tore it up, eh?" said the second clerk.

Head and Shoulders

In 1915 Horace Tarbox was thirteen years old. In that year he took the examinations for entrance to Princeton University and received the Grade A—excellent—in Cæsar, Cicero, Vergil, Xenophon, Homer, Algebra, Plane Geometry, Solid Geometry, and Chemistry.

Two years later, while George M. Cohan[1] was composing "Over There," Horace was leading the sophomore class by several lengths and digging out theses on "The Syllogism as an Obsolete Scholastic Form," and during the battle of Château-Thierry[2] he was sitting at his desk deciding whether or not to wait until his seventeenth birthday before beginning his series of essays on "The Pragmatic Bias of the New Realists."

After a while some newsboy told him that the war was over, and he was glad, because it meant that Peat Brothers, publishers, would get out their new edition of "Spinoza's Improvement of the Understanding."[3] Wars were all very well in their way, made young men self-reliant or something, but Horace felt that he could never forgive the President for allowing a brass band to play under his window on the night of the false armistice, causing him to leave three important sentences out of his thesis on "German Idealism."

The next year he went up to Yale to take his degree as Master of Arts.

He was seventeen then, tall and slender, with near-sighted gray eyes and an air of keeping himself utterly detached from the mere words he let drop.

"I never feel as though I'm talking to him," expostulated Professor Dillinger to a sympathetic colleague. "He makes me feel as though I were talking to his representative. I always expect him to say: 'Well, I'll ask myself and find out.' "

And then, just as nonchalantly as though Horace Tarbox had been Mr. Beef the butcher or Mr. Hat the haberdasher, life reached in, seized him, handled him, stretched him, and unrolled him like a piece of Irish lace on a Saturday-afternoon bargain-counter.

To move in the literary fashion I should say that this was all because when way back in colonial days the hardy pioneers had come to a bald place in Connecticut and asked of each other, "Now, what shall we build here?" the hardiest one among 'em had answered: "Let's build a town where theatrical managers can try out musical comedies!" How afterward they founded Yale College there, to try the musical comedies on, is a story every one knows. At any rate one December, "Home James"[4] opened at the Shubert, and all the students encored Marcia Meadow, who sang a song about the Blundering Blimp[5] in the first act and did a shaky, shivery, celebrated dance in the last.

Marcia was nineteen. She didn't have wings, but audiences agreed generally that she didn't need them. She was a blonde by natural pigment, and she wore no paint on the streets at high noon. Outside of that she was no better than most women.

It was Charlie Moon who promised her five thousand Pall Malls[6] if she would pay a call on Horace Tarbox, prodigy extraordinary. Charlie was a senior in Sheffield,[7] and he and Horace were first cousins. They liked and pitied each other.

Horace had been particularly busy that night. The failure of the Frenchman Laurier to appreciate the significance of the new realists was preying on his mind. In fact, his only reaction to a low, clear-cut rap at his study was to make him speculate as to whether any rap would have actual existence without an ear there to hear it. He fancied he was verging more and more toward pragmatism. But at that moment, though he did not know it, he was verging with astounding rapidity toward something quite different.

The rap sounded—three seconds leaked by—the rap sounded.

"Come in," muttered Horace automatically.

He heard the door open and then close, but, bent over his book in the big armchair before the fire, he did not look up.

"Leave it on the bed in the other room," he said absently.

"Leave what on the bed in the other room?"

Marcia Meadow had to talk her songs, but her speaking voice was like byplay on a harp.

"The laundry."

"I can't."

Horace stirred impatiently in his chair.

"Why can't you?"

"Why, because I haven't got it."

"Hm!" he replied testily. "Suppose you go back and get it."

Across the fire from Horace was another easy-chair. He was accustomed to change to it in the course of an evening by way of exercise and variety. One chair he called Berkeley,[8] the other he called Hume.[9] He suddenly heard a sound as of a rustling, diaphanous form sinking into Hume. He glanced up.

"Well," said Marcia with the sweet smile she used in Act Two ("Oh, so the Duke liked my dancing!"), "Well, Omar Khayyam,[10] here I am beside you singing in the wilderness."

Horace stared at her dazedly. The momentary suspicion came to him that she existed there only as a phantom of his imagination. Women didn't come into men's rooms and sink into men's Humes. Women brought laundry and took your seat in the street-car and married you later on when you were old enough to know fetters.

This woman had clearly materialized out of Hume. The very froth of her brown gauzy dress was an emanation from Hume's leather arm there! If he looked long enough he would see Hume right through her and then he would be alone again in the room. He passed his fist across his eyes. He really must take up those trapeze exercises again.

"For Pete's sake, don't look so critical!" objected the emanation pleasantly. "I feel as if you were going to wish me away with that patent dome of yours. And then there wouldn't be anything left of me except my shadow in your eyes."

Horace coughed. Coughing was one of his two gestures. When he talked you forgot he had a body at all. It was like hearing a phonograph record by a singer who had been dead a long time.

"What do you want?" he asked.

"I want them letters," whined Marcia melodramatically—"them letters of mine you bought from my grandsire in 1881."

Horace considered.

"I haven't got your letters," he said evenly. "I am only seventeen years old. My father was not born until March 3, 1879. You evidently have me confused with some one else."

"You're only seventeen?" repeated Marcia suspiciously.

"Only seventeen."

"I knew a girl," said Marcia reminiscently, "who went on the ten-twenty-thirty[11] when she was sixteen. She was so stuck on herself that she could never say 'sixteen' without putting the 'only' before it. We got to calling her 'Only Jessie.' And she's just where she was when she started—only worse. 'Only' is a bad habit, Omar—it sounds like an alibi."

"My name is not Omar."

"I know," agreed Marcia, nodding—"your name's Horace. I just call you Omar because you remind me of a smoked cigarette."

"And I haven't your letters. I doubt if I've ever met your grandfather. In fact, I think it very improbable that you yourself were alive in 1881."

Marcia stared at him in wonder.

"Me—1881? Why sure! I was second-line stuff when the Florodora Sextette[12] was still in the convent. I was the original nurse to Mrs. Sol Smith's[13] Juliette. Why, Omar, I was a canteen singer during the War of 1812."

Horace's mind made a sudden successful leap, and he grinned.

"Did Charlie Moon put you up to this?"

Marcia regarded him inscrutably.

"Who's Charlie Moon?"

"Small—wide nostrils—big ears."

She grew several inches and sniffed.

"I'm not in the habit of noticing my friends' nostrils."

"Then it was Charlie?"

Marcia bit her lip—and then yawned.

"Oh, let's change the subject, Omar. I'll pull a snore in this chair in a minute."

"Yes," replied Horace gravely, "Hume has often been considered soporific."

"Who's your friend—and will he die?"

Then of a sudden Horace Tarbox rose slenderly and began to pace the room with his hands in his pockets. This was his other gesture.

"I don't care for this," he said as if he were talking to himself—"at all. Not that I mind your being here—I don't. You're quite a pretty little thing, but I don't like Charlie Moon's sending you up here. Am I a laboratory experiment on which the janitors as well as the chemists can make experiments? Is my intellectual development humorous in any way? Do I look like the pictures of the little Boston boy in the comic magazines?[14] Has that callow ass, Moon, with his eternal tales about his week in Paris, any right to——"

"No," interrupted Marcia emphatically. "And you're a sweet boy. Come here and kiss me."

Horace stopped quickly in front of her.

"Why do you want me to kiss you?" he asked intently. "Do you just go round kissing people?"

"Why, yes," admitted Marcia, unruffled. "'At's all life is. Just going round kissing people."

"Well," replied Horace emphatically, "I must say your ideas are horribly garbled! In the first place life isn't just that, and in the second place I won't kiss you. It might get to be a habit and I can't get rid of habits. This year I've got in the habit of lolling in bed until seven-thirty."

Marcia nodded understandingly.

"Do you ever have any fun?" she asked.

"What do you mean by fun?"

"See here," said Marcia sternly, "I like you, Omar, but I wish you'd talk as if you had a line on what you were saying. You sound as if you were gargling a lot of words in your mouth and lost a bet every time you spilled a few. I asked you if you ever had any fun."

Horace shook his head.

"Later, perhaps," he answered. "You see I'm a plan. I'm an experiment. I don't say that I don't get tired of it sometimes—I do. Yet—oh, I can't explain! But what you and Charlie Moon call fun wouldn't be fun to me."

"Please explain."

Horace stared at her, started to speak and then, changing his mind, resumed his walk. After an unsuccessful attempt to determine whether or not he was looking at her Marcia smiled at him.

"Please explain."

Horace turned.

"If I do, will you promise to tell Charlie Moon that I wasn't in?"

"Uh-uh."

"Very well, then. Here's my history: I was a 'why' child. I wanted to see the wheels go round. My father was a young economics professor at Princeton. He brought me up on the system of answering every question I asked him to the best of his ability. My response to that gave him the idea of making an experiment in precocity. To aid in the massacre I had ear trouble—seven operations between the ages of nine and twelve. Of course this kept me apart from other boys and made me ripe for forcing. Anyway, while my generation was laboring through Uncle Remus[15] I was honestly enjoying Catullus[16] in the original.

"I passed off my college examinations when I was thirteen because I couldn't help it. My chief associates were professors, and I took a tremendous pride in knowing that I had a fine intelligence, for though I was unusually gifted I was not abnormal in other ways. When I was sixteen I got tired of being a freak; I decided that some one had made a bad mistake. Still as I'd gone that far I concluded to finish it up by taking my degree of Master of Arts. My chief interest in life is the study of modern philosophy. I am a realist of the School of Anton Laurier—with Bergsonian trimmings[17]—and I'll be eighteen years old in two months. That's all."

"Whew!" exclaimed Marcia. "That's enough! You do a neat job with the parts of speech."

"Satisfied?"

"No, you haven't kissed me."

"It's not in my programme," demurred Horace. "Understand that I don't pretend to be above physical things. They have their place, but——"

"Oh, don't be so darned reasonable!"

"I can't help it."

"I hate these slot-machine people."

"I assure you I—" began Horace.

"Oh, shut up!"

"My own rationality——"

"I didn't say anything about your nationality. You're an Amuricun, ar'n't you?"

"Yes."

"Well, that's O.K. with me. I got a notion I want to see you do something that isn't in your highbrow programme. I want to see if a what-ch-call-em with Brazilian trimmings—that thing you said you were—can be a little human."

Horace shook his head again.

"I won't kiss you."

"My life is blighted," muttered Marcia tragically. "I'm a beaten woman. I'll go through life without ever having a kiss with Brazilian trimmings." She sighed. "Anyways, Omar, will you come and see my show?"

"What show?"

"I'm a wicked actress from 'Home James'!"

"Light opera?"

"Yes—at a stretch. One of the characters is a Brazilian rice-planter. That might interest you."

"I saw 'The Bohemian Girl'[18] once," reflected Horace aloud. "I enjoyed it—to some extent."

"Then you'll come?"

"Well, I'm—I'm——"

"Oh, I know—you've got to run down to Brazil for the week-end."

"Not at all. I'd be delighted to come."

Marcia clapped her hands.

"Goodyforyou! I'll mail you a ticket—Thursday night?"

"Why, I——"

"Good! Thursday night it is."

She stood up and walking close to him laid both hands on his shoulders.

"I like you, Omar. I'm sorry I tried to kid you. I thought you'd be sort of frozen, but you're a nice boy."

He eyed her sardonically.

"I'm several thousand generations older than you are."

"You carry your age well."

They shook hands gravely.

"My name's Marcia Meadow," she said emphatically. "'Member it—Marcia Meadow. And I won't tell Charlie Moon you were in."

An instant later as she was skimming down the last flight of stairs three at a time she heard a voice call over the upper banister: "Oh, say——"

She stopped and looked up—made out a vague form leaning over.

"Oh, say!" called the prodigy again. "Can you hear me?"

"Here's your connection, Omar."

"I hope I haven't given you the impression that I consider kissing intrinsically irrational."

"Impression? Why, you didn't even give me the kiss! Never fret—so long."

Two doors near her opened curiously at the sound of a feminine voice. A tentative cough sounded from above. Gathering her skirts, Marcia dived wildly down the last flight, and was swallowed up in the murky Connecticut air outside.

Up-stairs Horace paced the floor of his study. From time to time he glanced toward Berkeley waiting there in suave dark-red respectability, an open book lying suggestively on his cushions. And then he found that his circuit of the floor was bringing him each time nearer to Hume. There was something about Hume that was strangely and inexpressibly different. The diaphanous form still seemed hovering near, and had Horace sat there he would have felt as if he were sitting on a lady's lap. And though Horace couldn't have named the quality of difference, there was such a quality—quite intangible to the speculative mind, but real, nevertheless. Hume was radiating something that in all the two hundred years of his influence he had never radiated before.

Hume was radiating attar of roses.

II

On Thursday night Horace Tarbox sat in an aisle seat in the fifth row and witnessed "Home James." Oddly enough he found that he was enjoying himself. The cynical students near him were annoyed at his audible appreciation of time-honored jokes in the Hammerstein[19] tradition. But Horace was waiting with anxiety for Marcia Meadow singing her song about a Jazz-bound Blundering Blimp. When she did appear, radiant under a floppity flower-faced hat, a warm glow settled over him, and when the song was over he did not join in the storm of applause. He felt somewhat numb.

In the intermission after the second act an usher materialized beside him, demanded to know if he were Mr. Tarbox, and then handed him a note written in a round adolescent hand. Horace read it in some confusion, while the usher lingered with withering patience in the aisle.

"DEAR OMAR: After the show I always grow an awful hunger. If you want to satisfy it for me in the Taft Grill just communicate your answer to the big-timber guide that brought this and oblige.

Your friend,

MARCIA MEADOW."

"Tell her"—he coughed—"tell her that it will be quite all right. I'll meet her in front of the theatre."

The big-timber guide smiled arrogantly.

"I giss she meant for you to come roun' t' the stage door."

"Where—where is it?"

"Ou'side. Tunayulef. Down ee alley."

"What?"

"Ou'side. Turn to y' left! Down ee alley!"

The arrogant person withdrew. A freshman behind Horace snickered.

Then half an hour later, sitting in the Taft Grill opposite the hair that was yellow by natural pigment, the prodigy was saying an odd thing.

"Do you have to do that dance in the last act?" he was asking earnestly—"I mean, would they dismiss you if you refused to do it?"

Marcia grinned.

"It's fun to do it. I like to do it."

And then Horace came out with a *faux pas.*

"I should think you'd detest it," he remarked succinctly. "The people behind me were making remarks about your bosom."

Marcia blushed fiery red.

"I can't help that," she said quickly. "The dance to me is only a sort of acrobatic stunt. Lord, it's hard enough to do! I rub liniment into my shoulders for an hour every night."

"Do you have—fun while you're on the stage?"

"Uh-huh—sure! I got in the habit of having people look at me, Omar, and I like it."

"Hm!" Horace sank into a brownish study.

"How's the Brazilian trimmings?"

"Hm!" repeated Horace, and then after a pause: "Where does the play go from here?"

"New York."

"For how long?"

"All depends. Winter—maybe."

"Oh!"

"Coming up to lay eyes on me, Omar, or aren't you int'rested? Not as nice here, is it, as it was up in your room? I wish we was there now."

"I feel idiotic in this place," confessed Horace, looking round him nervously.

"Too bad! We got along pretty well."

At this he looked suddenly so melancholy that she changed her tone, and reaching over patted his hand.

"Ever take an actress out to supper before?"

"No," said Horace miserably, "and I never will again. I don't know why I came to-night. Here under all these lights and with all these people laughing and chattering I feel completely out of my sphere. I don't know what to talk to you about."

"We'll talk about me. We talked about you last time."

"Very well."

"Well, my name really is Meadow, but my first name isn't Marcia—it's Veronica. I'm nineteen. Question—how did the girl make her leap to the footlights? Answer—she was born in Passaic, New Jersey, and up to a year ago she got the right to breathe by pushing Nabiscoes in Marcel's tea-room in Trenton. She started going with a guy named Robbins, a singer in the Trent House cabaret, and he got her to try a song and dance with him one evening. In a month we were filling the supper-room every night. Then we went to New York with meet-my-friend letters thick as a pile of napkins.

"In two days we'd landed a job at Divinerries', and I learned to shimmy[20] from a kid at the Palais Royal. We stayed at Divinerries' six months until one night Peter Boyce Wendell, the columnist, ate his milk-toast there. Next morning a poem about Marvellous Marcia came out in his newspaper, and within two days I had three vaudeville offers and a chance at the Midnight Frolic. I wrote Wendell a thank-you letter, and he printed it in his column—said that the style was like Carlyle's,[21] only more rugged, and that I ought to quit dancing and do North American literature. This got me a coupla more vaudeville offers and a chance as an ingénue in a regular show. I took it—and here I am, Omar."

When she finished they sat for a moment in silence, she draping the last skeins of a Welsh rabbit on her fork and waiting for him to speak.

"Let's get out of here," he said suddenly.

Marcia's eyes hardened.

"What's the idea? Am I making you sick?"

"No, but I don't like it here. I don't like to be sitting here with you."

Without another word Marcia signalled for the waiter.

"What's the check?" she demanded briskly. "My part—the rabbit and the ginger ale."

Horace watched blankly as the waiter figured it.

"See here," he began, "I intended to pay for yours too. You're my guest."

With a half-sigh Marcia rose from the table and walked from the room. Horace, his face a document in bewilderment, laid a bill down and followed her out, up the stairs and into the lobby. He overtook her in front of the elevator and they faced each other.

"See here," he repeated, "you're my guest. Have I said something to offend you?"

After an instant of wonder Marcia's eyes softened.

"You're a rude fella," she said slowly. "Don't you know you're rude?"

"I can't help it," said Horace with a directness she found quite disarming. "You know I like you."

"You said you didn't like being with me."

"I didn't like it."

"Why not?"

Fire blazed suddenly from the gray forests of his eyes.

"Because I didn't. I've formed the habit of liking you. I've been thinking of nothing much else for two days."

"Well, if you——"

"Wait a minute," he interrupted. "I've got something to say. It's this: in six weeks I'll be eighteen years old. When I'm eighteen years old I'm coming up to New York to see you. Is there some place in New York where we can go and not have a lot of people in the room?"

"Sure!" smiled Marcia. "You can come up to my 'partment. Sleep on the couch, if you want to."

"I can't sleep on couches," he said shortly. "But I want to talk to you."

"Why, sure," repeated Marcia—"in my 'partment."

In his excitement Horace put his hands in his pockets.

"All right—just so I can see you alone. I want to talk to you as we talked up in my room."

"Honey boy," cried Marcia, laughing, "is it that you want to kiss me?"

"Yes," Horace almost shouted. "I'll kiss you if you want me to."

The elevator man was looking at them reproachfully. Marcia edged toward the grated door.

"I'll drop you a post-card," she said.

Horace's eyes were quite wild.

"Send me a post-card! I'll come up any time after January first. I'll be eighteen then."

And as she stepped into the elevator he coughed enigmatically, yet with a vague challenge, at the ceiling, and walked quickly away.

III

He was there again. She saw him when she took her first glance at the restless Manhattan audience—down in the front row with his head bent a bit forward and his gray eyes fixed on her. And she knew that to him they were alone together in a world where the high-rouged row of ballet faces and the massed whines of the violins were as imperceivable as powder on a marble Venus. An instinctive defiance rose within her.

"Silly boy!" she said to herself hurriedly, and she didn't take her encore.

"What do they expect for a hundred a week—perpetual motion?" she grumbled to herself in the wings.

"What's the trouble, Marcia?"

"Guy I don't like down in front."

During the last act as she waited for her specialty she had an odd attack of stage fright. She had never sent Horace the promised post-card. Last night she had pretended not to see him—had hurried from the theatre immediately after her dance to pass a sleepless night in her apartment, thinking—as she had so often in the last month—of his pale, rather intent face, his slim, boyish figure, the merciless, unworldly abstraction that made him charming to her.

And now that he had come she felt vaguely sorry—as though an unwonted responsibility was being forced on her.

"Infant prodigy!" she said aloud.

"What?" demanded the negro comedian standing beside her.

"Nothing—just talking about myself."

On the stage she felt better. This was her dance—and she always felt that the way she did it wasn't suggestive any more than to some men every pretty girl is suggestive. She made it a stunt.

"Uptown, downtown, jelly on a spoon,
After sundown shiver by the moon."

He was not watching her now. She saw that clearly. He was looking very deliberately at a castle on the back drop, wearing that expression he had worn in the Taft Grill. A wave of exasperation swept over her—he was criticising her.

"That's the vibration that thr-ills me,
Funny how affection fi-lls me,
Uptown, downtown——"

Unconquerable revulsion seized her. She was suddenly and horribly conscious of her audience as she had never been since her first appearance. Was that a leer on a pallid face in the front row, a droop of disgust on one young girl's mouth? These shoulders of hers—these shoulders shaking—were they hers? Were they real? Surely shoulders weren't made for this!

"Then—you'll see at a glance
I'll need some funeral ushers with St. Vitus dance[22]
At the end of the world I'll——"

The bassoon and two cellos crashed into a final chord. She paused and poised a moment on her toes with every muscle tense, her young face looking out dully at the audience in what one young girl afterward called "such a curious, puzzled look," and then without bowing rushed from the stage. Into the dressing-room she sped, kicked out of one dress and into another, and caught a taxi outside.

Her apartment was very warm—small, it was, with a row of professional pictures and sets of Kipling[23] and O. Henry[24] which she had bought once from a blue-eyed agent and read occasionally. And there were several chairs which matched, but were none of them comfortable, and a pink-shaded lamp with blackbirds painted on it and an atmosphere of rather stifled pink throughout. There were nice things in it—nice things unrelentingly hostile to each other, offsprings of a vicarious, impatient taste acting in stray moments. The worst was typified by a great picture framed in oak bark of Passaic as seen from the Erie Railroad—altogether a frantic, oddly extravagant, oddly penurious attempt to make a cheerful room. Marcia knew it was a failure.

Into this room came the prodigy and took her two hands awkwardly.

"I followed you this time," he said.

"Oh!"

"I want you to marry me," he said.

Her arms went out to him. She kissed his mouth with a sort of passionate wholesomeness.

"There!"

"I love you," he said.

She kissed him again and then with a little sigh flung herself into an armchair and half lay there, shaken with absurd laughter.

"Why, you infant prodigy!" she cried.

"Very well, call me that if you want to. I once told you that I was ten thousand years older than you—I am."

She laughed again.

"I don't like to be disapproved of."

"No one's ever going to disapprove of you again."

"Omar," she asked, "why do you want to marry me?"

The prodigy rose and put his hands in his pockets.

"Because I love you, Marcia Meadow."

And then she stopped calling him Omar.

"Dear boy," she said, "you know I sort of love you. There's something about you—I can't tell what—that just puts my heart through the wringer every time I'm round you. But, honey—" She paused.

"But what?"

"But lots of things. But you're only just eighteen, and I'm nearly twenty."

"Nonsense!" he interrupted. "Put it this way—that I'm in my nineteenth year and you're nineteen. That makes us pretty close—without counting that other ten thousand years I mentioned."

Marcia laughed.

"But there are some more 'buts.' Your people——"

"My people!" exclaimed the prodigy ferociously. "My people tried to make a monstrosity out of me." His face grew quite crimson at the enormity of what he was going to say. "My people can go way back and sit down!"

"My heavens!" cried Marcia in alarm. "All that? On tacks, I suppose."

"Tacks—yes," he agreed wildly—"on anything. The more I think of how they allowed me to become a little dried-up mummy——"

"What makes you think you're that?" asked Marcia quietly—"me?"

"Yes. Every person I've met on the streets since I met you has made me jealous because they knew what love was before I did. I used to call it the 'sex impulse.' Heavens!"

"There's more 'buts,' " said Marcia.

"What are they?"

"How could we live?"

"I'll make a living."

"You're in college."

"Do you think I care anything about taking a Master of Arts degree?"

"You want to be Master of Me, hey?"

"Yes! What? I mean, no!"

Marcia laughed, and crossing swiftly over sat in his lap. He put his arm round her wildly and implanted the vestige of a kiss somewhere near her neck.

"There's something white about you," mused Marcia, "but it doesn't sound very logical."

"Oh, don't be so darned reasonable!"

"I can't help it," said Marcia.

"I hate these slot-machine people!"

"But we——"

"Oh, shut up!"

And as Marcia couldn't talk through her ears she had to.

IV

Horace and Marcia were married early in February. The sensation in academic circles both at Yale and Princeton was tremendous. Horace

Tarbox, who at fourteen had been played up in the Sunday magazines sections of metropolitan newspapers, was throwing over his career, his chance of being a world authority on American philosophy, by marrying a chorus girl—they made Marcia a chorus girl. But like all modern stories it was a four-and-a-half-day wonder.

They took a flat in Harlem. After two weeks' search, during which his idea of the value of academic knowledge faded unmercifully, Horace took a position as clerk with a South American export company—some one had told him that exporting was the coming thing. Marcia was to stay in her show for a few months—anyway until he got on his feet. He was getting a hundred and twenty-five to start with, and though of course they told him it was only a question of months until he would be earning double that, Marcia refused even to consider giving up the hundred and fifty a week that she was getting at the time.

"We'll call ourselves Head and Shoulders, dear," she said softly, "and the shoulders'll have to keep shaking a little longer until the old head gets started."

"I hate it," he objected gloomily.

"Well," she replied emphatically, "your salary wouldn't keep us in a tenement. Don't think I want to be public—I don't. I want to be yours. But I'd be a half-wit to sit in one room and count the sunflowers on the wall-paper while I waited for you. When you pull down three hundred a month I'll quit."

And much as it hurt his pride, Horace had to admit that hers was the wiser course.

March mellowed into April. May read a gorgeous riot act to the parks and waters of Manhattan, and they were very happy. Horace, who had no habits whatsoever—he had never had time to form any—proved the most adaptable of husbands, and as Marcia entirely lacked opinions on the subjects that engrossed him there were very few joltings and bumpings. Their minds moved in different spheres. Marcia acted as practical factotum, and Horace lived either in his old world of abstract ideas or in a sort of triumphantly earthy worship and adoration of his wife. She was a continual source of astonishment to him—the freshness and originality of her mind, her dynamic, clear-headed energy, and her unfailing good humor.

And Marcia's co-workers in the nine-o'clock show, whither she had transferred her talents, were impressed with her tremendous pride in her husband's mental powers. Horace they knew only as a very slim, tight-lipped, and immature-looking young man, who waited every night to take her home.

"Horace," said Marcia one evening when she met him as usual at eleven, "you looked like a ghost standing there against the street lights. You losing weight?"

He shook his head vaguely.

"I don't know. They raised me to a hundred and thirty-five dollars to-day, and——"

"I don't care," said Marcia severely. "You're killing yourself working at night. You read those big books on economy——"

"Economics," corrected Horace.

"Well, you read 'em every night long after I'm asleep. And you're getting all stooped over like you were before we were married."

"But, Marcia, I've got to——"

"No, you haven't, dear. I guess I'm running this shop for the present, and I won't let my fella ruin his health and eyes. You got to get some exercise."

"I do. Every morning I——"

"Oh, I know! But those dumb-bells of yours wouldn't give a consumptive two degrees of fever. I mean real exercise. You've got to join a gymnasium. 'Member you told me you were such a trick gymnast once that they tried to get you out for the team in college and they couldn't because you had a standing date with Herb Spencer?"[25]

"I used to enjoy it," mused Horace, "but it would take up too much time now."

"All right," said Marcia. "I'll make a bargain with you. You join a gym and I'll read one of those books from the brown row of 'em."

" 'Pepys' Diary'?[26] Why, that ought to be enjoyable. He's very light."

"Not for me—he isn't. It'll be like digesting plate glass. But you been telling me how much it'd broaden my lookout. Well, you go to a gym three nights a week and I'll take one big dose of Sammy."

Horace hesitated.

"Well——"

"Come on, now! You do some giant swings for me and I'll chase some culture for you."

So Horace finally consented, and all through a baking summer he spent three and sometimes four evenings a week experimenting on the trapeze in Skipper's Gymnasium. And in August he admitted to Marcia that it made him capable of more mental work during the day.

"Mens sana in corpore sano,"[27] he said.

"Don't believe in it," replied Marcia. "I tried one of those patent medicines once and they're all bunk. You stick to gymnastics."

One night in early September while he was going through one of his contortions on the rings in the nearly deserted room he was addressed by a meditative fat man whom he had noticed watching him for several nights.

"Say, lad, do that stunt you were doin' last night."

Horace grinned at him from his perch.

"I invented it," he said. "I got the idea from the fourth proposition of Euclid."[28]

"What circus he with?"

"He's dead."

"Well, he must of broke his neck doin' that stunt. I set here last night thinkin' sure you was goin' to break yours."

"Like this!" said Horace, and swinging onto the trapeze he did his stunt.

"Don't it kill your neck an' shoulder muscles?"

"It did at first, but inside of a week I wrote the *quod erat demonstrandum*[29] on it."

"Hm!"

Horace swung idly on the trapeze.

"Ever think of takin' it up professionally?" asked the fat man.

"Not I."

"Good money in it if you're willin' to do stunts like 'at an' can get away with it."

"Here's another," chirped Horace eagerly, and the fat man's mouth dropped suddenly agape as he watched this pink-jerseyed Prometheus[30] again defy the gods and Isaac Newton.[31]

The night following this encounter Horace got home from work to find a rather pale Marcia stretched out on the sofa waiting for him.

"I fainted twice to-day," she began without preliminaries.

"What?"

"Yep. You see baby's due in four months now. Doctor says I ought to have quit dancing two weeks ago."

Horace sat down and thought it over.

"I'm glad, of course," he said pensively—"I mean glad that we're going to have a baby. But this means a lot of expense."

"I've got two hundred and fifty in the bank," said Marcia hopefully, "and two weeks' pay coming."

Horace computed quickly.

"Including my salary, that'll give us nearly fourteen hundred for the next six months."

Marcia looked blue.

"That all? Course I can get a job singing somewhere this month. And I can go to work again in March."

"Of course nothing!" said Horace gruffly. "You'll stay right here. Let's see now—there'll be doctor's bills and a nurse, besides the maid. We've got to have some more money."

"Well," said Marcia wearily, "I don't know where it's coming from. It's up to the old head now. Shoulders is out of business."

Horace rose and pulled on his coat.

"Where are you going?"

"I've got an idea," he answered. "I'll be right back."

Ten minutes later as he headed down the street toward Skipper's Gymnasium he felt a placid wonder, quite unmixed with humor, at what he was going to do. How he would have gaped at himself a year before! How every one would have gaped! But when you opened your door at the rap of life you let in many things.

The gymnasium was brightly lit, and when his eyes became accustomed to the glare he found the meditative fat man seated on a pile of canvas mats smoking a big cigar.

"Say," began Horace directly, "were you in earnest last night when you said I could make money on my trapeze stunts?"

"Why, yes," said the fat man in surprise.

"Well, I've been thinking it over, and I believe I'd like to try it. I could work at night and on Saturday afternoons—and regularly if the pay is high enough."

The fat man looked at his watch.

"Well," he said, "Charlie Paulson's the man to see. He'll book you inside of four days, once he sees you work out. He won't be in now, but I'll get hold of him for to-morrow night."

The fat man was as good as his word. Charlie Paulson arrived next night and put in a wondrous hour watching the prodigy swoop through the air in amazing parabolas, and on the night following he brought two large men with him who looked as though they had been born smoking black cigars and talking about money in low, passionate voices. Then on the succeeding Saturday Horace Tarbox's torso made its first professional appearance in a gymnastic exhibition at the Coleman Street Gardens. But though the audience numbered nearly five thousand people, Horace felt no nervousness. From his childhood he had read papers to audiences—learned that trick of detaching himself.

"Marcia," he said cheerfully later that same night, "I think we're out of the woods. Paulson thinks he can get me an opening at the Hippodrome,[32] and that means an all-winter engagement. The Hippodrome, you know, is a big——"

"Yes, I believe I've heard of it," interrupted Marcia, "but I want to know about this stunt you're doing. It isn't any spectacular suicide, is it?"

"It's nothing," said Horace quietly. "But if you can think of any nicer way of a man killing himself than taking a risk for you, why that's the way I want to die."

Marcia reached up and wound both arms tightly round his neck.

"Kiss me," she whispered, "and call me 'dear heart.' I love to hear you say 'dear heart.' And bring me a book to read to-morrow. No more Sam Pepys, but something trick and trashy. I've been wild for something to do all day. I felt like writing letters, but I didn't have anybody to write to."

"Write to me," said Horace. "I'll read them."

"I wish I could," breathed Marcia. "If I knew words enough I could write you the longest love-letter in the world—and never get tired."

But after two more months Marcia grew very tired indeed, and for a row of nights it was a very anxious, weary-looking young athlete who walked out before the Hippodrome crowd. Then there were two days when his place was taken by a young man who wore pale blue instead of white, and got very little applause. But after the two days Horace appeared again, and those who sat close to the stage remarked an expression of beatific happiness on that young acrobat's face, even when he was twisting breathlessly in the air in the middle of his amazing and original shoulder swing. After that performance he laughed at the elevator man and dashed up the stairs to the flat five steps at a time—and then tiptoed very carefully into a quiet room.

"Marcia," he whispered.

"Hello!" She smiled up at him wanly. "Horace, there's something I want you to do. Look in my top bureau drawer and you'll find a big stack of paper. It's a book—sort of—Horace. I wrote it down in these last three months while I've been laid up. I wish you'd take it to that Peter Boyce Wendell who put my letter in his paper. He could tell you whether it'd be a good book. I wrote it just the way I talk, just the way I wrote that letter to him. It's just a story about a lot of things that happened to me. Will you take it to him, Horace?"

"Yes, darling."

He leaned over the bed until his head was beside her on the pillow, and began stroking back her yellow hair.

"Dearest Marcia," he said softly.

"No," she murmured, "call me what I told you to call me."

"Dear heart," he whispered passionately—"dearest, dearest heart."

"What'll we call her?"

They rested a minute in happy, drowsy content, while Horace considered.

"We'll call her Marcia Hume Tarbox," he said at length.

"Why the Hume?"

"Because he's the fellow who first introduced us."

"That so?" she murmured, sleepily surprised. "I thought his name was Moon."

Her eyes closed, and after a moment the slow, lengthening surge of the bedclothes over her breast showed that she was asleep.

Horace tiptoed over to the bureau and opening the top drawer found a heap of closely scrawled, lead-smeared pages. He looked at the first sheet:

SANDRA PEPYS, SYNCOPATED
BY MARCIA TARBOX

He smiled. So Samuel Pepys had made an impression on her after all. He turned a page and began to read. His smile deepened—he read on. Half an hour passed and he became aware that Marcia had waked and was watching him from the bed.

"Honey," came in a whisper.

"What, Marcia?"

"Do you like it?"

Horace coughed.

"I seem to be reading on. It's bright."

"Take it to Peter Boyce Wendell. Tell him you got the highest marks in Princeton once and that you ought to know when a book's good. Tell him this one's a world beater."

"All right, Marcia," said Horace gently.

Her eyes closed again and Horace crossing over kissed her forehead—stood there for a moment with a look of tender pity. Then he left the room.

All that night the sprawly writing on the pages, the constant mistakes in spelling and grammar, and the weird punctuation danced before his eyes. He woke several times in the night, each time full of a welling chaotic sympathy for this desire of Marcia's soul to express itself in words. To him there was something infinitely pathetic about it, and for the first time in months he began to turn over in his mind his own half-forgotten dreams.

He had meant to write a series of books, to popularize the new realism as Schopenhauer[33] had popularized pessimism and William James pragmatism.[34]

But life hadn't come that way. Life took hold of people and forced them into flying rings. He laughed to think of that rap at his door, the diaphanous shadow in Hume, Marcia's threatened kiss.

"And it's still me," he said aloud in wonder as he lay awake in the darkness. "I'm the man who sat in Berkeley with temerity to wonder if that rap would have had actual existence had my ear not been there to hear it. I'm still that man. I could be electrocuted for the crimes he committed.

"Poor gauzy souls trying to express ourselves in something tangible. Marcia with her written book; I with my unwritten ones. Trying to choose our mediums and then taking what we get—and being glad."

V

"Sandra Pepys, Syncopated," with an introduction by Peter Boyce Wendell, the columnist, appeared serially in *Jordan's Magazine,* and came out in book form in March. From its first published instalment it attracted attention far and wide. A trite enough subject—a girl from a small New Jersey town coming to New York to go on the stage—

treated simply, with a peculiar vividness of phrasing and a haunting undertone of sadness in the very inadequacy of its vocabulary, it made an irresistible appeal.

Peter Boyce Wendell, who happened at that time to be advocating the enrichment of the American language by the immediate adoption of expressive vernacular words, stood as its sponsor and thundered his indorsement over the placid bromides of the conventional reviewers.

Marcia received three hundred dollars an instalment for the serial publication, which came at an opportune time, for though Horace's monthly salary at the Hippodrome was now more than Marcia's had ever been, young Marcia was emitting shrill cries which they interpreted as a demand for country air. So early April found them installed in a bungalow in Westchester County, with a place for a lawn, a place for a garage, and a place for everything, including a sound-proof impregnable study, in which Marcia faithfully promised Mr. Jordan she would shut herself up when her daughter's demands began to be abated, and compose immortally illiterate literature.

"It's not half bad," thought Horace one night as he was on his way from the station to his house. He was considering several prospects that had opened up, a four months' vaudeville offer in five figures, a chance to go back to Princeton in charge of all gymnasium work. Odd! He had once intended to go back there in charge of all philosophic work, and now he had not even been stirred by the arrival in New York of Anton Laurier, his old idol.

The gravel crunched raucously under his heel. He saw the lights of his sitting-room gleaming and noticed a big car standing in the drive. Probably Mr. Jordan again, come to persuade Marcia to settle down to work.

She had heard the sound of his approach and her form was silhouetted against the lighted door as she came out to meet him.

"There's some Frenchman here," she whispered nervously. "I can't pronounce his name, but he sounds awful deep. You'll have to jaw with him."

"What Frenchman?"

"You can't prove it by me. He drove up an hour ago with Mr. Jordan, and said he wanted to meet Sandra Pepys, and all that sort of thing."

Two men rose from chairs as they went inside.

"Hello, Tarbox," said Jordan. "I've just been bringing together two celebrities. I've brought M'sieur Laurier out with me. M'sieur Laurier, let me present Mr. Tarbox, Mrs. Tarbox's husband."

"Not Anton Laurier!" exclaimed Horace.

"But, yes. I must come. I have to come. I have read the book of Madame, and I have been charmed"—he fumbled in his pocket—"ah, I have read of you too. In this newspaper which I read to-day it has your name."

He finally produced a clipping from a magazine.

"Read it!" he said eagerly. "It has about you too."

Horace's eye skipped down the page.

"A distinct contribution to American dialect literature," it said. "No attempt at literary tone; the book derives its very quality from this fact, as did 'Huckleberry Finn.' "

Horace's eyes caught a passage lower down; he became suddenly aghast—read on hurriedly:

"Marcia Tarbox's connection with the stage is not only as a spectator but as the wife of a performer. She was married last year to Horace Tarbox, who every evening delights the children at the Hippodrome with his wondrous flying-ring performance. It is said that the young couple have dubbed themselves Head and Shoulders, referring doubtless to the fact that Mrs. Tarbox supplies the literary and mental qualities, while the supple and agile shoulders of her husband contribute their share to the family fortunes.

"Mrs. Tarbox seems to merit that much-abused title—'prodigy.' Only twenty——"

Horace stopped reading, and with a very odd expression in his eyes gazed intently at Anton Laurier.

"I want to advise you—" he began hoarsely.

"What?"

"About raps. Don't answer them! Let them alone—have a padded door."

The Ice Palace

The sunlight dripped over the house like golden paint over an art jar, and the freckling shadows here and there only intensified the rigor of the bath of light. The Butterworth and Larkin houses flanking were intrenched behind great stodgy trees; only the Happer house took the full sun, and all day long faced the dusty road-street with a tolerant kindly patience. This was the city of Tarleton in southernmost Georgia, September afternoon.

Up in her bedroom window Sally Carrol Happer rested her nineteen-year-old chin on a fifty-two-year-old sill and watched Clark Darrow's ancient Ford turn the corner. The car was hot—being partly metallic it retained all the heat it absorbed or evolved—and Clark Darrow sitting bolt upright at the wheel wore a pained, strained expression as though he considered himself a spare part, and rather likely to break. He laboriously crossed two dust ruts, the wheels squeaking indignantly at the encounter, and then with a terrifying expression he gave the steering-gear a final wrench and deposited self and car approximately in front of the Happer steps. There was a plaintive heaving sound, a death-rattle, followed by a short silence; and then the air was rent by a startling whistle.

Sally Carrol gazed down sleepily. She started to yawn, but finding this quite impossible unless she raised her chin from the window-sill, changed her mind and continued silently to regard the car, whose owner sat brilliantly if perfunctorily at attention as he waited for an answer to his signal. After a moment the whistle once more split the dusty air.

"Good mawnin'."

With difficulty Clark twisted his tall body round and bent a distorted glance on the window.

"'Tain't mawnin', Sally Carrol."

"Isn't it, sure enough?"

"What you doin'?"

"Eatin' 'n apple."

"Come on go swimmin'—want to?"

"Reckon so."

"How 'bout hurryin' up?"

"Sure enough."

Sally Carrol sighed voluminously and raised herself with profound inertia from the floor, where she had been occupied in alternately destroying parts of a green apple and painting paper dolls for her younger sister. She approached a mirror, regarded her expression with a pleased and pleasant languor, dabbed two spots of rouge on her lips and a grain of powder on her nose, and covered her bobbed corn-colored hair with a rose-littered sunbonnet. Then she kicked over the painting water, said, "Oh, damn!"—but let it lay—and left the room.

"How you, Clark?" she inquired a minute later as she slipped nimbly over the side of the car.

"Mighty fine, Sally Carrol."

"Where we go swimmin'?"

"Out to Walley's Pool. Told Marylyn we'd call by an' get her an' Joe Ewing."

Clark was dark and lean, and when on foot was rather inclined to stoop. His eyes were ominous and his expression somewhat petulant except when startlingly illuminated by one of his frequent smiles. Clark had "a income"—just enough to keep himself in ease and his car in gasolene—and he had spent the two years since he graduated from Georgia Tech in dozing round the lazy streets of his home town, discussing how he could best invest his capital for an immediate fortune.

Hanging round he found not at all difficult; a crowd of little girls had grown up beautifully, the amazing Sally Carrol foremost among them; and they enjoyed being swum with and danced with and made love to in the flower-filled summery evenings—and they all liked Clark immensely. When feminine company palled there were half a dozen other youths who were always just about to do something, and meanwhile were quite willing to join him in a few holes of golf, or a game of billiards, or the consumption of a quart of "hard yella licker." Every once in a while one of these contemporaries made a farewell round of calls before going up to New York or Philadelphia or Pittsburgh to go into business, but mostly they just stayed round in this languid paradise of dreamy skies and firefly evenings and noisy niggery street fairs—and especially of gracious, soft-voiced girls, who were brought up on memories instead of money.

The Ford having been excited into a sort of restless resentful life Clark and Sally Carrol rolled and rattled down Valley Avenue into Jefferson Street, where the dust road became a pavement; along opiate Millicent Place, where there were half a dozen prosperous, substantial mansions; and on into the down-town section. Driving was perilous here, for it was shopping time; the population idled casually across the streets and a drove of low-moaning oxen were being urged along in front of a placid street-car; even the shops seemed only yawning their doors and blinking their windows in the sunshine before retiring into a state of utter and finite coma.

"Sally Carrol," said Clark suddenly, "it a fact that you're engaged?"

She looked at him quickly.

"Where'd you hear that?"

"Sure enough, you engaged?"

"'At's a nice question!"

"Girl told me you were engaged to a Yankee you met up in Asheville last summer."

Sally Carrol sighed.

"Never saw such an old town for rumors."

"Don't marry a Yankee, Sally Carrol. We need you round here."

Sally Carrol was silent a moment.

"Clark," she demanded suddenly, "who on earth shall I marry?"

"I offer my services."

"Honey, you couldn't support a wife," she answered cheerfully. "Anyway, I know you too well to fall in love with you."

"'At doesn't mean you ought to marry a Yankee," he persisted.

"S'pose I love him?"

He shook his head.

"You couldn't. He'd be a lot different from us, every way."

He broke off as he halted the car in front of a rambling, dilapidated house. Marylyn Wade and Joe Ewing appeared in the doorway.

"'Lo, Sally Carrol."

"Hi!"

"How you-all?"

"Sally Carrol," demanded Marylyn as they started off again, "you engaged?"

"Lawdy, where'd all this start? Can't I look at a man 'thout everybody in town engagin' me to him?"

Clark stared straight in front of him at a bolt on the clattering windshield.

"Sally Carrol," he said with a curious intensity, "don't you like us?"

"What?"

"Us down here?"

"Why, Clark, you know I do. I adore all you boys."

"Then why you gettin' engaged to a Yankee?"

"Clark, I don't know. I'm not sure what I'll do, but—well, I want to go places and see people. I want my mind to grow. I want to live where things happen on a big scale."

"What you mean?"

"Oh, Clark, I love you, and I love Joe here, and Ben Arrot, and you-all, but you'll—you'll——"

"We'll all be failures?"

"Yes. I don't mean only money failures, but just sort of—of ineffectual and sad, and—oh, how can I tell you?"

"You mean because we stay here in Tarleton?"

"Yes, Clark; and because you like it and never want to change things or think or go ahead."

He nodded and she reached over and pressed his hand.

"Clark," she said softly, "I wouldn't change you for the world. You're sweet the way you are. The things that'll make you fail I'll love always—the living in the past, the lazy days and nights you have, and all your carelessness and generosity."

"But you're goin' away?"

"Yes—because I couldn't ever marry you. You've a place in my heart no one else ever could have, but tied down here I'd get restless.

I'd feel I was—wastin' myself. There's two sides to me, you see. There's the sleepy old side you love; an' there's a sort of energy—the feelin' that makes me do wild things. That's the part of me that may be useful somewhere, that'll last when I'm not beautiful any more."

She broke off with characteristic suddenness and sighed, "Oh, sweet cooky!" as her mood changed.

Half closing her eyes and tipping back her head till it rested on the seat-back she let the savory breeze fan her eyes and ripple the fluffy curls of her bobbed hair. They were in the country now, hurrying between tangled growths of bright-green coppice and grass and tall trees that sent sprays of foliage to hang a cool welcome over the road. Here and there they passed a battered negro cabin, its oldest white-haired inhabitant smoking a corncob pipe beside the door, and half a dozen scantily clothed pickaninnies parading tattered dolls on the wild-grown grass in front. Farther out were lazy cotton-fields, where even the workers seemed intangible shadows lent by the sun to the earth, not for toil, but to while away some age-old tradition in the golden September fields. And round the drowsy picturesqueness, over the trees and shacks and muddy rivers, flowed the heat, never hostile, only comforting, like a great warm nourishing bosom for the infant earth.

"Sally Carrol, we're here!"

"Poor chile's soun' asleep."

"Honey, you dead at last outa sheer laziness?"

"Water, Sally Carrol! Cool water waitin' for you!"

Her eyes opened sleepily.

"Hi!" she murmured, smiling.

II

In November Harry Bellamy, tall, broad, and brisk, came down from his Northern city to spend four days. His intention was to settle a matter that had been hanging fire since he and Sally Carrol had met in Asheville, North Carolina, in midsummer. The settlement took only a quiet afternoon and an evening in front of a glowing open fire, for Harry Bellamy had everything she wanted; and, besides, she loved him—loved him with that side of her she kept especially for loving. Sally Carrol had several rather clearly defined sides.

On his last afternoon they walked, and she found their steps tending half-unconsciously toward one of her favorite haunts, the cemetery.

When it came in sight, gray-white and golden-green under the cheerful late sun, she paused, irresolute, by the iron gate.

"Are you mournful by nature, Harry?" she asked with a faint smile.

"Mournful? Not I."

"Then let's go in here. It depresses some folks, but I like it."

They passed through the gateway and followed a path that led through a wavy valley of graves—dusty-gray and mouldy for the fifties; quaintly carved with flowers and jars for the seventies; ornate and hideous for the nineties, with fat marble cherubs lying in sodden sleep on stone pillows, and great impossible growths of nameless granite flowers. Occasionally they saw a kneeling figure with tributary flowers, but over most of the graves lay silence and withered leaves with only the fragrance that their own shadowy memories could waken in living minds.

They reached the top of a hill where they were fronted by a tall, round head-stone, freckled with dark spots of damp and half grown over with vines.

"Margery Lee," she read; "1844–1873. Wasn't she nice? She died when she was twenty-nine. Dear Margery Lee," she added softly. "Can't you see her, Harry?"

"Yes, Sally Carrol."

He felt a little hand insert itself into his.

"She was dark, I think; and she always wore her hair with a ribbon in it, and gorgeous hoop-skirts of alice blue and old rose."

"Yes."

"Oh, she was sweet, Harry! And she was the sort of girl born to stand on a wide, pillared porch and welcome folks in. I think perhaps a lot of men went away to war meanin' to come back to her; but maybe none of 'em ever did."

He stooped down close to the stone, hunting for any record of marriage.

"There's nothing here to show."

"Of course not. How could there be anything there better than just 'Margery Lee,' and that eloquent date?"

She drew close to him and an unexpected lump came into his throat as her yellow hair brushed his cheek.

"You see how she was, don't you, Harry?"

"I see," he agreed gently. "I see through your precious eyes. You're beautiful now, so I know she must have been."

Silent and close they stood, and he could feel her shoulders trembling a little. An ambling breeze swept up the hill and stirred the brim of her floppidy hat.

"Let's go down there!"

She was pointing to a flat stretch on the other side of the hill where along the green turf were a thousand grayish-white crosses stretching in endless, ordered rows like the stacked arms of a battalion.

"Those are the Confederate dead," said Sally Carrol simply.

They walked along and read the inscriptions, always only a name and a date, sometimes quite indecipherable.

"The last row is the saddest—see, 'way over there. Every cross has just a date on it, and the word 'Unknown.' "

She looked at him and her eyes brimmed with tears.

"I can't tell you how real it is to me, darling—if you don't know."

"How you feel about it is beautiful to me."

"No, no, it's not me, it's them—that old time that I've tried to have live in me. These were just men, unimportant evidently or they wouldn't have been 'unknown'; but they died for the most beautiful thing in the world—the dead South. You see," she continued, her voice still husky, her eyes glistening with tears, "people have these dreams they fasten onto things, and I've always grown up with that dream. It was so easy because it was all dead and there weren't any disillusions comin' to me. I've tried in a way to live up to those past standards of noblesse oblige—there's just the last remnants of it, you know, like the roses of an old garden dying all round us—streaks of strange courtliness and chivalry in some of these boys an' stories I used to hear from a Confederate soldier who lived next door, and a few old darkies. Oh, Harry, there was something, there was something! I couldn't ever make you understand, but it was there."

"I understand," he assured her again quietly.

Sally Carrol smiled and dried her eyes on the tip of a handkerchief protruding from his breast pocket.

"You don't feel depressed, do you, lover? Even when I cry I'm happy here, and I get a sort of strength from it."

Hand in hand they turned and walked slowly away. Finding soft grass she drew him down to a seat beside her with their backs against the remnants of a low broken wall.

"Wish those three old women would clear out," he complained. "I want to kiss you, Sally Carrol."

"Me, too."

They waited impatiently for the three bent figures to move off, and then she kissed him until the sky seemed to fade out and all her smiles and tears to vanish in an ecstasy of eternal seconds.

Afterward they walked slowly back together, while on the corners twilight played at somnolent black-and-white checkers with the end of day.

"You'll be up about mid-January," he said, "and you've got to stay a month at least. It'll be slick. There's a winter carnival on, and if you've never really seen snow it'll be like fairy-land to you. There'll be skating and skiing and tobogganing and sleigh-riding, and all sorts of torchlight parades on snow-shoes. They haven't had one for years, so they're going to make it a knock-out."

"Will I be cold, Harry?" she asked suddenly.

"You certainly won't. You may freeze your nose, but you won't be shivery cold. It's hard and dry, you know."

"I guess I'm a summer child. I don't like any cold I've ever seen."

She broke off and they were both silent for a minute.

"Sally Carrol," he said very slowly, "what do you say to—March?"

"I say I love you."

"March?"

"March, Harry."

III

All night in the Pullman it was very cold. She rang for the porter to ask for another blanket, and when he couldn't give her one she tried vainly, by squeezing down into the bottom of her berth and doubling back the bedclothes, to snatch a few hours' sleep. She wanted to look her best in the morning.

She rose at six and sliding uncomfortably into her clothes stumbled up to the diner for a cup of coffee. The snow had filtered into the vestibules and covered the floor with a slippery coating. It was intriguing, this cold, it crept in everywhere. Her breath was quite visible and she blew into the air with a naïve enjoyment. Seated in the diner she stared out the window at white hills and valleys and scattered pines whose every branch was a green platter for a cold feast of snow. Sometimes a solitary farmhouse would fly by, ugly and bleak and lone on the white waste; and with each one she had an instant of chill compassion for the souls shut in there waiting for spring.

As she left the diner and swayed back into the Pullman she experienced a surging rush of energy and wondered if she was feeling the bracing air of which Harry had spoken. This was the North, the North—her land now!

"Then blow, ye winds, heigho!
A-roving I will go,"[1]

she chanted exultantly to herself.

"What's 'at?" inquired the porter politely.

"I said: 'Brush me off.' ".

The long wires of the telegraph-poles doubled; two tracks ran up beside the train—three—four; came a succession of white-roofed houses, a glimpse of a trolley-car with frosted windows, streets—more streets—the city.

She stood for a dazed moment in the frosty station before she saw three fur-bundled figures descending upon her.

"There she is!"

"Oh, Sally Carrol!"

Sally Carrol dropped her bag.

"Hi!"

A faintly familiar icy-cold face kissed her, and then she was in a group of faces all apparently emitting great clouds of heavy smoke; she was shaking hands. There were Gordon, a short, eager man of thirty who looked like an amateur knocked-about model for Harry, and his wife, Myra, a listless lady with flaxen hair under a fur automobile cap. Almost immediately Sally Carrol thought of her as vaguely Scandinavian. A cheerful chauffeur adopted her bag, and amid ricochets of half-phrases, exclamations, and perfunctory listless "my dears" from Myra, they swept each other from the station.

Then they were in a sedan bound through a crooked succession of snowy streets where dozens of little boys were hitching sleds behind grocery wagons and automobiles.

"Oh," cried Sally Carrol, "I want to do that! Can we, Harry?"

"That's for kids. But we might——"

"It looks like such a circus!" she said regretfully.

Home was a rambling frame house set on a white lap of snow, and there she met a big, gray-haired man of whom she approved, and a lady who was like an egg, and who kissed her—these were Harry's parents. There was a breathless indescribable hour crammed full of half-sentences, hot water, bacon and eggs and confusion; and after that she was alone with Harry in the library, asking him if she dared smoke.

It was a large room with a Madonna over the fireplace and rows upon rows of books in covers of light gold and dark gold and shiny red. All the chairs had little lace squares where one's head should rest, the couch was just comfortable, the books looked as if they had been read—some—and Sally Carrol had an instantaneous vision of the battered old library at home, with her father's huge medical books, and the oil-paintings of her three great-uncles, and the old couch that had been mended up for forty-five years and was still luxurious to dream in. This room struck her as being neither attractive nor particularly otherwise. It was simply a room with a lot of fairly expensive things in it that all looked about fifteen years old.

"What do you think of it up here?" demanded Harry eagerly. "Does it surprise you? Is it what you expected, I mean?"

"You are, Harry," she said quietly, and reached out her arms to him.

But after a brief kiss he seemed anxious to extort enthusiasm from her.

"The town, I mean. Do you like it? Can you feel the pep in the air?"

"Oh, Harry," she laughed, "you'll have to give me time. You can't just fling questions at me."

She puffed at her cigarette with a sigh of contentment.

"One thing I want to ask you," he began rather apologetically; "you Southerners put quite an emphasis on family, and all that—not that it isn't quite all right, but you'll find it a little different here. I mean—you'll notice a lot of things that'll seem to you sort of vulgar display at first, Sally Carrol; but just remember that this is a three-generation town. Everybody has a father, and about half of us have grandfathers. Back of that we don't go."

"Of course," she murmured.

"Our grandfathers, you see, founded the place, and a lot of them had to take some pretty queer jobs while they were doing the founding. For instance, there's one woman who at present is about the social model for the town; well, her father was the first public ash man—things like that."

"Why," said Sally Carrol, puzzled, "did you s'pose I was goin' to make remarks about people?"

"Not at all," interrupted Harry; "and I'm not apologizing for any one either. It's just that—well, a Southern girl came up here last summer and said some unfortunate things, and—oh, I just thought I'd tell you."

Sally Carrol felt suddenly indignant—as though she had been unjustly spanked—but Harry evidently considered the subject closed, for he went on with a great surge of enthusiasm.

"It's carnival time, you know. First in ten years. And there's an ice palace they're building now that's the first they've had since eighty-five. Built out of blocks of the clearest ice they could find—on a tremendous scale."

She rose and walking to the window pushed aside the heavy Turkish portières and looked out.

"Oh!" she cried suddenly. "There's two little boys makin' a snow man! Harry, do you reckon I can go out an' help 'em?"

"You dream! Come here and kiss me."

She left the window rather reluctantly.

"I don't guess this is a very kissable climate, is it? I mean, it makes you so you don't want to sit round, doesn't it?"

"We're not going to. I've got a vacation for the first week you're here, and there's a dinner-dance to-night."

"Oh, Harry," she confessed, subsiding in a heap, half in his lap, half in the pillows, "I sure do feel confused. I haven't got an idea whether I'll like it or not, an' I don't know what people expect, or anythin'. You'll have to tell me, honey."

"I'll tell you," he said softly, "if you'll just tell me you're glad to be here."

"Glad—just awful glad!" she whispered, insinuating herself into his arms in her own peculiar way. "Where you are is home for me, Harry."

And as she said this she had the feeling for almost the first time in her life that she was acting a part.

That night, amid the gleaming candles of a dinner-party, where the men seemed to do most of the talking while the girls sat in a haughty and expensive aloofness, even Harry's presence on her left failed to make her feel at home.

"They're a good-looking crowd, don't you think?" he demanded. "Just look round. There's Spud Hubbard, tackle at Princeton last year, and Junie Morton—he and the red-haired fellow next to him were both Yale hockey captains; Junie was in my class. Why, the best athletes in the world come from these States round here. This is a man's country, I tell you. Look at John J. Fishburn!"

"Who's he?" asked Sally Carrol innocently.

"Don't you know?"

"I've heard the name."

"Greatest wheat man in the Northwest, and one of the greatest financiers in the country."

She turned suddenly to a voice on her right.

"I guess they forgot to introduce us. My name's Roger Patton."

"My name is Sally Carrol Happer," she said graciously.

"Yes, I know. Harry told me you were coming."

"You a relative?"

"No, I'm a professor."

"Oh," she laughed.

"At the university. You're from the South, aren't you?"

"Yes; Tarleton, Georgia."

She liked him immediately—a reddish-brown mustache under watery blue eyes that had something in them that these other eyes lacked, some quality of appreciation. They exchanged stray sentences through dinner, and she made up her mind to see him again.

After coffee she was introduced to numerous good-looking young men who danced with conscious precision and seemed to take it for granted that she wanted to talk about nothing except Harry.

"Heavens," she thought, "they talk as if my being engaged made me older than they are—as if I'd tell their mothers on them!"

In the South an engaged girl, even a young married woman, expected the same amount of half-affectionate badinage and flattery that would be accorded a débutante, but here all that seemed banned. One young man, after getting well started on the subject of Sally Carrol's eyes, and how they had allured him ever since she entered the room, went into a violent confusion when he found she was visiting the

Bellamys—was Harry's fiancée. He seemed to feel as though he had made some risqué and inexcusable blunder, became immediately formal, and left her at the first opportunity.

She was rather glad when Roger Patton cut in on her and suggested that they sit out a while.

"Well," he inquired, blinking cheerily, "how's Carmen from the South?"

"Mighty fine. How's—how's Dangerous Dan McGrew?[2] Sorry, but he's the only Northerner I know much about."

He seemed to enjoy that.

"Of course," he confessed, "as a professor of literature I'm not supposed to have read Dangerous Dan McGrew."

"Are you a native?"

"No, I'm a Philadelphian. Imported from Harvard to teach French. But I've been here ten years."

"Nine years, three hundred an' sixty-four days longer than me."

"Like it here?"

"Uh-huh. Sure do!"

"Really?"

"Well, why not? Don't I look as if I were havin' a good time?"

"I saw you look out the window a minute ago—and shiver."

"Just my imagination," laughed Sally Carrol. "I'm used to havin' everythin' quiet outside, an' sometimes I look out an' see a flurry of snow, an' it's just as if somethin' dead was movin'."

He nodded appreciatively.

"Ever been North before?"

"Spent two Julys in Asheville, North Carolina."

"Nice-looking crowd, aren't they?" suggested Patton, indicating the swirling floor.

Sally Carrol started. This had been Harry's remark.

"Sure are! They're—canine."

"What?"

She flushed.

"I'm sorry; that sounded worse than I meant it. You see I always think of people as feline or canine, irrespective of sex."

"Which are you?"

"I'm feline. So are you. So are most Southern men an' most of these girls here."

"What's Harry?"

"Harry's canine distinctly. All the men I've met to-night seem to be canine."

"What does 'canine' imply? A certain conscious masculinity as opposed to subtlety?"

"Reckon so. I never analyzed it—only I just look at people an' say 'canine' or 'feline' right off. It's right absurd, I guess."

"Not at all. I'm interested. I used to have a theory about these people. I think they're freezing up."

"What?"

"I think they're growing like Swedes—Ibsenesque, you know. Very gradually getting gloomy and melancholy. It's these long winters. Ever read any Ibsen?"[3]

She shook her head.

"Well, you find in his characters a certain brooding rigidity. They're righteous, narrow, and cheerless, without infinite possibilities for great sorrow or joy."

"Without smiles or tears?"

"Exactly. That's my theory. You see there are thousands of Swedes up here. They come, I imagine, because the climate is very much like their own, and there's been a gradual mingling. There're probably not half a dozen here to-night, but—we've had four Swedish governors. Am I boring you?"

"I'm mighty interested."

"Your future sister-in-law is half Swedish. Personally I like her, but my theory is that Swedes react rather badly on us as a whole. Scandinavians, you know, have the largest suicide rate in the world."

"Why do you live here if it's so depressing?"

"Oh, it doesn't get me. I'm pretty well cloistered, and I suppose books mean more than people to me anyway."

"But writers all speak about the South being tragic. You know—Spanish señoritas, black hair and daggers an' haunting music."

He shook his head.

"No, the Northern races are the tragic races—they don't indulge in the cheering luxury of tears."

Sally Carrol thought of her graveyard. She supposed that that was vaguely what she had meant when she said it didn't depress her.

"The Italians are about the gayest people in the world—but it's a dull subject," he broke off. "Anyway, I want to tell you you're marrying a pretty fine man."

Sally Carrol was moved by an impulse of confidence.

"I know. I'm the sort of person who wants to be taken care of after a certain point, and I feel sure I will be."

"Shall we dance? You know," he continued as they rose, "it's encouraging to find a girl who knows what she's marrying for. Nine-tenths of them think of it as a sort of walking into a moving-picture sunset."

She laughed, and liked him immensely.

Two hours later on the way home she nestled near Harry in the back seat.

"Oh, Harry," she whispered, "it's so co-old!"

"But it's warm in here, darling girl."

"But outside it's cold; and oh, that howling wind!"

She buried her face deep in his fur coat and trembled involuntarily as his cold lips kissed the tip of her ear.

IV

The first week of her visit passed in a whirl. She had her promised toboggan-ride at the back of an automobile through a chill January twilight. Swathed in furs she put in a morning tobogganing on the country-club hill; even tried skiing, to sail through the air for a glorious moment and then land in a tangled laughing bundle on a soft snowdrift. She liked all the winter sports, except an afternoon spent snow-shoeing over a glaring plain under pale yellow sunshine, but she soon realized that these things were for children—that she was being humored and that the enjoyment round her was only a reflection of her own.

At first the Bellamy family puzzled her. The men were reliable and she liked them; to Mr. Bellamy especially, with his iron-gray hair and energetic dignity, she took an immediate fancy, once she found that he was born in Kentucky; this made of him a link between the old life and the new. But toward the women she felt a definite hostility. Myra, her future sister-in-law, seemed the essence of spiritless conventionality. Her conversation was so utterly devoid of personality that Sally Carrol, who came from a country where a certain amount of charm and assurance could be taken for granted in the women, was inclined to despise her.

"If those women aren't beautiful," she thought, "they're nothing. They just fade out when you look at them. They're glorified domestics. Men are the centre of every mixed group."

Lastly there was Mrs. Bellamy, whom Sally Carrol detested. The first day's impression of an egg had been confirmed—an egg with a cracked, veiny voice and such an ungracious dumpiness of carriage that Sally Carrol felt that if she once fell she would surely scramble. In addition, Mrs. Bellamy seemed to typify the town in being innately hostile to strangers. She called Sally Carrol "Sally," and could not be persuaded that the double name was anything more than a tedious ridiculous nickname. To Sally Carrol this shortening of her name was like presenting her to the public half clothed. She loved "Sally Carrol"; she loathed "Sally." She knew also that Harry's mother disapproved of her bobbed hair; and she had never dared smoke down-stairs after that first day when Mrs. Bellamy had come into the library sniffing violently.

Of all the men she met she preferred Roger Patton, who was a frequent visitor at the house. He never again alluded to the Ibsenesque tendency of the populace, but when he came in one day and found her curled upon the sofa bent over "Peer Gynt" he laughed and told her to forget what he'd said—that it was all rot.

And then one afternoon in her second week she and Harry hovered on the edge of a dangerously steep quarrel. She considered that he precipitated it entirely, though the Serbia in the case[4] was an unknown man who had not had his trousers pressed.

They had been walking homeward between mounds of high-piled snow and under a sun which Sally Carrol scarcely recognized. They passed a little girl done up in gray wool until she resembled a small Teddy bear, and Sally Carrol could not resist a gasp of maternal appreciation.

"Look! Harry!"

"What?"

"That little girl—did you see her face?"

"Yes, why?"

"It was red as a little strawberry. Oh, she was cute!"

"Why, your own face is almost as red as that already! Everybody's healthy here. We're out in the cold as soon as we're old enough to walk. Wonderful climate!"

She looked at him and had to agree. He was mighty healthy-looking;

so was his brother. And she had noticed the new red in her own cheeks that very morning.

Suddenly their glances were caught and held, and they stared for a moment at the street-corner ahead of them. A man was standing there, his knees bent, his eyes gazing upward with a tense expression as though he were about to make a leap toward the chilly sky. And then they both exploded into a shout of laughter, for coming closer they discovered it had been a ludicrous momentary illusion produced by the extreme bagginess of the man's trousers.

"Reckon that's one on us," she laughed.

"He must be a Southerner, judging by those trousers," suggested Harry mischievously.

"Why, Harry!"

Her surprised look must have irritated him.

"Those damn Southerners!"

Sally Carrol's eyes flashed.

"Don't call 'em that!"

"I'm sorry, dear," said Harry, malignantly apologetic, "but you know what I think of them. They're sort of—sort of degenerates—not at all like the old Southerners. They've lived so long down there with all the colored people that they've gotten lazy and shiftless."

"Hush your mouth, Harry!" she cried angrily. "They're not! They may be lazy—anybody would be in that climate—but they're my best friends, an' I don't want to hear 'em criticised in any such sweepin' way. Some of 'em are the finest men in the world."

"Oh, I know. They're all right when they come North to college, but of all the hangdog, ill-dressed, slovenly lot I ever saw, a bunch of small-town Southerners are the worst!"

Sally Carrol was clinching her gloved hands and biting her lip furiously.

"Why," continued Harry, "there was one in my class at New Haven, and we all thought that at last we'd found the true type of Southern aristocrat, but it turned out that he wasn't an aristocrat at all—just the son of a Northern carpetbagger, who owned about all the cotton round Mobile."

"A Southerner wouldn't talk the way you're talking now," she said evenly.

"They haven't the energy!"

"Or the somethin' else."

"I'm sorry, Sally Carrol, but I've heard you say yourself that you'd never marry——"

"That's quite different. I told you I wouldn't want to tie my life to any of the boys that are round Tarleton now, but I never made any sweepin' generalities."

They walked along in silence.

"I probably spread it on a bit thick, Sally Carrol. I'm sorry."

She nodded but made no answer. Five minutes later as they stood in the hallway she suddenly threw her arms round him.

"Oh, Harry," she cried, her eyes brimming with tears, "let's get married next week. I'm afraid of having fusses like that. I'm afraid, Harry. It wouldn't be that way if we were married."

But Harry, being in the wrong, was still irritated.

"That'd be idiotic. We decided on March."

The tears in Sally Carrol's eyes faded; her expression hardened slightly.

"Very well—I suppose I shouldn't have said that."

Harry melted.

"Dear little nut!" he cried. "Come and kiss me and let's forget."

That very night at the end of a vaudeville performance the orchestra played "Dixie" and Sally Carrol felt something stronger and more enduring than her tears and smiles of the day brim up inside her. She leaned forward gripping the arms of her chair until her face grew crimson.

"Sort of get you, dear?" whispered Harry.

But she did not hear him. To the spirited throb of the violins and the inspiring beat of the kettle-drums her own old ghosts were marching by and on into the darkness, and as fifes whistled and sighed in the low encore they seemed so nearly out of sight that she could have waved good-by.

"Away, Away,
    Away down South in Dixie!
Away, away,
    Away down South in Dixie!"

V

It was a particularly cold night. A sudden thaw had nearly cleared the streets the day before, but now they were traversed again with a powdery wraith of loose snow that travelled in wavy lines before the feet of the wind, and filled the lower air with a fine-particled mist. There was no sky—only a dark, ominous tent that draped in the tops of the streets and was in reality a vast approaching army of snowflakes—while over it all, chilling away the comfort from the brown-and-green glow of lighted windows and muffling the steady trot of the horse pulling their sleigh, interminably washed the north wind. It was a dismal town after all, she thought—dismal.

Sometimes at night it had seemed to her as though no one lived here—they had all gone long ago—leaving lighted houses to be covered in time by tombing heaps of sleet. Oh, if there should be snow on her grave! To be beneath great piles of it all winter long, where even her headstone would be a light shadow against light shadows. Her grave—a grave that should be flower-strewn and washed with sun and rain.

She thought again of those isolated country houses that her train had passed, and of the life there the long winter through—the ceaseless glare through the windows, the crust forming on the soft drifts of snow, finally the slow, cheerless melting, and the harsh spring of which Roger Patton had told her. Her spring—to lose it forever—with its lilacs and the lazy sweetness it stirred in her heart. She was laying away that spring—afterward she would lay away that sweetness.

With a gradual insistence the storm broke. Sally Carrol felt a film of flakes melt quickly on her eyelashes, and Harry reached over a furry arm and drew down her complicated flannel cap. Then the small flakes came in skirmish-line, and the horse bent his neck patiently as a transparency of white appeared momentarily on his coat.

"Oh, he's cold, Harry," she said quickly.

"Who? The horse? Oh, no, he isn't. He likes it!"

After another ten minutes they turned a corner and came in sight of their destination. On a tall hill outlined in vivid glaring green against the wintry sky stood the ice palace.[5] It was three stories in the air, with battlements and embrasures and narrow icicled windows, and the innumerable electric lights inside made a gorgeous transparency of the great central hall. Sally Carrol clutched Harry's hand under the fur robe.

"It's beautiful!" he cried excitedly. "My golly, it's beautiful, isn't it! They haven't had one here since eighty-five!"

Somehow the notion of there not having been one since eighty-five oppressed her. Ice was a ghost, and this mansion of it was surely peopled by those shades of the eighties, with pale faces and blurred snow-filled hair.

"Come on, dear," said Harry.

She followed him out of the sleigh and waited while he hitched the horse. A party of four—Gordon, Myra, Roger Patton, and another girl—drew up beside them with a mighty jingle of bells. There were quite a crowd already, bundled in fur or sheepskin, shouting and calling to each other as they moved through the snow, which was now so thick that people could scarcely be distinguished a few yards away.

"It's a hundred and seventy feet tall," Harry was saying to a muffled figure beside him as they trudged toward the entrance; "covers six thousand square yards."

She caught snatches of conversation: "One main hall"—"walls twenty to forty inches thick"—"and the ice cave has almost a mile of—"—"this Canuck who built it——"

They found their way inside, and dazed by the magic of the great crystal walls Sally Carrol found herself repeating over and over two lines from "Kubla Khan":

> "It was a miracle of rare device,
> A sunny pleasure-dome with caves of ice!"[6]

In the great glittering cavern with the dark shut out she took a seat on a wooden bench, and the evening's oppression lifted. Harry was right—it was beautiful; and her gaze travelled the smooth surface of the walls, the blocks for which had been selected for their purity and clearness to obtain this opalescent, translucent effect.

"Look! Here we go—oh, boy!" cried Harry.

A band in a far corner struck up "Hail, Hail, the Gang's All Here!" which echoed over to them in wild muddled acoustics, and then the lights suddenly went out; silence seemed to flow down the icy sides and sweep over them. Sally Carrol could still see her white breath in the darkness, and a dim row of pale faces over on the other side.

The music eased to a sighing complaint, and from outside drifted in the full-throated resonant chant of the marching clubs. It grew louder like some pæan of a viking tribe traversing an ancient wild; it swelled—

they were coming nearer; then a row of torches appeared, and another and another, and keeping time with their moccasined feet a long column of gray-mackinawed figures swept in, snow-shoes slung at their shoulders, torches soaring and flickering as their voices rose along the great walls.

The gray column ended and another followed, the light streaming luridly this time over red toboggan caps and flaming crimson mackinaws, and as they entered they took up the refrain; then came a long platoon of blue and white, of green, of white, of brown and yellow.

"Those white ones are the Wacouta Club,"[7] whispered Harry eagerly. "Those are the men you've met round at dances."

The volume of the voices grew; the great cavern was a phantasmagoria of torches waving in great banks of fire, of colors and the rhythm of soft-leather steps. The leading column turned and halted, platoon deployed in front of platoon until the whole procession made a solid flag of flame, and then from thousands of voices burst a mighty shout that filled the air like a crash of thunder, and sent the torches wavering. It was magnificent, it was tremendous! To Sally Carrol it was the North offering sacrifice on some mighty altar to the gray pagan God of Snow. As the shout died the band struck up again and there came more singing, and then long reverberating cheers by each club. She sat very quiet listening while the staccato cries rent the stillness; and then she started, for there was a volley of explosion, and great clouds of smoke went up here and there through the cavern—the flash-light photographers at work—and the council was over. With the band at their head the clubs formed in column once more, took up their chant, and began to march out.

"Come on!" shouted Harry. "We want to see the labyrinths downstairs before they turn the lights off!"

They all rose and started toward the chute—Harry and Sally Carrol in the lead, her little mitten buried in his big fur gauntlet. At the bottom of the chute was a long empty room of ice, with the ceiling so low that they had to stoop—and their hands were parted. Before she realized what he intended Harry had darted down one of the half-dozen glittering passages that opened into the room and was only a vague receding blot against the green shimmer.

"Harry!" she called.

"Come on!" he cried back.

She looked round the empty chamber; the rest of the party had evidently decided to go home, were already outside somewhere in the blundering snow. She hesitated and then darted in after Harry.

"Harry!" she shouted.

She had reached a turning-point thirty feet down; she heard a faint muffled answer far to the left, and with a touch of panic fled toward it. She passed another turning, two more yawning alleys.

"Harry!"

No answer. She started to run straight forward, and then turned like lightning and sped back the way she had come, enveloped in a sudden icy terror.

She reached a turn—was it here?—took the left and came to what should have been the outlet into the long, low room, but it was only another glittering passage with darkness at the end. She called again, but the walls gave back a flat, lifeless echo with no reverberations. Retracing her steps she turned another corner, this time following a wide passage. It was like the green lane between the parted waters of the Red Sea, like a damp vault connecting empty tombs.

She slipped a little now as she walked, for ice had formed on the bottom of her overshoes; she had to run her gloves along the half-slippery, half-sticky walls to keep her balance.

"Harry!"

Still no answer. The sound she made bounced mockingly down to the end of the passage.

Then on an instant the lights went out, and she was in complete darkness. She gave a small, frightened cry, and sank down into a cold little heap on the ice. She felt her left knee do something as she fell, but she scarcely noticed it as some deep terror far greater than any fear of being lost settled upon her. She was alone with this presence that came out of the North, the dreary loneliness that rose from ice-bound whalers in the Arctic seas, from smokeless, trackless wastes where were strewn the whitened bones of adventure. It was an icy breath of death; it was rolling down low across the land to clutch at her.

With a furious, despairing energy she rose again and started blindly down the darkness. She must get out. She might be lost in here for days, freeze to death and lie embedded in the ice like corpses she had read of, kept perfectly preserved until the melting of a glacier. Harry probably thought she had left with the others—he had gone by now; no one would know until late next day. She reached pitifully for the wall. Forty inches thick, they had said—forty inches thick!

"Oh!"

On both sides of her along the walls she felt things creeping, damp souls that haunted this palace, this town, this North.

"Oh, send somebody—send somebody!" she cried aloud.

Clark Darrow—he would understand; or Joe Ewing; she couldn't be left here to wander forever—to be frozen, heart, body, and soul. This her—this Sally Carrol! Why, she was a happy thing. She was a happy little girl. She liked warmth and summer and Dixie. These things were foreign—foreign.

"You're not crying," something said aloud. "You'll never cry any more. Your tears would just freeze; all tears freeze up here!"

She sprawled full length on the ice.

"Oh, God!" she faltered.

A long single file of minutes went by, and with a great weariness she felt her eyes closing. Then some one seemed to sit down near her and take her face in warm, soft hands. She looked up gratefully.

"Why, it's Margery Lee," she crooned softly to herself. "I knew you'd come." It really was Margery Lee, and she was just as Sally Carrol had known she would be, with a young, white brow, and wide, welcoming eyes, and a hoop-skirt of some soft material that was quite comforting to rest on.

"Margery Lee."

It was getting darker now and darker—all those tombstones ought to be repainted, sure enough, only that would spoil 'em, of course. Still, you ought to be able to see 'em.

Then after a succession of moments that went fast and then slow, but seemed to be ultimately resolving themselves into a multitude of blurred rays converging toward a pale-yellow sun, she heard a great cracking noise break her new-found stillness.

It was the sun, it was a light; a torch, and a torch beyond that, and another one, and voices; a face took flesh below the torch, heavy arms raised her, and she felt something on her cheek—it felt wet. Some one had seized her and was rubbing her face with snow. How ridiculous—with snow!

"Sally Carrol! Sally Carrol!"

It was Dangerous Dan McGrew; and two other faces she didn't know.

"Child, child! We've been looking for you two hours! Harry's half-crazy!"

Things came rushing back into place—the singing, the torches, the great shout of the marching clubs. She squirmed in Patton's arms and gave a long low cry.

"Oh, I want to get out of here! I'm going back home. Take me home"—her voice rose to a scream that sent a chill to Harry's heart as he came racing down the next passage—"to-morrow!" she cried with delirious, unrestrained passion—"To-morrow! To-morrow! To-morrow!"

VI

The wealth of golden sunlight poured a quite enervating yet oddly comforting heat over the house where day long it faced the dusty stretch of road. Two birds were making a great to-do in a cool spot found among the branches of a tree next door, and down the street a colored woman was announcing herself melodiously as a purveyor of strawberries. It was April afternoon.

Sally Carrol Happer, resting her chin on her arm, and her arm on an old window-seat, gazed sleepily down over the spangled dust whence the heat waves were rising for the first time this spring. She was watching a very ancient Ford turn a perilous corner and rattle and groan to a jolting stop at the end of the walk. She made no sound, and in a minute a strident familiar whistle rent the air. Sally Carrol smiled and blinked.

"Good mawnin'."

A head appeared tortuously from under the car-top below.

"'Tain't mawnin', Sally Carrol."

"Sure enough!" she said in affected surprise. "I guess maybe not."

"What you doin'?"

"Eatin' green peach. 'Spect to die any minute."

Clark twisted himself a last impossible notch to get a view of her face.

"Water's warm as a kettla steam, Sally Carrol. Wanta go swimmin'?"

"Hate to move," sighed Sally Carrol lazily, "but I reckon so."

Bernice Bobs Her Hair

After dark on Saturday night one could stand on the first tee of the golf-course and see the country-club windows as a yellow expanse over a very black and wavy ocean. The waves of this ocean, so to speak, were the heads of many curious caddies, a few of the more ingenious chauffeurs, the golf professional's deaf sister—and there were usually several stray, diffident waves who might have rolled inside had they so desired. This was the gallery.

The balcony was inside. It consisted of the circle of wicker chairs that lined the wall of the combination clubroom and ballroom. At these Saturday-night dances it was largely feminine; a great babel of middle-aged ladies with sharp eyes and icy hearts behind lorgnettes and large bosoms. The main function of the balcony was critical. It occasionally showed grudging admiration, but never approval, for it is well known among ladies over thirty-five that when the younger set dance in the summer-time it is with the very worst intentions in the world, and if they are not bombarded with stony eyes stray couples will dance weird barbaric interludes in the corners, and the more popular, more dangerous, girls will sometimes be kissed in the parked limousines of unsuspecting dowagers.

But, after all, this critical circle is not close enough to the stage to see the actors' faces and catch the subtler byplay. It can only frown and lean, ask questions and make satisfactory deductions from its set of postulates, such as the one which states that every young man with a large income leads the life of a hunted partridge. It never really appreciates the drama of the shifting, semicruel world of adolescence. No; boxes, orchestra-circle, principals, and chorus are represented by the medley of faces and voices that sway to the plaintive African rhythm of Dyer's dance orchestra.

From sixteen-year-old Otis Ormonde, who has two more years at Hill School,[1] to G. Reece Stoddard, over whose bureau at home hangs a Harvard law diploma; from little Madeleine Hogue, whose hair still feels strange and uncomfortable on top of her head, to Bessie MacRae, who has been the life of the party a little too long—more than ten years—the medley is not only the centre of the stage but contains the only people capable of getting an unobstructed view of it.

With a flourish and a bang the music stops. The couples exchange artificial, effortless smiles, facetiously repeat "*la*-de-*da-da* dum-*dum*," and then the clatter of young feminine voices soars over the burst of clapping.

A few disappointed stags caught in midfloor as they had been about to cut in subsided listlessly back to the walls, because this was not like the riotous Christmas dances—these summer hops were considered just pleasantly warm and exciting, where even the younger marrieds rose and performed ancient waltzes and terrifying fox trots to the tolerant amusement of their younger brothers and sisters.

Warren McIntyre, who casually attended Yale, being one of the unfortunate stags, felt in his dinner-coat pocket for a cigarette and strolled out onto the wide, semidark veranda, where couples were scattered at tables, filling the lantern-hung night with vague words and hazy laughter. He nodded here and there at the less absorbed and as he passed each couple some half-forgotten fragment of a story played in his mind, for it was not a large city and every one was Who's Who to every one else's past. There, for example, were Jim Strain and Ethel Demorest, who had been privately engaged for three years. Every one knew that as soon as Jim managed to hold a job for more than two months she would marry him. Yet how bored they both looked, and how wearily Ethel regarded Jim sometimes, as if she wondered why she had trained the vines of her affection on such a wind-shaken poplar.

Warren was nineteen and rather pitying with those of his friends who hadn't gone East to college. But, like most boys, he bragged tremendously about the girls of his city when he was away from it. There was Genevieve Ormonde, who regularly made the rounds of dances, house-parties, and football games at Princeton, Yale, Williams, and Cornell; there was black-eyed Roberta Dillon, who was quite as famous to her own generation as Hiram Johnson[2] or Ty Cobb;[3] and, of course, there was Marjorie Harvey, who besides having a fairylike face and a dazzling, bewildering tongue was already justly celebrated for having turned five cart-wheels in succession during the last pump-and-slipper dance at New Haven.

Warren, who had grown up across the street from Marjorie, had long been "crazy about her." Sometimes she seemed to reciprocate his feeling with a faint gratitude, but she had tried him by her infallible test and informed him gravely that she did not love him. Her test was that when she was away from him she forgot him and had affairs with other boys. Warren found this discouraging, especially as Marjorie had been making little trips all summer, and for the first two or three days after each arrival home he saw great heaps of mail on the Harveys' hall table addressed to her in various masculine handwritings. To make matters worse, all during the month of August she had been visited by her cousin Bernice from Eau Claire, and it seemed impossible to see her alone. It was always necessary to hunt round and find some one to take care of Bernice. As August waned this was becoming more and more difficult.

Much as Warren worshipped Marjorie, he had to admit that Cousin Bernice was sorta dopeless. She was pretty, with dark hair and high color, but she was no fun on a party. Every Saturday night he danced a long arduous duty dance with her to please Marjorie, but he had never been anything but bored in her company.

"Warren"—a soft voice at his elbow broke in upon his thoughts, and he turned to see Marjorie, flushed and radiant as usual. She laid a hand on his shoulder and a glow settled almost imperceptibly over him.

"Warren," she whispered, "do something for me—dance with Bernice. She's been stuck with little Otis Ormonde for almost an hour."

Warren's glow faded.

"Why—sure," he answered half-heartedly.

"You don't mind, do you? I'll see that you don't get stuck."

"'Sall right."

Marjorie smiled—that smile that was thanks enough.

"You're an angel, and I'm obliged loads."

With a sigh the angel glanced round the veranda, but Bernice and Otis were not in sight. He wandered back inside, and there in front of the women's dressing-room he found Otis in the centre of a group of young men who were convulsed with laughter. Otis was brandishing a piece of timber he had picked up, and discoursing volubly.

"She's gone in to fix her hair," he announced wildly. "I'm waiting to dance another hour with her."

Their laughter was renewed.

"Why don't some of you cut in?" cried Otis resentfully. "She likes more variety."

"Why, Otis," suggested a friend, "you've just barely got used to her."

"Why the two-by-four, Otis?" inquired Warren, smiling.

"The two-by-four? Oh, this? This is a club. When she comes out I'll hit her on the head and knock her in again."

Warren collapsed on a settee and howled with glee.

"Never mind, Otis," he articulated finally. "I'm relieving you this time."

Otis simulated a sudden fainting attack and handed the stick to Warren.

"If you need it, old man," he said hoarsely.

No matter how beautiful or brilliant a girl may be, the reputation of not being frequently cut in on makes her position at a dance unfortunate. Perhaps boys prefer her company to that of the butterflies with whom they dance a dozen times an evening, but youth in this jazz-nourished generation is temperamentally restless, and the idea of fox-trotting more than one full fox trot with the same girl is distasteful, not to say odious. When it comes to several dances and the intermissions between she can be quite sure that a young man, once relieved, will never tread on her wayward toes again.

Warren danced the next full dance with Bernice, and finally, thankful for the intermission, he led her to a table on the veranda. There was a moment's silence while she did unimpressive things with her fan.

"It's hotter here than in Eau Claire," she said.

Warren stifled a sigh and nodded. It might be for all he knew or cared. He wondered idly whether she was a poor conversationalist because she got no attention or got no attention because she was a poor conversationalist.

"You going to be here much longer?" he asked, and then turned rather red. She might suspect his reasons for asking.

"Another week," she answered, and stared at him as if to lunge at his next remark when it left his lips.

Warren fidgeted. Then with a sudden charitable impulse he decided to try part of his line on her. He turned and looked at her eyes.

"You've got an awfully kissable mouth," he began quietly.

This was a remark that he sometimes made to girls at college proms when they were talking in just such half dark as this. Bernice distinctly jumped. She turned an ungraceful red and became clumsy with her fan. No one had ever made such a remark to her before.

"Fresh!"—the word had slipped out before she realized it, and she bit her lip. Too late she decided to be amused, and offered him a flustered smile.

Warren was annoyed. Though not accustomed to have that remark taken seriously, still it usually provoked a laugh or a paragraph of sentimental banter. And he hated to be called fresh, except in a joking way. His charitable impulse died and he switched the topic.

"Jim Strain and Ethel Demorest sitting out as usual," he commented.

This was more in Bernice's line, but a faint regret mingled with her relief as the subject changed. Men did not talk to her about kissable mouths, but she knew that they talked in some such way to other girls.

"Oh, yes," she said, and laughed. "I hear they've been mooning round for years without a red penny.[4] Isn't it silly?"

Warren's disgust increased. Jim Strain was a close friend of his brother's, and anyway he considered it bad form to sneer at people for not having money. But Bernice had had no intention of sneering. She was merely nervous.

II

When Marjorie and Bernice reached home at half after midnight they said good night at the top of the stairs. Though cousins, they were not intimates. As a matter of fact Marjorie had no female intimates—she considered girls stupid. Bernice on the contrary all through this parent-arranged visit had rather longed to exchange those confidences flavored with giggles and tears that she considered an indispensable factor in all feminine intercourse. But in this respect she found Marjorie rather cold; felt somehow the same difficulty in talking to her that she had in talking to men. Marjorie never giggled, was never frightened, seldom embarrassed, and in fact had very few of the qualities which Bernice considered appropriately and blessedly feminine.

As Bernice busied herself with tooth-brush and paste this night she wondered for the hundredth time why she never had any attention when she was away from home. That her family were the wealthiest in Eau Claire; that her mother entertained tremendously, gave little dinners for her daughter before all dances and bought her a car of her own to drive round in, never occurred to her as factors in her home-town social success. Like most girls she had been brought up on the warm milk prepared by Annie Fellows Johnston[5] and on novels in which the female was beloved because of certain mysterious womanly qualities, always mentioned but never displayed.

Bernice felt a vague pain that she was not at present engaged in being popular. She did not know that had it not been for Marjorie's campaigning she would have danced the entire evening with one man; but she knew that even in Eau Claire other girls with less position and less pulchritude were given a much bigger rush. She attributed this to something subtly unscrupulous in those girls. It had never worried her, and if it had her mother would have assured her that the other girls cheapened themselves and that men really respected girls like Bernice.

She turned out the light in her bathroom, and on an impulse decided to go in and chat for a moment with her aunt Josephine, whose light was still on. Her soft slippers bore her noiselessly down the carpeted hall, but hearing voices inside she stopped near the partly opened door. Then she caught her own name, and without any definite intention of eavesdropping lingered—and the thread of the conversation going on inside pierced her consciousness sharply as if it had been drawn through with a needle.

"She's absolutely hopeless!" It was Marjorie's voice. "Oh, I know what you're going to say! So many people have told you how pretty and sweet she is, and how she can cook! What of it? She has a bum time. Men don't like her."

"What's a little cheap popularity?"

Mrs. Harvey sounded annoyed.

"It's everything when you're eighteen," said Marjorie emphatically.

"I've done my best. I've been polite and I've made men dance with her, but they just won't stand being bored. When I think of that gorgeous coloring wasted on such a ninny, and think what Martha Carey could do with it—oh!"

"There's no courtesy these days."

Mrs. Harvey's voice implied that modern situations were too much for her. When she was a girl all young ladies who belonged to nice families had glorious times.

"Well," said Marjorie, "no girl can permanently bolster up a lame-duck visitor, because these days it's every girl for herself. I've even tried to drop her hints about clothes and things, and she's been furious—given me the funniest looks. She's sensitive enough to know she's not getting away with much, but I'll bet she consoles herself by thinking that she's very virtuous and that I'm too gay and fickle and will come to a bad end. All unpopular girls think that way. Sour grapes! Sarah Hopkins refers to Genevieve and Roberta and me as gardenia girls! I'll bet she'd give ten years of her life and her European education to be a gardenia girl and have three or four men in love with her and be cut in on every few feet at dances."

"It seems to me," interrupted Mrs. Harvey rather wearily, "that you ought to be able to do something for Bernice. I know she's not very vivacious."

Marjorie groaned.

"Vivacious! Good grief! I've never heard her say anything to a boy except that it's hot or the floor's crowded or that she's going to school in New York next year. Sometimes she asks them what kind of car they have and tells them the kind she has. Thrilling!"

There was a short silence, and then Mrs. Harvey took up her refrain:

"All I know is that other girls not half so sweet and attractive get partners. Martha Carey, for instance, is stout and loud, and her mother is distinctly common. Roberta Dillon is so thin this year that she looks as though Arizona were the place for her. She's dancing herself to death."

"But, mother," objected Marjorie impatiently, "Martha is cheerful and awfully witty and an awfully slick girl, and Roberta's a marvellous dancer. She's been popular for ages!"

Mrs. Harvey yawned.

"I think it's that crazy Indian blood in Bernice," continued Marjorie. "Maybe she's a reversion to type. Indian women all just sat round and never said anything."

"Go to bed, you silly child," laughed Mrs. Harvey. "I wouldn't have told you that if I'd thought you were going to remember it. And I think most of your ideas are perfectly idiotic," she finished sleepily.

There was another silence, while Marjorie considered whether or not convincing her mother was worth the trouble. People over forty can seldom be permanently convinced of anything. At eighteen our convictions are hills from which we look; at forty-five they are caves in which we hide.

Having decided this, Marjorie said good night. When she came out into the hall it was quite empty.

III

While Marjorie was breakfasting late next day Bernice came into the room with a rather formal good morning, sat down opposite, stared intently over and slightly moistened her lips.

"What's on your mind?" inquired Marjorie, rather puzzled.

Bernice paused before she threw her hand-grenade.

"I heard what you said about me to your mother last night."

Marjorie was startled, but she showed only a faintly heightened color and her voice was quite even when she spoke.

"Where were you?"

"In the hall. I didn't mean to listen—at first."

After an involuntary look of contempt Marjorie dropped her eyes and became very interested in balancing a stray corn-flake on her finger.

"I guess I'd better go back to Eau Claire—if I'm such a nuisance." Bernice's lower lip was trembling violently and she continued on a wavering note: "I've tried to be nice, and—and I've been first neglected and then insulted. No one ever visited me and got such treatment."

Marjorie was silent.

"But I'm in the way, I see. I'm a drag on you. Your friends don't like me." She paused, and then remembered another one of her grievances. "Of course I was furious last week when you tried to hint to me that that dress was unbecoming. Don't you think I know how to dress myself?"

"No," murmured Marjorie less than half-aloud.

"What?"

"I didn't hint anything," said Marjorie succinctly. "I said, as I remember, that it was better to wear a becoming dress three times straight than to alternate it with two frights."

"Do you think that was a very nice thing to say?"

"I wasn't trying to be nice." Then after a pause: "When do you want to go?"

Bernice drew in her breath sharply.

"Oh!" It was a little half-cry.

Marjorie looked up in surprise.

"Didn't you say you were going?"

"Yes, but——"

"Oh, you were only bluffing!"

They stared at each other across the breakfast-table for a moment. Misty waves were passing before Bernice's eyes, while Marjorie's face wore that rather hard expression that she used when slightly intoxicated undergraduates were making love to her.

"So you were bluffing," she repeated as if it were what she might have expected.

Bernice admitted it by bursting into tears. Marjorie's eyes showed boredom.

"You're my cousin," sobbed Bernice. "I'm v-v-visiting you. I was to stay a month, and if I go home my mother will know and she'll wah-wonder——"

Marjorie waited until the shower of broken words collapsed into little sniffles.

"I'll give you my month's allowance," she said coldly, "and you can spend this last week anywhere you want. There's a very nice hotel——"

Bernice's sobs rose to a flute note, and rising of a sudden she fled from the room.

An hour later, while Marjorie was in the library absorbed in composing one of those non-committal, marvellously elusive letters that only a young girl can write, Bernice reappeared, very red-eyed and consciously calm. She cast no glance at Marjorie but took a book at random from the shelf and sat down as if to read. Marjorie seemed absorbed in her letter and continued writing. When the clock showed noon Bernice closed her book with a snap.

"I suppose I'd better get my railroad ticket."

This was not the beginning of the speech she had rehearsed upstairs, but as Marjorie was not getting her cues—wasn't urging her to be reasonable; it's all a mistake—it was the best opening she could muster.

"Just wait till I finish this letter," said Marjorie without looking round. "I want to get it off in the next mail."

After another minute, during which her pen scratched busily, she turned round and relaxed with an air of "at your service." Again Bernice had to speak.

"Do you want me to go home?"

"Well," said Marjorie, considering, "I suppose if you're not having a good time you'd better go. No use being miserable."

"Don't you think common kindness——"

"Oh, please don't quote 'Little Women'!"[6] cried Marjorie impatiently. "That's out of style."

"You think so?"

"Heavens, yes! What modern girl could live like those inane females?"

"They were the models for our mothers."

Marjorie laughed.

"Yes, they were—not! Besides, our mothers were all very well in their way, but they know very little about their daughters' problems."

Bernice drew herself up.

"Please don't talk about my mother."

Marjorie laughed.

"I don't think I mentioned her."

Bernice felt that she was being led away from her subject.

"Do you think you've treated me very well?"

"I've done my best. You're rather hard material to work with."

The lids of Bernice's eyes reddened.

"I think you're hard and selfish, and you haven't a feminine quality in you."

"Oh, my Lord!" cried Marjorie in desperation. "You little nut! Girls like you are responsible for all the tiresome colorless marriages; all those ghastly inefficiencies that pass as feminine qualities. What a blow it must be when a man with imagination marries the beautiful bundle of clothes that he's been building ideals round, and finds that she's just a weak, whining, cowardly mass of affectations!"

Bernice's mouth had slipped half open.

"The womanly woman!" continued Marjorie. "Her whole early life is occupied in whining criticisms of girls like me who really do have a good time."

Bernice's jaw descended farther as Marjorie's voice rose.

"There's some excuse for an ugly girl whining. If I'd been irretrievably ugly I'd never have forgiven my parents for bringing me into the world. But you're starting life without any handicap—" Marjorie's little fist clinched. "If you expect me to weep with you you'll be disappointed. Go or stay, just as you like." And picking up her letters she left the room.

Bernice claimed a headache and failed to appear at luncheon. They had a matinée date for the afternoon, but the headache persisting, Marjorie made explanation to a not very downcast boy. But when she returned late in the afternoon she found Bernice with a strangely set face waiting for her in her bedroom.

"I've decided," began Bernice without preliminaries, "that maybe you're right about things—possibly not. But if you'll tell me why your friends aren't—aren't interested in me I'll see if I can do what you want me to."

Marjorie was at the mirror shaking down her hair.

"Do you mean it?"

"Yes."

"Without reservations? Will you do exactly what I say?"

"Well, I——"

"Well nothing! Will you do exactly as I say?"

"If they're sensible things."

"They're not! You're no case for sensible things."

"Are you going to make—to recommend——"

"Yes, everything. If I tell you to take boxing-lessons you'll have to do it. Write home and tell your mother you're going to stay another two weeks."

"If you'll tell me——"

"All right—I'll just give you a few examples now. First, you have no ease of manner. Why? Because you're never sure about your personal appearance. When a girl feels that she's perfectly groomed and dressed she can forget that part of her. That's charm. The more parts of yourself you can afford to forget the more charm you have."

"Don't I look all right?"

"No; for instance, you never take care of your eyebrows. They're black and lustrous, but by leaving them straggly they're a blemish. They'd be beautiful if you'd take care of them in one-tenth the time you take doing nothing. You're going to brush them so that they'll grow straight."

Bernice raised the brows in question.

"Do you mean to say that men notice eyebrows?"

"Yes—subconsciously. And when you go home you ought to have your teeth straightened a little. It's almost imperceptible, still——"

"But I thought," interrupted Bernice in bewilderment, "that you despised little dainty feminine things like that."

"I hate dainty minds," answered Marjorie. "But a girl has to be dainty in person. If she looks like a million dollars she can talk about Russia, ping-pong, or the League of Nations[7] and get away with it."

"What else?"

"Oh, I'm just beginning! There's your dancing."

"Don't I dance all right?"

"No, you don't—you lean on a man; yes, you do—ever so slightly. I noticed it when we were dancing together yesterday. And you dance standing up straight instead of bending over a little. Probably some old lady on the side-line once told you that you looked so dignified that way. But except with a very small girl it's much harder on the man, and he's the one that counts."

"Go on." Bernice's brain was reeling.

"Well, you've got to learn to be nice to men who are sad birds. You look as if you'd been insulted whenever you're thrown with any except the most popular boys. Why, Bernice, I'm cut in on every few feet—and who does most of it? Why, those very sad birds. No girl can afford to neglect them. They're the big part of any crowd. Young boys too shy to talk are the very best conversational practice. Clumsy boys are the best dancing practice. If you can follow them and yet look graceful you can follow a baby tank across a barb-wire sky-scraper."

Bernice sighed profoundly, but Marjorie was not through.

"If you go to a dance and really amuse, say, three sad birds that dance with you; if you talk so well to them that they forget they're stuck with you, you've done something. They'll come back next time, and gradually so many sad birds will dance with you that the attractive boys will see there's no danger of being stuck—then they'll dance with you."

"Yes," agreed Bernice faintly. "I think I begin to see."

"And finally," concluded Marjorie, "poise and charm will just come. You'll wake up some morning knowing you've attained it, and men will know it too."

Bernice rose.

"It's been awfully kind of you—but nobody's ever talked to me like this before, and I feel sort of startled."

Marjorie made no answer but gazed pensively at her own image in the mirror.

"You're a peach to help me," continued Bernice.

Still Marjorie did not answer, and Bernice thought she had seemed too grateful.

"I know you don't like sentiment," she said timidly.

Marjorie turned to her quickly.

"Oh, I wasn't thinking about that. I was considering whether we hadn't better bob your hair."

Bernice collapsed backward upon the bed.

IV

On the following Wednesday evening there was a dinner-dance at the country club. When the guests strolled in Bernice found her place-card with a slight feeling of irritation. Though at her right sat G. Reece Stoddard, a most desirable and distinguished young bachelor, the all-important left held only Charley Paulson. Charley lacked height, beauty, and social shrewdness, and in her new enlightenment Bernice decided that his only qualification to be her partner was that he had never been stuck with her. But this feeling of irritation left with the last of the soup-plates, and Marjorie's specific instruction came to her. Swallowing her pride she turned to Charley Paulson and plunged.

"Do you think I ought to bob my hair, Mr. Charley Paulson?"

Charley looked up in surprise.

"Why?"

"Because I'm considering it. It's such a sure and easy way of attracting attention."

Charley smiled pleasantly. He could not know this had been rehearsed. He replied that he didn't know much about bobbed hair. But Bernice was there to tell him.

"I want to be a society vampire, you see," she announced coolly, and went on to inform him that bobbed hair was the necessary prelude. She added that she wanted to ask his advice, because she had heard he was so critical about girls.

Charley, who knew as much about the psychology of women as he did of the mental states of Buddhist contemplatives, felt vaguely flattered.

"So I've decided," she continued, her voice rising slightly, "that early next week I'm going down to the Sevier Hotel barber-shop, sit in the first chair, and get my hair bobbed." She faltered, noticing that the people near her had paused in their conversation and were listening; but after a confused second Marjorie's coaching told, and she finished her paragraph to the vicinity at large. "Of course I'm charging admission, but if you'll all come down and encourage me I'll issue passes for the inside seats."

There was a ripple of appreciative laughter, and under cover of it G. Reece Stoddard leaned over quickly and said close to her ear: "I'll take a box right now."

She met his eyes and smiled as if he had said something surpassingly brilliant.

"Do you believe in bobbed hair?" asked G. Reece in the same undertone.

"I think it's unmoral," affirmed Bernice gravely. "But, of course, you've either got to amuse people or feed 'em or shock 'em."[8] Marjorie had culled this from Oscar Wilde. It was greeted with a ripple of laughter from the men and a series of quick, intent looks from the girls. And then as though she had said nothing of wit or moment Bernice turned again to Charley and spoke confidentially in his ear.

"I want to ask you your opinion of several people. I imagine you're a wonderful judge of character."

Charley thrilled faintly—paid her a subtle compliment by overturning her water.

Two hours later, while Warren McIntyre was standing passively in the stag line abstractedly watching the dancers and wondering whither and with whom Marjorie had disappeared, an unrelated perception began to creep slowly upon him—a perception that Bernice, cousin to Marjorie, had been cut in on several times in the past five minutes. He closed his eyes, opened them and looked again. Several minutes back she had been dancing with a visiting boy, a matter easily accounted for; a visiting boy would know no better. But now she was dancing with some one else, and there was Charley Paulson headed for her with enthusiastic determination in his eye. Funny—Charley seldom danced with more than three girls an evening.

Warren was distinctly surprised when—the exchange having been effected—the man relieved proved to be none other than G. Reece Stoddard himself. And G. Reece seemed not at all jubilant at being relieved. Next time Bernice danced near, Warren regarded her intently. Yes, she was pretty, distinctly pretty; and to-night her face seemed really vivacious. She had that look that no woman, however histrionically proficient, can successfully counterfeit—she looked as if she were having a good time. He liked the way she had her hair arranged, wondered if it was brilliantine that made it glisten so. And that dress was becoming—a dark red that set off her shadowy eyes and high coloring. He remembered that he had thought her pretty when she first came to town, before he had realized that she was dull. Too bad she was dull—dull girls unbearable—certainly pretty though.

His thoughts zigzagged back to Marjorie. This disappearance would be like other disappearances. When she reappeared he would demand where she had been—would be told emphatically that it was none of his business. What a pity she was so sure of him! She basked in the knowledge that no other girl in town interested him; she defied him to fall in love with Genevieve or Roberta.

Warren sighed. The way to Marjorie's affections was a labyrinth indeed. He looked up. Bernice was again dancing with the visiting boy. Half unconsciously he took a step out from the stag line in her direction, and hesitated. Then he said to himself that it was charity. He walked toward her—collided suddenly with G. Reece Stoddard.

"Pardon me," said Warren.

But G. Reece had not stopped to apologize. He had again cut in on Bernice.

That night at one o'clock Marjorie, with one hand on the electric-light switch in the hall, turned to take a last look at Bernice's sparkling eyes.

"So it worked?"

"Oh, Marjorie, yes!" cried Bernice.

"I saw you were having a gay time."

"I did! The only trouble was that about midnight I ran short of talk. I had to repeat myself—with different men of course. I hope they won't compare notes."

"Men don't," said Marjorie, yawning, "and it wouldn't matter if they did—they'd think you were even trickier."

She snapped out the light, and as they started up the stairs Bernice grasped the banister thankfully. For the first time in her life she had been danced tired.

"You see," said Marjorie at the top of the stairs, "one man sees another man cut in and he thinks there must be something there. Well, we'll fix up some new stuff to-morrow. Good night."

"Good night."

As Bernice took down her hair she passed the evening before her in review. She had followed instructions exactly. Even when Charley Paulson cut in for the eighth time she had simulated delight and had apparently been both interested and flattered. She had not talked about the weather or Eau Claire or automobiles or her school, but had confined her conversation to me, you, and us.

But a few minutes before she fell asleep a rebellious thought was churning drowsily in her brain—after all, it was she who had done it. Marjorie, to be sure, had given her her conversation, but then Marjorie got much of her conversation out of things she read. Bernice had bought the red dress, though she had never valued it highly before Marjorie dug it out of her trunk—and her own voice had said the words, her own lips had smiled, her own feet had danced. Marjorie nice girl—vain, though—nice evening—nice boys—like Warren—Warren—Warren—what's-his-name—Warren——

She fell asleep.

V

To Bernice the next week was a revelation. With the feeling that people really enjoyed looking at her and listening to her came the foundation of self-confidence. Of course there were numerous mistakes at first. She did not know, for instance, that Draycott Deyo was studying for the ministry; she was unaware that he had cut in on her because he thought she was a quiet, reserved girl. Had she known these things she would not have treated him to the line which began "Hello, Shell Shock!" and continued with the bathtub story—"It takes a frightful lot of energy to fix my hair in the summer—there's so much of it—so I always fix it first and powder my face and put on my hat; then I get into the bathtub, and dress afterward. Don't you think that's the best plan?"

Though Draycott Deyo was in the throes of difficulties concerning baptism by immersion and might possibly have seen a connection, it must be admitted that he did not. He considered feminine bathing an immoral subject, and gave her some of his ideas on the depravity of modern society.

But to offset that unfortunate occurrence Bernice had several signal successes to her credit. Little Otis Ormonde pleaded off from a trip East and elected instead to follow her with a puppylike devotion, to the amusement of his crowd and to the irritation of G. Reece Stoddard, several of whose afternoon calls Otis completely ruined by the disgusting tenderness of the glances he bent on Bernice. He even told her the story of the two-by-four and the dressing-room to show her how frightfully mistaken he and every one else had been in their first judgment of her. Bernice laughed off that incident with a slight sinking sensation.

Of all Bernice's conversation perhaps the best known and most universally approved was the line about the bobbing of her hair.

"Oh, Bernice, when you goin' to get the hair bobbed?"

"Day after to-morrow maybe," she would reply, laughing. "Will you come and see me? Because I'm counting on you, you know."

"Will we? You know! But you better hurry up."

Bernice, whose tonsorial intentions were strictly dishonorable, would laugh again.

"Pretty soon now. You'd be surprised."

But perhaps the most significant symbol of her success was the gray car of the hypercritical Warren McIntyre, parked daily in front of the Harvey house. At first the parlor-maid was distinctly startled when he asked for Bernice instead of Marjorie; after a week of it she told the cook that Miss Bernice had gotta holda Miss Marjorie's best fella.

And Miss Bernice had. Perhaps it began with Warren's desire to rouse jealousy in Marjorie; perhaps it was the familiar though unrecognized strain of Marjorie in Bernice's conversation; perhaps it was both of these and something of sincere attraction besides. But somehow the collective mind of the younger set knew within a week that Marjorie's most reliable beau had made an amazing face-about and was giving an indisputable rush to Marjorie's guest. The question of the moment was how Marjorie would take it. Warren called Bernice on the 'phone twice a day, sent her notes, and they were frequently seen together in his roadster, obviously engrossed in one of those tense, significant conversations as to whether or not he was sincere.

Marjorie on being twitted only laughed. She said she was mighty glad that Warren had at last found some one who appreciated him. So the younger set laughed, too, and guessed that Marjorie didn't care and let it go at that.

One afternoon when there were only three days left of her visit Bernice was waiting in the hall for Warren, with whom she was going to a bridge party. She was in rather a blissful mood, and when Marjorie—also bound for the party—appeared beside her and began casually to adjust her hat in the mirror, Bernice was utterly unprepared for anything in the nature of a clash. Marjorie did her work very coldly and succinctly in three sentences.

"You may as well get Warren out of your head," she said coldly.

"What?" Bernice was utterly astounded.

"You may as well stop making a fool of yourself over Warren McIntyre. He doesn't care a snap of his fingers about you."

For a tense moment they regarded each other—Marjorie scornful, aloof; Bernice astounded, half-angry, half-afraid. Then two cars drove up in front of the house and there was a riotous honking. Both of them gasped faintly, turned, and side by side hurried out.

All through the bridge party Bernice strove in vain to master a rising uneasiness. She had offended Marjorie, the sphinx of sphinxes. With the most wholesome and innocent intentions in the world she had stolen Marjorie's property. She felt suddenly and horribly guilty. After the bridge game, when they sat in an informal circle and the conversation became general, the storm gradually broke. Little Otis Ormonde inadvertently precipitated it.

"When you going back to kindergarten, Otis?" some one had asked.

"Me? Day Bernice gets her hair bobbed."

"Then your education's over," said Marjorie quickly. "That's only a bluff of hers. I should think you'd have realized."

"That a fact?" demanded Otis, giving Bernice a reproachful glance.

Bernice's ears burned as she tried to think up an effectual come-back. In the face of this direct attack her imagination was paralyzed.

"There's a lot of bluffs in the world," continued Marjorie quite pleasantly. "I should think you'd be young enough to know that, Otis."

"Well," said Otis, "maybe so. But gee! With a line like Bernice's——"

"Really?" yawned Marjorie. "What's her latest bon mot?"

No one seemed to know. In fact, Bernice, having trifled with her muse's beau, had said nothing memorable of late.

"Was that really all a line?" asked Roberta curiously.

Bernice hesitated. She felt that wit in some form was demanded of her, but under her cousin's suddenly frigid eyes she was completely incapacitated.

"I don't know," she stalled.

"Splush!" said Marjorie. "Admit it!"

Bernice saw that Warren's eyes had left a ukulele he had been tinkering with and were fixed on her questioningly.

"Oh, I don't know!" she repeated steadily. Her cheeks were glowing.

"Splush!" remarked Marjorie again.

"Come through, Bernice," urged Otis. "Tell her where to get off."

Bernice looked round again—she seemed unable to get away from Warren's eyes.

"I like bobbed hair," she said hurriedly, as if he had asked her a question, "and I intend to bob mine."

"When?" demanded Marjorie.

"Any time."

"No time like the present," suggested Roberta.

Otis jumped to his feet.

"Good stuff!" he cried. "We'll have a summer bobbing party. Sevier Hotel barber-shop, I think you said."

In an instant all were on their feet. Bernice's heart throbbed violently.

"What?" she gasped.

Out of the group came Marjorie's voice, very clear and contemptuous.

"Don't worry—she'll back out!"

"Come on, Bernice!" cried Otis, starting toward the door.

Four eyes—Warren's and Marjorie's—stared at her, challenged her, defied her. For another second she wavered wildly.

"All right," she said swiftly, "I don't care if I do."

An eternity of minutes later, riding down-town through the late afternoon beside Warren, the others following in Roberta's car close behind, Bernice had all the sensations of Marie Antoinette[9] bound for the guillotine in a tumbrel. Vaguely she wondered why she did not cry out that it was all a mistake. It was all she could do to keep from clutching her hair with both hands to protect it from the suddenly hostile world. Yet she did neither. Even the thought of her mother was no deterrent now. This was the test supreme of her sportsmanship; her right to walk unchallenged in the starry heaven of popular girls.

Warren was moodily silent, and when they came to the hotel he drew up at the curb and nodded to Bernice to precede him out. Roberta's car emptied a laughing crowd into the shop, which presented two bold plate-glass windows to the street.

Bernice stood on the curb and looked at the sign, Sevier Barber-Shop. It was a guillotine indeed, and the hangman was the first barber, who, attired in a white coat and smoking a cigarette, leaned nonchalantly against the first chair. He must have heard of her; he must have been waiting all week, smoking eternal cigarettes beside that portentous, too-often-mentioned first chair. Would they blindfold her? No, but they would tie a white cloth round her neck lest any of her blood—nonsense—hair—should get on her clothes.

"All right, Bernice," said Warren quickly.

With her chin in the air she crossed the sidewalk, pushed open the swinging screen-door, and giving not a glance to the uproarious, riotous row that occupied the waiting bench, went up to the first barber.

"I want you to bob my hair."

The first barber's mouth slid somewhat open. His cigarette dropped to the floor.

"Huh?"

"My hair—bob it!"

Refusing further preliminaries, Bernice took her seat on high. A man in the chair next to her turned on his side and gave her a glance, half lather, half amazement. One barber started and spoiled little Willy Schuneman's monthly haircut. Mr. O'Reilly in the last chair grunted and swore musically in ancient Gaelic as a razor bit into his cheek. Two bootblacks became wide-eyed and rushed for her feet. No, Bernice didn't care for a shine.

Outside a passer-by stopped and stared; a couple joined him; half a dozen small boys' noses sprang into life, flattened against the glass; and snatches of conversation borne on the summer breeze drifted in through the screen-door.

"Lookada long hair on a kid!"

"Where'd yuh get 'at stuff? 'At's a bearded lady he just finished shavin'."

But Bernice saw nothing, heard nothing. Her only living sense told her that this man in the white coat had removed one tortoise-shell comb and then another; that his fingers were fumbling clumsily with unfamiliar hairpins; that this hair, this wonderful hair of hers, was going—she would never again feel its long voluptuous pull as it hung in a dark-brown glory down her back. For a second she was near breaking down, and then the picture before her swam mechanically into her vision—Marjorie's mouth curling in a faint ironic smile as if to say:

"Give up and get down! You tried to buck me and I called your bluff. You see you haven't got a prayer."

And some last energy rose up in Bernice, for she clinched her hands under the white cloth, and there was a curious narrowing of her eyes that Marjorie remarked on to some one long afterward.

Twenty minutes later the barber swung her round to face the mirror, and she flinched at the full extent of the damage that had been wrought. Her hair was not curly, and now it lay in lank lifeless blocks on both sides of her suddenly pale face. It was ugly as sin—she had known it would be ugly as sin. Her face's chief charm had been a Madonna-like simplicity. Now that was gone and she was—well, frightfully mediocre—not stagy; only ridiculous, like a Greenwich Villager who had left her spectacles at home.

As she climbed down from the chair she tried to smile—failed miserably. She saw two of the girls exchange glances; noticed Marjorie's mouth curved in attenuated mockery—and that Warren's eyes were suddenly very cold.

"You see"—her words fell into an awkward pause—"I've done it."

"Yes, you've—done it," admitted Warren.

"Do you like it?"

There was a half-hearted "Sure" from two or three voices, another awkward pause, and then Marjorie turned swiftly and with serpentlike intensity to Warren.

"Would you mind running me down to the cleaners?" she asked. "I've simply got to get a dress there before supper. Roberta's driving right home and she can take the others."

Warren stared abstractedly at some infinite speck out the window. Then for an instant his eyes rested coldly on Bernice before they turned to Marjorie.

"Be glad to," he said slowly.

VI

Bernice did not fully realize the outrageous trap that had been set for her until she met her aunt's amazed glance just before dinner.

"Why, Bernice!"

"I've bobbed it, Aunt Josephine."

"Why, child!"

"Do you like it?"

"Why, Ber-nice!"

"I suppose I've shocked you."

"No, but what'll Mrs. Deyo think to-morrow night? Bernice, you should have waited until after the Deyos' dance—you should have waited if you wanted to do that."

"It was sudden, Aunt Josephine. Anyway, why does it matter to Mrs. Deyo particularly?"

"Why, child," cried Mrs. Harvey, "in her paper on 'The Foibles of the Younger Generation' that she read at the last meeting of the Thursday Club she devoted fifteen minutes to bobbed hair. It's her pet abomination. And the dance is for you and Marjorie!"

"I'm sorry."

"Oh, Bernice, what'll your mother say? She'll think I let you do it."

"I'm sorry."

Dinner was an agony. She had made a hasty attempt with a curling-iron, and burned her finger and much hair. She could see that her aunt was both worried and grieved, and her uncle kept saying, "Well, I'll be darned!" over and over in a hurt and faintly hostile tone. And Marjorie sat very quietly, intrenched behind a faint smile, a faintly mocking smile.

Somehow she got through the evening. Three boys called; Marjorie disappeared with one of them, and Bernice made a listless unsuccessful attempt to entertain the two others—sighed thankfully as she climbed the stairs to her room at half past ten. What a day!

When she had undressed for the night the door opened and Marjorie came in.

"Bernice," she said, "I'm awfully sorry about the Deyo dance. I'll give you my word of honor I'd forgotten all about it."

"'Sall right," said Bernice shortly. Standing before the mirror she passed her comb slowly through her short hair.

"I'll take you down-town to-morrow," continued Marjorie, "and the hairdresser'll fix it so you'll look slick. I didn't imagine you'd go through with it. I'm really mighty sorry."

"Oh, 'sall right!"

"Still it's your last night, so I suppose it won't matter much."

Then Bernice winced as Marjorie tossed her own hair over her shoulders and began to twist it slowly into two long blond braids until in her cream-colored negligée she looked like a delicate painting of some Saxon princess. Fascinated, Bernice watched the braids grow. Heavy and luxurious they were, moving under the supple fingers like restive snakes—and to Bernice remained this relic and the curling-iron and a to-morrow full of eyes. She could see G. Reece Stoddard, who liked her, assuming his Harvard manner and telling his dinner partner that Bernice shouldn't have been allowed to go to the movies so much; she could see Draycott Deyo exchanging glances with his mother and then being conscientiously charitable to her. But then perhaps by to-morrow Mrs. Deyo would have heard the news; would send round an icy little note requesting that she fail to appear—and behind her back they would all laugh and know that Marjorie had made a fool of her; that her chance at beauty had been sacrificed to the jealous whim of a selfish girl. She sat down suddenly before the mirror, biting the inside of her cheek.

"I like it," she said with an effort. "I think it'll be becoming."

Marjorie smiled.

"It looks all right. For heaven's sake, don't let it worry you!"

"I won't."

"Good night, Bernice."

But as the door closed something snapped within Bernice. She sprang dynamically to her feet, clinching her hands, then swiftly and noiselessly crossed over to her bed and from underneath it dragged out her suitcase. Into it she tossed toilet articles and a change of clothing. Then she turned to her trunk and quickly dumped in two drawerfuls of lingerie and summer dresses. She moved quietly, but with deadly efficiency, and in three-quarters of an hour her trunk was locked and strapped and she was fully dressed in a becoming new travelling suit that Marjorie had helped her pick out.

Sitting down at her desk she wrote a short note to Mrs. Harvey, in which she briefly outlined her reasons for going. She sealed it, addressed it, and laid it on her pillow. She glanced at her watch. The train left at one, and she knew that if she walked down to the Marborough Hotel two blocks away she could easily get a taxicab.

Suddenly she drew in her breath sharply and an expression flashed into her eyes that a practised character reader might have connected vaguely with the set look she had worn in the barber's chair—somehow a development of it. It was quite a new look for Bernice—and it carried consequences.

She went stealthily to the bureau, picked up an article that lay there, and turning out all the lights stood quietly until her eyes became accustomed to the darkness. Softly she pushed open the door to Marjorie's room. She heard the quiet, even breathing of an untroubled conscience asleep.

She was by the bedside now, very deliberate and calm. She acted swiftly. Bending over she found one of the braids of Marjorie's hair, followed it up with her hand to the point nearest the head, and then holding it a little slack so that the sleeper would feel no pull, she reached down with the shears and severed it. With the pigtail in her hand she held her breath. Marjorie had muttered something in her sleep. Bernice deftly amputated the other braid, paused for an instant, and then flitted swiftly and silently back to her own room.

Down-stairs she opened the big front door, closed it carefully behind her, and feeling oddly happy and exuberant stepped off the porch into the moonlight, swinging her heavy grip like a shopping-bag. After a minute's brisk walk she discovered that her left hand still held the two blond braids. She laughed unexpectedly—had to shut her mouth hard to keep from emitting an absolute peal. She was passing Warren's house now, and on the impulse she set down her baggage, and swinging the braids like pieces of rope flung them at the wooden porch, where they landed with a slight thud. She laughed again, no longer restraining herself.

"Huh!" she giggled wildly. "Scalp the selfish thing!"

Then picking up her suitcase she set off at a half-run down the moonlit street.

The Offshore Pirate

This unlikely story begins on a sea that was a blue dream, as colorful as blue-silk stockings, and beneath a sky as blue as the irises of children's eyes. From the western half of the sky the sun was shying little golden disks at the sea—if you gazed intently enough you could see them skip from wave tip to wave tip until they joined a broad collar of golden coin that was collecting half a mile out and would eventually be a dazzling sunset. About half-way between the Florida shore and the golden collar a white steam-yacht, very young and graceful, was riding at anchor and under a blue-and-white awning aft a yellow-haired girl reclined in a wicker settee reading The Revolt of the Angels, by Anatole France.[1]

She was about nineteen, slender and supple, with a spoiled alluring mouth and quick gray eyes full of a radiant curiosity. Her feet, stockingless, and adorned rather than clad in blue-satin slippers which swung nonchalantly from her toes, were perched on the arm of a settee adjoining the one she occupied. And as she read she intermittently regaled herself by a faint application to her tongue of a half-lemon that she held in her hand. The other half, sucked dry, lay on the deck at her feet and rocked very gently to and fro at the almost imperceptible motion of the tide.

The second half-lemon was well-nigh pulpless and the golden collar had grown astonishing in width, when suddenly the drowsy silence which enveloped the yacht was broken by the sound of heavy footsteps and an elderly man topped with orderly gray hair and clad in a white-flannel suit appeared at the head of the companionway. There he paused for a moment until his eyes became accustomed to the sun, and then seeing the girl under the awning he uttered a long even grunt of disapproval.

If he had intended thereby to obtain a rise of any sort he was doomed to disappointment. The girl calmly turned over two pages, turned back one, raised the lemon mechanically to tasting distance, and then very faintly but quite unmistakably yawned.

"Ardita!" said the gray-haired man sternly.

Ardita uttered a small sound indicating nothing.

"Ardita!" he repeated. "Ardita!"

Ardita raised the lemon languidly, allowing three words to slip out before it reached her tongue.

"Oh, shut up."

"Ardita!"

"What?"

"Will you listen to me—or will I have to get a servant to hold you while I talk to you?"

The lemon descended slowly and scornfully.

"Put it in writing."

"Will you have the decency to close that abominable book and discard that damn lemon for two minutes?"

"Oh, can't you lemme alone for a second?"

"Ardita, I have just received a telephone message from the shore——"

"Telephone?" She showed for the first time a faint interest.

"Yes, it was——"

"Do you mean to say," she interrupted wonderingly, "'at they let you run a wire out here?"

"Yes, and just now——"

"Won't other boats bump into it?"

"No. It's run along the bottom. Five min——"

"Well, I'll be darned! Gosh! Science is golden or something—isn't it?"

"Will you let me say what I started to?"

"Shoot!"

"Well, it seems—well, I am up here—" He paused and swallowed several times distractedly. "Oh, yes. Young woman, Colonel Moreland has called up again to ask me to be sure to bring you in to dinner. His son Toby has come all the way from New York to meet you and he's invited several other young people. For the last time, will you——"

"No," said Ardita shortly, "I won't. I came along on this darn cruise with the one idea of going to Palm Beach, and you knew it, and I absolutely refuse to meet any darn old colonel or any darn young Toby or any darn old young people or to set foot in any other darn old town in this crazy state. So you either take me to Palm Beach or else shut up and go away."

"Very well. This is the last straw. In your infatuation for this man—a man who is notorious for his excesses, a man your father would not have allowed to so much as mention your name—you have reflected the demi-monde rather than the circles in which you have presumably grown up. From now on——"

"I know," interrupted Ardita ironically, "from now on you go your way and I go mine. I've heard that story before. You know I'd like nothing better."

"From now on," he announced grandiloquently, "you are no niece of mine. I——"

"O-o-o-oh!" The cry was wrung from Ardita with the agony of a lost soul. "Will you stop boring me! Will you go 'way! Will you jump overboard and drown! Do you want me to throw this book at you!"

"If you dare do any——"

Smack! The Revolt of the Angels sailed through the air, missed its target by the length of a short nose, and bumped cheerfully down the companionway.

The gray-haired man made an instinctive step backward and then two cautious steps forward. Ardita jumped to her five feet four and stared at him defiantly, her gray eyes blazing.

"Keep off!"

"How dare you!" he cried.

"Because I darn please!"

"You've grown unbearable! Your disposition——"

"You've made me that way! No child ever has a bad disposition unless it's her family's fault! Whatever I am, you did it."

Muttering something under his breath her uncle turned and, walking forward, called in a loud voice for the launch. Then he returned to the awning, where Ardita had again seated herself and resumed her attention to the lemon.

"I am going ashore," he said slowly. "I will be out again at nine o'clock to-night. When I return we will start back to New York, where I shall turn you over to your aunt for the rest of your natural, or rather unnatural, life."

He paused and looked at her, and then all at once something in the utter childishness of her beauty seemed to puncture his anger like an inflated tire, and render him helpless, uncertain, utterly fatuous.

"Ardita," he said not unkindly, "I'm no fool. I've been round. I know men. And, child, confirmed libertines don't reform until they're tired—and then they're not themselves—they're husks of themselves." He looked at her as if expecting agreement, but receiving no sight or sound of it he continued. "Perhaps the man loves you—that's possible. He's loved many women and he'll love many more. Less than a month ago, one month, Ardita, he was involved in a notorious affair with that red-haired woman, Mimi Merril; promised to give her the diamond bracelet that the Czar of Russia gave his mother. You know—you read the papers."

"Thrilling scandals by an anxious uncle," yawned Ardita. "Have it filmed. Wicked clubman making eyes at virtuous flapper. Virtuous flapper conclusively vamped by his lurid past. Plans to meet him at Palm Beach. Foiled by anxious uncle."

"Will you tell me why the devil you want to marry him?"

"I'm sure I couldn't say," said Ardita shortly. "Maybe because he's the only man I know, good or bad, who has an imagination and the courage of his convictions. Maybe it's to get away from the young fools that spend their vacuous hours pursuing me around the country. But as for the famous Russian bracelet, you can set your mind at rest on that score. He's going to give it to me at Palm Beach—if you'll show a little intelligence."

"How about the—red-haired woman?"

"He hasn't seen her for six months," she said angrily. "Don't you suppose I have enough pride to see to that? Don't you know by this time that I can do any darn thing with any darn man I want to?"

She put her chin in the air like the statue of France Aroused,[2] and then spoiled the pose somewhat by raising the lemon for action.

"Is it the Russian bracelet that fascinates you?"

"No, I'm merely trying to give you the sort of argument that would appeal to your intelligence. And I wish you'd go 'way," she said, her temper rising again. "You know I never change my mind. You've been boring me for three days until I'm about to go crazy. I won't go ashore! Won't! Do you hear? Won't!"

"Very well," he said, "and you won't go to Palm Beach either. Of all the selfish, spoiled, uncontrolled, disagreeable, impossible girls I have——"

Splush! The half-lemon caught him in the neck. Simultaneously came a hail from over the side.

"The launch is ready, Mr. Farnam."

Too full of words and rage to speak, Mr. Farnam cast one utterly condemning glance at his niece and, turning, ran swiftly down the ladder.

II

Five o'clock rolled down from the sun and plumped soundlessly into the sea. The golden collar widened into a glittering island; and a faint breeze that had been playing with the edges of the awning and swaying one of the dangling blue slippers became suddenly freighted with song. It was a chorus of men in close harmony and in perfect rhythm to an accompanying sound of oars cleaving the blue waters. Ardita lifted her head and listened.

"Carrots and peas,
Beans on their knees,
Pigs in the seas,
    Lucky fellows!
Blow us a breeze,
Blow us a breeze,
Blow us a breeze,
    With your bellows."

Ardita's brow wrinkled in astonishment. Sitting very still she listened eagerly as the chorus took up a second verse.

"Onions and beans,
Marshalls and Deans,

Goldbergs and Greens
And Costellos.
Blow us a breeze,
Blow us a breeze,
Blow us a breeze,
With your bellows."

With an exclamation she tossed her book to the desk, where it sprawled at a straddle, and hurried to the rail. Fifty feet away a large rowboat was approaching containing seven men, six of them rowing and one standing up in the stern keeping time to their song with an orchestra leader's baton.

"Oysters and rocks,
Sawdust and socks,
Who could make clocks
Out of cellos?—"

The leader's eyes suddenly rested on Ardita, who was leaning over the rail spellbound with curiosity. He made a quick movement with his baton and the singing instantly ceased. She saw that he was the only white man in the boat—the six rowers were negroes.

"Narcissus ahoy!"[3] he called politely.

"What's the idea of all the discord?" demanded Ardita cheerfully. "Is this the varsity crew from the county nut farm?"

By this time the boat was scraping the side of the yacht and a great hulking negro in the bow turned round and grasped the ladder. Thereupon the leader left his position in the stern and before Ardita had realized his intention he ran up the ladder and stood breathless before her on the deck.

"The women and children will be spared!" he said briskly. "All crying babies will be immediately drowned and all males put in double irons!"

Digging her hands excitedly down into the pockets of her dress Ardita stared at him, speechless with astonishment.

He was a young man with a scornful mouth and the bright blue eyes of a healthy baby set in a dark sensitive face. His hair was pitch black, damp and curly—the hair of a Grecian statue gone brunette. He was trimly built, trimly dressed, and graceful as an agile quarter-back.

"Well, I'll be a son of a gun!" she said dazedly.

They eyed each other coolly.

"Do you surrender the ship?"

"Is this an outburst of wit?" demanded Ardita. "Are you an idiot—or just being initiated to some fraternity?"

"I asked you if you surrendered the ship."

"I thought the country was dry," said Ardita disdainfully. "Have you been drinking finger-nail enamel? You better get off this yacht!"

"What?" The young man's voice expressed incredulity.

"Get off the yacht! You heard me!"

He looked at her for a moment as if considering what she had said.

"No," said his scornful mouth slowly; "no, I won't get off the yacht. You can get off if you wish."

Going to the rail he gave a curt command and immediately the crew of the rowboat scrambled up the ladder and ranged themselves in line before him, a coal-black and burly darky at one end and a miniature mulatto of four feet nine at the other. They seemed to be uniformly dressed in some sort of blue costume ornamented with dust, mud, and tatters; over the shoulder of each was slung a small, heavy-looking white sack, and under their arms they carried large black cases apparently containing musical instruments.

"'Ten-*shun!*" commanded the young man, snapping his own heels together crisply. "Right *driss!* Front! Step out here, Babe!"

The smallest negro took a quick step forward and saluted.

"Yas-suh!"

"Take command, go down below, catch the crew and tie 'em up—all except the engineer. Bring him up to me. Oh, and pile those bags by the rail there."

"Yas-suh!"

Babe saluted again and wheeling about motioned for the five others to gather about him. Then after a short whispered consultation they all filed noiselessly down the companionway.

"Now," said the young man cheerfully to Ardita, who had witnessed this last scene in withering silence, "if you will swear on your honor as a flapper—which probably isn't worth much—that you'll keep that spoiled little mouth of yours tight shut for forty-eight hours, you can row yourself ashore in our rowboat."

"Otherwise what?"

"Otherwise you're going to sea in a ship."

With a little sigh as for a crisis well passed, the young man sank into the settee Ardita had lately vacated and stretched his arms lazily. The corners of his mouth relaxed appreciatively as he looked round at the rich striped awning, the polished brass, and the luxurious fittings of the deck. His eye fell on the book, and then on the exhausted lemon.

"Hm," he said, "Stonewall Jackson[4] claimed that lemon-juice cleared his head. Your head feel pretty clear?"

Ardita disdained to answer.

"Because inside of five minutes you'll have to make a clear decision whether it's go or stay."

He picked up the book and opened it curiously.

"The Revolt of the Angels. Sounds pretty good. French, eh?" He stared at her with new interest. "You French?"

"No."

"What's your name?"

"Farnam."

"Farnam what?"

"Ardita Farnam."

"Well, Ardita, no use standing up there and chewing out the insides of your mouth. You ought to break those nervous habits while you're young. Come over here and sit down."

Ardita took a carved jade case from her pocket, extracted a cigarette and lit it with a conscious coolness, though she knew her hand was trembling a little; then she crossed over with her supple, swinging walk, and sitting down in the other settee blew a mouthful of smoke at the awning.

"You can't get me off this yacht," she said steadily; "and you haven't got very much sense if you think you'll get far with it. My uncle'll have wirelesses zigzagging all over this ocean by half past six."

"Hm."

She looked quickly at his face, caught anxiety stamped there plainly in the faintest depression of the mouth's corners.

"It's all the same to me," she said, shrugging her shoulders. "'Tisn't my yacht. I don't mind going for a coupla hours' cruise. I'll even lend you that book so you'll have something to read on the revenue boat that takes you up to Sing Sing."[5]

He laughed scornfully.

"If that's advice you needn't bother. This is part of a plan arranged before I ever knew this yacht existed. If it hadn't been this one it'd have been the next one we passed anchored along the coast."

"Who are you?" demanded Ardita suddenly. "And what are you?"

"You've decided not to go ashore?"

"I never even faintly considered it."

"We're generally known," he said, "all seven of us, as Curtis Carlyle and his Six Black Buddies, late of the Winter Garden and the Midnight Frolic."[6]

"You're singers?"

"We were until to-day. At present, due to those white bags you see there, we're fugitives from justice, and if the reward offered for our capture hasn't by this time reached twenty thousand dollars I miss my guess."

"What's in the bags?" asked Ardita curiously.

"Well," he said, "for the present we'll call it—mud—Florida mud."

III

Within ten minutes after Curtis Carlyle's interview with a very frightened engineer the yacht Narcissus was under way, steaming south through a balmy tropical twilight. The little mulatto, Babe, who seemed to have Carlyle's implicit confidence, took full command of the situation. Mr. Farnam's valet and the chef, the only members of the crew on board except the engineer, having shown fight, were now reconsidering, strapped securely to their bunks below. Trombone Mose, the biggest negro, was set busy with a can of paint obliterating the name Narcissus from the bow, and substituting the name Hula Hula, and the others congregated aft and became intently involved in a game of craps.

Having given orders for a meal to be prepared and served on deck at seven-thirty, Carlyle rejoined Ardita, and, sinking back into his settee, half closed his eyes and fell into a state of profound abstraction.

Ardita scrutinized him carefully—and classed him immediately as a romantic figure. He gave the effect of towering self-confidence erected on a slight foundation—just under the surface of each of his decisions she discerned a hesitancy that was in decided contrast to the arrogant curl of his lips.

"He's not like me," she thought. "There's a difference somewhere."

Being a supreme egotist Ardita frequently thought about herself; never having had her egotism disputed she did it entirely naturally and with no detraction from her unquestioned charm. Though she was nineteen she gave the effect of a high-spirited precocious child, and in the present glow of her youth and beauty all the men and women she had known were but driftwood on the ripples of her temperament. She had met other egotists—in fact she found that selfish people bored her rather less than unselfish people—but as yet there had not been one she had not eventually defeated and brought to her feet.

But though she recognized an egotist in the settee next to her, she felt none of that usual shutting of doors in her mind which meant clearing ship for action; on the contrary her instinct told her that this man was somehow completely pregnable and quite defenseless. When Ardita defied convention—and of late it had been her chief amusement—it was from an intense desire to be herself, and she felt that this man, on the contrary, was preoccupied with his own defiance.

She was much more interested in him than she was in her own situation, which affected her as the prospect of a matinée might affect a ten-year-old child. She had implicit confidence in her ability to take care of herself under any and all circumstances.

The night deepened. A pale new moon smiled misty-eyed upon the sea, and as the shore faded dimly out and dark clouds were blown like leaves along the far horizon a great haze of moonshine suddenly bathed the yacht and spread an avenue of glittering mail in her swift path. From time to time there was the bright flare of a match as one of them lighted a cigarette, but except for the low undertone of the throbbing engines and the even wash of the waves about the stern the yacht was quiet as a dream boat star-bound through the heavens. Round them flowed the smell of the night sea, bringing with it an infinite languor.

Carlyle broke the silence at last.

"Lucky girl," he sighed, "I've always wanted to be rich—and buy all this beauty."

Ardita yawned.

"I'd rather be you," she said frankly.

"You would—for about a day. But you do seem to possess a lot of nerve for a flapper."

"I wish you wouldn't call me that."

"Beg your pardon."

"As to nerve," she continued slowly, "it's my one redeeming feature. I'm not afraid of anything in heaven or earth."

"Hm, I am."

"To be afraid," said Ardita, "a person has either to be very great and strong—or else a coward. I'm neither." She paused for a moment, and eagerness crept into her tone. "But I want to talk about you. What on earth have you done—and how did you do it?"

"Why?" he demanded cynically. "Going to write a movie about me?"

"Go on," she urged. "Lie to me by the moonlight. Do a fabulous story."

A negro appeared, switched on a string of small lights under the awning, and began setting the wicker table for supper. And while they ate cold sliced chicken, salad, artichokes, and strawberry jam from the plentiful larder below, Carlyle began to talk, hesitatingly at first, but eagerly as he saw she was interested. Ardita scarcely touched her food as she watched his dark young face—handsome, ironic, faintly ineffectual.

He began life as a poor kid in a Tennessee town, he said, so poor that his people were the only white family in their street. He never remembered any white children—but there were inevitably a dozen pickaninnies streaming in his trail, passionate admirers whom he kept in tow by the vividness of his imagination and the amount of trouble he was always getting them in and out of. And it seemed that this association diverted a rather unusual musical gift into a strange channel.

There had been a colored woman named Belle Pope Calhoun who played the piano at parties given for white children—nice white children that would have passed Curtis Carlyle with a sniff. But the ragged little "poh white" used to sit beside her piano by the hour and try to get in an alto with one of those kazoos that boys hum through. Before he was thirteen he was picking up a living teasing ragtime out of a battered violin in little cafés round Nashville. Eight years later the ragtime craze hit the country, and he took six darkies on the Orpheum circuit.[7] Five of them were boys he had grown up with; the other was the little mulatto, Babe Divine, who was a wharf nigger round New York, and long before that a plantation hand in Bermuda, until he stuck an eight-inch stiletto in his master's back. Almost before Carlyle realized his good fortune he was on Broadway, with offers of engagements on all sides, and more money than he had ever dreamed of.

It was about then that a change began in his whole attitude, a rather curious, embittering change. It was when he realized that he was spending the golden years of his life gibbering round a stage with a lot of black men. His act was good of its kind—three trombones, three saxophones, and Carlyle's flute—and it was his own peculiar sense of rhythm that made all the difference; but he began to grow strangely sensitive about it, began to hate the thought of appearing, dreaded it from day to day.

They were making money—each contract he signed called for more—but when he went to managers and told them that he wanted to separate from his sextet and go on as a regular pianist, they laughed at him and told him he was crazy—it would be an artistic suicide. He used to laugh afterward at the phrase "artistic suicide." They all used it.

Half a dozen times they played at private dances at three thousand dollars a night, and it seemed as if these crystallized all his distaste for his mode of livelihood. They took place in clubs and houses that he couldn't have gone into in the daytime. After all, he was merely playing the rôle of the eternal monkey, a sort of sublimated chorus man. He was sick of the very smell of the theatre, of powder and rouge and the chatter of the greenroom, and the patronizing approval of the boxes. He couldn't put his heart into it any more. The idea of a slow approach to the luxury of leisure drove him wild. He was, of course, progressing toward it, but, like a child, eating his ice-cream so slowly that he couldn't taste it at all.

He wanted to have a lot of money and time, and opportunity to read and play, and the sort of men and women round him that he could never have—the kind who, if they thought of him at all, would have considered him rather contemptible; in short he wanted all those things which he was beginning to lump under the general head of aristocracy, an aristocracy which it seemed almost any money could buy except money made as he was making it. He was twenty-five then, without family or education or any promise that he would succeed in a business career. He began speculating wildly, and within three weeks he had lost every cent he had saved.

Then the war came. He went to Plattsburg,[8] and even there his profession followed him. A brigadier-general called him up to headquarters and told him he could serve the country better as a band leader—so he spent the war entertaining celebrities behind the line with a headquarters band. It was not so bad—except that when the infantry came limping back from the trenches he wanted to be one of them. The sweat and mud they wore seemed only one of those ineffable symbols of aristocracy that were forever eluding him.

"It was the private dances that did it. After I came back from the war the old routine started. We had an offer from a syndicate of Florida hotels. It was only a question of time then."

He broke off and Ardita looked at him expectantly, but he shook his head.

"No," he said, "I'm not going to tell you about it. I'm enjoying it too much, and I'm afraid I'd lose a little of that enjoyment if I shared it with any one else. I want to hang on to those few breathless, heroic moments when I stood out before them all and let them know I was more than a damn bobbing, squawking clown."

From up forward came suddenly the low sound of singing. The negroes had gathered together on the deck and their voices rose together in a haunting melody that soared in poignant harmonics toward the moon. And Ardita listened in enchantment.

"Oh down—
    Oh down,
Mammy wanna take me downa milky way,
Oh down—
    Oh down,
Pappy say to-morra-a-a-ah!
But mammy say to-day,
Yes—mammy say to-day!"

Carlyle sighed and was silent for a moment, looking up at the gathered host of stars blinking like arclights in the warm sky. The negroes' song had died away to a plaintive humming and it seemed as if minute by minute the brightness and the great silence were increasing until he could almost hear the midnight toilet of the mermaids as they combed their silver dripping curls under the moon and gossiped to each other of the fine wrecks they lived in on the green opalescent avenues below.

"You see," said Carlyle softly, "this is the beauty I want. Beauty has got to be astonishing, astounding—it's got to burst in on you like a dream, like the exquisite eyes of a girl."

He turned to her, but she was silent.

"You see, don't you, Anita—I mean, Ardita?"

Again she made no answer. She had been sound asleep for some time.

IV

In the dense sun-flooded noon of next day a spot in the sea before them resolved casually into a green-and-gray islet, apparently composed of a great granite cliff at its northern end which slanted south through a mile of vivid coppice and grass to a sandy beach melting lazily into the surf. When Ardita, reading in her favorite seat, came to the last page of The Revolt of the Angels, and slamming the book shut looked up and saw it, she gave a little cry of delight, and called to Carlyle, who was standing moodily by the rail.

"Is this it? Is this where you're going?"

Carlyle shrugged his shoulders carelessly.

"You've got me." He raised his voice and called up to the acting skipper: "Oh, Babe, is this your island?"

The mulatto's miniature head appeared from round the corner of the deck-house.

"Yas-suh! This yeah's it."

Carlyle joined Ardita.

"Looks sort of sporting, doesn't it?"

"Yes," she agreed; "but it doesn't look big enough to be much of a hiding-place."

"You still putting your faith in those wirelesses your uncle was going to have zigzagging round?"

"No," said Ardita frankly. "I'm all for you. I'd really like to see you make a get-away."

He laughed.

"You're our Lady Luck. Guess we'll have to keep you with us as a mascot—for the present, anyway."

"You couldn't very well ask me to swim back," she said coolly. "If you do I'm going to start writing dime novels founded on that interminable history of your life you gave me last night."

He flushed and stiffened slightly.

"I'm very sorry I bored you."

"Oh, you didn't—until just at the end with some story about how furious you were because you couldn't dance with the ladies you played music for."

He rose angrily.

"You have got a darn mean little tongue."

"Excuse me," she said, melting into laughter, "but I'm not used to having men regale me with the story of their life ambitions—especially if they've lived such deathly platonic lives."

"Why? What do men usually regale you with?"

"Oh, they talk about me," she yawned. "They tell me I'm the spirit of youth and beauty."

"What do you tell them?"

"Oh, I agree quietly."

"Does every man you meet tell you he loves you?"

Ardita nodded.

"Why shouldn't he? All life is just a progression toward, and then a recession from, one phrase—'I love you.' "

Carlyle laughed and sat down.

"That's very true. That's—that's not bad. Did you make that up?"

"Yes—or rather I found it out. It doesn't mean anything especially. It's just clever."

"It's the sort of remark," he said gravely, "that's typical of your class."

"Oh," she interrupted impatiently, "don't start that lecture on aristocracy again! I distrust people who can be intense at this hour in the morning. It's a mild form of insanity—a sort of breakfast-food jag. Morning's the time to sleep, swim, and be careless."

Ten minutes later they had swung round in a wide circle as if to approach the island from the north.

"There's a trick somewhere," commented Ardita thoughtfully. "He can't mean just to anchor up against this cliff."

They were heading straight in now toward the solid rock, which must have been well over a hundred feet tall, and not until they were within fifty yards of it did Ardita see their objective. Then she clapped her hands in delight. There was a break in the cliff entirely hidden by a curious overlapping of rock, and through this break the yacht entered and very slowly traversed a narrow channel of crystal-clear water between high gray walls. Then they were riding at anchor in a miniature world of green and gold, a gilded bay smooth as glass and set round with tiny palms, the whole resembling the mirror lakes and twig trees that children set up in sand piles.

"Not so darned bad!" cried Carlyle excitedly.

"I guess that little coon knows his way round this corner of the Atlantic."

His exuberance was contagious, and Ardita became quite jubilant.

"It's an absolutely sure-fire hiding-place!"

"Lordy, yes! It's the sort of island you read about."

The rowboat was lowered into the golden lake and they pulled ashore.

"Come on," said Carlyle as they landed in the slushy sand, "we'll go exploring."

The fringe of palms was in turn ringed in by a round mile of flat, sandy country. They followed it south and brushing through a farther rim of tropical vegetation came out on a pearl-gray virgin beach where Ardita kicked off her brown golf shoes—she seemed to have permanently abandoned stockings—and went wading. Then they sauntered back to the yacht, where the indefatigable Babe had luncheon ready for them. He had posted a lookout on the high cliff to the north to watch the sea on both sides, though he doubted if the entrance to the cliff was generally known—he had never even seen a map on which the island was marked.

"What's its name," asked Ardita—"the island, I mean?"

"No name 'tall," chuckled Babe. "Reckin she jus' island, 'at's all."

In the late afternoon they sat with their backs against great boulders on the highest part of the cliff and Carlyle sketched for her his vague plans. He was sure they were hot after him by this time. The total proceeds of the coup he had pulled off, and concerning which he still refused to enlighten her, he estimated as just under a million dollars. He counted on lying up here several weeks and then setting off southward, keeping well outside the usual channels of travel, rounding the Horn and heading for Callao, in Peru. The details of coaling and provisioning he was leaving entirely to Babe, who, it seemed, had sailed these seas in every capacity from cabin-boy aboard a coffee trader to virtual first mate on a Brazilian pirate craft, whose skipper had long since been hung.

"If he'd been white he'd have been king of South America long ago," said Carlyle emphatically. "When it comes to intelligence he makes Booker T. Washington[9] look like a moron. He's got the guile of every race and nationality whose blood is in his veins, and that's half a dozen or I'm a liar. He worships me because I'm the only man in the world who can play better ragtime than he can. We used to sit together on the wharfs down on the New York water-front, he with a bassoon and me with an oboe, and we'd blend minor keys in African harmonics a thousand years old until the rats would crawl up the posts and sit round groaning and squeaking like dogs will in front of a phonograph."

Ardita roared.

"How you can tell 'em!"

Carlyle grinned.

"I swear that's the gos——"

"What you going to do when you get to Callao?"[10] she interrupted.

"Take ship for India. I want to be a rajah.[11] I mean it. My idea is to go up into Afghanistan somewhere, buy up a palace and a reputation, and then after about five years appear in England with a foreign accent and a mysterious past. But India first. Do you know, they say that all the gold in the world drifts very gradually back to India. Something fascinating about that to me. And I want leisure to read—an immense amount."

"How about after that?"

"Then," he answered defiantly, "comes aristocracy. Laugh if you want to—but at least you'll have to admit that I know what I want—which I imagine is more than you do."

"On the contrary," contradicted Ardita, reaching in her pocket for her cigarette case, "when I met you I was in the midst of a great uproar of all my friends and relatives because I did know what I wanted."

"What was it?"

"A man."

He started.

"You mean you were engaged?"

"After a fashion. If you hadn't come aboard I had every intention of slipping ashore yesterday evening—how long ago it seems—and meeting him in Palm Beach. He's waiting there for me with a bracelet that once belonged to Catharine of Russia.[12] Now don't mutter anything about aristocracy," she put in quickly. "I liked him simply because he had had an imagination and the utter courage of his convictions."

"But your family disapproved, eh?"

"What there is of it—only a silly uncle and a sillier aunt. It seems he got into some scandal with a red-haired woman named Mimi something—it was frightfully exaggerated, he said, and men don't lie to me—and anyway I didn't care what he'd done; it was the future that counted. And I'd see to that. When a man's in love with me he doesn't care for other amusements. I told him to drop her like a hot cake, and he did."

"I feel rather jealous," said Carlyle, frowning—and then he laughed. "I guess I'll just keep you along with us until we get to Callao. Then I'll lend you enough money to get back to the States. By that time you'll have had a chance to think that gentleman over a little more."

"Don't talk to me like that!" fired up Ardita. "I won't tolerate the parental attitude from anybody! Do you understand me?"

He chuckled and then stopped, rather abashed, as her cold anger seemed to fold him about and chill him.

"I'm sorry," he offered uncertainly.

"Oh, don't apologize! I can't stand men who say 'I'm sorry' in that manly, reserved tone. Just shut up!"

A pause ensued, a pause which Carlyle found rather awkward, but which Ardita seemed not to notice at all as she sat contentedly enjoying her cigarette and gazing out at the shining sea. After a minute she crawled out on the rock and lay with her face over the edge looking down. Carlyle, watching her, reflected how it seemed impossible for her to assume an ungraceful attitude.

"Oh, look!" she cried. "There's a lot of sort of ledges down there. Wide ones of all different heights."

He joined her and together they gazed down the dizzy height.

"We'll go swimming to-night!" she said excitedly. "By moonlight."

"Wouldn't you rather go in at the beach on the other end?"

"Not a chance. I like to dive. You can use my uncle's bathing-suit, only it'll fit you like a gunny sack, because he's a very flabby man. I've got a one-piece affair that's shocked the natives all along the Atlantic coast from Biddeford Pool to St. Augustine."[13]

"I suppose you're a shark."

"Yes, I'm pretty good. And I look cute too. A sculptor up at Rye last summer told me my calves were worth five hundred dollars."

There didn't seem to be any answer to this, so Carlyle was silent, permitting himself only a discreet interior smile.

V

When the night crept down in shadowy blue and silver they threaded the shimmering channel in the rowboat and, tying it to a jutting rock, began climbing the cliff together. The first shelf was ten feet up, wide, and furnishing a natural diving platform. There they sat down in the bright moonlight and watched the faint incessant surge of the waters, almost stilled now as the tide set seaward.

"Are you happy?" he asked suddenly.

She nodded.

"Always happy near the sea. You know," she went on, "I've been thinking all day that you and I are somewhat alike. We're both rebels—only for different reasons. Two years ago, when I was just eighteen, and you were——"

"Twenty-five."

"—well, we were both conventional successes. I was an utterly devastating débutante and you were a prosperous musician just commissioned in the army——"

"Gentleman by act of Congress," he put in ironically.

"Well, at any rate, we both fitted. If our corners were not rubbed off they were at least pulled in. But deep in us both was something that made us require more for happiness. I didn't know what I wanted. I went from man to man, restless, impatient, month by month getting less acquiescent and more dissatisfied. I used to sit sometimes chewing at the insides of my mouth and thinking I was going crazy—I had a frightful sense of transiency. I wanted things now—now—now! Here I was—beautiful—I am, aren't I?"

"Yes," agreed Carlyle tentatively.

Ardita rose suddenly.

"Wait a second. I want to try this delightful-looking sea."

She walked to the end of the ledge and shot out over the sea, doubling up in mid-air and then straightening out and entering the water straight as a blade in a perfect jack-knife dive.

In a minute her voice floated up to him.

"You see, I used to read all day and most of the night. I began to resent society——"

"Come on up here," he interrupted. "What on earth are you doing?"

"Just floating round on my back. I'll be up in a minute. Let me tell you. The only thing I enjoyed was shocking people; wearing something quite impossible and quite charming to a fancy-dress party, going round with the fastest men in New York, and getting into some of the most hellish scrapes imaginable."

The sounds of splashing mingled with her words, and then he heard her hurried breathing as she began climbing up the side to the ledge.

"Go on in!" she called.

Obediently he rose and dived. When he emerged, dripping, and made the climb he found that she was no longer on the ledge, but after a frightened second he heard her light laughter from another shelf ten feet up. There he joined her and they both sat quietly for a moment, their arms clasped round their knees, panting a little from the climb.

"The family were wild," she said suddenly. "They tried to marry me off. And then when I'd begun to feel that after all life was scarcely worth living I found something"—her eyes went skyward exultantly—"I found something!"

Carlyle waited and her words came with a rush.

"Courage—just that; courage as a rule of life, and something to cling to always. I began to build up this enormous faith in myself. I began to see that in all my idols in the past some manifestation of courage had unconsciously been the thing that attracted me. I began separating courage from the other things of life. All sorts of courage—the beaten, bloody prize-fighter coming up for more—I used to make men take me to prize-fights; the déclassé woman sailing through a nest of cats and looking at them as if they were mud under her feet; the liking what you like always; the utter disregard for other people's opinions—just to live as I liked always and to die in my own way—Did you bring up the cigarettes?"

He handed one over and held a match for her silently.

"Still," Ardita continued, "the men kept gathering—old men and young men, my mental and physical inferiors, most of them, but all intensely desiring to have me—to own this rather magnificent proud tradition I'd built up round me. Do you see?"

"Sort of. You never were beaten and you never apologized."

"Never!"

She sprang to the edge, poised for a moment like a crucified figure against the sky; then describing a dark parabola plunked without a slash between two silver ripples twenty feet below.

Her voice floated up to him again.

"And courage to me meant ploughing through that dull gray mist that comes down on life—not only overriding people and circumstances but overriding the bleakness of living. A sort of insistence on the value of life and the worth of transient things."

She was climbing up now, and at her last words her head, with the damp yellow hair slicked symmetrically back, appeared on his level.

"All very well," objected Carlyle. "You can call it courage, but your courage is really built, after all, on a pride of birth. You were bred to that defiant attitude. On my gray days even courage is one of the things that's gray and lifeless."

She was sitting near the edge, hugging her knees and gazing abstractedly at the white moon; he was farther back, crammed like a grotesque god into a niche in the rock.

"I don't want to sound like Pollyanna,"[14] she began, "but you haven't grasped me yet. My courage is faith—faith in the eternal resilience of me—that joy'll come back, and hope and spontaneity. And I feel that till it does I've got to keep my lips shut and my chin high, and my eyes wide—not necessarily any silly smiling. Oh, I've been through hell without a whine quite often—and the female hell is deadlier than the male."

"But supposing," suggested Carlyle, "that before joy and hope and all that came back the curtain was drawn on you for good?"

Ardita rose, and going to the wall climbed with some difficulty to the next ledge, another ten or fifteen feet above.

"Why," she called back, "then I'd have won!"

He edged out till he could see her.

"Better not dive from there! You'll break your back," he said quickly.

She laughed.

"Not I!"

Slowly she spread her arms and stood there swanlike, radiating a pride in her young perfection that lit a warm glow in Carlyle's heart.

"We're going through the black air with our arms wide," she called, "and our feet straight out behind like a dolphin's tail, and we're going to think we'll never hit the silver down there till suddenly it'll be all warm round us and full of little kissing, caressing waves."

Then she was in the air, and Carlyle involuntarily held his breath. He had not realized that the dive was nearly forty feet. It seemed an eternity before he heard the swift compact sound as she reached the sea.

And it was with his glad sigh of relief when her light watery laughter curled up the side of the cliff and into his anxious ears that he knew he loved her.

VI

Time, having no axe to grind, showered down upon them three days of afternoons. When the sun cleared the port-hole of Ardita's cabin an hour after dawn she rose cheerily, donned her bathing-suit, and went up on deck. The negroes would leave their work when they saw her, and crowd, chuckling and chattering, to the rail as she floated, an agile minnow, on and under the surface of the clear water. Again in the cool of the afternoon she would swim—and loll and smoke with Carlyle upon the cliff; or else they would lie on their sides in the sands of the southern beach, talking little, but watching the day fade colorfully and tragically into the infinite languor of a tropical evening.

And with the long, sunny hours Ardita's idea of the episode as incidental, madcap, a sprig of romance in a desert of reality, gradually left her. She dreaded the time when he would strike off southward; she dreaded all the eventualities that presented themselves to her; thoughts were suddenly troublesome and decisions odious. Had prayers found place in the pagan rituals of her soul she would have asked of life only to be unmolested for a while, lazily acquiescent to the ready, naïf flow of Carlyle's ideas, his vivid boyish imagination, and the vein of monomania that seemed to run crosswise through his temperament and colored his every action.

But this is not a story of two on an island, nor concerned primarily with love bred of isolation. It is merely the presentation of two personalities, and its idyllic setting among the palms of the Gulf Stream is quite incidental. Most of us are content to exist and breed and fight for the right to do both, and the dominant idea, the foredoomed attempt to control one's destiny, is reserved for the fortunate or unfortunate few. To me the interesting thing about Ardita is the courage that will tarnish with her beauty and youth.

"Take me with you," she said late one night as they sat lazily in the grass under the shadowy spreading palms. The negroes had brought ashore their musical instruments, and the sound of weird ragtime was drifting softly over on the warm breath of the night. "I'd love to reappear in ten years as a fabulously wealthy high-caste Indian lady," she continued.

Carlyle looked at her quickly.

"You can, you know."

She laughed.

"Is it a proposal of marriage? Extra! Ardita Farnam becomes pirate's bride. Society girl kidnapped by ragtime bank robber."

"It wasn't a bank."

"What was it? Why won't you tell me?"

"I don't want to break down your illusions."

"My dear man, I have no illusions about you."

"I mean your illusions about yourself."

She looked up in surprise.

"About myself! What on earth have I got to do with whatever stray felonies you've committed?"

"That remains to be seen."

She reached over and patted his hand.

"Dear Mr. Curtis Carlyle," she said softly, "are you in love with me?"

"As if it mattered."

"But it does—because I think I'm in love with you."

He looked at her ironically.

"Thus swelling your January total to half a dozen," he suggested. "Suppose I call your bluff and ask you to come to India with me?"

"Shall I?"

He shrugged his shoulders.

"We can get married in Callao."

"What sort of life can you offer me? I don't mean that unkindly, but seriously; what would become of me if the people who want that twenty-thousand-dollar reward ever catch up with you?"

"I thought you weren't afraid."

"I never am—but I won't throw my life away just to show one man I'm not."

"I wish you'd been poor. Just a little poor girl dreaming over a fence in a warm cow country."

"Wouldn't it have been nice?"

"I'd have enjoyed astonishing you—watching your eyes open on things. If you only wanted things! Don't you see?"

"I know—like girls who stare into the windows of jewelry-stores."

"Yes—and want the big oblong watch that's platinum and has diamonds all round the edge. Only you'd decide it was too expensive and choose one of white gold for a hundred dollars. Then I'd say: 'Expensive? I should say not!' And we'd go into the store and pretty soon the platinum one would be gleaming on your wrist."

"That sounds so nice and vulgar—and fun, doesn't it?" murmured Ardita.

"Doesn't it? Can't you see us travelling round and spending money right and left, and being worshipped by bell-boys and waiters? Oh, blessed are the simple rich, for they inherit the earth!"[15]

"I honestly wish we were that way."

"I love you, Ardita," he said gently.

Her face lost its childish look for a moment and became oddly grave.

"I love to be with you," she said, "more than with any man I've ever met. And I like your looks and your dark old hair, and the way you go over the side of the rail when we come ashore. In fact, Curtis Carlyle, I like all the things you do when you're perfectly natural. I think you've got nerve, and you know how I feel about that. Sometimes when you're around I've been tempted to kiss you suddenly and tell you that you were just an idealistic boy with a lot of caste nonsense in his head. Perhaps if I were just a little bit older and a little more bored I'd go with you. As it is, I think I'll go back and marry—that other man."

Over across the silver lake the figures of the negroes writhed and squirmed in the moonlight, like acrobats who, having been too long inactive, must go through their tricks from sheer surplus energy. In single file they marched, weaving in concentric circles, now with their heads thrown back, now bent over their instruments like piping fauns. And from trombone and saxophone ceaselessly whined a blended melody, sometimes riotous and jubilant, sometimes haunting and plaintive as a death-dance from the Congo's heart.

"Let's dance!" cried Ardita. "I can't sit still with that perfect jazz going on."

Taking her hand he led her out into a broad stretch of hard sandy soil that the moon flooded with great splendor. They floated out like drifting moths under the rich hazy light, and as the fantastic symphony wept and exulted and wavered and despaired Ardita's last sense of reality dropped away, and she abandoned her imagination to the dreamy summer scents of tropical flowers and the infinite starry spaces overhead, feeling that if she opened her eyes it would be to find herself dancing with a ghost in a land created by her own fancy.

"This is what I should call an exclusive private dance," he whispered.

"I feel quite mad—but delightfully mad!"

"We're enchanted. The shades of unnumbered generations of cannibals are watching us from high up on the side of the cliff there."

"And I'll bet the cannibal women are saying that we dance too close, and that it was immodest of me to come without my nose-ring."

They both laughed softly—and then their laughter died as over across the lake they heard the trombones stop in the middle of a bar, and the saxaphones give a startled moan and fade out.

"What's the matter?" called Carlyle.

After a moment's silence they made out the dark figure of a man rounding the silver lake at a run. As he came closer they saw it was Babe in a state of unusual excitement. He drew up before them and gasped out his news in a breath.

"Ship stan'in' off sho' 'bout half a mile, suh. Mose, he uz on watch, he say look's if she's done ancho'd."

"A ship—what kind of a ship?" demanded Carlyle anxiously.

Dismay was in his voice, and Ardita's heart gave a sudden wrench as she saw his whole face suddenly droop.

"He say he don't know, suh."

"Are they landing a boat?"

"No, suh."

"We'll go up," said Carlyle.

They ascended the hill in silence, Ardita's hand still resting in Carlyle's as it had when they finished dancing. She felt it clinch nervously from time to time as though he were unaware of the contact, but though he hurt her she made no attempt to remove it. It seemed an hour's climb before they reached the top and crept cautiously across the silhouetted plateau to the edge of the cliff. After one short look Carlyle involuntarily gave a little cry. It was a revenue boat with six-inch guns mounted fore and aft.

"They know!" he said with a short intake of breath. "They know! They picked up the trail somewhere."

"Are you sure they know about the channel? They may be only standing by to take a look at the island in the morning. From where they are they couldn't see the opening in the cliff."

"They could with field-glasses," he said hopelessly. He looked at his wrist-watch. "It's nearly two now. They won't do anything until dawn, that's certain. Of course there's always the faint possibility that they're waiting for some other ship to join; or for a coaler."

"I suppose we may as well stay right here."

The hours passed and they lay there side by side, very silently, their chins in their hands like dreaming children. In back of them squatted the negroes, patient, resigned, acquiescent, announcing now and then with sonorous snores that not even the presence of danger could subdue their unconquerable African craving for sleep.

Just before five o'clock Babe approached Carlyle. There were half a dozen rifles aboard the Narcissus he said. Had it been decided to offer no resistance? A pretty good fight might be made, he thought, if they worked out some plan.

Carlyle laughed and shook his head.

"That isn't a Spic army out there, Babe. That's a revenue boat. It'd be like a bow and arrow trying to fight a machine-gun. If you want to bury those bags somewhere and take a chance on recovering them later, go on and do it. But it won't work—they'd dig this island over from one end to the other. It's a lost battle all round, Babe."

Babe inclined his head silently and turned away, and Carlyle's voice was husky as he turned to Ardita.

"There's the best friend I ever had. He'd die for me, and be proud to, if I'd let him."

"You've given up?"

"I've no choice. Of course there's always one way out—the sure way—but that can wait. I wouldn't miss my trial for anything—it'll be an interesting experiment in notoriety. 'Miss Farnam testifies that the pirate's attitude to her was at all times that of a gentleman.' "

"Don't!" she said. "I'm awfully sorry."

When the color faded from the sky and lustreless blue changed to leaden gray a commotion was visible on the ship's deck, and they made out a group of officers clad in white duck, gathered near the rail. They had field-glasses in their hands and were attentively examining the islet.

"It's all up," said Carlyle grimly.

"Damn!" whispered Ardita. She felt tears gathering in her eyes.

"We'll go back to the yacht," he said. "I prefer that to being hunted out up here like a 'possum."

Leaving the plateau they descended the hill, and reaching the lake were rowed out to the yacht by the silent negroes. Then, pale and weary, they sank into the settees and waited.

Half an hour later in the dim gray light the nose of the revenue boat appeared in the channel and stopped, evidently fearing that the bay might be too shallow. From the peaceful look of the yacht, the man and the girl in the settees, and the negroes lounging curiously against the rail, they evidently judged that there would be no resistance, for two boats were lowered casually over the side, one containing an officer and six bluejackets, and the other, four rowers and in the stern two gray-haired men in yachting flannels. Ardita and Carlyle stood up, and half unconsciously started toward each other. Then he paused and putting his hand suddenly into his pocket he pulled out a round, glittering object and held it out to her.

"What is it?" she asked wonderingly.

"I'm not positive, but I think from the Russian inscription inside that it's your promised bracelet."

"Where—where on earth——"

"It came out of one of those bags. You see, Curtis Carlyle and his Six Black Buddies, in the middle of their performance in the tea-room of the hotel at Palm Beach, suddenly changed their instruments for automatics and held up the crowd. I took this bracelet from a pretty, overrouged woman with red hair."

Ardita frowned and then smiled.

"So that's what you did! You *have* got nerve!"

He bowed.

"A well-known bourgeois quality," he said.

And then dawn slanted dynamically across the deck and flung the shadows reeling into gray corners. The dew rose and turned to golden mist, thin as a dream, enveloping them until they seemed gossamer relics of the late night, infinitely transient and already fading. For a moment sea and sky were breathless, and dawn held a pink hand over the young mouth of life—then from out in the lake came the complaint of a rowboat and the swish of oars.

Suddenly against the golden furnace low in the east their two graceful figures melted into one, and he was kissing her spoiled young mouth.

"It's a sort of glory," he murmured after a second.

She smiled up at him.

"Happy, are you?"

Her sigh was a benediction—an ecstatic surety that she was youth and beauty now as much as she would ever know. For another instant life was radiant and time a phantom and their strength eternal—then there was a bumping, scraping sound as the rowboat scraped alongside.

Up the ladder scrambled the two gray-haired men, the officer and two of the sailors with their hands on their revolvers. Mr. Farnam folded his arms and stood looking at his niece.

"So," he said, nodding his head slowly.

With a sigh her arms unwound from Carlyle's neck, and her eyes, transfigured and far away, fell upon the boarding party. Her uncle saw her upper lip slowly swell into that arrogant pout he knew so well.

"So," he repeated savagely. "So this is your idea of—of romance. A runaway affair, with a high-seas pirate."

Ardita glanced at him carelessly.

"What an old fool you are!" she said quietly.

"Is that the best you can say for yourself?"

"No," she said as if considering. "No, there's something else. There's that well-known phrase with which I have ended most of our conversations for the past few years—'Shut up!' "

And with that she turned, included the two old men, the officer, and the two sailors in a curt glance of contempt, and walked proudly down the companionway.

But had she waited an instant longer she would have heard a sound from her uncle quite unfamiliar in most of their interviews. He gave vent to a whole-hearted amused chuckle, in which the second old man joined.

The latter turned briskly to Carlyle, who had been regarding this scene with an air of cryptic amusement.

"Well, Toby," he said genially, "you incurable, hare-brained, romantic chaser of rainbows, did you find that she was the person you wanted?"

Carlyle smiled confidently.

"Why—naturally," he said. "I've been perfectly sure ever since I first heard tell of her wild career. That's why I had Babe send up the rocket last night."

"I'm glad you did," said Colonel Moreland gravely. "We've been keeping pretty close to you in case you should have trouble with those six strange niggers. And we hoped we'd find you two in some such compromising position," he sighed. "Well, set a crank to catch a crank!"

"Your father and I sat up all night hoping for the best—or perhaps it's the worst. Lord knows you're welcome to her, my boy. She's run me crazy. Did you give her the Russian bracelet my detective got from that Mimi woman?"

Carlyle nodded.

"Sh!" he said. "She's coming on deck."

Ardita appeared at the head of the companionway and gave a quick involuntary glance at Carlyle's wrists. A puzzled look passed across her face. Back aft the negroes had begun to sing, and the cool lake, fresh with dawn, echoed serenely to their low voices.

"Ardita," said Carlyle unsteadily.

She swayed a step toward him.

"Ardita," he repeated breathlessly, "I've got to tell you the—the truth. It was all a plant, Ardita. My name isn't Carlyle. It's Moreland, Toby Moreland. The story was invented, Ardita, invented out of thin Florida air."

She stared at him, bewildered amazement, disbelief, and anger flowing in quick waves across her face. The three men held their breaths. Moreland, Senior, took a step toward her; Mr. Farnam's mouth dropped a little open as he waited, panic-stricken, for the expected crash.

But it did not come. Ardita's face became suddenly radiant, and with a little laugh she went swiftly to young Moreland and looked up at him without a trace of wrath in her gray eyes.

"Will you swear," she said quietly, "that it was entirely a product of your own brain?"

"I swear," said young Moreland eagerly.

She drew his head down and kissed him gently.

"What an imagination!" she said softly and almost enviously. "I want you to lie to me just as sweetly as you know how for the rest of my life."

The negroes' voices floated drowsily back, mingled in an air that she had heard them sing before.

"Time is a thief;
Gladness and grief
Cling to the leaf
As it yellows——"

"What was in the bags?" she asked softly.

"Florida mud," he answered. "That was one of the two true things I told you."

"Perhaps I can guess the other one," she said; and reaching up on her tiptoes she kissed him softly in the illustration.

May Day

There had been a war fought and won and the great city of the conquering people was crossed with triumphal arches and vivid with thrown flowers of white, red, and rose. All through the long spring days the returning soldiers marched up the chief highway behind the strump of drums and the joyous, resonant wind of the brasses, while merchants and clerks left their bickerings and figurings and, crowding to the windows, turned their white-bunched faces gravely upon the passing battalions.

Never had there been such splendor in the great city, for the victorious war had brought plenty in its train, and the merchants had flocked thither from the South and West with their households to taste of all the luscious feasts and witness the lavish entertainments prepared—and to buy for their women furs against the next winter and bags of golden mesh and varicolored slippers of silk and silver and rose satin and cloth of gold.

So gaily and noisily were the peace and prosperity impending hymned by the scribes and poets of the conquering people that more and more spenders had gathered from the provinces to drink the wine of excitement, and faster and faster did the merchants dispose of their trinkets and slippers until they sent up a mighty cry for more trinkets and more slippers in order that they might give in barter what was demanded of them. Some even of them flung up their hands helplessly, shouting:

"Alas! I have no more slippers! and alas! I have no more trinkets! May Heaven help me, for I know not what I shall do!"

But no one listened to their great outcry, for the throngs were far too busy—day by day, the foot-soldiers trod jauntily the highway and all exulted because the young men returning were pure and brave, sound of tooth and pink of cheek, and the young women of the land were virgins and comely both of face and of figure.

So during all this time there were many adventures that happened in the great city, and, of these, several—or perhaps one—are here set down.

I

At nine o'clock on the morning of the first of May, 1919, a young man spoke to the room clerk at the Biltmore Hotel,[1] asking if Mr. Philip Dean were registered there, and if so, could he be connected with Mr. Dean's rooms. The inquirer was dressed in a well-cut, shabby suit. He was small, slender, and darkly handsome; his eyes were framed above with unusually long eyelashes and below with the blue semicircle of ill health, this latter effect heightened by an unnatural glow which colored his face like a low, incessant fever.

Mr. Dean was staying there. The young man was directed to a telephone at the side.

After a second his connection was made; a sleepy voice hello'd from somewhere above.

"Mr. Dean?"—this very eagerly—"it's Gordon, Phil. It's Gordon Sterrett. I'm down-stairs. I heard you were in New York and I had a hunch you'd be here."

The sleepy voice became gradually enthusiastic. Well, how was Gordy, old boy! Well, he certainly was surprised and tickled! Would Gordy come right up, for Pete's sake!

A few minutes later Philip Dean, dressed in blue silk pajamas, opened his door and the two young men greeted each other with a half-embarrassed exuberance. They were both about twenty-four, Yale graduates of the year before the war; but there the resemblance stopped abruptly. Dean was blond, ruddy, and rugged under his thin pajamas. Everything about him radiated fitness and bodily comfort. He smiled frequently, showing large and prominent teeth.

"I was going to look you up," he cried enthusiastically. "I'm taking a couple of weeks off. If you'll sit down a sec I'll be right with you. Going to take a shower."

As he vanished into the bathroom his visitor's dark eyes roved nervously around the room, resting for a moment on a great English travelling bag in the corner and on a family of thick silk shirts littered on the chairs amid impressive neckties and soft woollen socks.

Gordon rose and, picking up one of the shirts, gave it a minute examination. It was of very heavy silk, yellow, with a pale blue stripe—and there were nearly a dozen of them. He stared involuntarily at his own shirt-cuffs—they were ragged and linty at the edges and soiled to a faint gray. Dropping the silk shirt, he held his coat-sleeves down and worked the frayed shirt-cuffs up till they were out of sight. Then he went to the mirror and looked at himself with listless, unhappy interest. His tie, of former glory, was faded and thumb-creased—it served no longer to hide the jagged buttonholes of his collar. He thought, quite without amusement, that only three years before he had received a scattering vote in the senior elections at college for being the best-dressed man in his class.

Dean emerged from the bathroom polishing his body.

"Saw an old friend of yours last night," he remarked. "Passed her in the lobby and couldn't think of her name to save my neck. That girl you brought up to New Haven senior year."

Gordon started.

"Edith Bradin? That whom you mean?"

"'At's the one. Damn good looking. She's still sort of a pretty doll—you know what I mean: as if you touched her she'd smear."

He surveyed his shining self complacently in the mirror, smiled faintly, exposing a section of teeth.

"She must be twenty-three anyway," he continued.

"Twenty-two last month," said Gordon absently.

"What? Oh, last month. Well, I imagine she's down for the Gamma Psi dance. Did you know we're having a Yale Gamma Psi dance tonight at Delmonico's?[2] You better come up, Gordy. Half of New Haven'll probably be there. I can get you an invitation."

Draping himself reluctantly in fresh underwear, Dean lit a cigarette and sat down by the open window, inspecting his calves and knees under the morning sunshine which poured into the room.

"Sit down, Gordy," he suggested, "and tell me all about what you've been doing and what you're doing now and everything."

Gordon collapsed unexpectedly upon the bed; lay there inert and spiritless. His mouth, which habitually dropped a little open when his face was in repose, became suddenly helpless and pathetic.

"What's the matter?" asked Dean quickly.

"Oh, God!"

"What's the matter?"

"Every God damn thing in the world," he said miserably. "I've absolutely gone to pieces, Phil. I'm all in."

"Huh?"

"I'm all in." His voice was shaking.

Dean scrutinized him more closely with appraising blue eyes.

"You certainly look all shot."

"I am. I've made a hell of a mess of everything." He paused. "I'd better start at the beginning—or will it bore you?"

"Not at all; go on." There was, however, a hesitant note in Dean's voice. This trip East had been planned for a holiday—to find Gordon Sterrett in trouble exasperated him a little.

"Go on," he repeated, and then added half under his breath, "Get it over with."

"Well," began Gordon unsteadily, "I got back from France in February, went home to Harrisburg for a month, and then came down to New York to get a job. I got one—with an export company. They fired me yesterday."

"Fired you?"

"I'm coming to that, Phil. I want to tell you frankly. You're about the only man I can turn to in a matter like this. You won't mind if I just tell you frankly, will you, Phil?"

Dean stiffened a bit more. The pats he was bestowing on his knees grew perfunctory. He felt vaguely that he was being unfairly saddled with responsibility; he was not even sure he wanted to be told. Though never surprised at finding Gordon Sterrett in mild difficulty, there was something in this present misery that repelled him and hardened him, even though it excited his curiosity.

"Go on."

"It's a girl."

"Hm." Dean resolved that nothing was going to spoil his trip. If Gordon was going to be depressing, then he'd have to see less of Gordon.

"Her name is Jewel Hudson," went on the distressed voice from the bed. "She used to be 'pure,' I guess, up to about a year ago. Lived here in New York—poor family. Her people are dead now and she lives with an old aunt. You see it was just about the time I met her that everybody began to come back from France in droves—and all I did was to welcome the newly arrived and go on parties with 'em. That's the way it started, Phil, just from being glad to see everybody and having them glad to see me."

"You ought to've had more sense."

"I know," Gordon paused, and then continued listlessly. "I'm on my own now, you know, and Phil, I can't stand being poor. Then came this darn girl. She sort of fell in love with me for a while and, though I never intended to get so involved, I'd always seem to run into her somewhere. You can imagine the sort of work I was doing for those exporting people—of course, I always intended to draw; do illustrating for magazines; there's a pile of money in it."

"Why didn't you? You've got to buckle down if you want to make good," suggested Dean with cold formalism.

"I tried, a little, but my stuff's crude. I've got talent, Phil; I can draw—but I just don't know how. I ought to go to art school and I can't afford it. Well, things came to a crisis about a week ago. Just as I was down to about my last dollar this girl began bothering me. She wants some money; claims she can make trouble for me if she doesn't get it."

"Can she?"

"I'm afraid she can. That's one reason I lost my job—she kept calling up the office all the time, and that was sort of the last straw down there. She's got a letter all written to send to my family. Oh, she's got me, all right. I've got to have some money for her."

There was an awkward pause. Gordon lay very still, his hands clenched by his side.

"I'm all in," he continued, his voice trembling. "I'm half crazy, Phil. If I hadn't known you were coming East, I think I'd have killed myself. I want you to lend me three hundred dollars."

Dean's hands, which had been patting his bare ankles, were suddenly quiet—and the curious uncertainty playing between the two became taut and strained.

After a second Gordon continued:

"I've bled the family until I'm ashamed to ask for another nickel."

Still Dean made no answer.

"Jewel says she's got to have two hundred dollars."

"Tell her where she can go."

"Yes, that sounds easy, but she's got a couple of drunken letters I wrote her. Unfortunately she's not at all the flabby sort of person you'd expect."

Dean made an expression of distaste.

"I can't stand that sort of woman. You ought to have kept away."

"I know," admitted Gordon wearily.

"You've got to look at things as they are. If you haven't got money you've got to work and stay away from women."

"That's easy for you to say," began Gordon, his eyes narrowing. "You've got all the money in the world."

"I most certainly have not. My family keep darn close tab on what I spend. Just because I have a little leeway I have to be extra careful not to abuse it."

He raised the blind and let in a further flood of sunshine.

"I'm no prig, Lord knows," he went on deliberately. "I like pleasure—and I like a lot of it on a vacation like this, but you're—you're in awful shape. I never heard you talk just this way before. You seem to be sort of bankrupt—morally as well as financially."

"Don't they usually go together?"

Dean shook his head impatiently.

"There's a regular aura about you that I don't understand. It's a sort of evil."

"It's an air of worry and poverty and sleepless nights," said Gordon, rather defiantly.

"I don't know."

"Oh, I admit I'm depressing. I depress myself. But, my God, Phil, a week's rest and a new suit and some ready money and I'd be like—like I was. Phil, I can draw like a streak, and you know it. But half the time I haven't had the money to buy decent drawing materials—and I can't draw when I'm tired and discouraged and all in. With a little ready money I can take a few weeks off and get started."

"How do I know you wouldn't use it on some other woman?"

"Why rub it in?" said Gordon quietly.

"I'm not rubbing it in. I hate to see you this way."

"Will you lend me the money, Phil?"

"I can't decide right off. That's a lot of money and it'll be darn inconvenient for me."

"It'll be hell for me if you can't—I know I'm whining, and it's all my own fault but—that doesn't change it."

"When could you pay it back?"

This was encouraging. Gordon considered. It was probably wisest to be frank.

"Of course, I could promise to send it back next month, but—I'd better say three months. Just as soon as I start to sell drawings."

"How do I know you'll sell any drawings?"

A new hardness in Dean's voice sent a faint chill of doubt over Gordon. Was it possible that he wouldn't get the money?

"I supposed you had a little confidence in me."

"I did have—but when I see you like this I begin to wonder."

"Do you suppose if I wasn't at the end of my rope I'd come to you like this? Do you think I'm enjoying it?" He broke off and bit his lip, feeling that he had better subdue the rising anger in his voice. After all, he was the suppliant.

"You seem to manage it pretty easily," said Dean angrily. "You put me in the position where, if I don't lend it to you, I'm a sucker—oh, yes, you do. And let me tell you it's no easy thing for me to get hold of three hundred dollars. My income isn't so big but that a slice like that won't play the deuce with it."

He left his chair and began to dress, choosing his clothes carefully. Gordon stretched out his arms and clenched the edges of the bed, fighting back a desire to cry out. His head was splitting and whirring, his mouth was dry and bitter and he could feel the fever in his blood resolving itself into innumerable regular counts like a slow dripping from a roof.

Dean tied his tie precisely, brushed his eyebrows, and removed a piece of tobacco from his teeth with solemnity. Next he filled his cigarette case, tossed the empty box thoughtfully into the waste basket, and settled the case in his vest pocket.

"Had breakfast?" he demanded.

"No; I don't eat it any more."

"Well, we'll go out and have some. We'll decide about that money later. I'm sick of the subject. I came East to have a good time.

"Let's go over to the Yale Club," he continued moodily, and then added with an implied reproof: "You've given up your job. You've got nothing else to do."

"I'd have a lot to do if I had a little money," said Gordon pointedly.

"Oh, for Heaven's sake drop the subject for a while! No point in glooming on my whole trip. Here, here's some money."

He took a five-dollar bill from his wallet and tossed it over to Gordon, who folded it carefully and put it in his pocket. There was an added spot of color in his cheeks, an added glow that was not fever. For an instant before they turned to go out their eyes met and in that instant each found something that made him lower his own glance quickly. For in that instant they quite suddenly and definitely hated each other.

II

Fifth Avenue and Forty-fourth Street swarmed with the noon crowd. The wealthy, happy sun glittered in transient gold through the thick windows of the smart shops, lighting upon mesh bags and purses and strings of pearls in gray velvet cases; upon gaudy feather fans of many colors; upon the laces and silks of expensive dresses; upon the bad paintings and the fine period furniture in the elaborate show rooms of interior decorators.

Working-girls, in pairs and groups and swarms, loitered by these windows, choosing their future boudoirs from some resplendent display which included even a man's silk pajamas laid domestically across the bed. They stood in front of the jewelry stores and picked out their engagement rings, and their wedding rings and their platinum wrist watches, and then drifted on to inspect the feather fans and opera cloaks; meanwhile digesting the sandwiches and sundaes they had eaten for lunch.

All through the crowd were men in uniform, sailors from the great fleet anchored in the Hudson, soldiers with divisional insignia from Massachusetts to California, wanting fearfully to be noticed, and finding the great city thoroughly fed up with soldiers unless they were nicely massed into pretty formations and uncomfortable under the weight of a pack and rifle.

Through this medley Dean and Gordon wandered; the former interested, made alert by the display of humanity at its frothiest and gaudiest; the latter reminded of how often he had been one of the crowd, tired, casually fed, overworked, and dissipated. To Dean the struggle was significant, young, cheerful; to Gordon it was dismal, meaningless, endless.

In the Yale Club they met a group of their former classmates who greeted the visiting Dean vociferously. Sitting in a semicircle of lounges and great chairs, they had a highball all around.

Gordon found the conversation tiresome and interminable. They lunched together *en masse,* warmed with liquor as the afternoon began. They were all going to the Gamma Psi dance that night—it promised to be the best party since the war.

"Edith Bradin's coming," said some one to Gordon. "Didn't she used to be an old flame of yours? Aren't you both from Harrisburg?"

"Yes." He tried to change the subject. "I see her brother occasionally. He's sort of a socialistic nut. Runs a paper or something here in New York."

"Not like his gay sister, eh?" continued his eager informant. "Well, she's coming to-night with a junior named Peter Himmel."

Gordon was to meet Jewel Hudson at eight o'clock—he had promised to have some money for her. Several times he glanced nervously at his wrist watch. At four, to his relief, Dean rose and announced that he was going over to Rivers Brothers to buy some collars and ties. But as they left the Club another of the party joined them, to Gordon's great dismay. Dean was in a jovial mood now, happy, expectant of the evening's party, faintly hilarious. Over in Rivers' he chose a dozen neckties, selecting each one after long consultations with the other man. Did he think narrow ties were coming back? And wasn't it a shame that Rivers couldn't get any more Welsh Margotson collars? There never was a collar like the "Covington."[3]

Gordon was in something of a panic. He wanted the money immediately. And he was now inspired also with a vague idea of attending the Gamma Psi dance. He wanted to see Edith—Edith whom he hadn't met since one romantic night at the Harrisburg Country Club just before he went to France. The affair had died, drowned in the turmoil of the war and quite forgotten in the arabesque of these three months, but a picture of her, poignant, debonnaire, immersed in her own inconsequential chatter, recurred to him unexpectedly and brought a hundred memories with it. It was Edith's face that he had cherished through college with a sort of detached yet affectionate admiration. He had loved to draw her—around his room had been a dozen sketches of her—playing golf, swimming—he could draw her pert, arresting profile with his eyes shut.

They left Rivers' at five-thirty and paused for a moment on the sidewalk.

"Well," said Dean genially, "I'm all set now. Think I'll go back to the hotel and get a shave, haircut, and massage."

"Good enough," said the other man, "I think I'll join you."

Gordon wondered if he was to be beaten after all. With difficulty he restrained himself from turning to the man and snarling out, "Go on away, damn you!" In despair he suspected that perhaps Dean had spoken to him, was keeping him along in order to avoid a dispute about the money.

They went into the Biltmore—a Biltmore alive with girls—mostly from the West and South, the stellar débutantes of many cities gathered for the dance of a famous fraternity of a famous university. But to Gordon they were faces in a dream. He gathered together his forces for a last appeal, was about to come out with he knew not what, when Dean suddenly excused himself to the other man and taking Gordon's arm led him aside.

"Gordy," he said quickly, "I've thought the whole thing over carefully and I've decided that I can't lend you that money. I'd like to oblige you, but I don't feel I ought to—it'd put a crimp in me for a month."

Gordon, watching him dully, wondered why he had never before noticed how much those upper teeth projected.

"—I'm mighty sorry, Gordon," continued Dean, "but that's the way it is."

He took out his wallet and deliberately counted out seventy-five dollars in bills.

"Here," he said, holding them out, "here's seventy-five; that makes eighty all together. That's all the actual cash I have with me, besides what I'll actually spend on the trip."

Gordon raised his clenched hand automatically, opened it as though it were a tongs he was holding, and clenched it again on the money.

"I'll see you at the dance," continued Dean. "I've got to get along to the barber-shop."

"So-long," said Gordon in a strained and husky voice.

"So-long."

Dean began to smile, but seemed to change his mind. He nodded briskly and disappeared.

But Gordon stood there, his handsome face awry with distress, the roll of bills clenched tightly in his hand. Then, blinded by sudden tears, he stumbled clumsily down the Biltmore steps.

III

About nine o'clock of the same night two human beings came out of a cheap restaurant in Sixth Avenue. They were ugly, ill-nourished, devoid of all except the very lowest form of intelligence, and without even that animal exuberance that in itself brings color into life; they were lately vermin-ridden, cold, and hungry in a dirty town of a strange land; they were poor, friendless; tossed as driftwood from their births, they would be tossed as driftwood to their deaths. They were dressed in the uniform of the United States Army, and on the shoulder of each was the insignia of a drafted division from New Jersey, landed three days before.

The taller of the two was named Carrol Key, a name hinting that in his veins, however thinly diluted by generations of degeneration, ran blood of some potentiality. But one could stare endlessly at the long, chinless face, the dull, watery eyes, and high cheek-bones, without finding a suggestion of either ancestral worth or native resourcefulness.

His companion was swart and bandy-legged, with rat-eyes and a much-broken hooked nose. His defiant air was obviously a pretense, a weapon of protection borrowed from that world of snarl and snap, of physical bluff and physical menace, in which he had always lived. His name was Gus Rose.

Leaving the café they sauntered down Sixth Avenue, wielding toothpicks with great gusto and complete detachment.

"Where to?" asked Rose, in a tone which implied that he would not be surprised if Key suggested the South Sea Islands.

"What you say we see if we can getta holda some liquor?" Prohibition was not yet. The ginger in the suggestion was caused by the law forbidding the selling of liquor to soldiers.

Rose agreed enthusiastically.

"I got an idea," continued Key, after a moment's thought, "I got a brother somewhere."

"In New York?"

"Yeah. He's an old fella." He meant that he was an elder brother. "He's a waiter in a hash joint."

"Maybe he can get us some."

"I'll say he can!"

"B'lieve me, I'm goin' to get this darn uniform off me to-morra. Never get me in it again, neither. I'm goin' to get me some regular clothes."

"Say, maybe I'm not."

As their combined finances were something less than five dollars, this intention can be taken largely as a pleasant game of words, harmless and consoling. It seemed to please both of them, however, for they reinforced it with chuckling and mention of personages high in biblical circles, adding such further emphasis as "Oh, boy!" "You know!" and "I'll say so!" repeated many times over.

The entire mental pabulum of these two men consisted of an offended nasal comment extended through the years upon the institution—army, business, or poor-house—which kept them alive, and toward their immediate superior in that institution. Until that very morning the institution had been the "government" and the immediate superior had been the "Cap'n"—from these two they had glided out and were now in the vaguely uncomfortable state before they should adopt their next bondage. They were uncertain, resentful, and somewhat ill at ease. This they hid by pretending an elaborate relief at being out of the army, and by assuring each other that military discipline should never again rule their stubborn, liberty-loving wills. Yet, as a matter of fact, they would have felt more at home in a prison than in this new-found and unquestionable freedom.

Suddenly Key increased his gait. Rose, looking up and following his glance, discovered a crowd that was collecting fifty yards down the street. Key chuckled and began to run in the direction of the crowd; Rose thereupon also chuckled and his short bandy legs twinkled beside the long, awkward strides of his companion.

Reaching the outskirts of the crowd they immediately became an indistinguishable part of it. It was composed of ragged civilians somewhat the worse for liquor, and of soldiers representing many divisions and many stages of sobriety, all clustered around a gesticulating little Jew with long black whiskers, who was waving his arms and delivering an excited but succinct harangue. Key and Rose, having wedged themselves into the approximate parquet, scrutinized him with acute suspicion, as his words penetrated their common consciousness.

"—What have you got outa the war?" he was crying fiercely. "Look arounja, look arounja! Are you rich? Have you got a lot of money offered you?—no; you're lucky if you're alive and got both your legs; you're lucky if you came back an' find your wife ain't gone off with some other fella that had the money to buy himself out of the war! That's when you're lucky! Who got anything out of it except J. P. Morgan[4] an' John D. Rockerfeller?"[5]

At this point the little Jew's oration was interrupted by the hostile impact of a fist upon the point of his bearded chin and he toppled backward to a sprawl on the pavement.

"God damn Bolsheviki!"[6] cried the big soldier-blacksmith who had delivered the blow. There was a rumble of approval, the crowd closed in nearer.

The Jew staggered to his feet, and immediately went down again before a half-dozen reaching-in fists. This time he stayed down, breathing heavily, blood oozing from his lip where it was cut within and without.

There was a riot of voices, and in a minute Rose and Key found themselves flowing with the jumbled crowd down Sixth Avenue under the leadership of a thin civilian in a slouch hat and the brawny soldier who had summarily ended the oration. The crowd had marvellously swollen to formidable proportions and a stream of more noncommittal citizens followed it along the sidewalks lending their moral support by intermittent huzzas.

"Where we goin'?" yelled Key to the man nearest him.

His neighbor pointed up to the leader in the slouch hat.

"That guy knows where there's a lot of 'em! We're goin' to show 'em!"

"We're goin' to show 'em!" whispered Key delightedly to Rose, who repeated the phrase rapturously to a man on the other side.

Down Sixth Avenue swept the procession, joined here and there by soldiers and marines, and now and then by civilians, who came up with the inevitable cry that they were just out of the army themselves, as if presenting it as a card of admission to a newly formed Sporting and Amusement Club.

Then the procession swerved down a cross street and headed for Fifth Avenue and the word filtered here and there that they were bound for a Red meeting at Tolliver Hall.

"Where is it?"

The question went up the line and a moment later the answer floated back. Tolliver Hall was down on Tenth Street. There was a bunch of other sojers who was goin' to break it up and was down there now!

But Tenth Street had a far-away sound and at the word a general groan went up and a score of the procession dropped out. Among these were Rose and Key, who slowed down to a saunter and let the more enthusiastic sweep on by.

"I'd rather get some liquor," said Key as they halted and made their way to the sidewalk amid cries of "Shell hole!"[7] and "Quitters!"

"Does your brother work around here?" asked Rose, assuming the air of one passing from the superficial to the eternal.

"He oughta," replied Key. "I ain't seen him for a coupla years. I been out to Pennsylvania since. Maybe he don't work at night anyhow. It's right along here. He can get us some o'right if he ain't gone."

They found the place after a few minutes' patrol of the street—a shoddy tablecloth restaurant between Fifth Avenue and Broadway. Here Key went inside to inquire for his brother George, while Rose waited on the sidewalk.

"He ain't here no more," said Key emerging. "He's a waiter up to Delmonico's."

Rose nodded wisely, as if he'd expected as much. One should not be surprised at a capable man changing jobs occasionally. He knew a waiter once—there ensued a long conversation as they walked as to whether waiters made more in actual wages than in tips—it was decided that it depended on the social tone of the joint wherein the waiter labored. After having given each other vivid pictures of millionaires dining at Delmonico's and throwing away fifty-dollar bills after their first quart of champagne, both men thought privately of becoming waiters. In fact, Key's narrow brow was secreting a resolution to ask his brother to get him a job.

"A waiter can drink up all the champagne those fellas leave in bottles," suggested Rose with some relish, and then added as an afterthought, "Oh, boy!"

By the time they reached Delmonico's it was half past ten, and they were surprised to see a stream of taxis driving up to the door one after the other and emitting marvellous, hatless young ladies, each one attended by a stiff young gentleman in evening clothes.

"It's a party," said Rose with some awe. "Maybe we better not go in. He'll be busy."

"No, he won't. He'll be o'right."

After some hesitation they entered what appeared to them to be the least elaborate door and, indecision falling upon them immediately, stationed themselves nervously in an inconspicuous corner of the small dining-room in which they found themselves. They took off their caps and held them in their hands. A cloud of gloom fell upon them and both started when a door at one end of the room crashed open, emitting a comet-like waiter who streaked across the floor and vanished through another door on the other side.

There had been three of these lightning passages before the seekers mustered the acumen to hail a waiter. He turned, looked at them suspiciously, and then approached with soft, catlike steps, as if prepared at any moment to turn and flee.

"Say," began Key, "say, do you know my brother? He's a waiter here."

"His name is Key," annotated Rose.

Yes, the waiter knew Key. He was up-stairs, he thought. There was a big dance going on in the main ballroom. He'd tell him.

Ten minutes later George Key appeared and greeted his brother with the utmost suspicion; his first and most natural thought being that he was going to be asked for money.

George was tall and weak-chinned, but there his resemblance to his brother ceased. The waiter's eyes were not dull, they were alert and twinkling, and his manner was suave, in-door, and faintly superior. They exchanged formalities. George was married and had three children. He seemed fairly interested, but not impressed by the news that Carrol had been abroad in the army. This disappointed Carrol.

"George," said the younger brother, these amenities having been disposed of, "we want to get some booze, and they won't sell us none. Can you get us some?"

George considered.

"Sure. Maybe I can. It may be half an hour, though."

"All right," agreed Carrol, "we'll wait."

At this Rose started to sit down in a convenient chair, but was hailed to his feet by the indignant George.

"Hey! Watch out, you! Can't sit down here! This room's all set for a twelve o'clock banquet."

"I ain't goin' to hurt it," said Rose resentfully. "I been through the delouser."

"Never mind," said George sternly, "if the head waiter seen me here talkin' he'd romp all over me."

"Oh."

The mention of the head waiter was full explanation to the other two; they fingered their overseas caps nervously and waited for a suggestion.

"I tell you," said George, after a pause, "I got a place you can wait; you just come here with me."

They followed him out the far door, through a deserted pantry and up a pair of dark winding stairs, emerging finally into a small room chiefly furnished by piles of pails and stacks of scrubbing brushes, and illuminated by a single dim electric light. There he left them, after soliciting two dollars and agreeing to return in half an hour with a quart of whiskey.

"George is makin' money, I bet," said Key gloomily as he seated himself on an inverted pail. "I bet he's making fifty dollars a week."

Rose nodded his head and spat.

"I bet he is, too."

"What'd he say the dance was of?"

"A lot of college fellas. Yale College."

They both nodded solemnly at each other.

"Wonder where that crowda sojers is now?"

"I don't know. I know that's too damn long to walk for me."

"Me too. You don't catch me walkin' that far."

Ten minutes later restlessness seized them.

"I'm goin' to see what's out here," said Rose, stepping cautiously toward the other door.

It was a swinging door of green baize and he pushed it open a cautious inch.

"See anything?"

For answer Rose drew in his breath sharply.

"Doggone! Here's some liquor I'll say!"

"Liquor?"

Key joined Rose at the door, and looked eagerly.

"I'll tell the world that's liquor," he said, after a moment of concentrated gazing.

It was a room about twice as large as the one they were in—and in it was prepared a radiant feast of spirits. There were long walls of alternating bottles set along two white covered tables; whiskey, gin, brandy, French and Italian vermouths, and orange juice, not to mention an array of syphons and two great empty punch bowls. The room was as yet uninhabited.

"It's for this dance they're just starting," whispered Key; "hear the violins playin'? Say, boy, I wouldn't mind havin' a dance."

They closed the door softly and exchanged a glance of mutual comprehension. There was no need of feeling each other out.

"I'd like to get my hands on a coupla those bottles," said Rose emphatically.

"Me too."

"Do you suppose we'd get seen?"

Key considered.

"Maybe we better wait till they start drinkin' 'em. They got 'em all laid out now, and they know how many of them there are."

They debated this point for several minutes. Rose was all for getting his hands on a bottle now and tucking it under his coat before any one came into the room. Key, however, advocated caution. He was afraid he might get his brother in trouble. If they waited till some of the bottles were opened it'd be all right to take one, and everybody'd think it was one of the college fellas.

While they were still engaged in argument George Key hurried through the room and, barely grunting at them, disappeared by way of the green baize door. A minute later they heard several corks pop, and then the sound of cracking ice and splashing liquid. George was mixing the punch.

The soldiers exchanged delighted grins.

"Oh, boy!" whispered Rose.

George reappeared.

"Just keep low, boys," he said quickly. "I'll have your stuff for you in five minutes."

He disappeared through the door by which he had come.

As soon as his footsteps receded down the stairs, Rose, after a cautious look, darted into the room of delights and reappeared with a bottle in his hand.

"Here's what I say," he said, as they sat radiantly digesting their first drink. "We'll wait till he comes up, and we'll ask him if we can't just stay here and drink what he brings us—see. We'll tell him we haven't got any place to drink it—see. Then we can sneak in there whenever there ain't nobody in that there room and tuck a bottle under our coats. We'll have enough to last us a coupla days—see?"

"Sure," agreed Key[8] enthusiastically. "Oh, boy! And if we want to we can sell it to sojers any time we want to."

They were silent for a moment thinking rosily of this idea. Then Key reached up and unhooked the collar of his O. D. coat.

"It's hot in here, ain't it?"

Rose agreed earnestly.

"Hot as hell."

IV

She was still quite angry when she came out of the dressing-room and crossed the intervening parlor of politeness that opened onto the hall—angry not so much at the actual happening which was, after all, the merest commonplace of her social existence, but because it had occurred on this particular night. She had no quarrel with herself. She had acted with that correct mixture of dignity and reticent pity which she always employed. She had succinctly and deftly snubbed him.

It had happened when their taxi was leaving the Biltmore—hadn't gone half a block. He had lifted his right arm awkwardly—she was on his right side—and attempted to settle it snugly around the crimson fur-trimmed opera cloak she wore. This in itself had been a mistake. It was inevitably more graceful for a young man attempting to embrace a young lady of whose acquiescence he was not certain, to first put his far arm around her. It avoided that awkward movement of raising the near arm.

His second *faux pas* was unconscious. She had spent the afternoon at the hairdresser's; the idea of any calamity overtaking her hair was extremely repugnant—yet as Peter made his unfortunate attempt the point of his elbow had just faintly brushed it. That was his second *faux pas.* Two were quite enough.

He had begun to murmur. At the first murmur she had decided that he was nothing but a college boy—Edith was twenty-two, and anyhow, this dance, first of its kind since the war, was reminding her, with the accelerating rhythm of its associations, of something else—of another dance and another man, a man for whom her feelings had been little more than a sad-eyed, adolescent mooniness. Edith Bradin was falling in love with her recollection of Gordon Sterrett.

So she came out of the dressing-room at Delmonico's and stood for a second in the doorway looking over the shoulders of a black dress in front of her at the groups of Yale men who flitted like dignified black moths around the head of the stairs. From the room she had left drifted out the heavy fragrance left by the passage to and fro of many scented young beauties—rich perfumes and the fragile memory-laden dust of fragrant powders. This odor drifting out acquired the tang of cigarette smoke in the hall, and then settled sensuously down the stairs and permeated the ballroom where the Gamma Psi dance was to be held. It was an odor she knew well, exciting, stimulating, restlessly sweet—the odor of a fashionable dance.

She thought of her own appearance. Her bare arms and shoulders were powdered to a creamy white. She knew they looked very soft and would gleam like milk against the black backs that were to silhouette them to-night. The hairdressing had been a success; her reddish mass of hair was piled and crushed and creased to an arrogant marvel of mobile curves. Her lips were finely made of deep carmine; the irises of her eyes were delicate, breakable blue, like china eyes. She was a complete, infinitely delicate, quite perfect thing of beauty, flowing in an even line from a complex coiffure to two small slim feet.

She thought of what she would say to-night at this revel, faintly prestiged already by the sounds of high and low laughter and slippered footsteps, and movements of couples up and down the stairs. She would talk the language she had talked for many years—her line—made up of the current expressions, bits of journalese and college slang strung together into an intrinsic whole, careless, faintly provocative, delicately sentimental. She smiled faintly as she heard a girl sitting on the stairs near her say: "You don't know the half of it, dearie!"

And as she smiled her anger melted for a moment, and closing her eyes she drew in a deep breath of pleasure. She dropped her arms to her side until they were faintly touching the sleek sheath that covered and suggested her figure. She had never felt her own softness so much nor so enjoyed the whiteness of her own arms.

"I smell sweet," she said to herself simply, and then came another thought—"I'm made for love."

She liked the sound of this and thought it again; then in inevitable succession came her new-born riot of dreams about Gordon. The twist of her imagination which, two months before, had disclosed to her her unguessed desire to see him again, seemed now to have been leading up to this dance, this hour.

For all her sleek beauty, Edith was a grave, slow-thinking girl. There was a streak in her of that same desire to ponder, of that adolescent idealism that had turned her brother socialist and pacifist. Henry Bradin had left Cornell, where he had been an instructor in economics, and had come to New York to pour the latest cures for incurable evils into the columns of a radical weekly newspaper.

Edith, less fatuously, would have been content to cure Gordon Sterrett. There was a quality of weakness in Gordon that she wanted to take care of; there was a helplessness in him that she wanted to protect. And she wanted someone she had known a long while, someone who had loved her a long while. She was a little tired; she wanted to get married. Out of a pile of letters, half a dozen pictures and as many memories, and this weariness, she had decided that next time she saw Gordon their relations were going to be changed. She would say something that would change them. There was this evening. This was her evening. All evenings were her evenings.

Then her thoughts were interrupted by a solemn undergraduate with a hurt look and an air of strained formality who presented himself before her and bowed unusually low. It was the man she had come with, Peter Himmel. He was tall and humorous, with horned-rimmed glasses and an air of attractive whimsicality. She suddenly rather disliked him—probably because he had not succeeded in kissing her.

"Well," she began, "are you still furious at me?"

"Not at all."

She stepped forward and took his arm.

"I'm sorry," she said softly. "I don't know why I snapped out that way. I'm in a bum humor to-night for some strange reason. I'm sorry."

"S'all right," he mumbled, "don't mention it."

He felt disagreeably embarrassed. Was she rubbing in the fact of his late failure?

"It was a mistake," she continued, on the same consciously gentle key. "We'll both forget it." For this he hated her.

A few minutes later they drifted out on the floor while the dozen swaying, sighing members of the specially hired jazz orchestra informed the crowded ballroom that "if a saxophone and me are left alone why then two is com-pan-ee!"

A man with a mustache cut in.

"Hello," he began reprovingly. "You don't remember me."

"I can't just think of your name," she said lightly—"and I know you so well."

"I met you up at—" His voice trailed disconsolately off as a man with very fair hair cut in. Edith murmured a conventional "Thanks, loads—cut in later," to the *inconnu*.[9]

The very fair man insisted on shaking hands enthusiastically. She placed him as one of the numerous Jims of her acquaintance—last name a mystery. She remembered even that he had a peculiar rhythm in dancing and found as they started that she was right.

"Going to be here long?" he breathed confidentially.

She leaned back and looked up at him.

"Couple of weeks."

"Where are you?"

"Biltmore. Call me up some day."

"I mean it," he assured her. "I will. We'll go to tea."

"So do I—Do."

A dark man cut in with intense formality.

"You don't remember me, do you?" he said gravely.

"I should say I do. Your name's Harlan."

"No-ope. Barlow."

"Well, I knew there were two syllables anyway. You're the boy that played the ukulele so well up at Howard Marshall's house-party."

"I played—but not——"

A man with prominent teeth cut in. Edith inhaled a slight cloud of whiskey. She liked men to have had something to drink; they were so much more cheerful, and appreciative and complimentary—much easier to talk to.

"My name's Dean, Philip Dean," he said cheerfully. "You don't remember me, I know, but you used to come up to New Haven with a fellow I roomed with senior year, Gordon Sterrett."

Edith looked up quickly.

"Yes, I went up with him twice—to the Pump and Slipper and the Junior prom."

"You've seen him, of course," said Dean carelessly. "He's here tonight. I saw him just a minute ago."

Edith started. Yet she had felt quite sure he would be here.

"Why, no, I haven't——"

A fat man with red hair cut in.

"Hello, Edith," he began.

"Why—hello there——"

She slipped, stumbled lightly.

"I'm sorry, dear," she murmured mechanically.

She had seen Gordon—Gordon very white and listless, leaning against the side of a doorway, smoking and looking into the ballroom. Edith could see that his face was thin and wan—that the hand he raised to his lips with a cigarette was trembling. They were dancing quite close to him now.

"—They invite so darn many extra fellas that you—" the short man was saying.

"Hello, Gordon," called Edith over her partner's shoulder. Her heart was pounding wildly.

His large dark eyes were fixed on her. He took a step in her direction. Her partner turned her away—she heard his voice bleating——

"—but half the stags get lit and leave before long, so——"

Then a low tone at her side.

"May I, please?"

She was dancing suddenly with Gordon; one of his arms was around her; she felt it tighten spasmodically; felt his hand on her back with the fingers spread. Her hand holding the little lace handkerchief was crushed in his.

"Why Gordon," she began breathlessly.

"Hello, Edith."

She slipped again—was tossed forward by her recovery until her face touched the black cloth of his dinner coat. She loved him—she knew she loved him—then for a minute there was silence while a strange feeling of uneasiness crept over her. Something was wrong.

Of a sudden her heart wrenched, and turned over as she realized what it was. He was pitiful and wretched, a little drunk, and miserably tired.

"Oh——" she cried involuntarily.

His eyes looked down at her. She saw suddenly that they were blood-streaked and rolling uncontrollably.

"Gordon," she murmured, "we'll sit down; I want to sit down."

They were nearly in mid-floor, but she had seen two men start toward her from opposite sides of the room, so she halted, seized Gordon's limp hand and led him bumping through the crowd, her mouth tight shut, her face a little pale under her rouge, her eyes trembling with tears.

She found a place high up on the soft-carpeted stairs, and he sat down heavily beside her.

"Well," he began, staring at her unsteadily, "I certainly am glad to see you, Edith."

She looked at him without answering. The effect of this on her was immeasurable. For years she had seen men in various stages of intoxication, from uncles all the way down to chauffeurs, and her feelings had varied from amusement to disgust, but here for the first time she was seized with a new feeling—an unutterable horror.

"Gordon," she said accusingly and almost crying, "you look like the devil."

He nodded. "I've had trouble, Edith."

"Trouble?"

"All sorts of trouble. Don't you say anything to the family, but I'm all gone to pieces. I'm a mess, Edith."

His lower lip was sagging. He seemed scarcely to see her.

"Can't you—can't you," she hesitated, "can't you tell me about it, Gordon? You know I'm always interested in you."

She bit her lip—she had intended to say something stronger, but found at the end that she couldn't bring it out.

Gordon shook his head dully. "I can't tell you. You're a good woman. I can't tell a good woman the story."

"Rot," she said, defiantly. "I think it's a perfect insult to call any one a good woman in that way. It's a slam. You've been drinking, Gordon."

"Thanks." He inclined his head gravely. "Thanks for the information."

"Why do you drink?"

"Because I'm so damn miserable."

"Do you think drinking's going to make it any better?"

"What you doing—trying to reform me?"

"No; I'm trying to help you, Gordon. Can't you tell me about it?"

"I'm in an awful mess. Best thing you can do is to pretend not to know me."

"Why, Gordon?"

"I'm sorry I cut in on you—it's unfair to you. You're pure woman—and all that sort of thing. Here, I'll get some one else to dance with you."

He rose clumsily to his feet, but she reached up and pulled him down beside her on the stairs.

"Here, Gordon. You're ridiculous. You're hurting me. You're acting like a—like a crazy man——"

"I admit it. I'm a little crazy. Something's wrong with me, Edith. There's something left me. It doesn't matter."

"It does, tell me."

"Just that. I was always queer—little bit different from other boys. All right in college, but now it's all wrong. Things have been snapping inside me for four months like little hooks on a dress, and it's about to come off when a few more hooks go. I'm very gradually going loony."

He turned his eyes full on her and began to laugh, and she shrank away from him.

"What *is* the matter?"

"Just me," he repeated. "I'm going loony. This whole place is like a dream to me—this Delmonico's——"

As he talked she saw he had changed utterly. He wasn't at all light and gay and careless—a great lethargy and discouragement had come over him. Revulsion seized her, followed by a faint, surprising boredom. His voice seemed to come out of a great void.

"Edith," he said, "I used to think I was clever, talented, an artist. Now I know I'm nothing. Can't draw, Edith. Don't know why I'm telling you this."

She nodded absently.

"I can't draw, I can't do anything. I'm poor as a church mouse." He laughed, bitterly and rather too loud. "I've become a damn beggar, a leech on my friends. I'm a failure. I'm poor as hell."

Her distaste was growing. She barely nodded this time, waiting for her first possible cue to rise.

Suddenly Gordon's eyes filled with tears.

"Edith," he said, turning to her with what was evidently a strong effort at self-control, "I can't tell you what it means to me to know there's one person left who's interested in me."

He reached out and patted her hand, and involuntarily she drew it away.

"It's mighty fine of you," he repeated.

"Well," she said slowly, looking him in the eye, "any one's always glad to see an old friend—but I'm sorry to see you like this, Gordon."

There was a pause while they looked at each other, and the momentary eagerness in his eyes wavered. She rose and stood looking at him, her face quite expressionless.

"Shall we dance?" she suggested, coolly.

—Love is fragile—she was thinking—but perhaps the pieces are saved, the things that hovered on lips, that might have been said. The new love words, the tendernesses learned, are treasured up for the next lover.

V

Peter Himmel, escort to the lovely Edith, was unaccustomed to being snubbed; having been snubbed, he was hurt and embarrassed, and ashamed of himself. For a matter of two months he had been on special delivery terms with Edith Bradin, and knowing that the one excuse and explanation of the special delivery letter is its value in sentimental correspondence, he had believed himself quite sure of his ground. He searched in vain for any reason why she should have taken this attitude in the matter of a simple kiss.

Therefore when he was cut in on by the man with the mustache he went out into the hall and, making up a sentence, said it over to himself several times. Considerably deleted, this was it:

"Well, if any girl ever led a man on and then jolted him, she did—and she has no kick coming if I go out and get beautifully boiled."

So he walked through the supper room into a small room adjoining it, which he had located earlier in the evening. It was a room in which there were several large bowls of punch flanked by many bottles. He took a seat beside the table which held the bottles.

At the second highball, boredom, disgust, the monotony of time, the turbidity of events, sank into a vague background before which glittering cobwebs formed. Things became reconciled to themselves, things lay quietly on their shelves; the troubles of the day arranged themselves in trim formation and at his curt wish of dismissal, marched off and disappeared. And with the departure of worry came brilliant, permeating symbolism. Edith became a flighty, negligible girl, not to be worried over; rather to be laughed at. She fitted like a figure of his own dream into the surface world forming about him. He himself became in a measure symbolic, a type of the continent bacchanal, the brilliant dreamer at play.

Then the symbolic mood faded and as he sipped his third highball his imagination yielded to the warm glow and he lapsed into a state similar to floating on his back in pleasant water. It was at this point that he noticed that a green baize door near him was open about two inches, and that through the aperture a pair of eyes were watching him intently.

"Hm," murmured Peter calmly.

The green door closed—and then opened again—a bare half inch this time.

"Peek-a-boo," murmured Peter.

The door remained stationary and then he became aware of a series of tense intermittent whispers.

"One guy."

"What's he doin'?"

"He's sittin' lookin'."

"He better beat it off. We gotta get another li'l' bottle."

Peter listened while the words filtered into his consciousness.

"Now this," he thought, "is most remarkable."

He was excited. He was jubilant. He felt that he had stumbled upon a mystery. Affecting an elaborate carelessness he arose and walked around the table—then, turning quickly, pulled open the green door, precipitating Private Rose into the room.

Peter bowed.

"How do you do?" he said.

Private Rose set one foot slightly in front of the other, poised for fight, flight, or compromise.

"How do you do?" repeated Peter politely.

"I'm o'right."

"Can I offer you a drink?"

Private Rose looked at him searchingly, suspecting possible sarcasm.

"O'right," he said finally.

Peter indicated a chair.

"Sit down."

"I got a friend," said Rose, "I got a friend in there." He pointed to the green door.

"By all means let's have him in."

Peter crossed over, opened the door and welcomed in Private Key, very suspicious and uncertain and guilty. Chairs were found and the three took their seats around the punch bowl. Peter gave them each a highball and offered them a cigarette from his case. They accepted both with some diffidence.

"Now," continued Peter easily, "may I ask why you gentlemen prefer to lounge away your leisure hours in a room which is chiefly furnished, as far as I can see, with scrubbing brushes. And when the human race has progressed to the stage where seventeen thousand chairs are manufactured on every day except Sunday—" he paused. Rose and Key regarded him vacantly. "Will you tell me," went on Peter, "why you choose to rest yourselves on articles intended for the transportation of water from one place to another?"

At this point Rose contributed a grunt to the conversation.

"And lastly," finished Peter, "will you tell me why, when you are in a building beautifully hung with enormous candelabra, you prefer to spend these evening hours under one anemic electric light?"

Rose looked at Key; Key looked at Rose. They laughed; they laughed uproariously; they found it was impossible to look at each other without laughing. But they were not laughing with this man—they were laughing at him. To them a man who talked after this fashion was either raving drunk or raving crazy.

"You are Yale men, I presume," said Peter, finishing his highball and preparing another.

They laughed again.

"Na-ah."

"So? I thought perhaps you might be members of that lowly section of the university known as the Sheffield Scientific School."

"Na-ah."

"Hm. Well, that's too bad. No doubt you are Harvard men, anxious to preserve your incognito in this—this paradise of violet blue, as the newspapers say."

"Na-ah," said Key scornfully, "we was just waitin' for somebody."

"Ah," exclaimed Peter, rising and filling their glasses, "very interestin'. Had a date with a scrublady, eh?"

They both denied this indignantly.

"It's all right," Peter reassured them, "don't apologize. A scrublady's as good as any lady in the world. Kipling says 'Any lady and Judy O'Grady under the skin.' "

"Sure," said Key, winking broadly at Rose.

"My case, for instance," continued Peter, finishing his glass. "I got a girl up here that's spoiled. Spoildest darn girl I ever saw. Refused to kiss me; no reason whatsoever. Led me on deliberately to think sure I want to kiss you and then plunk! Threw me over! What's the younger generation comin' to?"

"Say tha's hard luck," said Key—"that's awful hard luck."

"Oh, boy!" said Rose.

"Have another?" said Peter.

"We got in a sort of fight for a while," said Key after a pause, "but it was too far away."

"A fight?—tha's stuff!" said Peter, seating himself unsteadily. "Fight 'em all! I was in the army."

"This was with a Bolshevik fella."

"Tha's stuff!" exclaimed Peter, enthusiastic. "That's what I say! Kill the Bolshevik! Exterminate 'em!"

"We're Americuns," said Rose, implying a sturdy, defiant patriotism.

"Sure," said Peter. "Greatest race in the world! We're all Americuns! Have another."

They had another.

VI

At one o'clock a special orchestra, special even in a day of special orchestras, arrived at Delmonico's, and its members, seating themselves arrogantly around the piano, took up the burden of providing music for the Gamma Psi Fraternity. They were headed by a famous flute-player, distinguished throughout New York for his feat of standing on his head and shimmying with his shoulders while he played the latest jazz on his flute. During his performance the lights were extinguished except for the spotlight on the flute-player and another roving beam that threw flickering shadows and changing kaleidoscopic colors over the massed dancers.

Edith had danced herself into that tired, dreamy state habitual only with débutantes, a state equivalent to the glow of a noble soul after several long highballs. Her mind floated vaguely on the bosom of her music; her partners changed with the unreality of phantoms under the colorful shifting dusk, and to her present coma it seemed as if days had passed since the dance began. She had talked on many fragmentary subjects with many men. She had been kissed once and made love to six times. Earlier in the evening different undergraduates had danced with her, but now, like all the more popular girls there, she had her own entourage—that is, half a dozen gallants had singled her out or were alternating her charms with those of some other chosen beauty; they cut in on her in regular, inevitable succession.

Several times she had seen Gordon—he had been sitting a long time on the stairway with his palm to his head, his dull eyes fixed at an infinite speck on the floor before him, very depressed, he looked, and quite drunk—but Edith each time had averted her glance hurriedly. All that seemed long ago; her mind was passive now, her senses were lulled to trance-like sleep; only her feet danced and her voice talked on in hazy sentimental banter.

But Edith was not nearly so tired as to be incapable of moral indignation when Peter Himmel cut in on her, sublimely and happily drunk. She gasped and looked up at him.

"Why, *Peter!*"

"I'm a li'l' stewed, Edith."

"Why, Peter, you're a *peach,* you are! Don't you think it's a bum way of doing—when you're with me?"

Then she smiled unwillingly, for he was looking at her with owlish sentimentality varied with a silly spasmodic smile.

"Darlin' Edith," he began earnestly, "you know I love you, don't you?"

"You tell it well."

"I love you—and I merely wanted you to kiss me," he added sadly.

His embarrassment, his shame, were both gone. She was a mos' beautiful girl in whole worl'. Mos' beautiful eyes, like stars above. He wanted to 'pologize—firs', for presuming try to kiss her; second, for drinking—but he'd been so discouraged 'cause he had thought she was mad at him——

The red-fat man cut in, and looking up at Edith smiled radiantly.

"Did you bring any one?" she asked.

No. The red-fat man was a stag.

"Well, would you mind—would it be an awful bother for you to—to take me home to-night?" (this extreme diffidence was a charming affectation on Edith's part—she knew that the red-fat man would immediately dissolve into a paroxysm of delight).

"Bother? Why, good Lord, I'd be darn glad to! You know I'd be darn glad to."

"Thanks *loads!* You're awfully sweet."

She glanced at her wrist-watch. It was half-past one. And, as she said "half-past one" to herself, it floated vaguely into her mind that her brother had told her at luncheon that he worked in the office of his newspaper until after one-thirty every evening.

Edith turned suddenly to her current partner.

"What street is Delmonico's on, anyway?"

"Street? Oh, why Fifth Avenue, of course."

"I mean, what cross street?"

"Why—let's see—it's on Forty-fourth Street."

This verified what she had thought. Henry's office must be across the street and just around the corner, and it occurred to her immediately that she might slip over for a moment and surprise him, float in on him, a shimmering marvel in her new crimson opera cloak and "cheer him up." It was exactly the sort of thing Edith revelled in doing—an unconventional, jaunty thing. The idea reached out and gripped at her imagination—after an instant's hesitation she had decided.

"My hair is just about to tumble entirely down," she said pleasantly to her partner; "would you mind if I go and fix it?"

"Not at all."

"You're a peach."

A few minutes later, wrapped in her crimson opera cloak, she flitted down a side-stairs, her cheeks glowing with excitement at her little adventure. She ran by a couple who stood at the door—a weak-chinned waiter and an over-rouged young lady, in hot dispute—and opening the outer door stepped into the warm May night.

VII

The over-rouged young lady followed her with a brief, bitter glance—then turned again to the weak-chinned waiter and took up her argument.

"You better go up and tell him I'm here," she said defiantly, "or I'll go up myself."

"No, you don't!" said George sternly.

The girl smiled sardonically.

"Oh, I don't, don't I? Well, let me tell you I know more college fellas and more of 'em know me, and are glad to take me out on a party, than you ever saw in your whole life."

"Maybe so——"

"Maybe so," she interrupted. "Oh, it's all right for any of 'em like that one that just ran out—God knows where *she* went—it's all right for them that are asked here to come or go as they like—but when I want to see a friend they have some cheap, ham-slinging, bring-me-a-doughnut waiter to stand here and keep me out."

"See here," said the elder Key indignantly, "I can't lose my job. Maybe this fella you're talkin' about doesn't want to see you."

"Oh, he wants to see me all right."

"Anyways, how could I find him in all that crowd?"

"Oh, he'll be there," she asserted confidently. "You just ask anybody for Gordon Sterrett and they'll point him out to you. They all know each other, those fellas."

She produced a mesh bag, and taking out a dollar bill handed it to George.

"Here," she said, "here's a bribe. You find him and give him my message. You tell him if he isn't here in five minutes I'm coming up."

George shook his head pessimistically, considered the question for a moment, wavered violently, and then withdrew.

In less than the allotted time Gordon came down-stairs. He was drunker than he had been earlier in the evening and in a different way. The liquor seemed to have hardened on him like a crust. He was heavy and lurching—almost incoherent when he talked.

"'Lo, Jewel," he said thickly. "Came right away. Jewel, I couldn't get that money. Tried my best."

"Money nothing!" she snapped. "You haven't been near me for ten days. What's the matter?"

He shook his head slowly.

"Been very low, Jewel. Been sick."

"Why didn't you tell me if you were sick. I don't care about the money that bad. I didn't start bothering you about it at all until you began neglecting me."

Again he shook his head.

"Haven't been neglecting you. Not at all."

"Haven't! You haven't been near me for three weeks, unless you been so drunk you didn't know what you were doing."

"Been sick, Jewel," he repeated, turning his eyes upon her wearily.

"You're well enough to come and play with your society friends here all right. You told me you'd meet me for dinner, and you said you'd have some money for me. You didn't even bother to ring me up."

"I couldn't get any money."

"Haven't I just been saying that doesn't matter? I wanted to see *you,* Gordon, but you seem to prefer your somebody else."

He denied this bitterly.

"Then get your hat and come along," she suggested.

Gordon hesitated—and she came suddenly close to him and slipped her arms around his neck.

"Come on with me, Gordon," she said in a half whisper. "We'll go over to Devineries' and have a drink, and then we can go up to my apartment."

"I can't, Jewel,——"

"You can," she said intensely.

"I'm sick as a dog!"

"Well, then, you oughtn't to stay here and dance."

With a glance around him in which relief and despair were mingled, Gordon hesitated; then she suddenly pulled him to her and kissed him with soft, pulpy lips.

"All right," he said heavily. "I'll get my hat."

VIII

When Edith came out into the clear blue of the May night she found the Avenue deserted. The windows of the big shops were dark; over their doors were drawn great iron masks until they were only shadowy tombs of the late day's splendor. Glancing down toward Forty-second Street she saw a commingled blur of lights from the all-night restaurants. Over on Sixth Avenue the elevated, a flare of fire, roared across the street between the glimmering parallels of light at the station and streaked along into the crisp dark. But at Forty-fourth Street it was very quiet.

Pulling her cloak close about her Edith darted across the Avenue. She started nervously as a solitary man passed her and said in a hoarse whisper—"Where bound, kiddo?" She was reminded of a night in her childhood when she had walked around the block in her pajamas and a dog had howled at her from a mystery-big back yard.

In a minute she had reached her destination, a two-story, comparatively old building on Forty-fourth, in the upper window of which she thankfully detected a wisp of light. It was bright enough outside for her to make out the sign beside the window—the *New York Trumpet.* She stepped inside a dark hall and after a second saw the stairs in the corner.

Then she was in a long, low room furnished with many desks and hung on all sides with file copies of newspapers. There were only two occupants. They were sitting at different ends of the room, each wearing a green eye-shade and writing by a solitary desk light.

For a moment she stood uncertainly in the doorway, and then both men turned around simultaneously and she recognized her brother.

"Why, Edith!" He rose quickly and approached her in surprise, removing his eye-shade. He was tall, lean, and dark, with black, piercing eyes under very thick glasses. They were faraway eyes that seemed always fixed just over the head of the person to whom he was talking.

He put his hands on her arms and kissed her cheek.

"What is it?" he repeated in some alarm.

"I was at a dance across at Delmonico's, Henry," she said excitedly, "and I couldn't resist tearing over to see you."

"I'm glad you did." His alertness gave way quickly to a habitual vagueness. "You oughtn't to be out alone at night though, ought you?"

The man at the other end of the room had been looking at them curiously, but at Henry's beckoning gesture he approached. He was loosely fat with little twinkling eyes, and, having removed his collar and tie, he gave the impression of a Middle-Western farmer on a Sunday afternoon.

"This is my sister," said Henry. "She dropped in to see me."

"How do you do?" said the fat man, smiling. "My name's Bartholomew, Miss Bradin. I know your brother has forgotten it long ago."

Edith laughed politely.

"Well," he continued, "not exactly gorgeous quarters we have here, are they?"

Edith looked around the room.

"They seem very nice," she replied. "Where do you keep the bombs?"

"The bombs?" repeated Bartholomew, laughing. "That's pretty good—the bombs. Did you hear her, Henry? She wants to know where we keep the bombs. Say, that's pretty good."

Edith swung herself onto a vacant desk and sat dangling her feet over the edge. Her brother took a seat beside her.

"Well," he asked, absent-mindedly, "how do you like New York this trip?"

"Not bad. I'll be over at the Biltmore with the Hoyts until Sunday. Can't you come to luncheon to-morrow?"

He thought a moment.

"I'm especially busy," he objected, "and I hate women in groups."

"All right," she agreed, unruffled. "Let's you and me have luncheon together."

"Very well."

"I'll call for you at twelve."

Bartholomew was obviously anxious to return to his desk, but apparently considered that it would be rude to leave without some parting pleasantry.

"Well"—he began awkwardly.

They both turned to him.

"Well, we—we had an exciting time earlier in the evening."

The two men exchanged glances.

"You should have come earlier," continued Bartholomew, somewhat encouraged. "We had a regular vaudeville."

"Did you really?"

"A serenade," said Henry. "A lot of soldiers gathered down there in the street and began to yell at the sign."

"Why?" she demanded.

"Just a crowd," said Henry, abstractedly. "All crowds have to howl. They didn't have anybody with much initiative in the lead, or they'd probably have forced their way in here and smashed things up."

"Yes," said Bartholomew, turning again to Edith, "you should have been here."

He seemed to consider this a sufficient cue for withdrawal, for he turned abruptly and went back to his desk.

"Are the soldiers all set against the Socialists?" demanded Edith of her brother. "I mean do they attack you violently and all that?"

Henry replaced his eye-shade and yawned.

"The human race has come a long way," he said casually, "but most of us are throw-backs; the soldiers don't know what they want, or what they hate, or what they like. They're used to acting in large bodies, and they seem to have to make demonstrations. So it happens to be against us. There've been riots all over the city to-night. It's May Day, you see."

"Was the disturbance here pretty serious?"

"Not a bit," he said scornfully. "About twenty-five of them stopped in the street about nine o'clock, and began to bellow at the moon."

"Oh"— She changed the subject. "You're glad to see me, Henry?"

"Why, sure."

"You don't seem to be."

"I am."

"I suppose you think I'm a—a waster. Sort of the World's Worst Butterfly."

Henry laughed.

"Not at all. Have a good time while you're young. Why? Do I seem like the priggish and earnest youth?"

"No—" She paused, "—but somehow I began thinking how absolutely different the party I'm on is from—from all your purposes. It seems sort of—of incongruous, doesn't it?—me being at a party like that, and you over here working for a thing that'll make that sort of party impossible ever any more, if your ideas work."

"I don't think of it that way. You're young, and you're acting just as you were brought up to act. Go ahead—have a good time."

Her feet, which had been idly swinging, stopped and her voice dropped a note.

"I wish you'd—you'd come back to Harrisburg and have a good time. Do you feel sure that you're on the right track——"

"You're wearing beautiful stockings," he interrupted. "What on earth are they?"

"They're embroidered," she replied, glancing down. "Aren't they cunning?" She raised her skirts and uncovered slim, silk-sheathed calves. "Or do you disapprove of silk stockings?"

He seemed slightly exasperated, bent his dark eyes on her piercingly.

"Are you trying to make me out as criticising you in any way, Edith?"

"Not at all——"

She paused. Bartholomew had uttered a grunt. She turned and saw that he had left his desk and was standing at the window.

"What is it?" demanded Henry.

"People," said Bartholomew, and then after an instant: "Whole jam of them. They're coming from Sixth Avenue."

"People?"

The fat man pressed his nose to the pane.

"Soldiers, by God!" he said emphatically. "I had an idea they'd come back."

Edith jumped to her feet, and running over joined Bartholomew at the window.

"There's a lot of them!" she cried excitedly. "Come here, Henry!"

Henry readjusted his shade, but kept his seat.

"Hadn't we better turn out the lights?" suggested Bartholomew.

"No. They'll go away in a minute."

"They're not," said Edith, peering from the window. "They're not even thinking of going away. There's more of them coming. Look—there's a whole crowd turning the corner of Sixth Avenue."

By the yellow glow and blue shadows of the street lamp she could see that the sidewalk was crowded with men. They were mostly in uniform, some sober, some enthusiastically drunk, and over the whole swept an incoherent clamor and shouting.

Henry rose, and going to the window exposed himself as a long silhouette against the office lights. Immediately the shouting became a steady yell, and a rattling fusillade of small missiles, corners of tobacco plugs, cigarette-boxes, and even pennies beat against the window. The sounds of the racket now began floating up the stairs as the folding doors revolved.

"They're coming up!" cried Bartholomew.

Edith turned anxiously to Henry.

"They're coming up, Henry."

From down-stairs in the lower hall their cries were now quite audible.

"—God damn Socialists!"

"Pro-Germans! Boche-lovers!"[10]

"Second floor, front! Come on!"

"We'll get the sons——"

The next five minutes passed in a dream. Edith was conscious that the clamor burst suddenly upon the three of them like a cloud of rain, that there was a thunder of many feet on the stairs, that Henry had seized her arm and drawn her back toward the rear of the office. Then the door opened and an overflow of men were forced into the room—not the leaders, but simply those who happened to be in front.

"Hello, Bo!"

"Up late, ain't you?"

"You an' your girl. Damn *you!*"

She noticed that two very drunken soldiers had been forced to the front, where they wobbled fatuously—one of them was short and dark, the other was tall and weak of chin.

Henry stepped forward and raised his hand.

"Friends!" he said.

The clamor faded into a momentary stillness, punctuated with mutterings.

"Friends!" he repeated, his faraway eyes fixed over the heads of the crowd, "you're injuring no one but yourselves by breaking in here tonight. Do we look like rich men? Do we look like Germans? I ask you in all fairness——"

"Pipe down!"

"I'll say you do!"

"Say, who's your lady friend, buddy?"

A man in civilian clothes, who had been pawing over a table, suddenly held up a newspaper.

"Here it is!" he shouted. "They wanted the Germans to win the war!"

A new overflow from the stairs was shouldered in and of a sudden the room was full of men all closing around the pale little group at the back. Edith saw that the tall soldier with the weak chin was still in front. The short dark one had disappeared.

She edged slightly backward, stood close to the open window, through which came a clear breath of cool night air.

Then the room was a riot. She realized that the soldiers were surging forward, glimpsed the fat man swinging a chair over his head—instantly the lights went out, and she felt the push of warm bodies under rough cloth, and her ears were full of shouting and trampling and hard breathing.

A figure flashed by her out of nowhere, tottered, was edged sideways, and of a sudden disappeared helplessly out through the open window with a frightened, fragmentary cry that died staccato on the bosom of the clamor. By the faint light streaming from the building backing on the area Edith had a quick impression that it had been the tall soldier with the weak chin.

Anger rose astonishingly in her. She swung her arms wildly, edged blindly toward the thickest of the scuffling. She heard grunts, curses, the muffled impact of fists.

"Henry!" she called frantically, "Henry!"

Then, it was minutes later, she felt suddenly that there were other figures in the room. She heard a voice, deep, bullying, authoritative; she saw yellow rays of light sweeping here and there in the fracas. The cries became more scattered. The scuffling increased and then stopped.

Suddenly the lights were on and the room was full of policemen, clubbing left and right. The deep voice boomed out:

"Here now! Here now! Here now!"

And then:

"Quiet down and get out! Here now!"

The room seemed to empty like a wash-bowl. A policeman fast-grappled in the corner released his hold on his soldier antagonist and started him with a shove toward the door. The deep voice continued.

Edith perceived now that it came from a bull-necked police captain standing near the door.

"Here now! This is no way! One of your own sojers got shoved out of the back window an' killed hisself!"

"Henry!" called Edith, "Henry!"

She beat wildly with her fists on the back of the man in front of her; she brushed between two others; fought, shrieked, and beat her way to a very pale figure sitting on the floor close to a desk.

"Henry," she cried passionately, "what's the matter? What's the matter? Did they hurt you?"

His eyes were shut. He groaned and then looking up said disgustedly——

"They broke my leg. My God, the fools!"

"Here now!" called the police captain. "Here now! Here now!"

IX

"Childs',[11] Fifty-ninth Street," at eight o'clock of any morning differs from its sisters by less than the width of their marble tables or the degree of polish on the frying-pans. You will see there a crowd of poor people with sleep in the corners of their eyes, trying to look straight before them at their food so as not to see the other poor people. But Childs', Fifty-ninth, four hours earlier is quite unlike any Childs' restaurant from Portland, Oregon, to Portland, Maine. Within its pale but sanitary walls one finds a noisy medley of chorus girls, college boys, débutantes, rakes, *filles de joie*—a not unrepresentative mixture of the gayest of Broadway, and even of Fifth Avenue.

In the early morning of May the second it was unusually full. Over the marble-topped tables were bent the excited faces of flappers whose fathers owned individual villages. They were eating buckwheat cakes and scrambled eggs with relish and gusto, an accomplishment that it would have been utterly impossible for them to repeat in the same place four hours later.

Almost the entire crowd were from the Gamma Psi dance at Delmonico's except for several chorus girls from a midnight revue who sat at a side table and wished they'd taken off a little more make-up after the show. Here and there a drab, mouse-like figure, desperately out of place, watched the butterflies with a weary, puzzled curiosity. But the drab figure was the exception. This was the morning after May Day, and celebration was still in the air.

Gus Rose, sober but a little dazed, must be classed as one of the drab figures. How he had got himself from Forty-fourth Street to Fifty-ninth Street after the riot was only a hazy half-memory. He had seen the body of Carrol Key put in an ambulance and driven off, and then he had started up town with two or three soldiers. Somewhere between Forty-fourth Street and Fifty-ninth Street the other soldiers had met some women and disappeared. Rose had wandered to Columbus Circle[12] and chosen the gleaming lights of Childs' to minister to his craving for coffee and doughnuts. He walked in and sat down.

All around him floated airy, inconsequential chatter and high-pitched laughter. At first he failed to understand, but after a puzzled five minutes he realized that this was the aftermath of some gay party. Here and there a restless, hilarious young man wandered fraternally and familiarly between the tables, shaking hands indiscriminately and pausing occasionally for a facetious chat, while excited waiters, bearing cakes and eggs aloft, swore at him silently, and bumped him out of the way. To Rose, seated at the most inconspicuous and least crowded table, the whole scene was a colorful circus of beauty and riotous pleasure.

He became gradually aware, after a few moments, that the couple seated diagonally across from him, with their backs to the crowd, were not the least interesting pair in the room. The man was drunk. He wore a dinner coat with a dishevelled tie and shirt swollen by spillings of water and wine. His eyes, dim and blood-shot, roved unnaturally from side to side. His breath came short between his lips.

"He's been on a spree!" thought Rose.

The woman was almost if not quite sober. She was pretty, with dark eyes and feverish high color, and she kept her active eyes fixed on her companion with the alertness of a hawk. From time to time she would lean and whisper intently to him, and he would answer by inclining his head heavily or by a particularly ghoulish and repellent wink.

Rose scrutinized them dumbly for some minutes, until the woman gave him a quick, resentful look; then he shifted his gaze to two of the most conspicuously hilarious of the promenaders who were on a protracted circuit of the tables. To his surprise he recognized in one of them the young man by whom he had been so ludicrously entertained at Delmonico's. This started him thinking of Key with a vague sentimentality, not unmixed with awe. Key was dead. He had fallen thirty-five feet and split his skull like a cracked cocoanut.

"He was a darn good guy," thought Rose mournfully. "He was a darn good guy, o'right. That was awful hard luck about him."

The two promenaders approached and started down between Rose's table and the next, addressing friends and strangers alike with jovial familiarity. Suddenly Rose saw the fair-haired one with the prominent teeth stop, look unsteadily at the man and girl opposite, and then begin to move his head disapprovingly from side to side.

The man with the blood-shot eyes looked up.

"Gordy," said the promenader with the prominent teeth, "Gordy."

"Hello," said the man with the stained shirt thickly.

Prominent Teeth shook his finger pessimistically at the pair, giving the woman a glance of aloof condemnation.

"What'd I tell you, Gordy?"

Gordon stirred in his seat.

"Go to hell!" he said.

Dean continued to stand there shaking his finger. The woman began to get angry.

"You go way!" she cried fiercely. "You're drunk, that's what you are!"

"So's he," suggested Dean, staying the motion of his finger and pointing it at Gordon.

Peter Himmel ambled up, owlish now and oratorically inclined.

"Here now," he began as if called upon to deal with some petty dispute between children. "Wha's all trouble?"

"You take your friend away," said Jewel tartly. "He's bothering us."

"What's at?"

"You heard me!" she said shrilly. "I said to take your drunken friend away."

Her rising voice rang out above the clatter of the restaurant and a waiter came hurrying up.

"You gotta be more quiet!"

"That fella's drunk," she cried. "He's insulting us."

"Ah-ha, Gordy," persisted the accused. "What'd I tell you." He turned to the waiter. "Gordy an' I friends. Been tryin' help him, haven't I, Gordy?"

Gordy looked up.

"Help me? Hell, no!"

Jewel rose suddenly, and seizing Gordon's arm assisted him to his feet.

"Come on, Gordy!" she said, leaning toward him and speaking in a half whisper. "Let's us get out of here. This fella's got a mean drunk on."

Gordon allowed himself to be urged to his feet and started toward the door. Jewel turned for a second and addressed the provoker of their flight.

"I know all about *you!*" she said fiercely. "Nice friend, you are, I'll say. He told me about you."

Then she seized Gordon's arm, and together they made their way through the curious crowd, paid their check, and went out.

"You'll have to sit down," said the waiter to Peter after they had gone.

"What's 'at? Sit down?"

"Yes—or get out."

Peter turned to Dean.

"Come on," he suggested. "Let's beat up this waiter."

"All right."

They advanced toward him, their faces grown stern. The waiter retreated.

Peter suddenly reached over to a plate on the table beside him and picking up a handful of hash tossed it into the air. It descended as a languid parabola in snowflake effect on the heads of those near by.

"Hey! Ease up!"

"Put him out!"

"Sit down, Peter!"

"Cut out that stuff!"

Peter laughed and bowed.

"Thank you for your kind applause, ladies and gents. If some one will lend me some more hash and a tall hat we will go on with the act."

The bouncer bustled up.

"You've gotta get out!" he said to Peter.

"Hell, no!"

"He's my friend!" put in Dean indignantly.

A crowd of waiters were gathering. "Put him out!"

"Better go, Peter."

There was a short struggle and the two were edged and pushed toward the door.

"I got a hat and a coat here!" cried Peter.

"Well, go get 'em and be spry about it!"

The bouncer released his hold on Peter, who, adopting a ludicrous air of extreme cunning, rushed immediately around to the other table, where he burst into derisive laughter and thumbed his nose at the exasperated waiters.

"Think I just better wait a l'il' longer," he announced.

The chase began. Four waiters were sent around one way and four another. Dean caught hold of two of them by the coat, and another struggle took place before the pursuit of Peter could be resumed; he was finally pinioned after overturning a sugar-bowl and several cups of coffee. A fresh argument ensued at the cashier's desk, where Peter attempted to buy another dish of hash to take with him and throw at policemen.

But the commotion upon his exit proper was dwarfed by another phenomenon which drew admiring glances and a prolonged involuntary "Oh-h-h!" from every person in the restaurant.

The great plate-glass front had turned to a deep creamy blue, the color of a Maxfield Parrish moonlight[13]—a blue that seemed to press close upon the pane as if to crowd its way into the restaurant. Dawn had come up in Columbus Circle, magical, breathless dawn, silhouetting the great statue of the immortal Christopher, and mingling in a curious and uncanny manner with the fading yellow electric light inside.

X

Mr. In and Mr. Out are not listed by the census-taker. You will search for them in vain through the social register or the births, marriages, and deaths, or the grocer's credit list. Oblivion has swallowed them and the testimony that they ever existed at all is vague and shadowy, and inadmissible in a court of law. Yet I have it upon the best authority that for a brief space Mr. In and Mr. Out lived, breathed, answered to their names and radiated vivid personalities of their own.

During the brief span of their lives they walked in their native garments down the great highway of a great nation; were laughed at, sworn at, chased, and fled from. Then they passed and were heard of no more.

They were already taking form dimly, when a taxicab with the top open breezed down Broadway in the faintest glimmer of May dawn. In this car sat the souls of Mr. In and Mr. Out discussing with amazement the blue light that had so precipitately colored the sky behind the statue of Christopher Columbus, discussing with bewilderment the old, gray faces of the early risers which skimmed palely along the street like blown bits of paper on a gray lake. They were agreed on all things, from the absurdity of the bouncer in Childs' to the absurdity of the business of life. They were dizzy with the extreme maudlin happiness that the morning had awakened in their glowing souls. Indeed, so fresh and vigorous was their pleasure in living that they felt it should be expressed by loud cries.

"Ye-ow-ow!" hooted Peter, making a megaphone with his hands—and Dean joined in with a call that, though equally significant and symbolic, derived its resonance from its very inarticulateness.

"Yo-ho! Yea! Yoho! Yo-buba!"

Fifty-third Street was a bus with a dark, bobbed-hair beauty atop; Fifty-second was a street cleaner who dodged, escaped, and sent up a yell of, "Look where you're aimin'!" in a pained and grieved voice. At Fiftieth Street a group of men on a very white sidewalk in front of a very white building turned to stare after them, and shouted:

"Some party, boys!"

At Forty-ninth Street Peter turned to Dean. "Beautiful morning," he said gravely, squinting up his owlish eyes.

"Probably is."

"Go get some breakfast, hey?"

Dean agreed—with additions.

"Breakfast and liquor."

"Breakfast and liquor," repeated Peter, and they looked at each other, nodding. "That's logical."

Then they both burst into loud laughter.

"Breakfast and liquor! Oh, gosh!"

"No such thing," announced Peter.

"Don't serve it? Ne'mind. We force 'em serve it. Bring pressure bear."

"Bring logic bear."

The taxi cut suddenly off Broadway, sailed along a cross street, and stopped in front of a heavy tomb-like building in Fifth Avenue.

"What's idea?"

The taxi-driver informed them that this was Delmonico's.

This was somewhat puzzling. They were forced to devote several minutes to intense concentration, for if such an order had been given there must have been a reason for it.

"Somep'm 'bouta coat," suggested the taxi-man.

That was it. Peter's overcoat and hat. He had left them at Delmonico's. Having decided this, they disembarked from the taxi and strolled toward the entrance arm in arm.

"Hey!" said the taxi-driver.

"Huh?"

"You better pay me."

They shook their heads in shocked negation.

"Later, not now—we give orders, you wait."

The taxi-driver objected; he wanted his money now. With the scornful condescension of men exercising tremendous self-control they paid him.

Inside Peter groped in vain through a dim, deserted check-room in search of his coat and derby.

"Gone, I guess. Somebody stole it."

"Some Sheff student."

"All probability."

"Never mind," said Dean, nobly. "I'll leave mine here too—then we'll both be dressed the same."

He removed his overcoat and hat and was hanging them up when his roving glance was caught and held magnetically by two large squares of cardboard tacked to the two coat-room doors. The one on the left-hand door bore the word "In" in big black letters, and the one on the right-hand door flaunted the equally emphatic word "Out."

"Look!" he exclaimed happily——

Peter's eyes followed his pointing finger.

"What?"

"Look at the signs. Let's take 'em."

"Good idea."

"Probably pair very rare an' valuable signs. Probably come in handy."

Peter removed the left-hand sign from the door and endeavored to conceal it about his person. The sign being of considerable proportions, this was a matter of some difficulty. An idea flung itself at him, and with an air of dignified mystery he turned his back. After an instant he wheeled dramatically around, and stretching out his arms displayed himself to the admiring Dean. He had inserted the sign in his vest, completely covering his shirt front. In effect, the word "In" had been painted upon his shirt in large black letters.

"Yoho!" cheered Dean. "Mister In."

He inserted his own sign in like manner.

"Mister Out!" he announced triumphantly. "Mr. In meet Mr. Out."

They advanced and shook hands. Again laughter overcame them and they rocked in a shaken spasm of mirth.

"Yoho!"

"We probably get a flock of breakfast."

"We'll go—go to the Commodore."[14]

Arm in arm they sallied out the door, and turning east in Forty-fourth Street set out for the Commodore.

As they came out a short dark soldier, very pale and tired, who had been wandering listlessly along the sidewalk, turned to look at them.

He started over as though to address them, but as they immediately bent on him glances of withering unrecognition, he waited until they had started unsteadily down the street, and then followed at about forty paces, chuckling to himself and saying "Oh, boy!" over and over under his breath, in delighted, anticipatory tones.

Mr. In and Mr. Out were meanwhile exchanging pleasantries concerning their future plans.

"We want liquor; we want breakfast. Neither without the other. One and indivisible."

"We want both 'em!"

"Both 'em!"

It was quite light now, and passers-by began to bend curious eyes on the pair. Obviously they were engaged in a discussion, which afforded each of them intense amusement, for occasionally a fit of laughter would seize upon them so violently that, still with their arms interlocked, they would bend nearly double.

Reaching the Commodore, they exchanged a few spicy epigrams with the sleepy-eyed doorman, navigated the revolving door with some difficulty, and then made their way through a thinly populated but startled lobby to the dining-room, where a puzzled waiter showed them an obscure table in a corner. They studied the bill of fare helplessly, telling over the items to each other in puzzled mumbles.

"Don't see any liquor here," said Peter reproachfully.

The waiter became audible but unintelligible.

"Repeat," continued Peter, with patient tolerance, "that there seems to be unexplained and quite distasteful lack of liquor upon bill of fare."

"Here!" said Dean confidently, "let me handle him." He turned to the waiter—"Bring us—bring us—" he scanned the bill of fare anxiously. "Bring us a quart of champagne and a—a—probably ham sandwich."

The waiter looked doubtful.

"Bring it!" roared Mr. In and Mr. Out in chorus.

The waiter coughed and disappeared. There was a short wait during which they were subjected without their knowledge to a careful scrutiny by the headwaiter. Then the champagne arrived, and at the sight of it Mr. In and Mr. Out became jubilant.

"Imagine their objecting to us having champagne for breakfast—jus' imagine."

They both concentrated upon the vision of such an awesome possibility, but the feat was too much for them. It was impossible for their joint imaginations to conjure up a world where any one might object to any one else having champagne for breakfast. The waiter drew the cork with an enormous *pop*—and their glasses immediately foamed with pale yellow froth.

"Here's health, Mr. In."

"Here's same to you, Mr. Out."

The waiter withdrew; the minutes passed; the champagne became low in the bottle.

"It's—it's mortifying," said Dean suddenly.

"Wha's mortifying?"

"The idea their objecting us having champagne breakfast."

"Mortifying?" Peter considered. "Yes, tha's word—mortifying."

Again they collapsed into laughter, howled, swayed, rocked back and forth in their chairs, repeating the word "mortifying" over and over to each other—each repetition seeming to make it only more brilliantly absurd.

After a few more gorgeous minutes they decided on another quart. Their anxious waiter consulted his immediate superior, and this discreet person gave implicit instructions that no more champagne should be served. Their check was brought.

Five minutes later, arm in arm, they left the Commodore and made their way through a curious, staring crowd along Forty-second Street, and up Vanderbilt Avenue to the Biltmore. There, with sudden cunning, they rose to the occasion and traversed the lobby, walking fast and standing unnaturally erect.

Once in the dining-room they repeated their performance. They were torn between intermittent convulsive laughter and sudden spasmodic discussions of politics, college, and the sunny state of their dispositions. Their watches told them that it was now nine o'clock, and a dim idea was born in them that they were on a memorable party, something that they would remember always. They lingered over the second bottle. Either of them had only to mention the word "mortifying" to send them both into riotous gasps. The dining-room was whirring and shifting now; a curious lightness permeated and rarefied the heavy air.

They paid their check and walked out into the lobby.

It was at this moment that the exterior doors revolved for the thousandth time that morning, and admitted into the lobby a very pale young beauty with dark circles under her eyes, attired in a much-rumpled evening dress. She was accompanied by a plain stout man, obviously not an appropriate escort.

At the top of the stairs this couple encountered Mr. In and Mr. Out.

"Edith," began Mr. In, stepping toward her hilariously and making a sweeping bow, "darling, good morning."

The stout man glanced questioningly at Edith, as if merely asking her permission to throw this man summarily out of the way.

"'Scuse familiarity," added Peter, as an afterthought. "Edith, good morning."

He seized Dean's elbow and impelled him into the foreground.

"Meet Mr. In, Edith, my bes' frien'. Inseparable. Mr. In and Mr. Out."

Mr. Out advanced and bowed; in fact, he advanced so far and bowed so low that he tipped slightly forward and only kept his balance by placing a hand lightly on Edith's shoulder.

"I'm Mr. Out, Edith," he mumbled pleasantly, "S'misterin Misterout."

"'Smisterinanout," said Peter proudly.

But Edith stared straight by them, her eyes fixed on some infinite speck in the gallery above her. She nodded slightly to the stout man, who advanced bull-like and with a sturdy brisk gesture pushed Mr. In and Mr. Out to either side. Through this alley he and Edith walked.

But ten paces farther on Edith stopped again—stopped and pointed to a short, dark soldier who was eying the crowd in general, and the tableau of Mr. In and Mr. Out in particular, with a sort of puzzled, spellbound awe.

"There," cried Edith. "See there!"

Her voice rose, became somewhat shrill. Her pointing finger shook slightly.

"There's the soldier who broke my brother's leg."

There were a dozen exclamations; a man in a cutaway coat left his place near the desk and advanced alertly; the stout person made a sort of lightning-like spring toward the short, dark soldier, and then the lobby closed around the little group and blotted them from the sight of Mr. In and Mr. Out.

But to Mr. In and Mr. Out this event was merely a particolored iridescent segment of a whirring, spinning world.

They heard loud voices; they saw the stout man spring; the picture suddenly blurred.

Then they were in an elevator bound skyward.

"What floor, please?" said the elevator man.

"Any floor," said Mr. In.

"Top floor," said Mr. Out.

"This is the top floor," said the elevator man.

"Have another floor put on," said Mr. Out.

"Higher," said Mr. In.

"Heaven," said Mr. Out.

XI

In a bedroom of a small hotel just off Sixth Avenue Gordon Sterrett awoke with a pain in the back of his head and a sick throbbing in all his veins. He looked at the dusky gray shadows in the corners of the room and at a raw place on a large leather chair in the corner where it had long been in use. He saw clothes, dishevelled, rumpled clothes on the floor and he smelt stale cigarette smoke and stale liquor. The windows were tight shut. Outside the bright sunlight had thrown a dust-filled beam across the sill—a beam broken by the head of the wide wooden bed in which he had slept. He lay very quiet—comatose, drugged, his eyes wide, his mind clicking wildly like an unoiled machine.

It must have been thirty seconds after he perceived the sunbeam with the dust on it and the rip on the large leather chair that he had the sense of life close beside him, and it was another thirty seconds after that before he realized that he was irrevocably married to Jewel Hudson.[15]

He went out half an hour later and bought a revolver at a sporting goods store. Then he took a taxi to the room where he had been living on East Twenty-seventh Street, and, leaning across the table that held his drawing materials, fired a cartridge into his head just behind the temple.

The Jelly-Bean

Jim Powell was a Jelly-bean. Much as I desire to make him an appealing character, I feel that it would be unscrupulous to deceive you on that point. He was a bred-in-the-bone, dyed-in-the-wool, ninety-nine three-quarters per cent Jelly-bean and he grew lazily all during Jelly-bean season, which is every season, down in the land of the Jelly-beans well below the Mason-Dixon line.

Now if you call a Memphis man a Jelly-bean he will quite possibly pull a long sinewy rope from his hip pocket and hang you to a convenient telegraph-pole. If you call a New Orleans man a Jelly-bean he will probably grin and ask you who is taking your girl to the Mardi Gras ball. The particular Jelly-bean patch which produced the protagonist of this history lies somewhere between the two—a little city of forty thousand that has dozed sleepily for forty thousand years in southern Georgia, occasionally stirring in its slumbers and muttering something about a war that took place sometime, somewhere, and that everyone else has forgotten long ago.

Jim was a Jelly-bean. I write that again because it has such a pleasant sound—rather like the beginning of a fairy story—as if Jim were nice. It somehow gives me a picture of him with a round, appetizing face and all sorts of leaves and vegetables growing out of his cap. But Jim was long and thin and bent at the waist from stooping over pool-tables, and he was what might have been known in the indiscriminating North as a corner loafer. "Jelly-bean" is the name throughout the undissolved Confederacy for one who spends his life conjugating the verb to idle in the first person singular—I am idling, I have idled, I will idle.

Jim was born in a white house on a green corner. It had four weather-beaten pillars in front and a great amount of lattice-work in the rear that made a cheerful criss-cross background for a flowery sun-drenched lawn. Originally the dwellers in the white house had owned the ground next door and next door to that and next door to that, but this had been so long ago that even Jim's father scarcely remembered it. He had, in fact, thought it a matter of so little moment that when he was dying from a pistol wound got in a brawl he neglected even to tell little Jim, who was five years old and miserably frightened. The white house became a boardinghouse run by a tight-lipped lady from Macon, whom Jim called Aunt Mamie and detested with all his soul.

He became fifteen, went to high school, wore his hair in black snarls, and was afraid of girls. He hated his home where four women and one old man prolonged an interminable chatter from summer to summer about what lots the Powell place had originally included and what sort of flowers would be out next. Sometimes the parents of little girls in town, remembering Jim's mother and fancying a resemblance in the dark eyes and hair, invited him to parties, but parties made him shy and he much preferred sitting on a disconnected axle in Tilly's Garage, rolling the bones or exploring his mouth endlessly with a long straw. For pocket money, he picked up odd jobs, and it was due to this that he stopped going to parties. At his third party little Marjorie Haight had whispered indiscreetly and within hearing distance that he was a boy who brought the groceries sometimes. So instead of the two-step and polka, Jim had learned to throw any number he desired on the dice and had listened to spicy tales of all the shootings that had occurred in the surrounding country during the past fifty years.

He became eighteen. The war broke out and he enlisted as a gob[1] and polished brass in the Charleston Navy-yard for a year. Then, by way of variety, he went North and polished brass in the Brooklyn Navy-yard for a year.

When the war was over he came home. He was twenty-one, his

trousers were too short and too tight. His buttoned shoes were long and narrow. His tie was an alarming conspiracy of purple and pink marvellously scrolled, and over it were two blue eyes faded like a piece of very good old cloth long exposed to the sun.

In the twilight of one April evening when a soft gray had drifted down along the cottonfields and over the sultry town, he was a vague figure leaning against a board fence, whistling and gazing at the moon's rim above the lights of Jackson Street. His mind was working persistently on a problem that had held his attention for an hour. The Jelly-bean had been invited to a party.

Back in the days when all the boys had detested all the girls, Clark Darrow and Jim had sat side by side in school. But, while Jim's social aspirations had died in the oily air of the garage, Clark had alternately fallen in and out of love, gone to college, taken to drink, given it up, and, in short, become one of the best beaux of the town. Nevertheless Clark and Jim had retained a friendship that, though casual, was perfectly definite. That afternoon Clark's ancient Ford had slowed up beside Jim, who was on the sidewalk and, out of a clear sky, Clark had invited him to a party at the country club. The impulse that made him do this was no stranger than the impulse which made Jim accept. The latter was probably an unconscious ennui, a half-frightened sense of adventure. And now Jim was soberly thinking it over.

He began to sing, drumming his long foot idly on a stone block in the sidewalk till it wobbled up and down in time to the low throaty tune:

> *"One mile from Home in Jelly-bean town,*
> *Lives Jeanne, the Jelly-bean Queen.*
> *She loves her dice and treats 'em nice;*
> *No dice would treat her mean."*

He broke off and agitated the sidewalk to a bumpy gallop.

"Daggone!" he muttered, half aloud.

They would all be there—the old crowd, the crowd to which, by right of the white house, sold long since, and the portrait of the officer in gray over the mantel, Jim should have belonged. But that crowd had grown up together into a tight little set as gradually as the girls' dresses had lengthened inch by inch, as definitely as the boys' trousers had dropped suddenly to their ankles. And to that society of first names and dead puppy-loves Jim was an outsider—a running mate of poor whites. Most of the men knew him, condescendingly; he tipped his hat to three or four girls. That was all.

When the dusk had thickened into a blue setting for the moon, he walked through the hot, pleasantly pungent town to Jackson Street. The stores were closing and the last shoppers were drifting homeward, as if borne on the dreamy revolution of a slow merry-go-round. A street-fair farther down made a brilliant alley of varicolored booths and contributed a blend of music to the night—an oriental dance on a calliope, a melancholy bugle in front of a freak show, a cheerful rendition of "Back Home in Tennessee"[2] on a hand-organ.

The Jelly-bean stopped in a store and bought a collar. Then he sauntered along toward Soda Sam's, where he found the usual three or four cars of a summer evening parked in front and the little darkies running back and forth with sundaes and lemonades.

"Hello, Jim."

It was a voice at his elbow—Joe Ewing sitting in an automobile with Marylyn Wade. Nancy Lamar and a strange man were in the back seat.

The Jelly-bean tipped his hat quickly.

"Hi, Ben—" then, after an almost imperceptible pause—"How y' all?"

Passing, he ambled on toward the garage where he had a room upstairs. His "How y' all" had been said to Nancy Lamar, to whom he had not spoken in fifteen years.

Nancy had a mouth like a remembered kiss and shadowy eyes and blue-black hair inherited from her mother who had been born in Budapest. Jim passed her often in the street, walking small-boy fashion with her hands in her pockets and he knew that with her inseparable Sally Carrol Hopper[3] she had left a trail of broken hearts from Atlanta to New Orleans.

For a few fleeting moments Jim wished he could dance. Then he laughed and as he reached his door began to sing softly to himself:

"Her Jelly Roll can twist your soul,
Her eyes are big and brown,
She's the Queen of the Queens of the Jelly-beans—
My Jeanne of Jelly-bean Town."

II

At nine-thirty Jim and Clark met in front of Soda Sam's and started for the Country Club in Clark's Ford.

"Jim," asked Clark casually, as they rattled through the jasmine-scented night, "how do you keep alive?"

The Jelly-bean paused, considered.

"Well," he said finally, "I got a room over Tilly's garage. I help him some with the cars in the afternoon an' he gives it to me free. Sometimes I drive one of his taxies and pick up a little thataway. I get fed up doin' that regular though."

"That all?"

"Well, when there's a lot of work I help him by the day—Saturdays usually—and then there's one main source of revenue I don't generally mention. Maybe you don't recollect I'm about the champion crap-shooter of this town. They make me shoot from a cup now because once I get the feel of a pair of dice they just roll for me."

Clark grinned appreciatively.

"I never could learn to set 'em so's they'd do what I wanted. Wish you'd shoot with Nancy Lamar some day and take all her money away from her. She will roll 'em with the boys and she loses more than her daddy can afford to give her. I happen to know she sold a good ring last month to pay a debt."

The Jelly-bean was non-committal.

"The white house on Elm Street still belong to you?"

Jim shook his head.

"Sold. Got a pretty good price, seein' it wasn't in a good part of town no more. Lawyer told me to put it into Liberty bonds.[4] But Aunt Mamie got so she didn't have no sense, so it takes all the interest to keep her up at Great Farms Sanitarium."

"Hm."

"I got an old uncle up-state an' I reckin I kin go up there if ever I get sure enough pore. Nice farm, but not enough niggers around to work it. He's asked me to come up and help him, but I don't guess I'd take much to it. Too doggone lonesome——" He broke off suddenly. "Clark, I want to tell you I'm much obliged to you for askin' me out, but I'd be a lot happier if you'd just stop the car right here an' let me walk back into town."

"Shucks!" Clark grunted. "Do you good to step out. You don't have to dance—just get out there on the floor and shake."

"Hold on," exclaimed Jim uneasily, "Don't you go leadin' me up to any girls and leavin' me there so I'll have to dance with 'em."

Clark laughed.

"'Cause," continued Jim desperately, "without you swear you won't do that I'm agoin' to get out right here an' my good legs goin' carry me back to Jackson Street."

They agreed after some argument that Jim, unmolested by females, was to view the spectacle from a secluded settee in the corner where Clark would join him whenever he wasn't dancing.

So ten o'clock found the Jelly-bean with his legs crossed and his arms conservatively folded, trying to look casually at home and politely uninterested in the dancers. At heart he was torn between overwhelming self-consciousness and an intense curiosity as to all that went on around him. He saw the girls emerge one by one from the dressing-room, stretching and pluming themselves like bright birds, smiling over their powdered shoulders at the chaperones, casting a quick glance around to take in the room and, simultaneously, the room's reaction to their entrance—and then, again like birds, alighting and nestling in the sober arms of their waiting escorts. Sally Carrol Hopper, blonde and lazy-eyed, appeared clad in her favorite pink and blinking like an awakened rose. Marjorie Haight, Marylyn Wade, Harriet Cary, all the girls he had seen loitering down Jackson Street by noon, now, curled and brilliantined and delicately tinted for the overhead lights, were miraculously strange Dresden figures[5] of pink and blue and red and gold, fresh from the shop and not yet fully dried.

He had been there half an hour, totally uncheered by Clark's jovial visits which were each one accompanied by a "Hello, old boy, how you making out?" and a slap at his knee. A dozen males had spoken to him or stopped for a moment beside him, but he knew that they were each one surprised at finding him there and fancied that one or two were even slightly resentful. But at half past ten his embarrassment suddenly left him and a pull of breathless interest took him completely out of himself—Nancy Lamar had come out of the dressing-room.

She was dressed in yellow organdie, a costume of a hundred cool corners, with three tiers of ruffles and a big bow in back until she shed black and yellow around her in a sort of phosphorescent lustre. The Jelly-bean's eyes opened wide and a lump arose in his throat. For a minute she stood beside the door until her partner hurried up. Jim recognized him as the stranger who had been with her in Joe Ewing's car that afternoon. He saw her set her arms akimbo and say something in a low voice, and laugh. The man laughed too and Jim experienced the quick pang of a weird new kind of pain. Some ray had passed between the pair, a shaft of beauty from that sun that had warmed him a moment since. The Jelly-bean felt suddenly like a weed in a shadow.

A minute later Clark approached him, bright-eyed and glowing.

"Hi, old man," he cried with some lack of originality. "How you making out?"

Jim replied that he was making out as well as could be expected.

"You come along with me," commanded Clark. "I've got something that'll put an edge on the evening."

Jim followed him awkwardly across the floor and up the stairs to the locker-room where Clark produced a flask of nameless yellow liquid.

"Good old corn."

Ginger ale arrived on a tray. Such potent nectar as "good old corn" needed some disguise beyond seltzer.

"Say, boy," exclaimed Clark breathlessly, "doesn't Nancy Lamar look beautiful?"

Jim nodded.

"Mighty beautiful," he agreed.

"She's all dolled up to a fare-you-well to-night," continued Clark. "Notice that fellow she's with?"

"Big fella? White pants?"

"Yeah. Well, that's Ogden Merritt from Savannah. Old man Merritt makes the Merritt safety razors. This fella's crazy about her. Been chasing after her all year.

"She's a wild baby," continued Clark, "but I like her. So does everybody. But she sure does do crazy stunts. She usually gets out alive, but she's got scars all over her reputation from one thing or another she's done."

"That so?" Jim passed over his glass. "That's good corn."

"Not so bad. Oh, she's a wild one. Shoots craps, say, boy! And she do like her highballs. Promised I'd give her one later on."

"She in love with this—Merritt?"

"Damned if I know. Seems like all the best girls around here marry fellas and go off somewhere."

He poured himself one more drink and carefully corked the bottle.

"Listen, Jim, I got to go dance and I'd be much obliged if you just stick this corn right on your hip as long as you're not dancing. If a man notices I've had a drink he'll come up and ask me and before I know it it's all gone and somebody else is having my good time."

So Nancy Lamar was going to marry. This toast of a town was to become the private property of an individual in white trousers—and all because white trousers' father had made a better razor than his neighbor. As they descended the stairs Jim found the idea inexplicably depressing. For the first time in his life he felt a vague and romantic yearning. A picture of her began to form in his imagination—Nancy walking boylike and debonnaire along the street, taking an orange as tithe from a worshipful fruit-dealer, charging a dope[6] on a mythical account at Soda Sam's, assembling a convoy of beaux and then driving off in triumphal state for an afternoon of splashing and singing.

The Jelly-bean walked out on the porch to a deserted corner, dark between the moon on the lawn and the single lighted door of the ballroom. There he found a chair and, lighting a cigarette, drifted into the thoughtless reverie that was his usual mood. Yet now it was a reverie made sensuous by the night and by the hot smell of damp powder puffs, tucked in the fronts of low dresses and distilling a thousand rich scents to float out through the open door. The music itself, blurred by a loud trombone, became hot and shadowy, a languorous overtone to the scraping of many shoes and slippers.

Suddenly the square of yellow light that fell through the door was obscured by a dark figure. A girl had come out of the dressing-room and was standing on the porch not more than ten feet away. Jim heard a low-breathed "doggone" and then she turned and saw him. It was Nancy Lamar.

Jim rose to his feet.

"Howdy?"

"Hello—" she paused, hesitated and then approached. "Oh, it's—Jim Powell."

He bowed slightly, tried to think of a casual remark.

"Do you suppose," she began quickly, "I mean—do you know anything about gum?"

"What?"

"I've got gum on my shoe. Some utter ass left his or her gum on the floor and of course I stepped in it."

Jim blushed, inappropriately.

"Do you know how to get it off?" she demanded petulantly. "I've tried a knife. I've tried every damn thing in the dressing-room. I've tried soap and water—and even perfume and I've ruined my powder puff trying to make it stick to that."

Jim considered the question in some agitation.

"Why—I think maybe gasolene——"

The words had scarcely left his lips when she grasped his hand and pulled him at a run off the low veranda, over a flower bed and at a gallop toward a group of cars parked in the moonlight by the first hole of the golf course.

"Turn on the gasolene," she commanded breathlessly.

"What?"

"For the gum of course. I've got to get it off. I can't dance with gum on."

Obediently Jim turned to the cars and began inspecting them with a view to obtaining the desired solvent. Had she demanded a cylinder he would have done his best to wrench one out.

"Here," he said after a moment's search. "Here's one that's easy. Got a handkerchief?"

"It's up-stairs wet. I used it for the soap and water."

Jim laboriously explored his pockets.

"Don't believe I got one either."

"Doggone it! Well, we can turn it on and let it run on the ground."

He turned the spout; a dripping began.

"More!"

He turned it on fuller. The dripping became a flow and formed an oily pool that glistened brightly, reflecting a dozen tremulous moons on its quivering bosom.

"Ah," she sighed contentedly, "let it all out. The only thing to do is to wade in it."

In desperation he turned on the tap full and the pool suddenly widened sending tiny rivers and trickles in all directions.

"That's fine. That's something like."

Raising her skirts she stepped gracefully in.

"I know this'll take it off," she murmured.

Jim smiled.

"There's lots more cars."

She stepped daintily out of the gasolene and began scraping her slippers, side and bottom, on the running-board of the automobile. The Jelly-bean contained himself no longer. He bent double with explosive laughter and after a second she joined in.

"You're here with Clark Darrow, aren't you?" she asked as they walked back toward the veranda.

"Yes."

"You know where he is now?"

"Out dancin', I reckin."

"The deuce. He promised me a highball."

"Well," said Jim, "I guess that'll be all right. I got his bottle right here in my pocket."

She smiled at him radiantly.

"I guess maybe you'll need ginger ale though," he added.

"Not me. Just the bottle."

"Sure enough?"

She laughed scornfully.

"Try me. I can drink anything any man can. Let's sit down."

She perched herself on the side of a table and he dropped into one of the wicker chairs beside her. Taking out the cork she held the flask to her lips and took a long drink. He watched her fascinated.

"Like it?"

She shook her head breathlessly.

"No, but I like the way it makes me feel. I think most people are that way."

Jim agreed.

"My daddy liked it too well. It got him."

"American men," said Nancy gravely, "don't know how to drink."

"What?" Jim was startled.

"In fact," she went on carelessly, "they don't know how to do anything very well. The one thing I regret in my life is that I wasn't born in England."

"In England?"

"Yes. It's the one regret of my life that I wasn't."

"Do you like it over there."

"Yes. Immensely. I've never been there in person, but I've met a lot of Englishmen who were over here in the army, Oxford and Cambridge men—you know, that's like Sewanee and University of Georgia are here—and of course I've read a lot of English novels."

Jim was interested, amazed.

"D' you ever hear of Lady Diana Manners?"[7] she asked earnestly.

No, Jim had not.

"Well, she's what I'd like to be. Dark, you know, like me, and wild as sin. She's the girl who rode her horse up the steps of some cathedral or church or something and all the novelists made their heroines do it afterwards."

Jim nodded politely. He was out of his depths.

"Pass the bottle," suggested Nancy. "I'm going to take another little one. A little drink wouldn't hurt a baby.

"You see," she continued, again breathless after a draught. "People over there have style. Nobody has style here. I mean the boys here aren't really worth dressing up for or doing sensational things for. Don't you know?"

"I suppose so—I mean I suppose not," murmured Jim.

"And I'd like to do 'em an' all. I'm really the only girl in town that has style."

She stretched out her arms and yawned pleasantly.

"Pretty evening."

"Sure is," agreed Jim.

"Like to have boat," she suggested dreamily. "Like to sail out on a silver lake, say the Thames, for instance. Have champagne and caviare sandwiches along. Have about eight people. And one of the men would jump overboard to amuse the party and get drowned like a man did with Lady Diana Manners once."

"Did he do it to please her?"

"Didn't mean drown himself to please her. He just meant to jump overboard and make everybody laugh."

"I reckin they just died laughin' when he drowned."

"Oh, I suppose they laughed a little," she admitted. "I imagine she did, anyway. She's pretty hard, I guess—like I am."

"You hard?"

"Like nails." She yawned again and added, "Give me a little more from that bottle."

Jim hesitated but she held out her hand defiantly.

"Don't treat me like a girl," she warned him. "I'm not like any girl *you* ever saw." She considered. "Still, perhaps you're right. You got—you got old head on young shoulders."

She jumped to her feet and moved toward the door. The Jelly-bean rose also.

"Good-bye," she said politely, "good-bye. Thanks, Jelly-bean."

Then she stepped inside and left him wide-eyed upon the porch.

III

At twelve o'clock a procession of cloaks issued single file from the women's dressing-room and, each one pairing with a coated beau like dancers meeting in a cotillion figure, drifted through the door with sleepy happy laughter—through the door into the dark where autos backed and snorted and parties called to one another and gathered around the water-cooler.

Jim, sitting in his corner, rose to look for Clark. They had met at eleven; then Clark had gone in to dance. So, seeking him, Jim wandered into the soft-drink stand that had once been a bar. The room was deserted except for a sleepy negro dozing behind the counter and two boys lazily fingering a pair of dice at one of the tables. Jim was about to leave when he saw Clark coming in. At the same moment Clark looked up.

"Hi, Jim!" he commanded. "C' mon over and help us with this bottle. I guess there's not much left, but there's one all around."

Nancy, the man from Savannah, Marylyn Wade, and Joe Ewing were lolling and laughing in the doorway. Nancy caught Jim's eye and winked at him humorously.

They drifted over to a table and arranging themselves around it waited for the waiter to bring ginger ale. Jim, faintly ill at ease, turned his eyes on Nancy, who had drifted into a nickel crap game with the two boys at the next table.

"Bring them over here," suggested Clark.

Joe looked around.

"We don't want to draw a crowd. It's against club rules."

"Nobody's around," insisted Clark, "except Mr. Taylor. He's walking up and down like a wild-man trying to find out who let all the gasolene out of his car."

There was a general laugh.

"I bet a million Nancy got something on her shoe again. You can't park when she's around."

"O Nancy, Mr. Taylor's looking for you!"

Nancy's cheeks were glowing with excitement over the game. "I haven't seen his silly little flivver in two weeks."

Jim felt a sudden silence. He turned and saw an individual of uncertain age standing in the doorway.

Clark's voice punctuated the embarrassment.

"Won't you join us, Mr. Taylor?"

"Thanks."

Mr. Taylor spread his unwelcome presence over a chair. "Have to, I guess. I'm waiting till they dig me up some gasolene. Somebody got funny with my car."

His eyes narrowed and he looked quickly from one to the other. Jim wondered what he had heard from the doorway—tried to remember what had been said.

"I'm right to-night," Nancy sang out, "and my four bits is in the ring."

"Faded!" snapped Taylor suddenly.

"Why, Mr. Taylor, I didn't know you shot craps!" Nancy was overjoyed to find that he had seated himself and instantly covered her bet. They had openly disliked each other since the night she had definitely discouraged a series of rather pointed advances.

"All right, babies, do it for your mamma. Just one little seven." Nancy was *cooing* to the dice. She rattled them with a brave underhand flourish, and rolled them out on the table.

"Ah-h! I suspected it. And now again with the dollar up."

Five passes to her credit found Taylor a bad loser. She was making it personal, and after each success Jim watched triumph flutter across her face. She was doubling with each throw—such luck could scarcely last.

"Better go easy," he cautioned her timidly.

"Ah, but watch this one," she whispered. It was eight on the dice and she called her number.

"Little Ada, this time we're going South."

Ada from Decatur rolled over the table. Nancy was flushed and half-hysterical, but her luck was holding. She drove the pot up and up, refusing to drag. Taylor was drumming with his fingers on the table, but he was in to stay.

Then Nancy tried for a ten and lost the dice. Taylor seized them avidly. He shot in silence, and in the hush of excitement the clatter of one pass after another on the table was the only sound.

Now Nancy had the dice again, but her luck had broken. An hour passed. Back and forth it went. Taylor had been at it again—and again and again. They were even at last—Nancy lost her ultimate five dollars.

"Will you take my check," she said quickly, "for fifty, and we'll shoot it all?" Her voice was a little unsteady and her hand shook as she reached to the money.

Clark exchanged an uncertain but alarmed glance with Joe Ewing. Taylor shot again. He had Nancy's check.

"How 'bout another?" she said wildly. "Jes' any bank'll do—money everywhere as a matter of fact."

Jim understood—the "good old corn" he had given her—the "good old corn" she had taken since. He wished he dared interfere—a girl of that age and position would hardly have two bank accounts. When the clock struck two he contained himself no longer.

"May I—can't you let me roll 'em for you?" he suggested, his low, lazy voice a little strained.

Suddenly sleepy and listless, Nancy flung the dice down before him.

"All right—old boy! As Lady Diana Manners says, 'Shoot 'em, Jelly-bean'—My luck's gone."

"Mr. Taylor," said Jim, carelessly, "we'll shoot for one of those there checks against the cash."

Half an hour later Nancy swayed forward and clapped him on the back.

"Stole my luck, you did." She was nodding her head sagely.

Jim swept up the last check and putting it with the others tore them into confetti and scattered them on the floor. Someone started singing, and Nancy kicking her chair backward rose to her feet.

"Ladies and gentlemen," she announced. "Ladies—that's you Marylyn. I want to tell the world that Mr. Jim Powell, who is a well-known Jelly-bean of this city, is an exception to a great rule—'lucky in dice—unlucky in love.' He's lucky in dice, and as matter fact I—I *love* him.

Ladies and gentlemen, Nancy Lamar, famous dark-haired beauty often featured in the *Herald* as one th' most popular members of younger set as other girls are often featured in this particular case. Wish to announce—wish to announce, anyway, Gentlemen——" She tipped suddenly. Clark caught her and restored her balance.

"My error," she laughed, "she stoops to—stoops to—anyways—— We'll drink to Jelly-bean . . . Mr. Jim Powell, King of the Jelly-beans."

And a few minutes later as Jim waited hat in hand for Clark in the darkness of that same corner of the porch where she had come searching for gasolene, she appeared suddenly beside him.

"Jelly-bean," she said, "are you here, Jelly-bean? I think—" and her slight unsteadiness seemed part of an enchanted dream—"I think you deserve one of my sweetest kisses for that, Jelly-bean."

For an instant her arms were around his neck—her lips were pressed to his.

"I'm a wild part of the world, Jelly-bean, but you did me a good turn."

Then she was gone, down the porch, over the cricket-loud lawn. Jim saw Merritt come out the front door and say something to her angrily—saw her laugh and, turning away, walk with averted eyes to his car. Marylyn and Joe followed, singing a drowsy song about a Jazz baby.

Clark came out and joined Jim on the steps. "All pretty lit, I guess," he yawned. "Merritt's in a mean mood. He's certainly off Nancy."

Over east along the golf course a faint rug of gray spread itself across the feet of the night. The party in the car began to chant a chorus as the engine warmed up.

"Good-night everybody," called Clark.

"Good-night, Clark."

"Good-night."

There was a pause, and then a soft, happy voice added,

"Good-night, Jelly-bean."

The car drove off to a burst of singing. A rooster on a farm across the way took up a solitary mournful crow, and behind them a last negro waiter turned out the porch light. Jim and Clark strolled over toward the Ford, their shoes crunching raucously on the gravel drive.

"Oh boy!" sighed Clark softly, "how you can set those dice!"

It was still too dark for him to see the flush on Jim's thin cheeks—or to know that it was a flush of unfamiliar shame.

IV

Over Tilly's garage a bleak room echoed all day to the rumble and snorting down-stairs and the singing of the negro washers as they turned the hose on the cars outside. It was a cheerless square of a room, punctuated with a bed and a battered table on which lay half a dozen books—Joe Miller's "Slow Train thru Arkansas,"[8] "Lucille,"[9] in an old edition very much annotated in an old-fashioned hand; "The Eyes of the World," by Harold Bell Wright,[10] and an ancient prayer-book of the Church of England with the name Alice Powell and the date 1831 written on the fly-leaf.

The East, gray when the Jelly-bean entered the garage, became a rich and vivid blue as he turned on his solitary electric light. He snapped it out again, and going to the window rested his elbows on the sill and stared into the deepening morning. With the awakening of his emotions, his first perception was a sense of futility, a dull ache at the utter grayness of his life. A wall had sprung up suddenly around him hedging him in, a wall as definite and tangible as the white wall of his bare room. And with his perception of this wall all that had been the romance of his existence, the casualness, the light-hearted improvidence, the miraculous open-handedness of life faded out. The Jelly-bean strolling up Jackson Street humming a lazy song, known at every shop and street stand, cropful of easy greeting and local wit, sad sometimes for only the sake of sadness and the flight of time—that Jelly-bean was suddenly vanished. The very name was a reproach, a triviality. With a flood of insight he knew that Merritt must despise him, that even Nancy's kiss in the dawn would have awakened not jealousy but only a contempt for Nancy's so lowering herself. And on his part the Jelly-bean had used for her a dingy subterfuge learned from the garage. He had been her moral laundry; the stains were his.

As the gray became blue, brightened and filled the room, he crossed to his bed and threw himself down on it, gripping the edges fiercely.

"I love her," he cried aloud, "God!"

As he said this something gave way within him like a lump melting in his throat. The air cleared and became radiant with dawn, and turning over on his face he began to sob dully into the pillow.

In the sunshine of three o'clock Clark Darrow chugging painfully along Jackson Street was hailed by the Jelly-bean, who stood on the curb with his fingers in his vest pockets.

"Hi!" called Clark, bringing his Ford to an astonishing stop alongside. "Just get up?"

The Jelly-bean shook his head.

"Never did go to bed. Felt sorta restless, so I took a long walk this morning out in the country. Just got into town this minute."

"Should think you *would* feel restless. I been feeling thataway all day——"

"I'm thinkin' of leavin' town," continued the Jelly-bean, absorbed by his own thoughts. "Been thinkin' of goin' up on the farm, and takin' a little that work off Uncle Dun. Reckin I been bummin' too long."

Clark was silent and the Jelly-bean continued:

"I reckin maybe after Aunt Mamie dies I could sink that money of mine in the farm and make somethin' out of it. All my people originally came from that part up there. Had a big place."

Clark looked at him curiously.

"That's funny," he said. "This—this sort of affected me the same way."

The Jelly-bean hesitated.

"I don't know," he began slowly, "somethin' about—about that girl last night talkin' about a lady named Diana Manners—an English lady, sorta got me thinkin'!" He drew himself up and looked oddly at Clark. "I had a family once," he said defiantly.

Clark nodded.

"I know."

"And I'm the last of 'em," continued the Jelly-bean, his voice rising slightly, "and I ain't worth shucks. Name they call me by means jelly—weak and wobbly like. People who weren't nothin' when my folks was a lot turn up their noses when they pass me on the street."

Again Clark was silent.

"So I'm through. I'm goin' to-day. And when I come back to this town it's going to be like a gentleman."

Clark took out his handkerchief and wiped his damp brow.

"Reckon you're not the only one it shook up," he admitted gloomily.

"All this thing of girls going round like they do is going to stop right quick. Too bad, too, but everybody'll have to see it thataway."

"Do you mean," demanded Jim in surprise, "that all that's leaked out?"

"Leaked out? How on earth could they keep it secret. It'll be announced in the papers to-night. Doctor Lamar's got to save his name somehow."

Jim put his hands on the sides of the car and tightened his long fingers on the metal.

"Do you mean Taylor investigated those checks?"

It was Clark's turn to be surprised.

"Haven't you heard what happened?"

Jim's startled eyes were answer enough.

"Why," announced Clark dramatically, "those four got another bottle of corn, got tight and decided to shock the town—so Nancy and that fella Merritt were married in Rockville at seven o'clock this morning."

A tiny indentation appeared in the metal under the Jelly-bean's fingers.

"Married?"

"Sure enough. Nancy sobered up and rushed back into town, crying and frightened to death—claimed it'd all been a mistake. First Doctor Lamar went wild and was going to kill Merritt, but finally they got it patched up some way, and Nancy and Merritt went to Savannah on the two-thirty train."

Jim closed his eyes and with an effort overcame a sudden sickness.

"It's too bad," said Clark philosophically. "I don't mean the wedding—reckon that's all right, though I don't guess Nancy cared a darn about him. But it's a crime for a nice girl like that to hurt her family that way."

The Jelly-bean let go the car and turned away. Again something was going on inside him, some inexplicable but almost chemical change.

"Where you going?" asked Clark.

The Jelly-bean turned and looked dully back over his shoulder.

"Got to go," he muttered. "Been up too long; feelin' right sick."

"Oh."

—

The street was hot at three and hotter still at four, the April dust seeming to enmesh the sun and give it forth again as a world-old joke forever played on an eternity of afternoons. But at half past four a first layer of quiet fell and the shades lengthened under the awnings and heavy foliaged trees. In this heat nothing mattered. All life was weather, a waiting through the hot where events had no significance for the cool that was soft and caressing like a woman's hand on a tired forehead. Down in Georgia there is a feeling—perhaps inarticulate—that this is the greatest wisdom of the South—so after a while the Jelly-bean turned into a pool-hall on Jackson Street where he was sure to find a congenial crowd who would make all the old jokes—the ones he knew.

The Diamond as Big as the Ritz

John T. Unger came from a family that had been well known in Hades—a small town on the Mississippi River—for several generations. John's father had held the amateur golf championship through many a heated contest; Mrs. Unger was known "from hot-box to hotbed," as the local phrase went, for her political addresses; and young John T. Unger, who had just turned sixteen, had danced all the latest dances from New York before he put on long trousers. And now, for a certain time, he was to be away from home. That respect for a New England education which is the bane of all provincial places, which drains them yearly of their most promising young men, had seized upon his parents. Nothing would suit them but that he should go to St. Midas' School[1] near Boston—Hades was too small to hold their darling and gifted son.

Now in Hades—as you know if you ever have been there—the names of the more fashionable preparatory schools and colleges mean very little. The inhabitants have been so long out of the world that, though they make a show of keeping up to date in dress and manners and literature, they depend to a great extent on hearsay, and a function that in Hades would be considered elaborate would doubtless be hailed by a Chicago beef-princess as "perhaps a little tacky."

John T. Unger was on the eve of departure. Mrs. Unger, with maternal fatuity, packed his trunks full of linen suits and electric fans, and

Mr. Unger presented his son with an asbestos pocket-book stuffed with money.

"Remember, you are always welcome here," he said. "You can be sure, boy, that we'll keep the home fires burning."

"I know," answered John huskily.

"Don't forget who you are and where you come from," continued his father proudly, "and you can do nothing to harm you. You are an Unger—from Hades."

So the old man and the young shook hands and John walked away with tears streaming from his eyes. Ten minutes later he had passed outside the city limits, and he stopped to glance back for the last time. Over the gates the old-fashioned Victorian motto seemed strangely attractive to him. His father had tried time and time again to have it changed to something with a little more push and verve about it, such as "Hades—Your Opportunity," or else a plain "Welcome" sign set over a hearty handshake pricked out in electric lights. The old motto was a little depressing, Mr. Unger had thought—but now....

So John took his look and then set his face resolutely toward his destination. And, as he turned away, the lights of Hades against the sky seemed full of a warm and passionate beauty.

St. Midas' School is half an hour from Boston in a Rolls-Pierce motor-car. The actual distance will never be known, for no one, except John T. Unger, had ever arrived there save in a Rolls-Pierce and probably no one ever will again. St. Midas' is the most expensive and the most exclusive boys' preparatory school in the world.

John's first two years there passed pleasantly. The fathers of all the boys were money-kings and John spent his summers visiting at fashionable resorts. While he was very fond of all the boys he visited, their fathers struck him as being much of a piece, and in his boyish way he often wondered at their exceeding sameness. When he told them where his home was they would ask jovially, "Pretty hot down there?" and John would muster a faint smile and answer, "It certainly is." His response would have been heartier had they not all made this joke—at best varying it with, "Is it hot enough for you down there?" which he hated just as much.

In the middle of his second year at school, a quiet, handsome boy named Percy Washington had been put in John's form. The newcomer was pleasant in his manner and exceedingly well dressed even for St. Midas', but for some reason he kept aloof from the other boys. The only person with whom he was intimate was John T. Unger, but even to John he was entirely uncommunicative concerning his home or his family. That he was wealthy went without saying, but beyond a few such deductions John knew little of his friend, so it promised rich confectionery for his curiosity when Percy invited him to spend the summer at his home "in the West." He accepted, without hesitation.

It was only when they were in the train that Percy became, for the first time, rather communicative. One day while they were eating lunch in the dining-car and discussing the imperfect characters of several of the boys at school, Percy suddenly changed his tone and made an abrupt remark.

"My father," he said, "is by far the richest man in the world."

"Oh," said John, politely. He could think of no answer to make to this confidence. He considered "That's very nice," but it sounded hollow and was on the point of saying, "Really?" but refrained since it would seem to question Percy's statement. And such an astounding statement could scarcely be questioned.

"By far the richest," repeated Percy.

"I was reading in the *World Almanac*," began John, "that there was one man in America with an income of over five million a year and four men with incomes of over three million a year, and——"

"Oh, they're nothing." Percy's mouth was a half-moon of scorn. "Catchpenny capitalists, financial small-fry, petty merchants and money-lenders. My father could buy them out and not know he'd done it."

"But how does he——"

"Why haven't they put down *his* income tax? Because he doesn't pay any. At least he pays a little one—but he doesn't pay any on his *real* income."

"He must be very rich," said John simply. "I'm glad. I like very rich people.

"The richer a fella is, the better I like him." There was a look of passionate frankness upon his dark face. "I visited the Schnlitzer-Murphys last Easter. Vivian Schnlitzer-Murphy had rubies as big as hen's eggs, and sapphires that were like globes with lights inside them——"

"I love jewels," agreed Percy enthusiastically. "Of course I wouldn't want any one at school to know about it, but I've got quite a collection myself. I used to collect them instead of stamps."

"And diamonds," continued John eagerly. "The Schnlitzer-Murphys had diamonds as big as walnuts——"

"That's nothing." Percy had leaned forward and dropped his voice to a low whisper. "That's nothing at all. My father has a diamond bigger than the Ritz-Carlton Hotel."[2]

II

The Montana sunset lay between two mountains like a gigantic bruise from which dark arteries spread themselves over a poisoned sky. An immense distance under the sky crouched the village of Fish, minute, dismal, and forgotten. There were twelve men, so it was said, in the village of Fish, twelve sombre and inexplicable souls who sucked a lean milk from the almost literally bare rock upon which a mysterious populatory force had begotten them. They had become a race apart, these twelve men of Fish, like some species developed by an early whim of nature, which on second thought had abandoned them to struggle and extermination.

Out of the blue-black bruise in the distance crept a long line of moving lights upon the desolation of the land, and the twelve men of Fish gathered like ghosts at the shanty depot to watch the passing of the seven o'clock train, the Transcontinental Express from Chicago. Six times or so a year the Transcontinental Express, through some inconceivable jurisdiction, stopped at the village of Fish, and when this occurred a figure or so would disembark, mount into a buggy that always appeared from out of the dusk, and drive off toward the bruised sunset. The observation of this pointless and preposterous phenomenon had become a sort of cult among the men of Fish. To observe, that was all; there remained in them none of the vital quality of illusion which would make them wonder or speculate, else a religion might have grown up around these mysterious visitations. But the men of Fish were beyond all religion—the barest and most savage tenets of even Christianity could gain no foothold on that barren rock—so there was no altar, no priest, no sacrifice; only each night at seven the silent concourse by the shanty depot, a congregation who lifted up a prayer of dim, anæmic wonder.

On this June night, the Great Brakeman, whom, had they deified any one, they might well have chosen as their celestial protagonist, had ordained that the seven o'clock train should leave its human (or inhuman) deposit at Fish. At two minutes after seven Percy Washington and John T. Unger disembarked, hurried past the spellbound, the agape, the fearsome eyes of the twelve men of Fish, mounted into a buggy which had obviously appeared from nowhere, and drove away.

After half an hour, when the twilight had coagulated into dark, the silent negro who was driving the buggy hailed an opaque body somewhere ahead of them in the gloom. In response to his cry, it turned upon them a luminous disk which regarded them like a malignant eye out of the unfathomable night. As they came closer, John saw that it was the tail-light of an immense automobile, larger and more magnificent than any he had ever seen. Its body was of gleaming metal richer than nickel and lighter than silver, and the hubs of the wheels were studded with iridescent geometric figures of green and yellow—John did not dare to guess whether they were glass or jewel.

Two negroes, dressed in glittering livery such as one sees in pictures of royal processions in London, were standing at attention beside the car and as the two young men dismounted from the buggy they were greeted in some language which the guest could not understand, but which seemed to be an extreme form of the Southern negro's dialect.

"Get in," said Percy to his friend, as their trunks were tossed to the ebony roof of the limousine. "Sorry we had to bring you this far in that buggy, but of course it wouldn't do for the people on the train or those God-forsaken fellas in Fish to see this automobile."

"Gosh! What a car!" This ejaculation was provoked by its interior. John saw that the upholstery consisted of a thousand minute and exquisite tapestries of silk, woven with jewels and embroideries, and set upon a background of cloth of gold. The two armchair seats in which the boys luxuriated were covered with stuff that resembled duvetyn,[3] but seemed woven in numberless colors of the ends of ostrich feathers.

"What a car!" cried John again, in amazement.

"This thing?" Percy laughed. "Why, it's just an old junk we use for a station wagon."

By this time they were gliding along through the darkness toward the break between the two mountains.

"We'll be there in an hour and a half," said Percy, looking at the clock. "I may as well tell you it's not going to be like anything you ever saw before."

If the car was any indication of what John would see, he was prepared to be astonished indeed. The simple piety prevalent in Hades has the earnest worship of and respect for riches as the first article of its creed—had John felt otherwise than radiantly humble before them, his parents would have turned away in horror at the blasphemy.

They had now reached and were entering the break between the two mountains and almost immediately the way became much rougher.

"If the moon shone down here, you'd see that we're in a big gulch," said Percy, trying to peer out of the window. He spoke a few words into the mouthpiece and immediately the footman turned on a search-light and swept the hillsides with an immense beam.

"Rocky, you see. An ordinary car would be knocked to pieces in half an hour. In fact, it'd take a tank to navigate it unless you knew the way. You notice we're going uphill now."

They were obviously ascending, and within a few minutes the car was crossing a high rise, where they caught a glimpse of a pale moon newly risen in the distance. The car stopped suddenly and several figures took shape out of the dark beside it—these were negroes also. Again the two young men were saluted in the same dimly recognizable dialect; then the negroes set to work and four immense cables dangling from overhead were attached with hooks to the hubs of the great jeweled wheels. At a resounding "Hey-yah!" John felt the car being lifted slowly from the ground—up and up—clear of the tallest rocks on both sides—then higher, until he could see a wavy, moonlit valley stretched out before him in sharp contrast to the quagmire of rocks that they had just left. Only on one side was there still rock—and then suddenly there was no rock beside them or anywhere around.

It was apparent that they had surmounted some immense knife-blade of stone, projecting perpendicularly into the air. In a moment they were going down again, and finally with a soft bump they were landed upon the smooth earth.

"The worst is over," said Percy, squinting out the window. "It's only five miles from here, and our own road—tapestry brick—all the way. This belongs to us. This is where the United States ends, father says."

"Are we in Canada?"

"We are not. We're in the middle of the Montana Rockies. But you are now on the only five square miles of land in the country that's never been surveyed."

"Why hasn't it? Did they forget it?"

"No," said Percy, grinning, "they tried to do it three times. The first time my grandfather corrupted a whole department of the State survey; the second time he had the official maps of the United States tinkered with—that held them for fifteen years. The last time was harder. My father fixed it so that their compasses were in the strongest magnetic field ever artificially set up. He had a whole set of surveying instruments made with a slight defection that would allow for this territory not to appear, and he substituted them for the ones that were to be used. Then he had a river deflected and he had what looked like a village built up on its banks—so that they'd see it, and think it was a town ten miles farther up the valley. There's only one thing my father's afraid of," he concluded, "only one thing in the world that could be used to find us out."

"What's that?"

Percy sank his voice to a whisper.

"Aeroplanes," he breathed. "We've got half a dozen anti-aircraft guns and we've arranged it so far—but there've been a few deaths and a great many prisoners. Not that we mind *that,* you know, father and I, but it upsets mother and the girls, and there's always the chance that some time we won't be able to arrange it."

Shreds and tatters of chinchilla, courtesy clouds in the green moon's heaven, were passing the green moon like precious Eastern stuffs paraded for the inspection of some Tartar Khan.[4] It seemed to John that it was day, and that he was looking at some lads sailing above him in the air, showering down tracts and patent medicine circulars, with their messages of hope for despairing, rock-bound hamlets. It seemed to him that he could see them look down out of the clouds and stare—and stare at whatever there was to stare at in this place whither he was bound— What then? Were they induced to land by some insidious device there to be immured far from patent medicines and from tracts until the judgment day—or, should they fail to fall into the trap, did a quick puff of smoke and the sharp round of a splitting shell bring them drooping to earth—and "upset" Percy's mother and sisters. John shook his head and the wraith of a hollow laugh issued silently from his parted lips. What desperate transaction lay hidden here? What a moral expedient of a bizarre Crœsus?[5] What terrible and golden mystery? . . .

The chinchilla clouds had drifted past now and outside the Montana night was bright as day. The tapestry brick of the road was smooth to the tread of the great tires as they rounded a still, moonlit lake; they passed into darkness for a moment, a pine grove, pungent and cool, then they came out into a broad avenue of lawn and John's exclamation of pleasure was simultaneous with Percy's taciturn "We're home."

Full in the light of the stars, an exquisite château rose from the borders of the lake, climbed in marble radiance half the height of an adjoining mountain, then melted in grace, in perfect symmetry, in translucent feminine languor, into the massed darkness of a forest of pine. The many towers, the slender tracery of the sloping parapets, the chiselled wonder of a thousand yellow windows with their oblongs and hectagons and triangles of golden light, the shattered softness of the intersecting planes of star-shine and blue shade, all trembled on John's spirit like a chord of music. On one of the towers, the tallest, the blackest at its base, an arrangement of exterior lights at the top made a sort of floating fairyland—and as John gazed up in warm enchantment the faint acciaccare[6] sound of violins drifted down in a rococo harmony that was like nothing he had ever heard before. Then in a moment the car stopped before wide, high marble steps around which the night air was fragrant with a host of flowers. At the top of the steps two great doors swung silently open and amber light flooded out upon the darkness, silhouetting the figure of an exquisite lady with black, high-piled hair, who held out her arms toward them.

"Mother," Percy was saying, "this is my friend, John Unger, from Hades."

Afterward John remembered that first night as a daze of many colors, of quick sensory impressions, of music soft as a voice in love, and of the beauty of things, lights and shadows, and motions and faces. There was a white-haired man who stood drinking a many-hued cordial from a crystal thimble set on a golden stem. There was a girl with a flowery face, dressed like Titania[7] with braided sapphires in her hair. There was a room where the solid, soft gold of the walls yielded to the pressure of his hand, and a room that was like a platonic conception of the ultimate prison—ceiling, floor, and all, it was lined with an unbroken mass of diamonds, diamonds of every size and shape, until, lit with tall violet lamps in the corners, it dazzled the eyes with a whiteness that could be compared only with itself, beyond human wish or dream.

Through a maze of these rooms the two boys wandered. Sometimes the floor under their feet would flame in brilliant patterns from lighting below, patterns of barbaric clashing colors, of pastel delicacy, of sheer whiteness, or of subtle and intricate mosaic, surely from some mosque on the Adriatic Sea. Sometimes beneath layers of thick crystal he would see blue or green water swirling, inhabited by vivid fish and growths of rainbow foliage. Then they would be treading on furs of every texture and color or along corridors of palest ivory, unbroken as though carved complete from the gigantic tusks of dinosaurs extinct before the age of man....

Then a hazily remembered transition, and they were at dinner—where each plate was of two almost imperceptible layers of solid diamond between which was curiously worked a filigree of emerald design, a shaving sliced from green air. Music, plangent and unobtrusive, drifted down through far corridors—his chair, feathered and curved insidiously to his back, seemed to engulf and overpower him as he drank his first glass of port. He tried drowsily to answer a question that had been asked him, but the honeyed luxury that clasped his body added to the illusion of sleep—jewels, fabrics, wines, and metals blurred before his eyes into a sweet mist....

"Yes," he replied with a polite effort, "it certainly is hot enough for me down there."

He managed to add a ghostly laugh; then, without movement, without resistance, he seemed to float off and away, leaving an iced dessert that was pink as a dream.... He fell asleep.

When he awoke he knew that several hours had passed. He was in a great quiet room with ebony walls and a dull illumination that was too faint, too subtle, to be called a light. His young host was standing over him.

"You fell asleep at dinner," Percy was saying. "I nearly did, too—it was such a treat to be comfortable again after this year of school. Servants undressed and bathed you while you were sleeping."

"Is this a bed or a cloud?" sighed John. "Percy, Percy—before you go, I want to apologize."

"For what?"

"For doubting you when you said you had a diamond as big as the Ritz-Carlton Hotel."

Percy smiled.

"I thought you didn't believe me. It's that mountain, you know."

"What mountain?"

"The mountain the château rests on. It's not very big, for a mountain. But except about fifty feet of sod and gravel on top it's solid diamond. *One* diamond, one cubic mile without a flaw. Aren't you listening? Say——"

But John T. Unger had again fallen asleep.

III

Morning. As he awoke he perceived drowsily that the room had at the same moment become dense with sunlight. The ebony panels of one wall had slid aside on a sort of track, leaving his chamber half open to the day. A large negro in a white uniform stood beside his bed.

"Good-evening," muttered John, summoning his brains from the wild places.

"Good-morning, sir. Are you ready for your bath, sir? Oh, don't get up—I'll put you in, if you'll just unbutton your pajamas—there. Thank you, sir."

John lay quietly as his pajamas were removed—he was amused and delighted; he expected to be lifted like a child by this black Gargantua[8] who was tending him, but nothing of the sort happened; instead he felt the bed tilt up slowly on its side—he began to roll, startled at first, in the direction of the wall, but when he reached the wall its drapery gave way, and sliding two yards farther down a fleecy incline he plumped gently into water the same temperature as his body.

He looked about him. The runway or rollway on which he had arrived had folded gently back into place. He had been projected into another chamber and was sitting in a sunken bath with his head just above the level of the floor. All about him, lining the walls of the room and the sides and bottom of the bath itself, was a blue aquarium, and gazing through the crystal surface on which he sat, he could see fish swimming among amber lights and even gliding without curiosity past his outstretched toes, which were separated from them only by the thickness of the crystal. From overhead, sunlight came down through sea-green glass.

"I suppose, sir, that you'd like hot rosewater and soapsuds this morning, sir—and perhaps cold salt water to finish."

The negro was standing beside him.

"Yes," agreed John, smiling inanely, "as you please." Any idea of ordering this bath according to his own meagre standards of living would have been priggish and not a little wicked.

The negro pressed a button and a warm rain began to fall, apparently from overhead, but really, so John discovered after a moment, from a fountain arrangement near by. The water turned to a pale rose color and jets of liquid soap spurted into it from four miniature walrus heads at the corners of the bath. In a moment a dozen little paddle-wheels, fixed to the sides, had churned the mixture into a radiant rainbow of pink foam which enveloped him softly with its delicious lightness, and burst in shining, rosy bubbles here and there about him.

"Shall I turn on the moving-picture machine, sir?" suggested the negro deferentially. "There's a good one-reel comedy in this machine to-day, or I can put in a serious piece in a moment, if you prefer it."

"No, thanks," answered John, politely but firmly. He was enjoying his bath too much to desire any distraction. But distraction came. In a moment he was listening intently to the sound of flutes from just outside, flutes dripping a melody that was like a waterfall, cool and green as the room itself, accompanying a frothy piccolo, in play more fragile than the lace of suds that covered and charmed him.

After a cold salt-water bracer and a cold fresh finish, he stepped out and into a fleecy robe, and upon a couch covered with the same material he was rubbed with oil, alcohol, and spice. Later he sat in a voluptuous chair while he was shaved and his hair was trimmed.

"Mr. Percy is waiting in your sitting-room," said the negro, when these operations were finished. "My name is Gygsum, Mr. Unger, sir. I am to see to Mr. Unger every morning."

John walked out into the brisk sunshine of his living-room, where he found breakfast waiting for him and Percy, gorgeous in white kid knickerbockers, smoking in an easy chair.

IV

This is a story of the Washington family as Percy sketched it for John during breakfast.

The father of the present Mr. Washington had been a Virginian, a direct descendant of George Washington,[9] and Lord Baltimore.[10] At the close of the Civil War he was a twenty-five-year-old Colonel with a played-out plantation and about a thousand dollars in gold.

Fitz-Norman Culpepper Washington, for that was the young Colonel's name, decided to present the Virginia estate to his younger brother and go West. He selected two dozen of the most faithful blacks, who, of course, worshipped him, and bought twenty-five tickets to the West, where he intended to take out land in their names and start a sheep and cattle ranch.

When he had been in Montana for less than a month and things were going very poorly indeed, he stumbled on his great discovery. He had lost his way when riding in the hills, and after a day without food he began to grow hungry. As he was without his rifle, he was forced to pursue a squirrel, and in the course of the pursuit he noticed that it was carrying something shiny in its mouth. Just before it vanished into its hole—for Providence did not intend that this squirrel should alleviate his hunger—it dropped its burden. Sitting down to consider the situation Fitz-Norman's eye was caught by a gleam in the grass beside him. In ten seconds he had completely lost his appetite and gained one hundred thousand dollars. The squirrel, which had refused with annoying persistence to become food, had made him a present of a large and perfect diamond.

Late that night he found his way to camp and twelve hours later all the males among his darkies were back by the squirrel hole digging furiously at the side of the mountain. He told them he had discovered a rhinestone mine, and, as only one or two of them had ever seen even a small diamond before, they believed him, without question. When the magnitude of his discovery became apparent to him, he found himself in a quandary. The mountain was *a* diamond—it was literally nothing else but solid diamond. He filled four saddle bags full of glittering samples and started on horseback for St. Paul. There he managed to dispose of half a dozen small stones—when he tried a larger one a storekeeper fainted and Fitz-Norman was arrested as a public disturber. He escaped from jail and caught the train for New York, where he sold a few medium-sized diamonds and received in exchange about two hundred thousand dollars in gold. But he did not dare to produce any exceptional gems—in fact, he left New York just in time. Tremendous excitement had been created in jewelry circles, not so much by the size of his diamonds as by their appearance in the city from mysterious sources. Wild rumors became current that a diamond mine had been discovered in the Catskills, on the Jersey coast, on Long Island, beneath Washington Square. Excursion trains, packed with men carrying picks and shovels, began to leave New York hourly, bound for various neighboring El Dorados.[11] But by that time young Fitz-Norman was on his way back to Montana.

By the end of a fortnight he had estimated that the diamond in the mountain was approximately equal in quantity to all the rest of the diamonds known to exist in the world. There was no valuing it by any regular computation, however, for it was *one solid diamond*—and if it were offered for sale not only would the bottom fall out of the market, but also, if the value should vary with its size in the usual arithmetical progression, there would not be enough gold in the world to buy a tenth part of it. And what could any one do with a diamond that size?

It was an amazing predicament. He was, in one sense, the richest man that ever lived—and yet was he worth anything at all? If his secret should transpire there was no telling to what measures the Government might resort in order to prevent a panic, in gold as well as in jewels. They might take over the claim immediately and institute a monopoly.

There was no alternative—he must market his mountain in secret. He sent South for his younger brother and put him in charge of his colored following—darkies who had never realized that slavery was abolished. To make sure of this, he read them a proclamation that he had composed, which announced that General Forrest[12] had reorganized the shattered Southern armies and defeated the North in one pitched battle. The negroes believed him implicitly. They passed a vote declaring it a good thing and held revival services immediately.

Fitz-Norman himself set out for foreign parts with one hundred thousand dollars and two trunks filled with rough diamonds of all sizes. He sailed for Russia in a Chinese junk and six months after his departure from Montana he was in St. Petersburg. He took obscure lodgings and called immediately upon the court jeweller, announcing that he had a diamond for the Czar. He remained in St. Petersburg for two weeks, in constant danger of being murdered, living from lodging to lodging, and afraid to visit his trunks more than three or four times during the whole fortnight.

On his promise to return in a year with larger and finer stones, he was allowed to leave for India. Before he left, however, the Court Treasurers had deposited to his credit, in American banks, the sum of fifteen million dollars—under four different aliases.

He returned to America in 1868, having been gone a little over two years. He had visited the capitals of twenty-two countries and talked with five emperors, eleven kings, three princes, a shah, a khan, and a sultan. At that time Fitz-Norman estimated his own wealth at one billion dollars. One fact worked consistently against the disclosure of his secret. No one of his larger diamonds remained in the public eye for a week before being invested with a history of enough fatalities, amours, revolutions, and wars to have occupied it from the days of the first Babylonian Empire.[13]

From 1870 until his death in 1900, the history of Fitz-Norman Washington was a long epic in gold. There were side issues, of course—he evaded the surveys, he married a Virginia lady, by whom he had a single son, and he was compelled, due to a series of unfortunate complications, to murder his brother, whose unfortunate habit of drinking himself into an indiscreet stupor had several times endangered their safety. But very few other murders stained these happy years of progress and expansion.

Just before he died he changed his policy, and with all but a few million dollars of his outside wealth bought up rare minerals in bulk, which he deposited in the safety vaults of banks all over the world, marked as bric-à-brac. His son, Braddock Tarleton Washington, followed this policy on an even more tensive scale. The minerals were converted into the rarest of all elements—radium—so that the equivalent of a billion dollars in gold could be placed in a receptacle no bigger than a cigar box.

When Fitz-Norman had been dead three years his son, Braddock, decided that the business had gone far enough. The amount of wealth that he and his father had taken out of the mountain was beyond all exact computation. He kept a note-book in cipher in which he set down the approximate quantity of radium in each of the thousand banks he patronized, and recorded the alias under which it was held. Then he did a very simple thing—he sealed up the mine.

He sealed up the mine. What had been taken out of it would support all the Washingtons yet to be born in unparalleled luxury for generations. His one care must be the protection of his secret, lest in the possible panic attendant on its discovery he should be reduced with all the property-holders in the world to utter poverty.

This was the family among whom John T. Unger was staying. This was the story he heard in his silver-walled living-room the morning after his arrival.

V

After breakfast, John found his way out the great marble entrance, and looked curiously at the scene before him. The whole valley, from the diamond mountain to the steep granite cliff five miles away, still gave off a breath of golden haze which hovered idly above the fine sweep of lawns and lakes and gardens. Here and there clusters of elms made delicate groves of shade, contrasting strangely with the tough masses of pine forest that held the hills in a grip of dark-blue green. Even as John looked he saw three fawns in single file patter out from one clump about a half mile away and disappear with awkward gayety into the black-ribbed half-light of another. John would not have been surprised to see a goat-foot piping his way among the trees or to catch a glimpse of pink nymph-skin and flying yellow hair between the greenest of the green leaves.

In some such cool hope he descended the marble steps, disturbing faintly the sleep of two silky Russian wolfhounds at the bottom, and set off along a walk of white and blue brick that seemed to lead in no particular direction.

He was enjoying himself as much as he was able. It is youth's felicity as well as its insufficiency that it can never live in the present, but must always be measuring up the day against its own radiantly imagined future—flowers and gold, girls and stars, they are only prefigurations and prophecies of that incomparable, unattainable young dream.

John rounded a soft corner where the massed rose bushes filled the air with heavy scent, and struck off across a park toward a patch of moss under some trees. He had never lain upon moss, and he wanted to see whether it was really soft enough to justify the use of its name as an adjective. Then he saw a girl coming toward him over the grass. She was the most beautiful person he had ever seen.

She was dressed in a white little gown that came just below her knees, and a wreath of mignonettes clasped with blue slices of sapphire bound up her hair. Her pink bare feet scattered the dew before them as she came. She was younger than John—not more than sixteen.

"Hello," she cried softly, "I'm Kismine."

She was much more than that to John already. He advanced toward her, scarcely moving as he drew near lest he should tread on her bare toes.

"You haven't met me," said her soft voice. Her blue eyes added, "Oh, but you've missed a great deal!" . . . "You met my sister, Jasmine, last night. I was sick with lettuce poisoning," went on her soft voice, and her eyes continued, "and when I'm sick I'm sweet—and when I'm well."

"You have made an enormous impression on me," said John's eyes, "and I'm not so slow myself"—"How do you do?" said his voice. "I hope you're better this morning."—"You darling," added his eyes tremulously.

John observed that they had been walking along the path. On her suggestion they sat down together upon the moss, the softness of which he failed to determine.

He was critical about women. A single defect—a thick ankle, a hoarse voice, a glass eye—was enough to make him utterly indifferent. And here for the first time in his life he was beside a girl who seemed to him the incarnation of physical perfection.

"Are you from the East?" asked Kismine with charming interest.

"No," answered John simply. "I'm from Hades."

Either she had never heard of Hades, or she could think of no pleasant comment to make upon it, for she did not discuss it further.

"I'm going East to school this fall," she said. "D'you think I'll like it? I'm going to New York to Miss Bulge's. It's very strict, but you see over the weekends I'm going to live at home with the family in our New York house, because father heard that the girls had to go walking two by two."

"Your father wants you to be proud," observed John.

"We are," she answered, her eyes shining with dignity. "None of us has ever been punished. Father said we never should be. Once when my sister Jasmine was a little girl she pushed him down-stairs and he just got up and limped away.

"Mother was—well, a little startled," continued Kismine, "when she heard that you were from—from where you *are* from, you know. She said that when she was a young girl—but then, you see, she's a Spaniard and old-fashioned."

"Do you spend much time out here?" asked John, to conceal the fact that he was somewhat hurt by this remark. It seemed an unkind allusion to his provincialism.

"Percy and Jasmine and I are here every summer, but next summer Jasmine is going to Newport. She's coming out in London a year from this fall. She'll be presented at court."

"Do you know," began John hesitantly, "you're much more sophisticated than I thought you were when I first saw you?"

"Oh, no, I'm not," she exclaimed hurriedly. "Oh, I wouldn't think of being. I think that sophisticated young people are *terribly* common, don't you? I'm not at all, really. If you say I am, I'm going to cry."

She was so distressed that her lip was trembling. John was impelled to protest:

"I didn't mean that; I only said it to tease you."

"Because I wouldn't mind if I *were*," she persisted, "but I'm *not*. I'm very innocent and girlish. I never smoke, or drink, or read anything except poetry. I know scarcely any mathematics or chemistry. I dress *very* simply—in fact, I scarcely dress at all. I think sophisticated is the last thing you can say about me. I believe that girls ought to enjoy their youths in a wholesome way."

"I do, too," said John heartily.

Kismine was cheerful again. She smiled at him, and a still-born tear dripped from the corner of one blue eye.

"I like you," she whispered, intimately. "Are you going to spend all your time with Percy while you're here, or will you be nice to me? Just think—I'm absolutely fresh ground. I've never had a boy in love with me in all my life. I've never been allowed even to *see* boys alone—except Percy. I came all the way out here into this grove hoping to run into you, where the family wouldn't be around."

Deeply flattered, John bowed from the hips as he had been taught at dancing school in Hades.

"We'd better go now," said Kismine sweetly. "I have to be with mother at eleven. You haven't asked me to kiss you once. I thought boys always did that nowadays."

John drew himself up proudly.

"Some of them do," he answered, "but not me. Girls don't do that sort of thing—in Hades."

Side by side they walked back toward the house.

VI

John stood facing Mr. Braddock Washington in the full sunlight. The elder man was about forty with a proud, vacuous face, intelligent eyes, and a robust figure. In the mornings he smelt of horses—the best horses. He carried a plain walking-stick of gray birch with a single large opal for a grip. He and Percy were showing John around.

"The slaves' quarters are there." His walking-stick indicated a cloister of marble on their left that ran in graceful Gothic along the side of the mountain. "In my youth I was distracted for a while from the business of life by a period of absurd idealism. During that time they lived in luxury. For instance, I equipped every one of their rooms with a tile bath."

"I suppose," ventured John, with an ingratiating laugh, "that they used the bathtubs to keep coal in. Mr. Schnlitzer-Murphy told me that once he——"

"The opinions of Mr. Schnlitzer-Murphy are of little importance, I should imagine," interrupted Braddock Washington, coldly. "My slaves did not keep coal in their bathtubs. They had orders to bathe every day, and they did. If they hadn't I might have ordered a sulphuric acid shampoo. I discontinued the baths for quite another reason. Several of them caught cold and died. Water is not good for certain races—except as a beverage."

John laughed, and then decided to nod his head in sober agreement. Braddock Washington made him uncomfortable.

"All these negroes are descendants of the ones my father brought North with him. There are about two hundred and fifty now. You notice that they've lived so long apart from the world that their original dialect has become an almost indistinguishable patois. We bring a few of them up to speak English—my secretary and two or three of the house servants.

"This is the golf course," he continued, as they strolled along the velvet winter grass. "It's all a green, you see—no fairway, no rough, no hazards."

He smiled pleasantly at John.

"Many men in the cage, father?" asked Percy suddenly.

Braddock Washington stumbled, and let forth an involuntary curse.

"One less than there should be," he ejaculated darkly—and then added after a moment, "We've had difficulties."

"Mother was telling me," exclaimed Percy, "that Italian teacher——"

"A ghastly error," said Braddock Washington angrily. "But of course there's a good chance that we may have got him. Perhaps he fell somewhere in the woods or stumbled over a cliff. And then there's always the probability that if he did get away his story wouldn't be believed. Nevertheless, I've had two dozen men looking for him in different towns around here."

"And no luck?"

"Some. Fourteen of them reported to my agent that they'd each killed a man answering to that description, but of course it was probably only the reward they were after——"

He broke off. They had come to a large cavity in the earth about the circumference of a merry-go-round and covered by a strong iron grating. Braddock Washington beckoned to John, and pointed his cane down through the grating. John stepped to the edge and gazed. Immediately his ears were assailed by a wild clamor from below.

"Come on down to Hell!"

"Hello, kiddo, how's the air up there?"

"Hey! Throw us a rope!"

"Got an old doughnut, Buddy, or a couple of second-hand sandwiches?"

"Say, fella, if you'll push down that guy you're with, we'll show you a quick disappearance scene."

"Paste him one for me, will you?"

It was too dark to see clearly into the pit below, but John could tell from the coarse optimism and rugged vitality of the remarks and voices that they proceeded from middle-class Americans of the more spirited type. Then Mr. Washington put out his cane and touched a button in the grass, and the scene below sprang into light.

"These are some adventurous mariners who had the misfortune to discover El Dorado," he remarked.

Below them there had appeared a large hollow in the earth shaped like the interior of a bowl. The sides were steep and apparently of polished glass, and on its slightly concave surface stood about two dozen men clad in the half costume, half uniform, of aviators. Their upturned faces, lit with wrath, with malice, with despair, with cynical humor, were covered by long growths of beard, but with the exception of a few who had pined perceptibly away, they seemed to be a well-fed, healthy lot.

Braddock Washington drew a garden chair to the edge of the pit and sat down.

"Well, how are you, boys?" he inquired genially.

A chorus of execration in which all joined except a few too dispirited to cry out, rose up into the sunny air, but Braddock Washington heard it with unruffled composure. When its last echo had died away he spoke again.

"Have you thought up a way out of your difficulty?"

From here and there among them a remark floated up.

"We decided to stay here for love!"

"Bring us up there and we'll find us a way!"

Braddock Washington waited until they were again quiet. Then he said:

"I've told you the situation. I don't want you here. I wish to heaven I'd never seen you. Your own curiosity got you here, and any time that you can think of a way out which protects me and my interests I'll be glad to consider it. But so long as you confine your efforts to digging tunnels—yes, I know about the new one you've started—you won't get very far. This isn't as hard on you as you make it out, with all your howling for the loved ones at home. If you were the type who worried much about the loved ones at home, you'd never have taken up aviation."

A tall man moved apart from the others, and held up his hand to call his captor's attention to what he was about to say.

"Let me ask you a few questions!" he cried. "You pretend to be a fair-minded man."

"How absurd. How could a man of *my* position be fair-minded toward *you?* You might as well speak of a Spaniard being fair-minded toward a piece of steak."

At this harsh observation the faces of the two dozen steaks fell, but the tall man continued:

"All right!" he cried. "We've argued this out before. You're not a humanitarian and you're not fair-minded, but you're human—at least you say you are—and you ought to be able to put yourself in our place for long enough to think how—how—how——"

"How what?" demanded Washington, coldly.

"—how unnecessary——"

"Not to me."

"Well,—how cruel——"

"We've covered that. Cruelty doesn't exist where self-preservation is involved. You've been soldiers; you know that. Try another."

"Well, then, how stupid."

"There," admitted Washington, "I grant you that. But try to think of an alternative. I've offered to have all or any of you painlessly executed if you wish. I've offered to have your wives, sweethearts, children, and mothers kidnapped and brought out here. I'll enlarge your place down there and feed and clothe you the rest of your lives. If there was some method of producing permanent amnesia I'd have all of you operated on and released immediately, somewhere outside of my preserves. But that's as far as my ideas go."

"How about trusting us not to peach on you?"[14] cried some one.

"You don't proffer that suggestion seriously," said Washington, with an expression of scorn. "I did take out one man to teach my daughter Italian. Last week he got away."

A wild yell of jubilation went up suddenly from two dozen throats and a pandemonium of joy ensued. The prisoners clog-danced and cheered and yodled and wrestled with one another in a sudden uprush of animal spirits. They even ran up the glass sides of the bowl as far as they could, and slid back to the bottom upon the natural cushions of their bodies. The tall man started a song in which they all joined——

"Oh, we'll hang the kaiser
On a sour apple tree——"

Braddock Washington sat in inscrutable silence until the song was over.

"You see," he remarked, when he could gain a modicum of attention. "I bear you no ill-will. I like to see you enjoying yourselves. That's why I didn't tell you the whole story at once. The man—what was his name? Critchtichiello?—was shot by some of my agents in fourteen different places."

Not guessing that the places referred to were cities, the tumult of rejoicing subsided immediately.

"Nevertheless," cried Washington with a touch of anger, "he tried to run away. Do you expect me to take chances with any of you after an experience like that?"

Again a series of ejaculations went up.

"Sure!"

"Would your daughter like to learn Chinese?"

"Hey, I can speak Italian! My mother was a wop."

"Maybe she'd like t'learna speak N'Yawk!"

"If she's the little one with the big blue eyes I can teach her a lot of things better than Italian."

"I know some Irish songs—and I could hammer brass once't."

Mr. Washington reached forward suddenly with his cane and pushed the button in the grass so that the picture below went out instantly, and there remained only that great dark mouth covered dismally with the black teeth of the grating.

"Hey!" called a single voice from below, "you ain't goin' away without givin' us your blessing?"

But Mr. Washington, followed by the two boys, was already strolling on toward the ninth hole of the golf course, as though the pit and its contents were no more than a hazard over which his facile iron had triumphed with ease.

VII

July under the lee of the diamond mountain was a month of blanket nights and of warm, glowing days. John and Kismine were in love. He did not know that the little gold football (inscribed with the legend *Pro deo et patria et St. Mida*)[15] which he had given her rested on a platinum chain next to her bosom. But it did. And she for her part was not aware that a large sapphire which had dropped one day from her simple coiffure was stowed away tenderly in John's jewel box.

Late one afternoon when the ruby and ermine music room was quiet, they spent an hour there together. He held her hand and she gave him such a look that he whispered her name aloud. She bent toward him—then hesitated.

"Did you say 'Kismine'?" she asked softly, "or——"

She had wanted to be sure. She thought she might have misunderstood.

Neither of them had ever kissed before, but in the course of an hour it seemed to make little difference.

The afternoon drifted away. That night when a last breath of music drifted down from the highest tower, they each lay awake, happily dreaming over the separate minutes of the day. They had decided to be married as soon as possible.

VIII

Every day Mr. Washington and the two young men went hunting or fishing in the deep forests or played golf around the somnolent course—games which John diplomatically allowed his host to win—or swam in the mountain coolness of the lake. John found Mr. Washington a somewhat exacting personality—utterly uninterested in any ideas or opinions except his own. Mrs. Washington was aloof and reserved at all times. She was apparently indifferent to her two daughters, and entirely absorbed in her son Percy, with whom she held interminable conversations in rapid Spanish at dinner.

Jasmine, the elder daughter, resembled Kismine in appearance—except that she was somewhat bow-legged, and terminated in large hands and feet—but was utterly unlike her in temperament. Her favorite books had to do with poor girls who kept house for widowed fathers. John learned from Kismine that Jasmine had never recovered from the shock and disappointment caused her by the termination of the World War, just as she was about to start for Europe as a canteen expert.[16] She had even pined away for a time, and Braddock Washington had taken steps to promote a new war in the Balkans—but she had seen a photograph of some wounded Serbian soldiers and lost interest in the whole proceedings. But Percy and Kismine seemed to have inherited the arrogant attitude in all its harsh magnificence from their father. A chaste and consistent selfishness ran like a pattern through their every idea.

John was enchanted by the wonders of the château and the valley. Braddock Washington, so Percy told him, had caused to be kidnapped a landscape gardener, an architect, a designer of state settings, and a French decadent poet left over from the last century. He had put his entire force of negroes at their disposal, guaranteed to supply them with any materials that the world could offer, and left them to work out some ideas of their own. But one by one they had shown their uselessness. The decadent poet had at once begun bewailing his separation from the boulevards in spring—he made some vague remarks about spices, apes, and ivories, but said nothing that was of any practical value. The stage designer on his part wanted to make the whole valley a series of tricks and sensational effects—a state of things that the Washingtons would soon have grown tired of. And as for the architect and the landscape gardener, they thought only in terms of convention. They must make this like this and that like that.

But they had, at least, solved the problem of what was to be done with them—they all went mad early one morning after spending the night in a single room trying to agree upon the location of a fountain, and were now confined comfortably in an insane asylum at Westport, Connecticut.

"But," inquired John curiously, "who did plan all your wonderful reception rooms and halls, and approaches and bathrooms——?"

"Well," answered Percy, "I blush to tell you, but it was a moving-picture fella. He was the only man we found who was used to playing with an unlimited amount of money, though he did tuck his napkin in his collar and couldn't read or write."

As August drew to a close John began to regret that he must soon go back to school. He and Kismine had decided to elope the following June.

"It would be nicer to be married here," Kismine confessed, "but of course I could never get father's permission to marry you at all. Next to that I'd rather elope. It's terrible for wealthy people to be married in America at present—they always have to send out bulletins to the press saying that they're going to be married in remnants, when what they mean is just a peck of old second-hand pearls and some used lace worn once by the Empress Eugénie."[17]

"I know," agreed John fervently. "When I was visiting the Schnlitzer-Murphys, the eldest daughter, Gwendolyn, married a man whose father owns half of West Virginia. She wrote home saying what a tough struggle she was carrying on on his salary as a bank clerk—and then she ended up by saying that 'Thank God, I have four good maids anyhow, and that helps a little.' "

"It's absurd," commented Kismine. "Think of the millions and millions of people in the world, laborers and all, who get along with only two maids."

One afternoon late in August a chance remark of Kismine's changed the face of the entire situation, and threw John into a state of terror.

They were in their favorite grove, and between kisses John was indulging in some romantic forebodings which he fancied added poignancy to their relations.

"Sometimes I think we'll never marry," he said sadly. "You're too wealthy, too magnificent. No one as rich as you are can be like other girls. I should marry the daughter of some well-to-do wholesale hardware man from Omaha or Sioux City, and be content with her half-million."

"I knew the daughter of a wholesale hardware man once," remarked Kismine. "I don't think you'd have been contented with her. She was a friend of my sister's. She visited here."

"Oh, then you've had other guests?" exclaimed John in surprise.

Kismine seemed to regret her words.

"Oh, yes," she said hurriedly, "we've had a few."

"But aren't you—wasn't your father afraid they'd talk outside?"

"Oh, to some extent, to some extent," she answered. "Let's talk about something pleasanter."

But John's curiosity was aroused.

"Something pleasanter!" he demanded. "What's unpleasant about that? Weren't they nice girls?"

To his great surprise Kismine began to weep.

"Yes—th—that's the—the whole t-trouble. I grew qu-quite attached to some of them. So did Jasmine, but she kept inv-viting them anyway. I couldn't under*stand* it."

A dark suspicion was born in John's heart.

"Do you mean that they *told,* and your father had them—removed?"

"Worse than that," she muttered brokenly. "Father took no chances—and Jasmine kept writing them to come, and they had *such* a good time!"

She was overcome by a paroxysm of grief.

Stunned with the horror of this revelation, John sat there openmouthed, feeling the nerves of his body twitter like so many sparrows perched upon his spinal column.

"Now, I've told you, and I shouldn't have," she said, calming suddenly and drying her dark blue eyes.

"Do you mean to say that your father had them *murdered* before they left?"

She nodded.

"In August usually—or early in September. It's only natural for us to get all the pleasure out of them that we can first."

"How abominable! How—why, I must be going crazy! Did you really admit that——"

"I did," interrupted Kismine, shrugging her shoulders. "We can't very well imprison them like those aviators, where they'd be a continual reproach to us every day. And it's always been made easier for Jasmine and me, because father had it done sooner than we expected. In that way we avoided any farewell scene——"

"So you murdered them! Uh!" cried John.

"It was done very nicely. They were drugged while they were asleep—and their families were always told that they died of scarlet fever in Butte."

"But—I fail to understand why you kept on inviting them!"

"I didn't," burst out Kismine. "I never invited one. Jasmine did. And they always had a very good time. She'd give them the nicest presents toward the last. I shall probably have visitors too—I'll harden up to it. We can't let such an inevitable thing as death stand in the way of enjoying life while we have it. Think how lonesome it'd be out here if we never had *any* one. Why, father and mother have sacrificed some of their best friends just as we have."

"And so," cried John accusingly, "and so you were letting me make love to you and pretending to return it, and talking about marriage, all the time knowing perfectly well that I'd never get out of here alive——"

"No," she protested passionately. "Not any more. I did at first. You were here. I couldn't help that, and I thought your last days might as well be pleasant for both of us. But then I fell in love with you, and—and I'm honestly sorry you're going to—going to be put away—though I'd rather you'd be put away than ever kiss another girl."

"Oh, you would, would you?" cried John ferociously.

"Much rather. Besides, I've always heard that a girl can have more fun with a man whom she knows she can never marry. Oh, why did I tell you? I've probably spoiled your whole good time now, and we were really enjoying things when you didn't know it. I knew it would make things sort of depressing for you."

"Oh, you did, did you?" John's voice trembled with anger. "I've heard about enough of this. If you haven't any more pride and decency than to have an affair with a fellow that you know isn't much better than a corpse, I don't want to have any more to do with you!"

"You're not a corpse!" she protested in horror. "You're not a corpse! I won't have you saying that I kissed a corpse!"

"I said nothing of the sort!"

"You did! You said I kissed a corpse!"

"I didn't!"

Their voices had risen, but upon a sudden interruption they both subsided into immediate silence. Footsteps were coming along the path in their direction, and a moment later the rose bushes were parted displaying Braddock Washington, whose intelligent eyes set in his good-looking vacuous face were peering in at them.

"Who kissed a corpse?" he demanded in obvious disapproval.

"Nobody," answered Kismine quickly. "We were just joking."

"What are you two doing here, anyhow?" he demanded gruffly. "Kismine, you ought to be—to be reading or playing golf with your sister. Go read! Go play golf! Don't let me find you here when I come back!"

Then he bowed at John and went up the path.

"See?" said Kismine crossly, when he was out of hearing. "You've spoiled it all. We can never meet any more. He won't let me meet you. He'd have you poisoned if he thought we were in love."

"We're not, any more!" cried John fiercely, "so he can set his mind at rest upon that. Moreover, don't fool yourself that I'm going to stay around here. Inside of six hours I'll be over those mountains, if I have to gnaw a passage through them, and on my way East."

They had both got to their feet, and at this remark Kismine came close and put her arm through his.

"I'm going, too."

"You must be crazy——"

"Of course I'm going," she interrupted impatiently.

"You most certainly are not. You——"

"Very well," she said quietly, "we'll catch up with father now and talk it over with him."

Defeated, John mustered a sickly smile.

"Very well, dearest," he agreed, with pale and unconvincing affection, "we'll go together."

His love for her returned and settled placidly on his heart. She was his—she would go with him to share his dangers. He put his arms about her and kissed her fervently. After all she loved him; she had saved him, in fact.

Discussing the matter, they walked slowly back toward the château. They decided that since Braddock Washington had seen them together they had best depart the next night. Nevertheless, John's lips were unusually dry at dinner, and he nervously emptied a great spoonful of peacock soup into his left lung. He had to be carried into the turquoise and sable card-room and pounded on the back by one of the under-butlers, which Percy considered a great joke.

IX

Long after midnight John's body gave a nervous jerk, and he sat suddenly upright, staring into the veils of somnolence that draped the room. Through the squares of blue darkness that were his open windows, he had heard a faint far-away sound that died upon a bed of wind before identifying itself on his memory, clouded with uneasy dreams. But the sharp noise that had succeeded it was nearer, was just outside the room—the click of a turned knob, a footstep, a whisper, he could not tell; a hard lump gathered in the pit of his stomach, and his whole body ached in the moment that he strained agonizingly to hear. Then one of the veils seemed to dissolve, and he saw a vague figure standing by the door, a figure only faintly limned and blocked in upon the darkness, mingled so with the folds of the drapery as to seem distorted, like a reflection seen in a dirty pane of glass.

With a sudden movement of fright or resolution John pressed the button by his bedside, and the next moment he was sitting in the green sunken bath of the adjoining room, waked into alertness by the shock of the cold water which half filled it.

He sprang out, and, his wet pajamas scattering a heavy trickle of water behind him, ran for the aquamarine door which he knew led out onto the ivory landing of the second floor. The door opened noiselessly. A single crimson lamp burning in a great dome above lit the magnificent sweep of the carved stairways with a poignant beauty. For a moment John hesitated, appalled by the silent splendor massed about him, seeming to envelop in its gigantic folds and contours the solitary drenched little figure shivering upon the ivory landing. Then simultaneously two things happened. The door of his own sitting-room swung open, precipitating three naked negroes into the hall—and, as John swayed in wild terror toward the stairway, another door slid back in the wall on the other side of the corridor, and John saw Braddock Washington standing in the lighted lift, wearing a fur coat and a pair of riding boots which reached to his knees and displayed, above, the glow of his rose-colored pajamas.

On the instant the three negroes—John had never seen any of them before, and it flashed through his mind that they must be the professional executioners—paused in their movement toward John, and turned expectantly to the man in the lift, who burst out with an imperious command:

"Get in here! All three of you! Quick as hell!"

Then, within the instant, the three negroes darted into the cage, the oblong of light was blotted out as the lift door slid shut, and John was again alone in the hall. He slumped weakly down against an ivory stair.

It was apparent that something portentous had occurred, something which, for the moment at least, had postponed his own petty disaster. What was it? Had the negroes risen in revolt? Had the aviators forced aside the iron bars of the grating? Or had the men of Fish stumbled blindly through the hills and gazed with bleak, joyless eyes upon the gaudy valley? John did not know. He heard a faint whir of air as the lift whizzed up again, and then, a moment later, as it descended. It was probable that Percy was hurrying to his father's assistance, and it occurred to John that this was his opportunity to join Kismine and plan an immediate escape. He waited until the lift had been silent for several minutes; shivering a little with the night cool that whipped in through his wet pajamas, he returned to his room and dressed himself quickly. Then he mounted a long flight of stairs and turned down the corridor carpeted with Russian sable which led to Kismine's suite.

The door of her sitting-room was open and the lamps were lighted. Kismine, in an angora kimono, stood near the window of the room in a listening attitude, and as John entered noiselessly she turned toward him.

"Oh, it's you!" she whispered, crossing the room to him. "Did you hear them?"

"I heard your father's slaves in my——"

"No," she interrupted excitedly. "Aeroplanes!"

"Aeroplanes? Perhaps that was the sound that woke me."

"There're at least a dozen. I saw one a few moments ago dead against the moon. The guard back by the cliff fired his rifle and that's what roused father. We're going to open on them right away."

"Are they here on purpose?"

"Yes—it's that Italian who got away——"

Simultaneously with her last word, a succession of sharp cracks tumbled in through the open window. Kismine uttered a little cry, took a penny with fumbling fingers from a box on her dresser, and ran to one of the electric lights. In an instant the entire château was in darkness—she had blown out the fuse.

"Come on!" she cried to him. "We'll go up to the roof garden, and watch it from there!"

Drawing a cape about her, she took his hand, and they found their way out the door. It was only a step to the tower lift, and as she pressed the button that shot them upward he put his arms around her in the darkness and kissed her mouth. Romance had come to John Unger at last. A minute later they had stepped out upon the star-white platform. Above, under the misty moon, sliding in and out of the patches of cloud that eddied below it, floated a dozen dark-winged bodies in a constant circling course. From here and there in the valley flashes of fire leaped toward them, followed by sharp detonations. Kismine clapped her hands with pleasure, which, a moment later, turned to dismay as the aeroplanes at some prearranged signal, began to release their bombs and the whole of the valley became a panorama of deep reverberate sound and lurid light.

Before long the aim of the attackers became concentrated upon the points where the anti-aircraft guns were situated, and one of them was almost immediately reduced to a giant cinder to lie smouldering in a park of rose bushes.

"Kismine," begged John, "you'll be glad when I tell you that this attack came on the eve of my murder. If I hadn't heard that guard shoot off his gun back by the pass I should now be stone dead——"

"I can't hear you!" cried Kismine, intent on the scene before her. "You'll have to talk louder!"

"I simply said," shouted John, "that we'd better get out before they begin to shell the château!"

Suddenly the whole portico of the negro quarters cracked asunder, a geyser of flame shot up from under the colonnades, and great fragments of jagged marble were hurled as far as the borders of the lake.

"There go fifty thousand dollars' worth of slaves," cried Kismine, "at prewar prices. So few Americans have any respect for property."

John renewed his efforts to compel her to leave. The aim of the aeroplanes was becoming more precise minute by minute, and only two of the anti-aircraft guns were still retaliating. It was obvious that the garrison, encircled with fire, could not hold out much longer.

"Come on!" cried John, pulling Kismine's arm, "we've got to go. Do you realize that those aviators will kill you without question if they find you?"

She consented reluctantly.

"We'll have to wake Jasmine!" she said, as they hurried toward the lift. Then she added in a sort of childish delight: "We'll be poor, won't we? Like people in books. And I'll be an orphan and utterly free. Free and poor! What fun!" She stopped and raised her lips to him in a delighted kiss.

"It's impossible to be both together," said John grimly. "People have found that out. And I should choose to be free as preferable of the two. As an extra caution you'd better dump the contents of your jewel box into your pockets."

Ten minutes later the two girls met John in the dark corridor and they descended to the main floor of the château. Passing for the last time through the magnificence of the splendid halls, they stood for a moment out on the terrace, watching the burning negro quarters and the flaming embers of two planes which had fallen on the other side of the lake. A solitary gun was still keeping up a sturdy popping, and the attackers seemed timorous about descending lower, but sent their thunderous fireworks in a circle around it, until any chance shot might annihilate its Ethiopian crew.

John and the two sisters passed down the marble steps, turned sharply to the left, and began to ascend a narrow path that wound like a garter about the diamond mountain. Kismine knew a heavily wooded spot half-way up where they could lie concealed and yet be able to observe the wild night in the valley—finally to make an escape, when it should be necessary, along a secret path laid in a rocky gully.

X

It was three o'clock when they attained their destination. The obliging and phlegmatic Jasmine fell off to sleep immediately, leaning against the trunk of a large tree, while John and Kismine sat, his arm around her, and watched the desperate ebb and flow of the dying battle among the ruins of a vista that had been a garden spot that morning. Shortly after four o'clock the last remaining gun gave out a clanging sound and went out of action in a swift tongue of red smoke. Though the moon was down, they saw that the flying bodies were circling closer to the earth. When the planes had made certain that the beleaguered possessed no further resources, they would land and the dark and glittering reign of the Washingtons would be over.

With the cessation of the firing the valley grew quiet. The embers of the two aeroplanes glowed like the eyes of some monster crouching in the grass. The château stood dark and silent, beautiful without light as it had been beautiful in the sun, while the woody rattles of Nemesis[18] filled the air above with a growing and receding complaint. Then John perceived that Kismine, like her sister, had fallen sound asleep.

It was long after four when he became aware of footsteps along the path they had lately followed, and he waited in breathless silence until the persons to whom they belonged had passed the vantage-point he occupied. There was a faint stir in the air now that was not of human origin, and the dew was cold; he knew that the dawn would break soon. John waited until the steps had gone a safe distance up the mountain and were inaudible. Then he followed. About half-way to the steep summit the trees fell away and a hard saddle of rock spread itself over the diamond beneath. Just before he reached this point he slowed down his pace, warned by an animal sense that there was life just ahead of him. Coming to a high boulder, he lifted his head gradually above its edge. His curiosity was rewarded; this is what he saw:

Braddock Washington was standing there motionless, silhouetted against the gray sky without sound or sign of life. As the dawn came up out of the east, lending a cold green color to the earth, it brought the solitary figure into insignificant contrast with the new day.

While John watched, his host remained for a few moments absorbed in some inscrutable contemplation; then he signalled to the two negroes who crouched at his feet to lift the burden which lay between them. As they struggled upright, the first yellow beam of the sun struck through the innumerable prisms of an immense and exquisitely chiselled diamond—and a white radiance was kindled that glowed upon the air like a fragment of the morning star. The bearers staggered beneath its weight for a moment—then their rippling muscles caught and hardened under the wet shine of the skins and the three figures were again motionless in their defiant impotency before the heavens.

After a while the white man lifted his head and slowly raised his arms in a gesture of attention, as one who would call a great crowd to hear—but there was no crowd, only the vast silence of the mountain and the sky, broken by faint bird voices down among the trees. The figure on the saddle of rock began to speak ponderously and with an inextinguishable pride.

"You out there—" he cried in a trembling voice. "You—there—!" He paused, his arms still uplifted, his head held attentively as though he were expecting an answer. John strained his eyes to see whether there might be men coming down the mountain, but the mountain was bare of human life. There was only sky and a mocking flute of wind along the tree-tops. Could Washington be praying? For a moment John wondered. Then the illusion passed—there was something in the man's whole attitude antithetical to prayer.

"Oh, you above there!"

The voice was become strong and confident. This was no forlorn supplication. If anything, there was in it a quality of monstrous condescension.

"You there——"

Words, too quickly uttered to be understood, flowing one into the other.... John listened breathlessly, catching a phrase here and there, while the voice broke off, resumed, broke off again—now strong and argumentative, now colored with a slow, puzzled impatience. Then a conviction commenced to dawn on the single listener, and as realization crept over him a spray of quick blood rushed through his arteries. Braddock Washington was offering a bribe to God!

That was it—there was no doubt. The diamond in the arms of his slaves was some advance sample, a promise of more to follow.

That, John perceived after a time, was the thread running through his sentences. Prometheus Enriched[19] was calling to witness forgotten sacrifices, forgotten rituals, prayers obsolete before the birth of Christ. For a while his discourse took the form of reminding God of this gift or that which Divinity had deigned to accept from men—great churches if he would rescue cities from the plague, gifts of myrrh and gold, of human lives and beautiful women and captive armies, of children and queens, of beasts of the forest and field, sheep and goats, harvests and cities, whole conquered lands that had been offered up in lust or blood for His appeasal, buying a meed's worth of alleviation from the Divine wrath—and now he, Braddock Washington, Emperor of Diamonds, king and priest of the age of gold, arbiter of splendor and luxury, would offer up a treasure such as princes before him had never dreamed of, offer it up not in suppliance, but in pride.

He would give to God, he continued, getting down to specifications, the greatest diamond in the world. This diamond would be cut with many more thousand facets than there were leaves on a tree, and yet the whole diamond would be shaped with the perfection of a stone no bigger than a fly. Many men would work upon it for many years. It would be set in a great dome of beaten gold, wonderfully carved and equipped with gates of opal and crusted sapphire. In the middle would be hollowed out a chapel presided over by an altar of iridescent, decomposing, ever-changing radium which would burn out the eyes of any worshipper who lifted up his head from prayer—and on this altar there would be slain for the amusement of the Divine Benefactor any victim He should choose, even though it should be the greatest and most powerful man alive.

In return he asked only a simple thing, a thing that for God would be absurdly easy—only that matters should be as they were yesterday at this hour and that they should so remain. So very simple! Let but the heavens open, swallowing these men and their aeroplanes—and then close again. Let him have his slaves once more, restored to life and well.

There was no one else with whom he had ever needed to treat or bargain.

He doubted only whether he had made his bribe big enough. God had His price, of course. God was made in man's image,[20] so it had been said: He must have His price. And the price would be rare—no cathedral whose building consumed many years, no pyramid constructed by ten thousand workmen, would be like this cathedral, this pyramid.

He paused here. That was his proposition. Everything would be up to specifications and there was nothing vulgar in his assertion that it would be cheap at the price. He implied that Providence could take it or leave it.

As he approached the end his sentences became broken, became short and uncertain, and his body seemed tense, seemed strained to catch the slightest pressure or whisper of life in the spaces around him. His hair had turned gradually white as he talked, and now he lifted his head high to the heavens like a prophet of old—magnificently mad.

Then, as John stared in giddy fascination, it seemed to him that a curious phenomenon took place somewhere around him. It was as though the sky had darkened for an instant, as though there had been a sudden murmur in a gust of wind, a sound of far-away trumpets, a sighing like the rustle of a great silken robe—for a time the whole of nature round about partook of this darkness; the birds' song ceased; the trees were still, and far over the mountain there was a mutter of dull, menacing thunder.

That was all. The wind died along the tall grasses of the valley. The dawn and the day resumed their place in a time, and the risen sun sent hot waves of yellow mist that made its path bright before it. The leaves laughed in the sun, and their laughter shook the trees until each bough was like a girl's school in fairyland. God had refused to accept the bribe.

For another moment John watched the triumph of the day. Then, turning, he saw a flutter of brown down by the lake, then another flutter, then another, like the dance of golden angels alighting from the clouds. The aeroplanes had come to earth.

John slid off the boulder and ran down the side of the mountain to the clump of trees, where the two girls were awake and waiting for him. Kismine sprang to her feet, the jewels in her pockets jingling, a question on her parted lips, but instinct told John that there was no time for words. They must get off the mountain without losing a moment. He seized a hand of each, and in silence they threaded the tree-trunks, washed with light now and with the rising mist. Behind them from the valley came no sound at all, except the complaint of the peacocks far away and the pleasant undertone of morning.

When they had gone about half a mile, they avoided the park land and entered a narrow path that led over the next rise of ground. At the highest point of this they paused and turned around. Their eyes rested upon the mountainside they had just left—oppressed by some dark sense of tragic impendency.

Clear against the sky a broken, white-haired man was slowly descending the steep slope, followed by two gigantic and emotionless negroes, who carried a burden between them which still flashed and glittered in the sun. Half-way down two other figures joined them—John could see that they were Mrs. Washington and her son, upon whose arm she leaned. The aviators had clambered from their machines to the sweeping lawn in front of the château, and with rifles in hand were starting up the diamond mountain in skirmishing formation.

But the little group of five which had formed farther up and was engrossing all the watchers' attention had stopped upon a ledge of rock. The negroes stooped and pulled up what appeared to be a trap-door in the side of the mountain. Into this they all disappeared, the white-haired man first, then his wife and son, finally the two negroes, the glittering tips of whose jeweled head-dresses caught the sun for a moment before the trap-door descended and engulfed them all.

Kismine clutched John's arm.

"Oh," she cried wildly, "where are they going? What are they going to do?"

"It must be some underground way of escape——"

A little scream from the two girls interrupted his sentence.

"Don't you see?" sobbed Kismine hysterically. "The mountain is wired!"

Even as she spoke John put up his hands to shield his sight. Before their eyes the whole surface of the mountain had changed suddenly to a dazzling burning yellow, which showed up through the jacket of turf as light shows through a human hand. For a moment the intolerable glow continued, and then like an extinguished filament it disappeared, revealing a black waste from which blue smoke arose slowly, carrying off with it what remained of vegetation and of human flesh. Of the aviators there was left neither blood nor bone—they were consumed as completely as the five souls who had gone inside.

Simultaneously, and with an immense concussion, the château literally threw itself into the air, bursting into flaming fragments as it rose, and then tumbling back upon itself in a smoking pile that lay projecting half into the water of the lake. There was no fire—what smoke there was drifted off mingling with the sunshine, and for a few minutes longer a powdery dust of marble drifted from the great featureless pile that had once been the house of jewels. There was no more sound and the three people were alone in the valley.

XI

At sunset John and his two companions reached the high cliff which had marked the boundaries of the Washingtons' dominion, and looking back found the valley tranquil and lovely in the dusk. They sat down to finish the food which Jasmine had brought with her in a basket.

"There!" she said, as she spread the table-cloth and put the sandwiches in a neat pile upon it. "Don't they look tempting? I always think that food tastes better outdoors."

"With that remark," remarked Kismine, "Jasmine enters the middle class."

"Now," said John eagerly, "turn out your pocket and let's see what jewels you brought along. If you made a good selection we three ought to live comfortably all the rest of our lives."

Obediently Kismine put her hand in her pocket and tossed two handfuls of glittering stones before him.

"Not so bad," cried John, enthusiastically. "They aren't very big, but—Hello!" His expression changed as he held one of them up to the declining sun. "Why, these aren't diamonds! There's something the matter!"

"By golly!" exclaimed Kismine, with a startled look. "What an idiot I am!"

"Why, these are rhinestones!" cried John.

"I know." She broke into a laugh. "I opened the wrong drawer. They belonged on the dress of a girl who visited Jasmine. I got her to give them to me in exchange for diamonds. I'd never seen anything but precious stones before."

"And this is what you brought?"

"I'm afraid so." She fingered the brilliants wistfully. "I think I like these better. I'm a little tired of diamonds."

"Very well," said John gloomily. "We'll have to live in Hades. And you will grow old telling incredulous women that you got the wrong drawer. Unfortunately your father's bank-books were consumed with him."

"Well, what's the matter with Hades?"

"If I come home with a wife at my age my father is just as liable as not to cut me off with a hot coal,[21] as they say down there."

Jasmine spoke up.

"I love washing," she said quietly. "I have always washed my own handkerchiefs. I'll take in laundry and support you both."

"Do they have washwomen in Hades?" asked Kismine innocently.

"Of course," answered John. "It's just like anywhere else."

"I thought—perhaps it was too hot to wear any clothes."

John laughed.

"Just try it!" he suggested. "They'll run you out before you're half started."

"Will father be there?" she asked.

John turned to her in astonishment.

"Your father is dead," he replied somberly. "Why should he go to Hades? You have it confused with another place that was abolished long ago."

After supper they folded up the table-cloth and spread their blankets for the night.

"What a dream it was," Kismine sighed, gazing up at the stars. "How strange it seems to be here with one dress and a penniless fiancé!

"Under the stars," she repeated. "I never noticed the stars before. I always thought of them as great big diamonds that belonged to some one. Now they frighten me. They make me feel that it was all a dream, all my youth."

"It *was* a dream," said John quietly. "Everybody's youth is a dream, a form of chemical madness."

"How pleasant then to be insane!"

"So I'm told," said John gloomily. "I don't know any longer. At any rate, let us love for a while, for a year or so, you and me. That's a form of divine drunkenness that we can all try. There are only diamonds in the whole world, diamonds and perhaps the shabby gift of disillusion. Well, I have that last and I will make the usual nothing of it." He shivered. "Turn up your coat collar, little girl, the night's full of chill and you'll get pneumonia. His was a great sin who first invented consciousness. Let us lose it for a few hours."

So wrapping himself in his blanket he fell off to sleep.

Winter Dreams

Some of the caddies were poor as sin and lived in one-room houses with a neurasthenic cow in the front yard, but Dexter Green's father owned the second best grocery store in Dillard—the best one was "The Hub," patronized by the wealthy people from Lake Erminie—and Dexter caddied only for pocket-money.

In the fall when the days became crisp and gray and the long Minnesota winter shut down like the white lid of a box, Dexter's skis moved over the snow that hid the fairways of the golf course. At these times the country gave him a feeling of profound melancholy—it offended him that the links should lie in enforced fallowness, haunted by ragged sparrows for the long season. It was dreary, too, that on the tees where the gay colors fluttered in summer there were now only the desolate sand boxes knee-deep in crusted ice. When he crossed the hills the wind blew cold as misery, and if the sun was out he tramped with his eyes squinted up against the hard dimensionless glare.

In April the winter ceased abruptly. The snow ran down into Lake Erminie scarcely tarrying for the early golfers to brave the season with red and black balls. Without elation, without an interval of moist glory the cold was gone.

Dexter knew that there was something dismal about this northern spring, just as he knew there was something gorgeous about the fall.

Fall made him clench his hands and tremble and repeat idiotic sentences to himself and make brisk abrupt gestures of command to imaginary audiences and armies. October filled him with hope which November raised to a sort of ecstatic triumph, and in this mood the fleeting brilliant impressions of the summer at Lake Erminie were ready grist to his mill. He became a golf champion and defeated Mr. T. A. Hedrick in a marvelous match played over a hundred times in the fairways of his imagination, a match each detail of which he changed about untiringly—sometimes winning with almost laughable ease, sometimes coming up magnificently from behind. Again, stepping from a Pierce-Arrow automobile, like Mr. Mortimer Jones, he strolled frigidly into the lounge of the Erminie Golf Club—or perhaps, surrounded by an admiring crowd, he gave an exhibition of fancy diving from the spring board of the Erminie Club raft.... Among those most impressed was Mr. Mortimer Jones.

And one day it came to pass that Mr. Jones, himself and not his ghost, came up to Dexter, almost with tears in his eyes and said that Dexter was the — — best caddy in the club and wouldn't he decide not to quit if Mr. Jones made it worth his while, because every other — — caddy in the club lost one ball a hole for him—regularly——

"No, sir," said Dexter, decisively, "I don't want to caddy any more." Then, after a pause, "I'm too old."

"You're—why, you're not more than fourteen. Why did you decide just this morning that you wanted to quit? You promised that next week you'd go over to the state tournament with me."

"I decided I was too old."

Dexter handed in his "A Class" badge, collected what money was due him from the caddy-master and caught the train for Dillard.

"The best — — caddy I ever saw," shouted Mr. Mortimer Jones over a drink that afternoon. "Never lost a ball! Willing! Intelligent! Quiet! Honest! Grateful!——"

The little girl who had done this was eleven—beautifully ugly as little girls are apt to be who are destined after a few years to be inexpressibly lovely and bring no end of misery to a great number of men. The spark, however, was perceptible. There was a general ungodliness in the way her lips twisted down at the corners when she smiled and in the—Heaven help us!—in the almost passionate quality of her eyes. Vitality is born early in such women. It was utterly in evidence now, shining through her thin frame in a sort of glow.

She had come eagerly out on to the course at nine o'clock with a white linen nurse and five small new golf clubs in a white canvas bag which the nurse was carrying. When Dexter first saw her she was standing by the caddy house, rather ill-at-ease and trying to conceal the fact by engaging her nurse in an obviously unnatural conversation illumined by startling and irrelevant smiles from herself.

"Well, it's certainly a nice day, Hilda," Dexter heard her say; then she drew down the corners of her mouth, smiled and glanced furtively around, her eyes in transit falling for an instant on Dexter.

Then to the nurse:

"Well, I guess there aren't very many people out here this morning, are there?"

The smile again radiant, blatantly artificial—convincing.

"I don't know what we're supposed to do now," said the nurse, looking nowhere in particular.

"Oh, that's all right"—the smile—"I'll fix it up."

Dexter stood perfectly still, his mouth faintly ajar. He knew that if he moved forward a step his stare would be in her line of vision—if he moved backward he would lose his full view of her face— For a moment he had not realized how young she was. Now he remembered having seen her several times the year before—in bloomers.[1]

Suddenly, involuntarily, he laughed, a short abrupt laugh—then, startled by himself, he turned and began to walk quickly away.

"Boy!"

Dexter stopped.

"Boy——"

Beyond question he was addressed. Not only that, but he was treated to that absurd smile, that preposterous smile—the memory of which at least half a dozen men were to carry to the grave.

"Boy, do you know where the golf teacher is?"

"He's giving a lesson."

"Well, do you know where the caddy-master is?"

"He's not here yet this morning."

"Oh." For a moment this baffled her. She stood alternately on her right and left foot.

"We'd like to get a caddy," said the nurse. "Mrs. Mortimer Jones sent us out to play golf and we don't know how without we get a caddy."

Here she was stopped by an ominous glance from Miss Jones, followed immediately by the smile.

"There aren't any caddies here except me," said Dexter to the nurse, "and I got to stay here in charge until the caddy-master gets here."

"Oh."

Miss Jones and her retinue now withdrew and at a proper distance from Dexter became involved in a heated conversation. The conversation was concluded by Miss Jones taking one of the clubs and hitting it on the ground with violence. For further emphasis she raised it again and was about to bring it down smartly upon the nurse's bosom, when the nurse seized the club and twisted it from her hands.

"You darn *fool*!" cried Miss Jones wildly.

Another argument ensued. Realizing that the elements of the comedy were implied in the scene, Dexter several times began to smile but each time slew the smile before it reached maturity. He could not resist the monstrous conviction that the little girl was justified in beating the nurse.

The situation was resolved by the fortuitous appearance of the caddy-master who was appealed to immediately by the nurse.

"Miss Jones is to have a little caddy and this one says he can't go."

"Mr. McKenna said I was to wait here till you came," said Dexter quickly.

"Well, he's here now." Miss Jones smiled cheerfully at the caddy-master. Then she dropped her bag and set off at a haughty mince toward the first tee.

"Well?" The caddy-master turned to Dexter. "What you standing there like a dummy for? Go pick up the young lady's clubs."

"I don't think I'll go out today," said Dexter.

"You don't——"

"I think I'll quit."

The enormity of his decision frightened him. He was a favorite caddy and the thirty dollars a month he earned through the summer was not to be made elsewhere in Dillard. But he had received a strong emotional shock and his perturbation required a violent and immediate outlet.

It is not so simple as that, either. As so frequently would be the case in the future, Dexter was unconsciously dictated to by his winter dreams.

Now, of course, the quality and the seasonability of these winter dreams varied, but the stuff of them remained. They persuaded Dexter several years later to pass up a business course at the State University—his father, prospering now, would have paid his way—for the precarious advantage of attending an older and more famous university in the East, where he was bothered by his scanty funds. But do not get the impression, because his winter dreams happened to be concerned at first with musings on the rich, that there was anything shoddy in the boy. He wanted not association with glittering things and glittering people—he wanted the glittering things themselves. Often he reached out for the best without knowing why he wanted it—and sometimes he ran up against the mysterious denials and prohibitions in which life indulges. It is with one of those denials and not with his career as a whole that this story deals.

He made money. It was rather amazing. After college he went to the city from which Lake Erminie draws its wealthy patrons. When he was only twenty-three and had been there not quite two years, there were already people who liked to say, "Now *there's* a boy—" All about him rich men's sons were peddling bonds precariously, or investing patrimonies precariously, or plodding through the two dozen volumes of canned rubbish in the "George Washington Commercial Course," but Dexter borrowed a thousand dollars on his college degree and his steady eyes, and bought a partnership in a *laundry*.

It was a small laundry when he went into it. Dexter made a specialty of learning how the English washed fine woolen golf stockings without shrinking them. Inside of a year he was catering to the trade who wore knickerbockers.[2] Men were insisting that their shetland hose and sweaters go to his laundry just as they had insisted on a caddy who could find golf balls. A little later he was doing their wives' lingerie as well—and running five branches in different parts of the city. Before he was twenty-seven he owned the largest string of laundries in his section of the country. It was then that he sold out and went to New York. But the part of his story that concerns us here goes back to when he was making his first big success.

When he was twenty-three Mr. W. L. Hart, one of the gray-haired men who like to say "Now there's a boy"—gave him a guest card to the Lake Erminie Club for over a week-end. So he signed his name one day on the register, and that afternoon played golf in a foursome with Mr. Hart and Mr. Sandwood and Mr. T. A. Hedrick. He did not consider it necessary to remark that he had once carried Mr. Hart's bag over this same links and that he knew every trap and gully with his eyes shut—but he found himself glancing at the four caddies who trailed them, trying to catch a gleam or gesture that would remind him of himself, that would lessen the gap which lay between his past and his future.

It was a curious day, slashed abruptly with fleeting, familiar impressions. One minute he had the sense of being a trespasser—in the next he was impressed by the tremendous superiority he felt toward Mr. T. A. Hedrick, who was a bore and not even a good golfer any more.

Then, because of a ball Mr. Hart lost near the fifteenth green an enormous thing happened. While they were searching the stiff grasses of the rough there was a clear call of "Fore!" from behind a hill in their rear. And as they all turned abruptly from their search a bright new ball sliced abruptly over the hill and caught Mr. T. A. Hedrick rather neatly in the stomach.

Mr. T. A. Hedrick grunted and cursed.

"By Gad!" cried Mr. Hedrick. "They ought to put some of these crazy women off the course. It's getting to be outrageous."

A head and a voice came up together over the hill:

"Do you mind if we go through?"

"You hit me in the stomach!" thundered Mr. Hedrick.

"Did I?" The girl approached the group of men. "I'm sorry. I yelled 'Fore!' "

Her glance fell casually on each of the men. She nodded to Sandwood and then scanned the fairway for her ball.

"Did I bounce off into the rough?"

It was impossible to determine whether this question was ingenuous or malicious. In a moment, however, she left no doubt, for as her partner came up over the hill she called cheerfully.

"Here I am! I'd have gone on the green except that I hit something."

As she took her stance for a short mashie shot, Dexter looked at her closely. She wore a blue gingham dress, rimmed at throat and shoulders with a white edging that accentuated her tan. The quality of exaggeration, of thinness that had made her passionate eyes and down-turning mouth absurd at eleven was gone now. She was arrestingly beautiful. The color in her cheeks was centered like the color in a picture—it was not a "high" color, but a sort of fluctuating and feverish warmth, so shaded that it seemed at any moment it would recede and disappear. This color and the mobility of her mouth gave a continual impression of flux, of intense life, of passionate vitality—balanced only partially by the sad luxury of her eyes.

She swung her mashie impatiently and without interest, pitching the ball into a sandpit on the other side of the green. With a quick insincere smile and a careless "Thank you!" she went on after it.

"That Judy Jones!" remarked Mr. Hedrick on the next tee, as they waited—some moments—for her to play on ahead. "All she needs is to be turned up and spanked for six months and then to be married off to an old-fashioned cavalry captain."

"Gosh, she's good-looking!" said Mr. Sandwood, who was just over thirty.

"Good-looking!" cried Mr. Hedrick contemptuously. "She always looks as if she wanted to be kissed! Turning those big cow-eyes on every young calf in town!"

It is doubtful if Mr. Hedrick intended a reference to the maternal instinct.

"She'd play pretty good golf if she'd try," said Mr. Sandwood.

"She has no form," said Mr. Hedrick solemnly.

"She has a nice figure," said Mr. Sandwood.

"Better thank the Lord she doesn't drive a swifter ball," said Mr. Hart, winking at Dexter. "Come on. Let's go."

Later in the afternoon the sun went down with a riotous swirl of gold and varying blues and scarlets, and left the dry rustling night of western summer. Dexter watched from the verandah of the Erminie Club, watched the even overlap of the waters in the little wind, silver molasses under the harvest moon. Then the moon held a finger to her lips and the lake became a clear pool, pale and quiet. Dexter put on his bathing suit and swam out to the farthest raft, where he stretched dripping on the wet canvas of the spring board.

There was a fish jumping and a star shining and the lights around the lake were gleaming. Over on a dark peninsula a piano was playing the songs of last summer and of summers before that—songs from "The Pink Lady" and "The Chocolate Soldier" and "Mlle. Modiste"[3]—and because the sound of a piano over a stretch of water had always seemed beautiful to Dexter he lay perfectly quiet and listened.

The tune the piano was playing at that moment had been gay and new five years before when Dexter was a sophomore at college. They had played it at a prom once and because he could not afford the luxury of proms in those days he had stood outside the gymnasium and listened. The sound of the tune and the splash of the fish jumping precipitated in him a sort of ecstasy and it was with that ecstasy he viewed what happened to him now. The ecstasy was a gorgeous appreciation. It was his sense that, for once, he was magnificently atune to life and that everything about him was radiating a brightness and a glamor he might never know again.

A low pale oblong detached itself suddenly from the darkness of the peninsula, spitting forth the reverberate sound of a racing motorboat. Two white streamers of cleft water rolled themselves out behind it and almost immediately the boat was beside him, drowning out the hot tinkle of the piano in the drone of its spray. Dexter, raising himself on his arms, was aware of a figure standing at the wheel, of two dark eyes regarding him over the lengthening space of water—then the boat had gone by and was sweeping in an immense and purposeless circle of spray round and round in the middle of the lake. With equal eccentricity one of the circles flattened out and headed back toward the raft.

"Who's that?" she called, shutting off her motor. She was so near now that Dexter could see her bathing suit, which consisted apparently of pink rompers. "Oh—you're one of the men I hit in the stomach."

The nose of the boat bumped the raft. After an inexpert struggle, Dexter managed to twist the line around a two-by-four. Then the raft tilted rakishly as she sprang on.

"Well, kiddo," she said huskily, "do you"—she broke off. She had sat herself upon the spring board, found it damp and jumped up quickly,—"do you want to go surf-board riding?"

He indicated that he would be delighted.

"The name is Judy Jones. Ghastly reputation but enormously popular." She favored him with an absurd smirk—rather, what tried to be a smirk, for, twist her mouth as she might, it was not grotesque, it was merely beautiful. "See that house over on the peninsula?"

"No."

"Well, there's a house there that I live in only you can't see it because it's too dark. And in that house there is a fella waiting for me. When he drove up by the door I drove out by the dock because he has watery eyes and asks me if I have an ideal."

There was a fish jumping and a star shining and the lights around the lake were gleaming. Dexter sat beside Judy Jones and she explained how her boat was driven. Then she was in the water, swimming to the floating surf-board with an exquisite crawl. Watching her was as without effort to the eye as watching a branch waving or a sea-gull flying. Her arms, burned to butternut, moved sinuously among the dull platinum ripples, elbow appearing first, casting the forearm back with a cadence of falling water, then reaching out and down stabbing a path ahead.

They moved out into the lake and, turning, Dexter saw that she was kneeling on the low rear of the now up-tilted surf-board.

"Go faster," she called, "fast as it'll go."

Obediently he jammed the lever forward and the white spray mounted at the bow. When he looked around again the girl was standing up on the rushing board, her arms spread ecstatically, her eyes lifted toward the moon.

"It's awful cold, kiddo," she shouted. "What's your name anyways."

"The name is Dexter Green. Would it amuse you to know how good you look back there?"

"Yes," she shouted, "it would amuse me. Except that I'm too cold. Come to dinner to-morrow night."

He kept thinking how glad he was that he had never caddied for this girl. The damp gingham clinging made her like a statue and turned her intense mobility to immobility at last.

"—At seven o'clock," she shouted. "Judy Jones, Girl, who hit man in stomach. Better write it down,"—and then, "Faster—oh, faster!"

Had he been as calm inwardly as he was in appearance, Dexter would have had time to examine his surroundings in detail. He received, however, an enduring impression that the house was the most elaborate he had ever seen. He had known for a long time that it was the finest on Lake Erminie, with a Pompeiian swimming pool and twelve acres of lawn and garden. But what gave it an air of breathless intensity was the sense that it was inhabited by Judy Jones—that it was as casual a thing to her as the little house in the village had once been to Dexter. There was a feeling of mystery in it, of bedrooms up-stairs more beautiful and strange than other bedrooms, of gay and radiant activities taking place through these deep corridors and of romances that were not musty and laid already in lavender, but were fresh and breathing and set forth in rich motor cars and in great dances whose flowers were scarcely withered. They were more real because he could feel them all about him, pervading the air with the shades and echoes of still vibrant emotion.

And so while he waited for her to appear he peopled the soft deep summer room and the sun porch that opened from it with the men who had already loved Judy Jones. He knew the sort of men they were—the men who when he first went to college had entered from the great prep-schools with graceful clothes and the deep tan of healthy summer, who did nothing or anything with the same debonair ease.

Dexter had seen that, in one sense, he was better than these men. He was newer and stronger. Yet in acknowledging to himself that he wished his children to be like them he was admitting that he was but the rough, strong stuff from which this graceful aristocracy eternally sprang.

When, a year before, the time had come when he could wear good clothes, he had known who were the best tailors in America, and the best tailor in America had made him the suit he wore this evening. He had acquired that particular reserve peculiar to his university, that set it off from other universities. He recognized the value to him of such a mannerism and he had adopted it; he knew that to be careless in dress and manner required more confidence than to be careful. But carelessness was for his children. His mother's name had been Krimslich. She was a Bohemian of the peasant class and she had talked broken English to the end of her days. Her son must keep to the set patterns.

He waited for Judy Jones in her house, and he saw these other young men around him. It excited him that many men had loved her. It increased her value in his eyes.

At a little after seven Judy Jones came downstairs. She wore a blue silk afternoon dress. He was disappointed at first that she had not put on something more elaborate, and this feeling was accentuated when, after a brief greeting, she went to the door of a butler's pantry and pushing it open called: "You can have dinner, Martha." He had rather expected that a butler would announce dinner, that there would be a cocktail perhaps. It even offended him that she should know the maid's name.

Then he put these thoughts behind him as they sat down together on a chintz-covered lounge.

"Father and mother won't be here," she said.

"Ought I to be sorry?"

"They're really quite nice," she confessed, as if it had just occurred to her. "I think my father's the best looking man of his age I've ever seen. And mother looks about thirty."

He remembered the last time he had seen her father, and found he was glad the parents were not to be here to-night. They would wonder who he was. He had been born in Keeble, a Minnesota village fifty miles farther north, and he always gave Keeble as his home instead of Dillard. Country towns were well enough to come from if they weren't inconveniently in sight and used as foot-stools by fashionable lakes.

Before dinner he found the conversation unsatisfactory. The beautiful Judy seemed faintly irritable—as much so as it was possible to be with a comparative stranger. They discussed Lake Erminie and its golf course, the surf-board riding of the night before and the cold she had caught, which made her voice more husky and charming than ever. They talked of his university which she had visited frequently during the past two years, and of the nearby city which supplied Lake Erminie with its patrons and whither Dexter would return next day to his prospering laundries.

During dinner she slipped into a moody depression which gave Dexter a feeling of guilt. Whatever petulance she uttered in her throaty voice worried him. Whatever she smiled at—at him, at a silver fork, at nothing—, it disturbed him that her smile could have no root in mirth, or even in amusement. When the red corners of her lips curved down, it was less a smile than an invitation to a kiss.

Then, after dinner, she led him out on the dark sun porch and deliberately changed the atmosphere.

"Do I seem gloomy?" she demanded.

"No, but I'm afraid I'm boring you," he answered quickly.

"You're not. I like you. But I've just had rather an unpleasant afternoon. There was a—man I cared about. He told me out of a clear sky that he was poor as a church-mouse. He'd never even hinted it before. Does this sound horribly mundane?"

"Perhaps he was afraid to tell you."

"I suppose he was," she answered thoughtfully. "He didn't start right. You see, if I'd thought of him as poor—well, I've been mad about loads of poor men, and fully intended to marry them all. But in this case, I hadn't thought of him that way and my interest in him wasn't strong enough to survive the shock."

"I know. As if a girl calmly informed her fiancé that she was a widow. He might not object to widows, but——"

"Let's start right," she suggested suddenly. "Who are you, anyhow?"

For a moment Dexter hesitated. There were two versions of his life that he could tell. There was Dillard and his caddying and his struggle through college, or——

"I'm nobody," he announced. "My career is largely a matter of futures."

"Are you poor?"

"No," he said frankly. "I'm probably making more money than any man my age in the northwest. I know that's an obnoxious remark, but you advised me to start right."

There was a pause. She smiled, and with a touch of amusement.

"You sound like a man in a play."

"It's your fault. You tempted me into being assertive."

Suddenly she turned her dark eyes directly upon him and the corners of her mouth drooped until her face seemed to open like a flower. He dared scarcely to breathe; he had the sense that she was exerting some force upon him, making him overwhelmingly conscious of the youth and mystery that wealth imprisons and preserves, the freshness of many clothes, of cool rooms and gleaming things, safe and proud above the hot struggles of the poor.

The porch was bright with the bought luxury of starshine. The wicker of the settee squeaked fashionably when he put his arm around her, commanded by her eyes. He kissed her curious and lovely mouth and committed himself to the following of a grail.

It began like that—and continued, with varying shades of intensity, on such a note right up to the dénouement. Dexter surrendered a part of himself to the most direct and unprincipled personality with which he had ever come in contact. Whatever the beautiful Judy Jones desired, she went after with the full pressure of her charm. There was no divergence of method, no jockeying for position or premeditation of effects—there was very little mental quality in any of her affairs. She simply made men conscious to the highest degree of her physical loveliness.

Dexter had no desire to change her. Her deficiencies were knit up with a passionate energy that transcended and justified them.

When, as Judy's head lay against his shoulder that first night, she whispered:

"I don't know what's the matter with me. Last night I thought I was in love with a man and tonight I think I'm in love with you——"

——it seemed to him a beautiful and romantic thing to say. It was the exquisite excitability that for the moment he controlled and owned. But a week later he was compelled to view this same quality in a different light. She took him in her roadster to a picnic supper and after supper she disappeared, likewise in her roadster, with another man. Dexter became enormously upset and was scarcely able to be decently civil to the other people present. When she assured him that she had not kissed the other man he knew she was lying—yet he was glad that she had taken the trouble to lie to him.

He was, as he found before the summer ended, one of a dozen, a varying dozen, who circulated about her. Each of them had at one time been favored above all others—about half of them still basked in the solace of occasional sentimental revivals. Whenever one showed signs of dropping out through long neglect she granted him a brief honeyed hour which encouraged him to tag along for a year or so longer. Judy made these forays upon the helpless and defeated without malice, indeed half unconscious that there was anything mischievous in what she did.

When a new man came to town everyone dropped out—dates were automatically cancelled.

The helpless part of trying to do anything about it was that she did it all herself. She was not a girl who could be "won" in the kinetic sense—she was proof against cleverness, she was proof against charm. If any of these assailed her too strongly she would immediately resolve the affair to a physical basis and under the magic of her physical splendor the strong as well as the brilliant played her game and not their own. She was entertained only by the gratification of her desires and by the direct exercise of her own charm. Perhaps from so much youthful love, so many youthful lovers, she had come, in self defense, to nourish herself wholly from within.

Succeeding Dexter's first exhilaration came restlessness and dissatisfaction. The helpless ecstasy of losing himself in her charm was a powerful opiate rather than a tonic. It was fortunate for his work during the winter that those moments of ecstasy came infrequently. Early in their acquaintance it had seemed for a while that there was a deep and spontaneous mutual attraction—that first August for example—three days of long evenings on her dusky verandah, of strange wan kisses through the late afternoon, in shadowy alcoves or behind the protecting trellises of the garden arbors, of mornings when she was fresh as a dream and almost shy at meeting him in the clarity of the rising day. There was all the ecstasy of an engagement about it, sharpened by his realization that there was no engagement. It was during those three days that, for the first time, he had asked her to marry him. She said "maybe some day," she said "kiss me," she said "I'd like to marry you," she said "I love you,"—she said—nothing.

The three days were interrupted by the arrival of a New York man who visited the Jones' for half September. To Dexter's agony, rumor engaged them. The man was the son of the president of a great trust company. But at the end of a month it was reported that Judy was yawning. At a dance one night she sat all evening in a motor boat with an old beau, while the New Yorker searched the club for her frantically. She told the old beau that she was bored with her visitor and two days later he left. She was seen with him at the station and it was reported that he looked very mournful indeed.

On this note the summer ended. Dexter was twenty-four and he found himself increasingly in a position to do as he wished. He joined two clubs in the city and lived at one of them. Though he was by no means an integral part of the stag-lines at these clubs he managed to be on hand at dances where Judy Jones was likely to appear. He could have gone out socially as much as he liked—he was an eligible young man, now, and popular with downtown fathers. His confessed devotion to

Judy Jones had rather solidified his position. But he had no social aspirations and rather despised the dancing men who were always on tap for the Thursday or Saturday parties and who filled in at dinners with the younger married set. Already he was playing with the idea of going east to New York. He wanted to take Judy Jones with him. No disillusion as to the world in which she had grown up could cure his illusion as to her desirability.

Remember that—for only in the light of it can what he did for her be understood.

Eighteen months after he first met Judy Jones he became engaged to another girl. Her name was Irene Scheerer and her father was one of the men who had always believed in Dexter. Irene was light haired and sweet and honorable and a little stout and she had two beaus whom she pleasantly relinquished when Dexter formally asked her to marry him.

Summer, fall, winter, spring, another summer, another fall—so much he had given of his active life to the curved lips of Judy Jones. She had treated him with interest, with encouragement, with malice, with indifference, with contempt. She had inflicted on him the innumerable little slights and indignities possible in such a case—as if in revenge for having ever cared for him at all. She had beckoned him and yawned at him and beckoned him again and he had responded often with bitterness and narrowed eyes. She had brought him ecstatic happiness and intolerable agony of spirit. She had caused him untold inconvenience and not a little trouble. She had insulted him and she had ridden over him and she had played his interest in her against his interest in his work—for fun. She had done everything to him except to criticise him—this she had not done—it seemed to him only because it might have sullied the utter indifference she manifested and sincerely felt toward him.

When autumn had come and gone again it occurred to him that he could not have Judy Jones. He had to beat this into his mind but he convinced himself at last. He lay awake at night for a while and argued it over. He told himself the trouble and the pain she had caused him, he enumerated her glaring deficiencies as a wife. Then he said to himself that he loved her and after a while he fell asleep. For a week, lest he imagine her husky voice over the telephone or her eyes opposite him at lunch, he worked hard and late, and at night he went to his office and plotted out his years.

At the end of a week he went to a dance and cut in on her once. For almost the first time since they had met he did not ask her to sit out with him or tell her that she was lovely. It hurt him that she did not miss these things—that was all. He was not jealous when he saw that there was a new man tonight. He had been hardened against jealousy long before.

He stayed late at the dance. He sat for an hour with Irene Scheerer and talked about books and about music. He knew very little about either. But he was beginning to be master of his own time now and he had a rather priggish notion that he—the young and already fabulously successful Dexter Green—should know more about such things.

That was in October when he was twenty-five. In January Dexter and Irene became engaged. It was to be announced in June and they were to be married three months later.

The Minnesota winter prolonged itself interminably and it was almost May when the winds came soft and the snow ran down into Lake Erminie at last. For the first time in over a year Dexter was enjoying a certain tranquility of spirit. Judy Jones had been in Florida and afterwards in Hot Springs and somewhere she had been engaged and somewhere she had broken it off. At first, when Dexter had definitely given her up, it had made him sad that people still linked them together and asked for news of her, but when he began to be placed at dinner next to Irene Scheerer people didn't ask him about her any more—they told him about her. He ceased to be an authority on her.

May at last. Dexter walked the streets at night when the darkness was damp as rain, wondering that so soon, with so little done, so much of ecstasy had gone from him. May, one year back had been marked by Judy's poignant, unforgivable, yet forgiven turbulence—it had been one of those rare times when he fancied she had grown to care for him. That old penny's worth of happiness he had spent for this bushel of content. He knew that Irene would be no more than a curtain spread behind him, a hand moving among gleaming tea cups, a voice calling to children... fire and loveliness were gone, magic of night and the hushed wonder of the hours and seasons... slender lips, down-turning, dropping to his lips like poppy petals, bearing him up into a heaven of eyes... a haunting gesture, light of a warm lamp on her hair. The thing was deep in him. He was too strong, too alive for it to die lightly.

In the middle of May when the weather balanced for a few days on the thin bridge that led to deep summer he turned in one night at Irene's house. Their engagement was to be announced in a week now—no one would be surprised at it. And tonight they would sit together on the lounge at the College Club and look on for an hour at the dancers. It gave him a sense of solidity to go with her——She was so sturdily popular, so intensely a "good egg."

He mounted the steps of the brown stone house and stepped inside.

"Irene," he called.

Mrs. Scheerer came out of the living-room to meet him.

"Dexter," she said, "Irene's gone up-stairs with a splitting headache. She wanted to go with you but I made her go to bed."

"Nothing serious I——"

"Oh, no. She's going to play golf with you in the morning. You can spare her for just one night, can't you, Dexter?"

Her smile was kind. She and Dexter liked each other. In the living-room he talked for a moment before he said goodnight.

Returning to the College Club, where he had rooms, he stood in the doorway for a moment and watched the dancers. He leaned against the door post, nodded at a man or two—yawned.

"Hello, kiddo."

The familiar voice at his elbow startled him. Judy Jones had left a man and crossed the room to him—Judy Jones, a slender enamelled doll in cloth of gold, gold in a band at her head, gold in two slipper points at her dress's hem. The fragile glow of her face seemed to blossom as she smiled at him. A breeze of warmth and light blew through the room. His hands in the pockets of his dinner jacket tightened spasmodically. He was filled with a sudden excitement.

"When did you get back?" he asked casually.

"Come here and I'll tell you about it."

She turned and he followed her. She had been away—he could have wept at the wonder of her return. She had passed through enchanted streets, doing young things that were like plaintive music. All mysterious happenings, all fresh and quickening hopes, had gone away with her, come back with her now.

She turned in the doorway.

"Have you a car here? If you haven't I have."

"I have a coupé."[4]

In, then, with a rustle of golden cloth. He slammed the door. Into so many cars she had stepped—like this—like that—her back against the leather, so—her elbow resting on the door—waiting. She would have been soiled long since had there been anything to soil her,—except herself—but these things were all her own outpouring.

With an effort he forced himself to start the car and avoiding her surprised glance backed into the street. This was nothing, he must remember. She had done this before and he had put her behind him, as he would have slashed a bad account from his books.

He drove slowly downtown and affecting a disinterested abstraction traversed the deserted streets of the business section, peopled here and there, where a movie was giving out its crowd or where consumptive or pugilistic youth lounged in front of pool halls. The clink of glasses and the slap of hands on the bars issued from saloons, cloisters of glazed glass and dirty yellow light.

She was watching him closely and the silence was embarrassing yet in this crisis he could find no casual word with which to profane the hour. At a convenient turning he began to zig-zag back toward the College Club.

"Have you missed me?" she asked suddenly.

"Everybody missed you."

He wondered if she knew of Irene Scheerer. She had been back only a day—her absence had been almost contemporaneous with his engagement.

"What a remark!" Judy laughed sadly—without sadness. She looked at him searchingly. He became absorbed for a moment in the dashboard.

"You're handsomer than you used to be," she said thoughtfully. "Dexter, you have the most rememberable eyes."

He could have laughed at this, but he did not laugh. It was the sort of thing that was said to sophomores. Yet it stabbed at him.

"I'm awfully tired of everything, kiddo." She called everyone kiddo, endowing the obsolete slang with careless, individual camaraderie. "I wish you'd marry me."

The directness of this confused him. He should have told her now that he was going to marry another girl but he could not tell her. He could as easily have sworn that he had never loved her.

"I think we'd get along," she continued, on the same note, "unless probably you've forgotten me and fallen in love with another girl."

Her confidence was obviously enormous. She had said, in effect, that she found such a thing impossible to believe, that if it were true he had merely committed a childish indiscretion—and probably to show off. She would forgive him, because it was not a matter of any moment but rather something to be brushed aside lightly.

"Of course you could never love anybody but me," she continued. "I like the way you love me. Oh, Dexter, have you forgotten last year?"

"No, I haven't forgotten."

"Neither have I!"

Was she sincerely moved—or was she carried along by the wave of her own acting?

"I wish we could be like that again," she said, and he forced himself to answer:

"I don't think we can."

"I suppose not.... I hear you're giving Irene Scheerer a violent rush."

There was not the faintest emphasis on the name, yet Dexter was suddenly ashamed.

"Oh, take me home," cried Judy suddenly, "I don't want to go back to that idiotic dance—with those children."

Then, as he turned up the street that led to the residence district, Judy began to cry quietly to herself. He had never seen her cry before.

The dark street lightened, the dwellings of the rich loomed up around them, he stopped his coupé in front of the great white bulk of the Mortimer Jones' house, somnolent, gorgeous, drenched with the splendor of the damp moonlight. Its solidity startled him. The strong walls, the fine steel of the girders, the breadth and beam and pomp of it were there only to bring out the contrast with the young beauty beside him. It was sturdy to accentuate her slightness—as if to show what a breeze could be generated by a butterfly's wing.

He sat perfectly quiet, his nerves in wild clamor, afraid that if he moved he would find her irresistibly in his arms. Two tears had rolled down her wet face and trembled on her upper lip.

"I'm more beautiful than anybody else," she said brokenly. "Why can't I be happy?" Her moist eyes tore at his stability—mouth turned slowly downward with an exquisite sadness. "I'd like to marry you if you'll have me, Dexter. I suppose you think I'm not worth having but I'll be so beautiful for you, Dexter."

A million phrases of anger, of pride, of passion, of hatred, of tenderness fought on his lips. Then a perfect wave of emotion washed over him, carrying off with it a sediment of wisdom, of convention, of doubt, of honor. This was his girl who was speaking, his own, his beautiful, his pride.

"Won't you come in?" he heard her draw in her breath sharply.

Waiting.

"All right," his voice was trembling, "I'll come in."

It seems strange to say that neither when it was over nor a long time afterward did he regret that night. Looking at it from the perspective of ten years, the fact that Judy's flare for him endured just one month seemed of little importance. Nor did it matter that by his yielding he subjected himself to a deeper agony in the end and gave serious hurt to Irene Scheerer and to Irene's parents who had befriended him. There was nothing sufficiently pictorial about Irene's grief to stamp itself on his mind.

Dexter was at bottom hard-minded. The attitude of the city on his action was of no importance to him, not because he was going to leave the city, but because any outside attitude on the situation seemed superficial. He was completely indifferent to popular opinion. Nor, when he had seen that it was no use, that he did not possess in himself the power to move fundamentally or to hold Judy Jones, did he bear any malice toward her. He loved her and he would love her until the day he was too old for loving—but he could not have her. So he tasted the deep pain that is reserved only for the strong, just as he had tasted for a little while the deep happiness.

Even the ultimate falsity of the grounds upon which Judy terminated the engagement—that she did not want to "take him away" from Irene, that it was on her conscience—did not revolt him. He was beyond any revulsion or any amusement.

He went east in February with the intention of selling out his laundries and settling in New York—but the war came to America[5] in March and changed his plans. He returned to the West, handed over the management of the business to his partner and went into the first officers' training camp in late April. He was one of those young thousands who greeted the war with a certain amount of relief, welcoming the liberation from webs of tangled emotion.

This story is not his biography, remember, although things creep into it which have nothing to do with those dreams he had when he was young. We are almost done with them and with him now. There is only one more incident to be related here and it happens seven years farther on.

It took place in New York, where he had done well—so well that there were no barriers too high for him now. He was thirty-two years old, and, except for one flying trip immediately after the war, he had not been west in seven years. A man named Devlin from Detroit came into his office to see him in a business way, and then and there this incident occurred, and closed out, so to speak, this particular side of his life.

"So you're from the Middle West," said the man Devlin with careless curiosity. "That's funny—I thought men like you were probably born and raised on Wall Street. You know—wife of one of my best friends in Detroit came from your city. I was an usher at the wedding."

Dexter waited with no apprehension of what was coming. There was a magic that his city would never lose for him. Just as Judy's house had always seemed to him more mysterious and gay than other houses, so his dream of the city itself, now that he had gone from it, was pervaded with a melancholy beauty.

"Judy Simms," said Devlin with no particular interest. "Judy Jones she was once."

"Yes, I knew her." A dull impatience spread over him. He had heard, of course, that she was married,—perhaps deliberately he had heard no more.

"Awfully nice girl," brooded Devlin, meaninglessly. "I'm sort of sorry for her."

"Why?" Something in Dexter was alert, receptive, at once.

"Oh, Joe Simms has gone to pieces in a way. I don't mean he beats her, you understand, or anything like that. But he drinks and runs around——"

"Doesn't she run around?"

"No. Stays at home with her kids."

"Oh."

"She's a little too old for him," said Devlin.

"Too old!" cried Dexter. "Why man, she's only twenty-seven."

He was possessed with a wild notion of rushing out into the streets and taking a train to Detroit. He rose to his feet, spasmodically, involuntarily.

"I guess you're busy," Devlin apologized quickly. "I didn't realize——"

"No, I'm not busy," said Dexter, steadying his voice, "I'm not busy at all. Not busy at all. Did you say she was—twenty-seven. No, I said she was twenty-seven."

"Yes, you did," agreed Devlin drily.

"Go on, then. Go on."

"What do you mean?"

"About Judy Jones."

Devlin looked at him helplessly.

"Well, that's—I told you all there is to it. He treats her like the devil. Oh, they're not going to get divorced or anything. When he's particularly outrageous she forgives him. In fact, I'm inclined to think she loves him. She was a pretty girl when she first came to Detroit."

A pretty girl! The phrase struck Dexter as ludicrous.

"Isn't she—a pretty girl any more?"

"Oh, she's all right."

"Look here," said Dexter, sitting down suddenly. "I don't understand. You say she was a 'pretty girl' and now you say she's 'all right.' I don't understand what you mean—Judy Jones wasn't a pretty girl, at all. She was a great beauty. Why, I knew her, I knew her. She was——"

Devlin laughed pleasantly.

"I'm not trying to start a row," he said. "I think Judy's a nice girl and I like her. I can't understand how a man like Joe Simms could fall madly in love with her, but he did." Then he added, "Most of the women like her."

Dexter looked closely at Devlin, thinking wildly that there must be a reason for this, some insensitivity in the man or some private malice.

"Lots of women fade just-like-*that,*" Devlin snapped his fingers.

"You must have seen it happen. Perhaps I've forgotten how pretty she was at her wedding. I've seen her so much since then, you see. She has nice eyes."

A sort of dullness settled down upon Dexter. For the first time in his life he felt like getting very drunk. He knew that he was laughing loudly at something Devlin had said but he did not know what it was or why it was funny. When Devlin went, in a few minutes, he lay down on his lounge and looked out the window at the New York skyline into which the sun was sinking in dull lovely shades of pink and gold.

He had thought that having nothing else to lose he was invulnerable at last—but he knew that he had just lost something more, as surely as if he had married Judy Jones and seen her fade away before his eyes.

The dream was gone. Something had been taken from him. In a sort of panic he pushed the palms of his hands into his eyes and tried to bring up a picture of the waters lapping at Lake Erminie and the moonlit verandah, and gingham on the golf links and the dry sun and the gold color of her neck's soft down. And her mouth damp to his kisses and her eyes plaintive with melancholy and her freshness like new fine linen in the morning. Why, these things were no longer in the world. They had existed and they existed no more.

For the first time in years the tears were streaming down his face. But they were for himself now. He did not care about mouth and eyes and moving hands. He wanted to care and he could not care. For he had gone away and he could never go back any more. The gates were closed, the sun was gone down and there was no beauty but the gray beauty of steel that withstands all time. Even the grief he could have borne was left behind in the country of illusion, of youth, of the richness of life, where his winter dreams had flourished.

"Long ago," he said, "long ago, there was something in me, but now that thing is gone. Now that thing is gone, that thing is gone. I cannot cry. I cannot care. That thing will come back no more."

Absolution

There was once a priest with cold, watery eyes, who, in the still of the night, wept cold tears. He wept because the afternoons were warm and long, and he was unable to attain a complete mystical union with our Lord. Sometimes, near four o'clock, there was a rustle of Swede girls along the path by his window, and in their shrill laughter he found a terrible dissonance that made him pray aloud for the twilight to come. At twilight the laughter and the voices were quieter, but several times he had walked past Romberg's Drug Store when it was dusk and the yellow lights shone inside and the nickel taps of the soda-fountain were gleaming, and he had found the scent of cheap toilet soap desperately sweet upon the air. He passed that way when he returned from hearing confessions on Saturday nights, and he grew careful to walk on the other side of the street so that the smell of the soap would float upward before it reached his nostrils as it drifted, rather like incense, toward the summer moon.

But there was no escape from the hot madness of four o'clock. From his window, as far as he could see, the Dakota wheat thronged the valley of the Red River.[1] The wheat was terrible to look upon and the carpet pattern to which in agony he bent his eyes sent his thought brooding through grotesque labyrinths, open always to the unavoidable sun.

One afternoon when he had reached the point where the mind runs down like an old clock, his housekeeper brought into his study a beautiful, intense little boy of eleven named Rudolph Miller. The little boy sat down in a patch of sunshine, and the priest, at his walnut desk, pretended to be very busy. This was to conceal his relief that some one had come into his haunted room.

Presently he turned around and found himself staring into two enormous, staccato eyes, lit with gleaming points of cobalt light. For a moment their expression startled him—then he saw that his visitor was in a state of abject fear.

"Your mouth is trembling," said Father Schwartz, in a haggard voice.

The little boy covered his quivering mouth with his hand.

"Are you in trouble?" asked Father Schwartz, sharply. "Take your hand away from your mouth and tell me what's the matter."

The boy—Father Schwartz recognized him now as the son of a parishioner, Mr. Miller, the freight-agent—moved his hand reluctantly off his mouth and became articulate in a despairing whisper.

"Father Schwartz—I've committed a terrible sin."

"A sin against purity?"

"No, Father... worse."

Father Schwartz's body jerked sharply.

"Have you killed somebody?"

"No—but I'm afraid—" the voice rose to a shrill whimper.

"Do you want to go to confession?"

The little boy shook his head miserably. Father Schwartz cleared his throat so that he could make his voice soft and say some quiet, kind thing. In this moment he should forget his own agony, and try to act like God. He repeated to himself a devotional phrase, hoping that in return God would help him to act correctly.

"Tell me what you've done," said his new soft voice.

The little boy looked at him through his tears, and was reassured by the impression of moral resiliency which the distraught priest had created. Abandoning as much of himself as he was able to this man, Rudolph Miller began to tell his story.

"On Saturday, three days ago, my father he said I had to go to confession, because I hadn't been for a month, and the family they go every week, and I hadn't been. So I just as leave go, I didn't care. So I put it off till after supper because I was playing with a bunch of kids and father asked me if I went, and I said 'no,' and he took me by the neck and he said 'You go now,' so I said 'All right,' so I went over to church. And he yelled after me: 'Don't come back till you go.' . . ."

II

"On Saturday, Three Days Ago."

The plush curtain of the confessional rearranged its dismal creases, leaving exposed only the bottom of an old man's old shoe. Behind the curtain an immortal soul was alone with God and the Reverend Adolphus Schwartz, priest of the parish. Sound began, a labored whispering, sibilant and discreet, broken at intervals by the voice of the priest in audible question.

Rudolph Miller knelt in the pew beside the confessional and waited, straining nervously to hear, and yet not to hear what was being said within. The fact that the priest was audible alarmed him. His own turn came next, and the three or four others who waited might listen unscrupulously while he admitted his violations of the Sixth and Ninth Commandments.

Rudolph had never committed adultery, nor even coveted his neighbor's wife—but it was the confession of the associate sins that was particularly hard to contemplate. In comparison he relished the less shameful fallings away—they formed a grayish background which relieved the ebony mark of sexual offenses upon his soul.

He had been covering his ears with his hands, hoping that his refusal to hear would be noticed, and a like courtesy rendered to him in turn, when a sharp movement of the penitent in the confessional made him sink his face precipitately into the crook of his elbow. Fear assumed solid form, and pressed out a lodging between his heart and his lungs. He must try now with all his might to be sorry for his sins—not because he was afraid, but because he had offended God. He must convince God that he was sorry and to do so he must first convince himself. After a tense emotional struggle he achieved a tremulous self-pity, and decided that he was now ready. If, by allowing no other thought to enter his head, he could preserve this state of emotion unimpaired until he went into that large coffin set on end, he would have survived another crisis in his religious life.

For some time, however, a demoniac notion had partially possessed him. He could go home now, before his turn came, and tell his mother that he had arrived too late, and found the priest gone. This, unfortunately, involved the risk of being caught in a lie. As an alternative he could say that he *had* gone to confession, but this meant that he must avoid communion next day, for communion taken upon an uncleansed soul would turn to poison in his mouth, and he would crumple limp and damned from the altar-rail.

Again Father Schwartz's voice became audible.

"And for your——"

The words blurred to a husky mumble, and Rudolph got excitedly to his feet. He felt that it was impossible for him to go to confession this afternoon. He hesitated tensely. Then from the confessional came a tap, a creak, and a sustained rustle. The slide had fallen and the plush curtain trembled. Temptation had come to him too late....

"Bless me, Father, for I have sinned.... I confess to Almighty God and to you, Father, that I have sinned.... Since my last confession it has been one month and three days.... I accuse myself of—taking the Name of the Lord in vain...."

This was an easy sin. His curses had been but bravado—telling of them was little less than a brag.

"... of being mean to an old lady."

The wan shadow moved a little on the latticed slat.

"How, my child?"

"Old lady Swenson," Rudolph's murmur soared jubilantly. "She got our baseball that we knocked in her window, and she wouldn't give it back, so we yelled 'Twenty-three, Skidoo,' at her all afternoon. Then about five o'clock she had a fit, and they had to have the doctor."

"Go on, my child."

"Of—of not believing I was the son of my parents."

"What?" The interrogation was distinctly startled.

"Of not believing that I was the son of my parents."

"Why not?"

"Oh, just pride," answered the penitent airily.

"You mean you thought you were too good to be the son of your parents?"

"Yes, Father." On a less jubilant note.

"Go on."

"Of being disobedient and calling my mother names. Of slandering people behind my back. Of smoking——"

Rudolph had now exhausted the minor offenses, and was approaching the sins it was agony to tell. He held his fingers against his face like bars as if to press out between them the shame in his heart.

"Of dirty words and immodest thoughts and desires," he whispered very low.

"How often?"

"I don't know."

"Once a week? Twice a week?"

"Twice a week."

"Did you yield to these desires?"

"No, Father."

"Were you alone when you had them?"

"No, Father. I was with two boys and a girl."

"Don't you know, my child, that you should avoid the occasions of sin as well as the sin itself? Evil companionship leads to evil desires and evil desires to evil actions. Where were you when this happened?"

"In a barn in back of——"

"I don't want to hear any names," interrupted the priest sharply.

"Well, it was up in the loft of this barn and this girl and—a fella, they were saying things—saying immodest things, and I stayed."

"You should have gone—you should have told the girl to go."

He should have gone! He could not tell Father Schwartz how his pulse had bumped in his wrist, how a strange, romantic excitement had possessed him when those curious things had been said. Perhaps in the houses of delinquency among the dull and hard-eyed incorrigible girls can be found those for whom has burned the whitest fire.

"Have you anything else to tell me?"

"I don't think so, Father."

Rudolph felt a great relief. Perspiration had broken out under his tight-pressed fingers.

"Have you told any lies?"

The question startled him. Like all those who habitually and instinctively lie, he had an enormous respect and awe for the truth. Something almost exterior to himself dictated a quick, hurt answer.

"Oh, no, Father, I never tell lies."

For a moment, like the commoner in the king's chair, he tasted the pride of the situation. Then as the priest began to murmur conventional admonitions he realized that in heroically denying he had told lies, he had committed a terrible sin—he had told a lie in confession.

In automatic response to Father Schwartz's "Make an act of contrition," he began to repeat aloud meaninglessly:

"Oh, my God, I am heartily sorry for having offended Thee. . . ."

He must fix this now—it was a bad mistake—but as his teeth shut on the last words of his prayer there was a sharp sound, and the slat was closed.

A minute later when he emerged into the twilight the relief in coming from the muggy church into an open world of wheat and sky postponed the full realization of what he had done. Instead of worrying he took a deep breath of the crisp air and began to say over and over to himself the words "Blatchford Sarnemington, Blatchford Sarnemington!"[2]

Blatchford Sarnemington was himself, and these words were in effect a lyric. When he became Blatchford Sarnemington a suave nobility flowed from him. Blatchford Sarnemington lived in great sweeping triumphs. When Rudolph half closed his eyes it meant that Blatchford had established dominance over him and, as he went by, there were envious mutters in the air: "Blatchford Sarnemington! There goes Blatchford Sarnemington."

He was Blatchford now for a while as he strutted homeward along the staggering road, but when the road braced itself in macadam in order to become the main street of Ludwig, Rudolph's exhilaration faded out and his mind cooled, and he felt the horror of his lie. God, of course, already knew of it—but Rudolph reserved a corner of his mind where he was safe from God, where he prepared the subterfuges with which he often tricked God. Hiding now in this corner he considered how he could best avoid the consequences of his misstatement.

At all costs he must avoid communion next day. The risk of angering God to such an extent was too great. He would have to drink water "by accident" in the morning, and thus, in accordance with a church law, render himself unfit to receive communion that day. In spite of its flimsiness this subterfuge was the most feasible that occurred to him. He accepted its risks and was concentrating on how best to put it into effect, as he turned the corner by Romberg's Drug Store and came in sight of his father's house.

III

Rudolph's father, the local freight-agent, had floated with the second wave of German and Irish stock[3] to the Minnesota-Dakota country.

Theoretically, great opportunities lay ahead of a young man of energy in that day and place, but Carl Miller had been incapable of establishing either with his superiors or his subordinates the reputation for approximate immutability which is essential to success in a hierarchic industry. Somewhat gross, he was, nevertheless, insufficiently hard-headed and unable to take fundamental relationships for granted, and this inability made him suspicious, unrestful, and continually dismayed.

His two bonds with the colorful life were his faith in the Roman Catholic Church and his mystical worship of the Empire Builder, James J. Hill.[4] Hill was the apotheosis of that quality in which Miller himself was deficient—the sense of things, the feel of things, the hint of rain in the wind on the cheek. Miller's mind worked late on the old decisions of other men, and he had never in his life felt the balance of any single thing in his hands. His weary, sprightly, undersized body was growing old in Hill's gigantic shadow. For twenty years he had lived alone with Hill's name and God.

On Sunday morning Carl Miller awoke in the dustless quiet of six o'clock. Kneeling by the side of the bed he bent his yellow-gray hair and the full dapple bangs of his mustache into the pillow, and prayed for several minutes. Then he drew off his night-shirt—like the rest of his generation he had never been able to endure pajamas—and clothed his thin, white, hairless body in woollen underwear.

He shaved. Silence in the other bedroom where his wife lay nervously asleep. Silence from the screened-off corner of the hall where his son's cot stood, and his son slept among his Alger books,[5] his collection of cigar-bands,[6] his mothy pennants—"Cornell," "Hamlin," and "Greetings from Pueblo, New Mexico"—and the other possessions of his private life. From outside Miller could hear the shrill birds and the whirring movement of the poultry, and, as an undertone, the low, swelling click-a-tick of the six-fifteen through-train for Montana and the green coast beyond. Then as the cold water dripped from the wash-rag in his hand he raised his head suddenly—he had heard a furtive sound from the kitchen below.

He dried his razor hastily, slipped his dangling suspenders to his shoulder, and listened. Some one was walking in the kitchen, and he knew by the light footfall that it was not his wife. With his mouth faintly ajar he ran quickly down the stairs and opened the kitchen door.

Standing by the sink, with one hand on the still dripping faucet and the other clutching a full glass of water, stood his son. The boy's eyes, still heavy with sleep, met his father's with a frightened, reproachful beauty. He was barefooted, and his pajamas were rolled up at the knees and sleeves.

For a moment they both remained motionless—Carl Miller's brow went down and his son's went up, as though they were striking a balance between the extremes of emotion which filled them. Then the bangs of the parent's moustache descended portentously until they obscured his mouth, and he gave a short glance around to see if anything had been disturbed.

The kitchen was garnished with sunlight which beat on the pans and made the smooth boards of the floor and table yellow and clean as wheat. It was the centre of the house where the fire burned and the tins fitted into tins like toys, and the steam whistled all day on a thin pastel note. Nothing was moved, nothing touched—except the faucet where beads of water still formed and dripped with a white flash into the sink below.

"What are you doing?"

"I got awful thirsty, so I thought I'd just come down and get——"

"I thought you were going to communion."

A look of vehement astonishment spread over his son's face.

"I forgot all about it."

"Have you drunk any water?"

"No——"

As the word left his mouth Rudolph knew it was the wrong answer, but the faded indignant eyes facing him had signalled up the truth before the boy's will could act. He realized, too, that he should never have come down-stairs; some vague necessity for verisimilitude had made him want to leave a wet glass as evidence by the sink; the honesty of his imagination had betrayed him.

"Pour it out," commanded his father, "that water!"

Rudolph despairingly inverted the tumbler.

"What's the matter with you, anyways?" demanded Miller angrily.

"Nothing."

"Did you go to confession yesterday?"

"Yes."

"Then why were you going to drink water?"

"I don't know—I forgot."

"Maybe you care more about being a little bit thirsty than you do about your religion."

"I forgot." Rudolph could feel the tears straining in his eyes.

"That's no answer."

"Well, I did."

"You better look out!" His father held to a high, persistent, inquisitory note: "If you're so forgetful that you can't remember your religion something better be done about it."

Rudolph filled a sharp pause with:

"I can remember it all right."

"First you begin to neglect your religion," cried his father, fanning his own fierceness, "the next thing you'll begin to lie and steal, and the *next* thing is the *reform* school!"[7]

Not even this familiar threat could deepen the abyss that Rudolph saw before him. He must either tell all now, offering his body for what he knew would be a ferocious beating, or else tempt the thunderbolts by receiving the Body and Blood of Christ with sacrilege upon his soul. And of the two the former seemed more terrible—it was not so much the beating he dreaded as the savage ferocity, outlet of the ineffectual man, which would lie behind it.

"Put down that glass and go up-stairs and dress!" his father ordered, "and when we get to church, before you go to communion, you better kneel down and ask God to forgive you for your carelessness."

Some accidental emphasis in the phrasing of this command acted like a catalytic agent on the confusion and terror of Rudolph's mind. A wild, proud anger rose in him, and he dashed the tumbler passionately into the sink.

His father uttered a strained, husky sound, and sprang for him. Rudolph dodged to the side, tipped over a chair, and tried to get beyond the kitchen table. He cried out sharply when a hand grasped his pajama shoulder, then he felt the dull impact of a fist against the side of his head, and glancing blows on the upper part of his body. As he slipped here and there in his father's grasp, dragged or lifted when he clung instinctively to an arm, aware of sharp smarts and strains, he made no sound except that he laughed hysterically several times. Then in less than a minute the blows abruptly ceased. After a lull during which Rudolph was tightly held, and during which they both trembled violently and uttered strange, truncated words, Carl Miller half dragged, half threatened his son up-stairs.

"Put on your clothes!"

Rudolph was now both hysterical and cold. His head hurt him, and there was a long, shallow scratch on his neck from his father's fingernail, and he sobbed and trembled as he dressed. He was aware of his mother standing at the doorway in a wrapper, her wrinkled face compressing and squeezing and opening out into new series of wrinkles which floated and eddied from neck to brow. Despising her nervous ineffectuality and avoiding her rudely when she tried to touch his neck with witch-hazel, he made a hasty, choking toilet. Then he followed his father out of the house and along the road toward the Catholic church.

IV

They walked without speaking except when Carl Miller acknowledged automatically the existence of passers-by. Rudolph's uneven breathing alone ruffled the hot Sunday silence.

His father stopped decisively at the door of the church.

"I've decided you'd better go to confession again. Go in and tell Father Schwartz what you did and ask God's pardon."

"You lost your temper, too!" said Rudolph quickly.

Carl Miller took a step toward his son, who moved cautiously backward.

"All right, I'll go."

"Are you going to do what I say?" cried his father in a hoarse whisper.

"All right."

Rudolph walked into the church, and for the second time in two days entered the confessional and knelt down. The slat went up almost at once.

"I accuse myself of missing my morning prayers."

"Is that all?"

"That's all."

A maudlin exultation filled him. Not easily ever again would he be able to put an abstraction before the necessities of his ease and pride. An invisible line had been crossed, and he had become aware of his isolation—aware that it applied not only to those moments when he was Blatchford Sarnemington but that it applied to all his inner life.

Hitherto such phenomena as "crazy" ambitions and petty shames and fears had been but private reservations, unacknowledged before the throne of his official soul. Now he realized unconsciously that his private reservations were himself—and all the rest a garnished front and a conventional flag. The pressure of his environment had driven him into the lonely secret road of adolescence.

He knelt in the pew beside his father. Mass began. Rudolph knelt up—when he was alone he slumped his posterior back against the seat—and tasted the consciousness of a sharp, subtle revenge. Beside him his father prayed that God would forgive Rudolph, and asked also that his own outbreak of temper would be pardoned. He glanced sidewise at this son, and was relieved to see that the strained, wild look had gone from his face and that he had ceased sobbing. The Grace of God, inherent in the Sacrament, would do the rest, and perhaps after Mass everything would be better. He was proud of Rudolph in his heart, and beginning to be truly as well as formally sorry for what he had done.

Usually, the passing of the collection box was a significant point for Rudolph in the services. If, as was often the case, he had no money to drop in he would be furiously ashamed and bow his head and pretend not to see the box, lest Jeanne Brady in the pew behind should take notice and suspect an acute family poverty. But to-day he glanced coldly into it as it skimmed under his eyes, noting with casual interest the large number of pennies it contained.

When the bell rang for communion, however, he quivered. There was no reason why God should not stop his heart. During the past twelve hours he had committed a series of mortal sins increasing in gravity, and he was now to crown them all with a blasphemous sacrilege.

"Domini, non sum dignus; ut interes sub tectum meum; sed tantum dic verbo, et sanabitur anima mea. . . ."[8]

There was a rustle in the pews, and the communicants worked their ways into the aisle with downcast eyes and joined hands. Those of larger piety pressed together their finger-tips to form steeples. Among these latter was Carl Miller. Rudolph followed him toward the altar-rail and knelt down, automatically taking up the napkin under his chin. The bell rang sharply, and the priest turned from the altar with the white Host held above the chalice:

"Corpus Domini nostri Jesu Christi custodiat animam meam in vitam æternam."[9]

A cold sweat broke out on Rudolph's forehead as the communion began. Along the line Father Schwartz moved, and with gathering nausea Rudolph felt his heart-valves weakening at the will of God. It seemed to him that the church was darker and that a great quiet had fallen, broken only by the inarticulate mumble which announced the approach of the Creator of Heaven and Earth. He dropped his head down between his shoulders and waited for the blow.

Then he felt a sharp nudge in his side. His father was poking him to sit up, not to slump against the rail; the priest was only two places away.

"Corpus Domini nostri Jesu Christi custodiat animam meam in vitam æternam."

Rudolph opened his mouth. He felt the sticky wax taste of the wafer on his tongue. He remained motionless for what seemed an interminable period of time, his head still raised, the wafer undissolved in his mouth. Then again he started at the pressure of his father's elbow, and saw that the people were falling away from the altar like leaves and turning with blind downcast eyes to their pews, alone with God.

Rudolph was alone with himself, drenched with perspiration and deep in mortal sin. As he walked back to his pew the sharp taps of his cloven hoofs were loud upon the floor, and he knew that it was a dark poison he carried in his heart.

V

"Sagitta Volante in Dei"[10]

The beautiful little boy with eyes like blue stones, and lashes that sprayed open from them like flower-petals had finished telling his sin to Father Schwartz—and the square of sunshine in which he sat had moved forward half an hour into the room. Rudolph had become less frightened now; once eased of the story a reaction had set in. He knew that as long as he was in the room with this priest God would not stop his heart, so he sighed and sat quietly, waiting for the priest to speak.

Father Schwartz's cold watery eyes were fixed upon the carpet pattern on which the sun had brought out the swastikas and the flat bloomless vines and the pale echoes of flowers. The hall-clock ticked insistently toward sunset, and from the ugly room and from the afternoon outside the window arose a stiff monotony, shattered now and then by the reverberate clapping of a far-away hammer on the dry air.

The priest's nerves were strung thin and the beads of his rosary were crawling and squirming like snakes upon the green felt of his table top. He could not remember now what it was he should say.

Of all the things in this lost Swede town he was most aware of this little boy's eyes—the beautiful eyes, with lashes that left them reluctantly and curved back as though to meet them once more.

For a moment longer the silence persisted while Rudolph waited, and the priest struggled to remember something that was slipping farther and farther away from him, and the clock ticked in the broken house. Then Father Schwartz stared hard at the little boy and remarked in a peculiar voice:

"When a lot of people get together in the best places things go glimmering."[11]

Rudolph started and looked quickly at Father Schwartz's face.

"I said—" began the priest, and paused, listening. "Do you hear the hammer and the clock ticking and the bees? Well, that's no good. The thing is to have a lot of people in the centre of the world, wherever that happens to be. Then"—his watery eyes widened knowingly—"things go glimmering."

"Yes, Father," agreed Rudolph, feeling a little frightened.

"What are you going to be when you grow up?"

"Well, I was going to be a baseball-player for a while," answered Rudolph nervously, "but I don't think that's a very good ambition, so I think I'll be an actor or a Navy officer."

Again the priest stared at him.

"I see *exactly* what you mean," he said, with a fierce air.

Rudolph had not meant anything in particular, and at the implication that he had, he became more uneasy.

"This man is crazy," he thought, "and I'm scared of him. He wants me to help him out some way, and I don't want to."

"You look as if things went glimmering," cried Father Schwartz wildly. "Did you ever go to a party?"

"Yes, Father."

"And did you notice that everybody was properly dressed? That's what I mean. Just as you went into the party there was a moment when everybody was properly dressed. Maybe two little girls were standing by the door and some boys were leaning over the banisters, and there were bowls around full of flowers."

"I've been to a lot of parties," said Rudolph, rather relieved that the conversation had taken this turn.

"Of course," continued Father Schwartz triumphantly, "I knew you'd agree with me. But my theory is that when a whole lot of people get together in the best places things go glimmering all the time."

Rudolph found himself thinking of Blatchford Sarnemington.

"Please listen to me!" commanded the priest impatiently. "Stop worrying about last Saturday. Apostasy implies an absolute damnation only on the supposition of a previous perfect faith. Does that fix it?"

Rudolph had not the faintest idea what Father Schwartz was talking about, but he nodded and the priest nodded back at him and returned to his mysterious preoccupation.

"Why," he cried, "they have lights now as big as stars—do you realize that? I heard of one light they had in Paris or somewhere that was as big as a star. A lot of people had it—a lot of gay people. They have all sorts of things now that you never dreamed of.

"Look here—" he came nearer to Rudolph, but the boy drew away, so Father Schwartz went back and sat down in his chair, his eyes dried out and hot. "Did you ever see an amusement park?"

"No, Father."

"Well, go and see an amusement park." The priest waved his hand vaguely. "It's a thing like a fair, only much more glittering. Go to one at night and stand a little way off from it in a dark place—under dark trees. You'll see a big wheel made of lights turning in the air, and a long slide shooting boats down into the water. A band playing somewhere, and a smell of peanuts—and everything will twinkle. But it won't remind you of anything, you see. It will all just hang out there in the night like a colored balloon—like a big yellow lantern on a pole."

Father Schwartz frowned as he suddenly thought of something.

"But don't get up close," he warned Rudolph, "because if you do you'll only feel the heat and the sweat and the life."

All this talking seemed particularly strange and awful to Rudolph, because this man was a priest. He sat there, half terrified, his beautiful eyes open wide and staring at Father Schwartz. But underneath his terror he felt that his own inner convictions were confirmed. There was something ineffably gorgeous somewhere that had nothing to do with God. He no longer thought that God was angry at him about the original lie, because He must have understood that Rudolph had done it to make things finer in the confessional, brightening up the dinginess of his admissions by saying a thing radiant and proud. At the moment when he had affirmed immaculate honor a silver pennon[12] had flapped out into the breeze somewhere and there had been the crunch of leather and the shine of silver spurs and a troop of horsemen waiting for dawn on a low green hill. The sun had made stars of light on their breastplates like the picture at home of the German cuirassiers at Sedan.[13]

But now the priest was muttering inarticulate and heart-broken words, and the boy became wildly afraid. Horror entered suddenly in at the open window, and the atmosphere of the room changed. Father Schwartz collapsed precipitously down on his knees, and let his body settle back against a chair.

"Oh, my God!" he cried out, in a strange voice, and wilted to the floor.

Then a human oppression rose from the priest's worn clothes, and mingled with the faint smell of old food in the corners. Rudolph gave a sharp cry and ran in a panic from the house—while the collapsed man lay there quite still, filling his room, filling it with voices and faces until it was crowded with echolalia, and rang loud with a steady, shrill note of laughter.

Outside the window the blue sirocco trembled over the wheat, and girls with yellow hair walked sensuously along roads that bounded the fields, calling innocent, exciting things to the young men who were working in the lines between the grain. Legs were shaped under starchless gingham, and rims of the necks of dresses were warm and damp. For five hours now hot fertile life had burned in the afternoon. It would be night in three hours, and all along the land there would be these blonde Northern girls and the tall young men from the farms lying out beside the wheat, under the moon.

METROPOLITAN, OCTOBER 1920.

Commentary and Illustrations

From *The American Magazine*, September 1922

F. Scott Fitzgerald (inset shows the author with his wife, Zelda Sayre Fitzgerald).
PHOTO BY BROWN BROS.

Two years ago a certain novel by a new writer was hailed as a work of remarkable talent. The novel was "This Side of Paradise," and the writer was Scott Fitzgerald, then only twenty-three years old. The book was followed by a score of short stories, later published under the title, "Flappers and Philosophers." Last winter a second novel, "The Beautiful and Damned," confirmed the belief that Fitzgerald was a writer of real genius.

He was born in St. Paul, Minnesota, went to preparatory school when he was fifteen, and entered Princeton University two years later. In his senior year he went into the army, where he became a first lieutenant. "This Side of Paradise" was begun while he was in training camp, and was finished in 1919, after he left the army. In 1920 he married Zelda Sayre, of Montgomery, Alabama; and the small picture at the right shows him with his young wife. They have one child, and their home is in St. Paul, where Mr. Fitzgerald was born, and where his parents still live.

FROM *THE AMERICAN MAGAZINE*,

SEPTEMBER 1922

SCOTT FITZGERALD IS THE MOST FAMOUS YOUNG WRITER IN AMERICA TO-DAY. READ HIS ARTICLE IF YOU WANT TO UNDERSTAND YOUTH'S POINT OF VIEW

WHAT I THINK AND FEEL AT 25

For one thing, I do not like old people—They are always talking about their "experience," and very few of them have any!—But it is the old folks that run the world; so they try to hide the fact that only young people are attractive or important

By F. Scott Fitzgerald

Author of "This Side of Paradise," "Flappers and Philosophers," and "The Beautiful and Damned"

The man stopped me on the street. He was ancient, but not a mariner. He had a long beard and a glittering eye. I think he was a friend of the family's, or something.

"Say, Fitzgerald," he said, "say! Will you tell me this: What in the blinkety-blank-blank has a—has a man of your age got to go saying these pessimistic things for? What's the idea?" I tried to laugh him off. He told me that he and my grandfather had been boys together. After that, I had no wish to corrupt him. So I tried to laugh him off.

"Ha-ha-ha!" I said determinedly. "Ha-ha-ha!" And then I added, "Ha-ha! Well, I'll see you later."

With this I attempted to pass him by, but he seized my arm firmly and showed symptoms of spending the afternoon in my company.

"When I was a boy—" he began, and then he drew the picture that people always draw of what excellent, happy, care-free souls they were at twenty-five. That is, he told me all the things he liked to *think* he thought in the misty past.

I allowed him to continue. I even made polite grunts at intervals to express my astonishment. For I will be doing it myself some day. I will concoct for my juniors a Scott Fitzgerald that, it's safe to say, none of my contemporaries would at present recognize. But they will be old themselves then; and they will respect my concoction as I shall respect theirs....

"And now," the happy ancient was concluding; "you are young, you have good health, you have made money, you are exceptionally happily married, you have achieved considerable success while you are still young enough to enjoy it—will you tell an innocent old man just why you write those—"

I succumbed. I would tell him. I began: "Well, you see, sir, it seems to me that as a man gets older he grows more vulner—"

But I got no further. As soon as I began to talk he hurriedly shook my hand and departed. He did not want to listen. He did not care why I thought what I thought. He had simply felt the need of giving a little speech, and I had been the victim. His receding form disappeared with a slight wobble around the next corner.

"All right, you old bore," I muttered; "*don't* listen, then. You wouldn't understand, anyhow." I took an awful kick at a curbstone, as a sort of proxy, and continued my walk.

The Chief Thing I Have Learned So Far

"I might as well declare," says Mr. Fitzgerald, "that the chief thing I've learned so far is: If you don't know much—well, nobody else knows much more. And nobody knows half as much about your own interests as *you* know.

"If you believe in anything very strongly—including yourself—and if you go after that thing alone, you end up in jail, in heaven, in the headlines, or in the largest house in the block, according to what you started after. If you *don't* believe in anything very strongly—including yourself—you go along, and enough money is made out of you to buy an automobile for some other fellow's son, and you marry if you've got time, and if you do, you have a lot of children whether you have time or not, and finally you get tired and you die.

"If you're in the second of those two classes you have the most fun before you're twenty-five. If you're in the first, you have it afterward."

Now, that's the first incident. The second was when a man came to me not long ago from a big newspaper syndicate, and said:

"Mr. Fitzgerald, there's a rumor around New York that you and—ah—you and Mrs. Fitzgerald are going to commit suicide at thirty because you hate and dread middle-age. I want to give you some publicity in this matter by getting it up as a story for the feature sections of five hundred and fourteen Sunday newspapers. In one corner of the page will be—"

"Don't!" I cried, "I know: In one corner will stand the doomed couple, she with an arsenic sundae, he with an Oriental dagger. Both of them will have their eyes fixed on a large clock, on the face of which will be a skull and crossbones. In the other corner will be a big calendar with the date marked in red."

"That's it!" cried the syndicate man enthusiastically. "You've grasped the idea. Now, what we—"

"Listen here!" I said severely. "There is nothing in that rumor. Nothing whatever. When I'm thirty I won't be *this* me—I'll be somebody else. I'll have a different body, because it said so in a book I read once, and I'll have a different attitude on everything. I'll even be married to a different person—"

"Ah!" he interrupted, with an eager light in his eye, and produced a notebook. "That's very interesting."

"No, no, no!" I cried hastily. "I mean my wife will be different."

"I see. You plan a divorce."

"No! I mean—"

"Well, it's all the same. Now, what we want, in order to fill out this story, is a lot of remarks about petting-parties. Do you think the—ah—petting-party is a serious menace to the Constitution? And, just to link it up, can we say that your suicide will be largely on account of past petting-parties?"

"See here!" I interrupted in despair. "Try to understand. I don't know what petting-parties have to do with the question. I have always dreaded age, because it invariably increases the vulner—"

But, as in the case of the family friend, I got no further. The syndicate man grasped my hand firmly. He shook it. Then he muttered something about interviewing a chorus girl who was reported to have an anklet of solid platinum, and hurried off.

That's the second incident. You see, I had managed to tell two different men that "age increased the vulner—" But they had not been interested. The old man had talked about himself and the syndicate man had talked about petting-parties. When I began to talk about the "vulner—" they both had sudden engagements.

So, with one hand on the Eighteenth Amendment and the other hand on the serious part of the Constitution, I have taken an oath that I will tell somebody my story.

As a man grows older it stands to reason that his vulnerability increases. Three years ago, for instance, I could be hurt in only one way—through myself. If my best friend's wife had her hair torn off by an electric washing-machine, I was grieved, of course. I would make my friend a long speech full of "old mans," and finish up with a paragraph from Washington's Farewell Address; but when I'd finished I could go to a good restaurant and enjoy my dinner as usual. If my second cousin's husband had an artery severed while having his nails manicured, I will not deny that it was a matter of considerable regret to me. But when I heard the news I did *not* faint and have to be taken home in a passing laundry wagon.

In fact I was pretty much invulnerable. I put up a conventional wail whenever a ship was sunk or a train got wrecked; but I don't suppose, if the whole city of Chicago had been wiped out, I'd have lost a night's sleep over it—unless something led me to believe that St. Paul was the next city on the list. Even then I could have moved my luggage over to Minneapolis and rested pretty comfortably all night.

But that was three years ago when I was still a young man. I was only twenty-two. When I said anything the book reviewers didn't like, they could say, "Gosh! That certainly is callow!" And that finished me. Label it "callow," and that was enough.

Well, now I'm twenty-five I'm not callow any longer—at least not so that I can notice it when I look in an ordinary mirror. Instead, I'm vulnerable. I'm vulnerable in every way.

For the benefit of revenue agents and moving-picture directors who may be reading this magazine I will explain that vulnerable means easily wounded. Well, that's it. I'm more easily wounded. I can not only be wounded in the chest, the feelings, the teeth, the bank account; but I can be wounded in the *dog*. Do I make myself clear? In the dog.

No, that isn't a new part of the body just discovered by the Rockefeller Institute. I mean a real dog. I mean if anyone gives my family dog to the dog-catcher he's hurting *me* almost as much as he's hurting the dog. He's hurting me *in* the dog. And if our doctor says to me tomorrow, "That child of yours isn't going to be a blonde after all," well, he's wounded me in a way I couldn't have been wounded in before, because I never before had a child to be wounded in. And if my daughter grows up and when she's sixteen elopes with some fellow from Zion City who believes the world is flat—I wouldn't write this except that she's only six months old and can't quite read yet, so it won't put any ideas in her head—why, then I'll be wounded again.

About being wounded through your wife I will not enter into, as it is a delicate subject. I will not say anything about my case. But I have private reasons for knowing that if anybody said to your wife one day that it was a shame she *would* wear yellow when it made her look so peaked, you would suffer violently, within six hours afterward, for what that person said.

"Attack him through his wife!" "Kidnap his child!" "Tie a tin can to his dog's tail!" How often do we hear those slogans in life, not to mention in the movies. And how they make me wince! Three years ago, you could have yelled them outside my window all through a summer night, and I wouldn't have batted an eye. The only thing that would have aroused me would have been: "Wait a minute. I think I can pot him from here."

I used to have about ten square feet of skin vulnerable to chills and fevers. Now I have about twenty. I have not personally enlarged—the twenty feet includes the skin of my family—but I might as well have, because if a chill or fever strikes any bit of that twenty feet of skin *I* begin to shiver.

And so I ooze gently into middle-age; for the true middle-age is not the acquirement of years, but the acquirement of a family. The incomes of the childless have wonderful elasticity. Two people require a room and a bath; couple with child require the millionaire's suite on the sunny side of the hotel.

So let me start the religious part of this article by saying that if the Editor thought he was going to get something young and happy—yes, and callow—I have got to refer him to my daughter, if she will give dictation. If anybody thinks that I am callow they ought to see her—she's so callow it makes me laugh. It even makes her laugh, too, to think how callow she is. If any literary critics saw her they'd have a nervous breakdown right on the spot. But, on the other hand, anybody writing to me, an editor or anybody else, is writing to a middle-aged man.

Well, I'm twenty-five, and I have to admit that I'm pretty well satisfied with *some* of that time. That is to say, the first five years seemed to go all right—but the last twenty! They have been a matter of violently contrasted extremes. In fact, this has struck me so forcibly that from time to time I have kept charts, trying to figure out the years when I was closest to happy. Then I get mad and tear up the charts.

Skipping that long list of mistakes which passes for my boyhood I will say that I went away to preparatory school at fifteen, and that my two years there were wasted, were years of utter and profitless unhappiness. I was unhappy because I was cast into a situation where everybody thought I ought to behave just as they behaved—and I didn't have the courage to shut up and go my own way, anyhow.

For example, there was a rather dull boy at school named Percy, whose approval, I felt, for some unfathomable reason, I must have. So, for the sake of this negligible cipher, I started out to let as much of my mind as I had under mild cultivation sink back into a state of heavy underbrush. I spent hours in a damp gymnasium fooling around with a muggy basket-ball and working myself into a damp, muggy rage, when I wanted, instead, to go walking in the country.

And all this to please Percy. He thought it was the thing to do. If you didn't go through the damp business every day you were "morbid." That was his favorite word, and it had me frightened. I didn't want to be morbid. So I became muggy instead.

Besides, Percy was dull in classes; so I used to pretend to be dull also. When I wrote stories I wrote them secretly, and felt like a criminal. If I gave birth to any idea that did not appeal to Percy's pleasant, vacant mind I discarded the idea at once and felt like apologizing.

Of course Percy never got into college. He went to work and I have scarcely seen him since, though I understand that he has since become an undertaker of considerable standing. The time I spent with him was wasted; but, worse than that, I did not enjoy the wasting of it. At least, he had nothing to give me, and I had not the faintest reasons for caring what he thought or said. But when I discovered this it was too late.

The worst of it is that this same business went on until I was twenty-two. That is, I'd be perfectly happy doing just what I wanted to do, when somebody would begin shaking his head and saying:

"Now see here, Fitzgerald, you mustn't go on doing that. It's—it's morbid."

And I was always properly awed by the word "morbid," so I quit what I wanted to do and what it was good for me to do, and did what some other fellow wanted me to do. Every once in a while, though, I used to tell somebody to go to the devil; otherwise I never would have done anything at all.

In officers' training camp during 1917 I started to write a novel. I would begin work at it every Saturday afternoon at one and work like mad until midnight. Then I would work at it from six Sunday morning until six Sunday night, when I had to report back to barracks. I was thoroughly enjoying myself.

After a month three friends came to me with scowling faces:

"See here, Fitzgerald, you ought to use the week-ends in getting some good rest and recreation. The way you use them is—is morbid!"

That word convinced me. It sent the usual shiver down my spine. The next week-end I laid the novel aside, went into town with the others and danced all night at a party. But I began to worry about my novel. I worried so much that I returned to camp, not rested, but utterly miserable. I *was* morbid then. But I never went to town again. I finished the novel. It was rejected; but a year later I rewrote it and it was published under the title, "This Side of Paradise."

But before I rewrote it I had a list of "morbids," chalked up against people that, placed end to end, would have reached to the nearest lunatic asylum. It was morbid:

1st. To get engaged without enough money to marry
2d. To leave the advertising business after three months
3d. To want to write at all
4th. To think I could
5th. To write about "silly little boys and girls that nobody wants to read about"

And so on, until a year later, when I found to my surprise that everybody had been only kidding—they had believed all their lives that writing was the only thing for me, and had hardly been able to keep from telling me all the time.

But I am really not old enough to begin drawing morals out of my own life to elevate the young. I will save that pastime until I am sixty; and then, as I have said, I will concoct a Scott Fitzgerald who will make Benjamin Franklin look like a lucky devil who loafed into prominence. Even in the above account I have managed to sketch the outline of a small but neat halo. I take it all back. I am twenty-five years old. I wish I had ten million dollars, and never had to do another lick of work as long as I live.

But as I *do* have to keep at it, I might as well declare that the chief thing I've learned so far is: If you don't know much—well, nobody else knows much more. And nobody knows half as much about your own interests as *you* know.

If you believe in anything very strongly—including yourself—and if you go after that thing alone, you end up in jail, in heaven, in the headlines, or in the largest house in the block, according to what you started after. If you *don't* believe in anything very strongly—including yourself—you go along, and enough money is made out of you to buy an automobile for some other fellow's son, and you marry if you've got time, and if you do you have a lot of children, whether you have time or not, and finally you get tired and you die.

If you're in the second of those two classes you have the most fun before you're twenty-five. If you're in the first, you have it afterward.

You see, if you're in the first class you'll frequently be called a darn fool—or worse. That was as true in Philadelphia about 1727 as it is to-day. Anybody knows that a kid that walked around town munching a loaf of bread and not caring what anybody thought was a darn fool. It stands to reason! But there are a lot of darn fools who get their pictures in the schoolbooks—with their names under the pictures. And the sensible fellows, the ones that had time to laugh, well, their pictures are in there, too. But their *names* aren't—and the laughs look sort of frozen on their faces.

The particular sort of darn fool I mean ought to remember that he's *least* a darn fool when he's being *called* a darn fool. The main thing is to be your own kind of a darn fool.

(The above advice is of course only for darn fools *under* twenty-five. It may be all wrong for darn fools over twenty-five.)

I don't know why it is that when I start to write about being twenty-five I suddenly begin to write about darn fools. I do not see any connection. Now, if I were asked to write about darn fools, I would write about people who have their front teeth filled with gold, because a friend of mine did that the other day, and after being mistaken for a jewelry store three times in one hour he came up and asked me if I thought it showed too much. As I am a kind man, I told him I would not have noticed it if the sun hadn't been so strong on it. I asked him why he had it done.

"Well," he said, "the dentist told me a porcelain filling never lasted more than ten years."

"Ten years! Why, you may be dead in ten years."

"That's true."

"Of course it'll be nice that all the time you're in your coffin you'll never have to worry about your teeth."

And it occurred to me that about half the people in the world are always having their front teeth filled with gold. That is, they're figuring on twenty years from now. Well, when you're young it's all right figuring your success a long ways ahead—if you don't make it *too* long. But as for your pleasure—your front teeth!—it's better to figure on to-day.

And that's the second thing I learned while getting vulnerable and middle-aged. Let me recapitulate:

1st. I think that compared to what you know about your own business nobody else knows *any*thing. And if anybody knows more about it than you do, then it's *his* business and you're *his* man, not your own. And as soon as your business becomes *your* business you'll know more about it than anybody else.

2d. Never have your front teeth filled with gold.

And now I will stop pretending to be a pleasant young fellow and disclose my real nature. I will prove to you, if you have not found it out already, that I have a mean streak and nobody would like to have me for a son.

I do not like old people. They are always talking about their "experience"—and very few of them have any. In fact, most of them go on making the same mistakes at fifty and believing in the same white list of approved twenty-carat lies that they did at seventeen. And it all starts with my old friend vulnerability.

Take a woman of thirty. She is considered lucky if she has allied herself to a multitude of things; her husband, her children, her home, her servant. If she has three homes, eight children, and fourteen servants, she is considered luckier still. (This, of course, does not generally apply to more husbands).

Now, when she was young she worried only about herself; but now she must be worried by *any* trouble occurring to *any* of these people or things. She is ten times as vulnerable. Moreover, she can never break one of these ties or relieve herself of one of these burdens except at the cost of great pain and sorrow to herself. They are the things that break her, and yet they are the most precious things in life.

In consequence, everything which doesn't go to make her secure, or at least to give her a sense of security, startles and annoys her. She acquires only the useless knowledge found in cheap movies, cheap novels, and the cheap memoirs of titled foreigners.

By this time her husband also has become suspicious of anything gay or new. He seldom addresses her, except in a series of profound grunts, or to ask whether she has sent his shirts out to the laundry. At the family dinner on Sunday he occasionally gives her some fascinating statistics on party politics, some opinions from that morning's newspaper editorial.

But after thirty, both husband and wife know in their hearts that the game is up. Without a few cocktails social intercourse becomes a torment. It is no longer spontaneous; it is a convention by which they agree to shut their eyes to the fact that the other men and women they know are tired and dull and fat, and yet must be put up with as politely as they themselves are put up with in their turn.

I have seen many happy young couples—but I have seldom seen a happy home after husband and wife are thirty. Most homes can be divided into four classes:

1st. Where the husband is a pretty conceited guy who thinks that a dinky insurance business is a lot harder than raising babies, and that everybody ought to kow-tow to him at home. He is the kind whose sons usually get away from home as soon as they can walk.

2d. When the wife has got a sharp tongue and the martyr complex, and thinks she's the only woman in the world that ever had a child. This is probably the unhappiest home of all.

3d. Where the children are always being reminded how nice it was of the parents to bring them into the world, and how they ought to respect their parents for being born in 1870 instead of 1902.

4th. Where everything is for the children. Where the parents pay much more for the children's education than they can afford, and spoil them unreasonably. This usually ends by the children being ashamed of the parents.

And yet I think that marriage is the most satisfactory institution we have. I'm simply stating my belief that when Life has used us for its purposes it takes away all our attractive qualities and gives us, instead, ponderous but shallow convictions of our own wisdom and "experience."

Needless to say, as old people run the world, an enormous camouflage has been built up to hide the fact that only young people are attractive or important.

Having got in wrong with many of the readers of this article, I will now proceed to close. If you don't agree with me on any minor points you have a right to say: "Gosh! He certainly is callow!" and turn to something else. Personally I do not consider that I am callow, because I do not see how anybody of my age could be callow. For instance, I was reading an article in this magazine a few months ago by a fellow named Ring Lardner that says he is thirty-five, and it seemed to me how young and happy and care-free he was in comparison with me.

Maybe he is vulnerable, too. He did not say so. Maybe when you get to be thirty-five you do not *know* any more how vulnerable you *are*. All I can say is that if he ever gets to be twenty-five again, which is very unlikely, maybe he will agree with me. The older I grow the more I get so I don't know anything. If I had been asked to do this article about five years ago it might have been worth reading.

"Bob It"

F. Scott Fitzgerald's story "Bernice Bobs Her Hair," illustrated here by May Wilson Preston, was published in *The Saturday Evening Post*, May 1, 1920.

"Is it a Proposal of Marriage? Extra! Ardita Farnam Becomes Pirate's Bride. Society Girl Kidnapped by Ragtime Bank Robber."

F. Scott Fitzgerald's story "The Offshore Pirate," illustrated by Leslie L. Benson, was published in *The Saturday Evening Post*, May 29, 1920.

From *Shadowland*,
January 1921

Fitzgerald, Flappers and Fame

An Interview with F. Scott Fitzgerald

By Frederick James Smith

F. Scott Fitzgerald is the recognized spokesman of the younger generation—the dancing, flirting, frivoling, lightly philosophizing young America—since the publication of his now famous flapper tale, "This Side of Paradise." Perhaps our elders were surprised to discover, as Mr. Fitzgerald relates, that the young folk, particularly the so-called gentler sex, were observing religion and morals slightly flippantly, that they had their own views on ethics, that they said damn and gotta and whatta and 'sall, that older viewpoints bored them and that they both smoked cigarets and admitted they were "just full of the devil."

All of which *is* the younger generation as Fitzgerald sees it. Indeed, the blond and youthful Fitzgerald, still in his twenties, is of, and a part of, it. He left Princeton in the class of '17 and, like certain young America, slipped into the world war *via* the training camp and an officership. We suspect he did it, much as the questioning hero of "This Side of Paradise," because "it was the thing to do." He was a lieutenant in the 45th Infantry and later an aide to Brigadier General Ryan. It was in training camp that he first drafted "This Side of Paradise."

"We all knew, of course, we were going to be killed," relates Fitzgerald with a smile, "and I, like everybody else, wanted to leave something for posterity." But the war ended and Fitzgerald tried writing advertising with a New York commercial firm. All the time he was endeavoring to write short stories and sell them, but every effort came back with a rejection slip. Finally, Fitzgerald resolved upon a desperate step. He would go back to his home in St. Paul and live a year with his parents, aiming consistently to "get over."

Then he sold his first story to *Smart Set* in June, 1918, receiving thirty dollars therefrom. He worked for three months rewriting "This

Side of Paradise"—and sold it to Scribner's. Success came with a bang and now Fitzgerald is contributing to most of the leading magazines. At the present moment he is completing his second novel, to be ready shortly.

"I realize that 'This Side of Paradise' was immature and callow, just as such critics as H. L. Mencken and others have said, altho they were kind enough to say I had possibilities. My new novel will, I hope, be more mature. It will be the story of two young married folk and it will show their gradual disintegration—broadly speaking, how they go to the devil. I have one ideal—to write honestly, as I see it.

"Of course, I know the sort of young folks I depict *are* as I paint them. I'm sick of the sexless animals writers have been giving us. I am tired, too, of hearing that the world war broke down the moral barriers of the younger generation. Indeed, except for leaving its touch of destruction here and there, I do not think the war left any real lasting effect. Why, it is almost forgotten right now.

"The younger generation has been changing all thru the last twenty years. The war had little or nothing to do with it. I put the change up to literature. Our skepticism or cynicism, if you wish to call it that, or, if you are older, our callow flippancy, is due to the way H. G. Wells and other intellectual leaders have been thinking and reflecting life. Our generation has grown up upon their work. So college-bred young people, here and in England, have made radical departures from the Victorian era.

"Girls, for instance, have found the accent shifted from chemical purity to breadth of viewpoint, intellectual charm and piquant cleverness. It is natural that they want to be interesting. And there is one fact that the younger generation could not overlook. All, or nearly all, the famous men and women of history—the kind who left a lasting mark—were, let us say, of broad moral views. Our generation has absorbed all this. Thus it is that we find the young woman of 1920 flirting, kissing; viewing life lightly, saying damn without a blush, playing along the danger line in an immature way—a sort of mental baby vamp. It is quite the same with the boys. They want to be like the interesting chaps they read about. Yes, I put it all up to the intellectuals like Wells.

"Personally, I prefer this sort of girl. Indeed, I married the heroine of my stories. I would not be interested in any other sort of woman."

We asked Fitzgerald about motion pictures. "I used to try scenarios in the old days," he laughed. "Invariably they came back. Now, however, I am being adapted to the screen. I suspect it must be difficult to mold my stuff into the conventional movie form with its creaky mid-Victorian sugar. Personally, when I go to the pictures, I like to see a pleasant flapper like Constance Talmadge or I want to see comedies like those of Chaplin's or Lloyd's. I'm not strong for the uplift stuff. It simply isn't life to me."

From *Metropolitan* Magazine, June 1922

Eulogy on the Flapper

By Zelda Sayre Fitzgerald

The Flapper is deceased. Her outer accoutrements have been bequeathed to several hundred girls' schools throughout the country, to several thousand big-town shop-girls, always imitative of the several hundred girls' schools, and to several million small-town belles always imitative of the big-town shop-girls via the "novelty stores" of their respective small towns. It is a great bereavement to me, thinking as I do that there will never be another product of circumstance to take the place of the dear departed.

I am assuming that the Flapper will live by her accomplishments and not by her Flapping. How can a girl say again, "I do not want to be respectable because respectable girls are not attractive," and how can she again so wisely arrive at the knowledge that "boys *do* dance most with the girls they kiss most," and that "men *will* marry the girls they could kiss before they had asked papa?" Perceiving these things, the Flapper awoke from her lethargy of subdeb-ism, bobbed her hair, put on her choicest pair of earrings and a great deal of audacity and rouge and went into the battle. She flirted because it was fun to flirt and wore a one-piece bathing suit because she had a good figure, she covered her face with powder and paint because she didn't need it and she refused to be bored chiefly because she wasn't boring. She was conscious that the things she did were the things she had always wanted to do. Mothers disapproved of their sons taking the Flapper to dances, to teas, to swim and most of all to heart. She had mostly masculine friends, but youth does not need friends—it needs only crowds, and the more masculine the crowds the more crowded for the Flapper. Of these things the Flapper was well aware!

Now audacity and earrings and one-piece bathing suits have become fashionable and the first Flappers are so secure in their positions

Houston Public Library
Check Out Summary

Title: Complete short stories of Ernest Hemingway : the
Call number: PAPERBACK CLASSIC
Item ID: 33477456597711
Date due: 6/4/2019,23:59

Title: Beowulf. English & English (Old English)
Call number: PAPERBACK CLASSIC
Item ID: 33477478213805
Date due: 6/4/2019,23:59

Title: The best early stories of F. Scott Fitzgerald
Call number: PAPERBACK CLASSIC
Item ID: 33477456473250
Date due: 6/4/2019,23:59

that their attitude toward themselves is scarcely distinguishable from that of their débutante sisters of ten years ago toward *themselves.* They have won their case. They are blasé. And the new Flappers galumping along in unfastened galoshes are striving not to do what is pleasant and what they please, but simply to outdo the founders of the Honorable Order of Flappers; to outdo *everything.* Flapperdom has become a game; it is no longer a philosophy.

I came across an amazing editorial a short time ago. It fixed the blame for all divorces, crime waves, high prices, unjust taxes, violations of the Volstead Act and crimes in Hollywood upon the head of the Flapper. The paper wanted back the dear old fireside of long ago, wanted to resuscitate "Hearts and Flowers" and have it instituted as the sole tune played at dances from now on and forever, wanted prayers before breakfast on Sunday morning—and to bring things back to this superb state it advocated restraining the Flapper. All neurotic "women of thirty" and all divorce cases, according to the paper, could be traced to the Flapper. As a matter of fact, she hasn't yet been given a chance. I know of no divorcées or neurotic women of thirty who were ever Flappers. Do you? And I should think that fully airing the desire for unadulterated gaiety, for romances that she knows will not last, and for dramatizing herself would make her more inclined to favor the "back to the fireside" movement than if she were repressed until age gives her those rights that only youth has the right to give.

I refer to the right to experiment with herself as a transient, poignant figure who will be dead tomorrow. Women, despite the fact that nine out of ten of them go through life with a death-bed air either of snatching-the-last-moment or with martyr-resignation, do not die tomorrow—or the next day. They have to live on to any one of many bitter ends, and I should think the sooner they learned that things weren't going to be over until they were too tired to care, the quicker the divorce court's popularity would decline.

"Out with inhibitions," gleefully shouts the Flapper, and elopes with the Arrow-collar boy that she had been thinking, for a week or two, might make a charming breakfast companion. The marriage is annulled by the proverbial irate parent and the Flapper comes home, none the worse for wear, to marry, years later, and live happily ever afterwards.

I see no logical reasons for keeping the young illusioned. Certainly disillusionment comes easier at twenty than at forty—the fundamental and inevitable disillusionments, I mean. Its effects on the Flappers I have known have simply been to crystallize their ambitious desires and give form to their code of living so that they *can* come home and live happily ever afterwards—or go into the movies or become social service "workers" or something. Older people, except a few geniuses, artistic and financial, simply throw up their hands, heave a great many heart-rending sighs and moan to themselves something about what a hard thing life is—and then, of course, turn to their children and wonder why they don't believe in Santa Claus and the kindness of their fellow men and in the tale that they will be happy if they are good and obedient. And yet the strongest cry against Flapperdom is that it is making the youth of the country cynical. It is making them intelligent and teaching them to capitalize their natural resources and get their money's worth. They are merely applying business methods to being young.

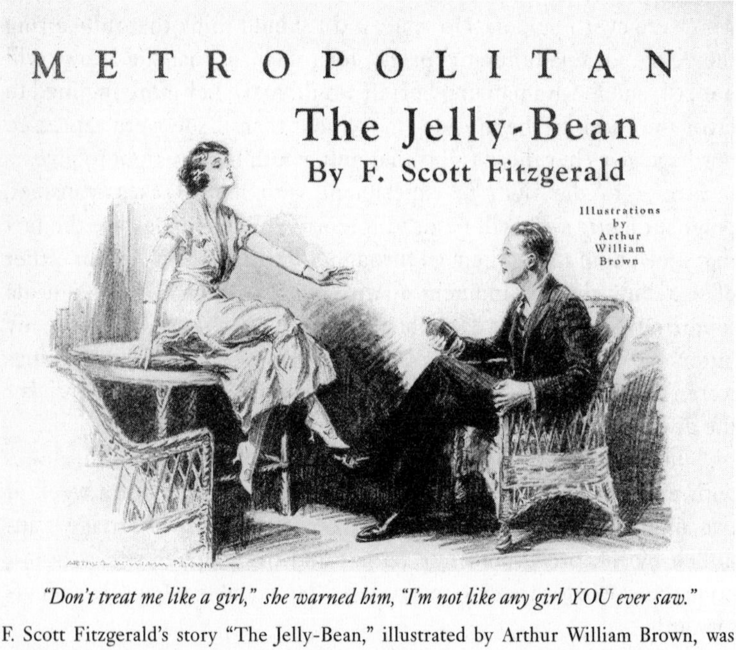

"Don't treat me like a girl," she warned him, "I'm not like any girl YOU ever saw."

F. Scott Fitzgerald's story "The Jelly-Bean," illustrated by Arthur William Brown, was published in *Metropolitan* magazine, October 1920.

Notes

Benediction

"Benediction" has its origins in an early story, "The Ordeal" (June 1915, *The Nassau Literary Magazine*), which Fitzgerald wrote and published as an undergraduate at Princeton, following a visit with his Jesuit-priest cousin and during a time when his association with Father Sigourney Webster Fay and Shane Leslie had led him to consider entering the priesthood. In "The Ordeal" a novice priest struggles with forces pulling him, on the one hand, toward the outside world and its sensual pleasures and, on the other, toward the vows of the priesthood and the ascetic life of the church. In reworking this story that would become "Benediction," Fitzgerald adds a female character, Lois, who does not appear in "The Ordeal," and shifts the spiritual crisis onto her. *The Smart Set* bought "Benediction" for $40 and published it in the February 1920 issue. With nineteen-year-old Lois in "Benediction" he introduces a forerunner of the "very romantic and curious and courageous" flapper who, as he explains in a later story, "is tendered the subtle compliment of being referred to by her [first] name alone." Fitzgerald included "Benediction" in his first story collection, *Flappers and Philosophers* (1920), which *The Smart Set* would review, singling out "Benediction" as the best story in the collection.

1. *thick volumes of Thomas Aquinas and Henry James and Cardinal Mercier and Immanuel Kant:* The volumes carried by the middle-aged monks suggest erudition and broad interests that extend across time (from the thirteenth through the twentieth centuries) and beyond church doctrine (Aquinas and Mercier) into fiction (James) and philosophy (Kant).

2. *the Society of Jesus, founded in Spain five hundred years before by a tough-minded soldier:* the Jesuits, founded by St. Ignatius Loyola (1491–1556).
3. *Farmington:* Miss Porter's School founded by Sarah Porter in 1843 and located in Farmington, Connecticut.
4. *the Jesuit College in Philadelphia:* likely referring to St. Joseph's College, the seventh oldest Jesuit college in America, founded in 1851.
5. *shimmys . . . maxixe:* Both the shimmy and the maxixe (pronounced max-ish) were popular American dances in the 1910s and '20s, but both have origins in other cultures. The shimmy is thought to have its origins in the Haitian voodoo dances, and in all of its various incarnations it has been a shoulder-shaking dance, while the maxixe originated in the Brazilian tango and emphasizes movement of the feet rather than the torso.
6. *Benediction:* The Benediction of the Blessed Sacrament is a complete rite, during which the Blessed Sacrament is exposed or displayed in a vessel, often ornate, called a monstrance. "O Salutaris Hostia" (literally "O Saving Host") is the second-to-last stanza of a hymn written by St. Thomas Aquinas, and it accompanies the Benediction rite.
7. *St. Francis Xavier:* a founding member of the Society of Jesus and canonized in the same year as the Society's primary founder, St. Ignatius Loyola. A converter of infidels, St. Francis Xavier is remembered as perhaps the greatest missionary since the era of the apostles.
8. *pietà, a life-size statue of the Blessed Virgin set within a semicircle of rocks:* A pietà is a representation of Mary mourning over the dead body of Jesus.

Head and Shoulders

Fitzgerald wrote "Head and Shoulders" (originally called "Nest Feathers") in November 1919 during what was, to him in retrospect, the most exciting period of his life. Harold Ober, who had in this same month become responsible for the marketing of Fitzgerald's stories at the Paul Revere Reynolds agency, sold "Head and Shoulders" for $400 to *The Saturday Evening Post.* This was nearly three times the amount Fitzgerald had received for any story he had sold thus far, and its appearance in the February 21, 1920, issue became Fitzgerald's first publication in a mass-circulation magazine: while he had previously published three stories in *The Smart Set,* its circulation was just above twenty thousand; the *Post*'s weekly audience was over two million. As he wrote about this to Ober in 1925, just months before the publication of *The Great Gatsby,* "I was twenty-two when I came to New York and found that you'd sold Head and Shoulders to the Post. I'd like to get a thrill like that again but I suppose its only once in a lifetime." From strictly a financial standpoint, the money that came from the sale of "Head and Shoulders" when coupled with the acceptance of his first novel, *This Side of Paradise,* enabled Fitzgerald to resume his courtship with the woman soon to become his wife, Zelda Sayre, who had called off their engagement until Fitzgerald could prove he was able to support her. "Head and Shoulders" marked the introduction of the flapper to middle America and in the process installed Fitzgerald as the flapper's historian, the chronicler of the Jazz Age in fiction. The appetite that "Head and Shoulders" created in the popular American magazine audience would prompt the *Post* to publish five more of his flapper stories (one of which, "The Ice Palace," introduced the combination of the flapper and Southern belle) in 1920 alone. Fitzgerald selected "Head and Shoulders" for inclusion in *Flappers and Philosophers,* placing it third after "The Offshore Pirate" and "The Ice Palace."

1. *George M. Cohan:* George M. Cohan (1878–1942), American actor, playwright, director, composer. The 1917 song "Over There" won him a Congressional medal.
2. *Château-Thierry:* French village where French and American troops halted the German advance into France in a July 1918 battle.
3. *"Spinoza's Improvement of the Understanding":* Baruch Spinoza (1632–77), Dutch philosopher, author of *Treatise on the Improvement of the Understanding.*
4. *"Home James":* 1917 Varsity Show at Columbia University, written by Oscar Hammerstein and Herman Axelrod.
5. *Blundering Blimp:* Song in Fitzgerald's play *Porcelain and Pink,* as published in *The Smart Set* in January 1920, has the lines, "As you blunder blindly, kindly through / The blinking, winking Blimp!"
6. *Pall Malls:* popular cigarette made by American Tobacco Company.
7. *Sheffield:* school for engineering and science at Yale.
8. *Berkeley:* George Berkeley (1685–1753), Irish bishop and philosopher.
9. *Hume:* David Hume (1711–76), Scottish philosopher.
10. *Omar Khayyam: Rubáiyát of Omar Khayyám,* poem attributed to the Persian scholar Omar Khayyám, who died circa 1123.
11. *ten-twenty-thirty:* vaudeville circuit where tickets cost ten, twenty, or thirty cents.
12. *Florodora Sextette:* performers in the long-running musical *Florodora,* which opened in New York in 1900. A group of six women and six men in the show sang the hit song "Tell Me Pretty Maiden."
13. *Mrs. Sol Smith's:* Sol Smith (1801–69), theater manager, ran a traveling show in the West and South in the 1830s and '40s.
14. *little Boston boy in the comic magazines:* perhaps a reference to Buster Brown, cartoon created by Richard Outcault.
15. *Uncle Remus:* narrator in Southern black folktales retold by Joel Chandler Harris (1848–1908). Uncle Remus, a slave, tells his master's children about Brer Rabbit's escapades.

16. *Catullus:* Gaius Valerius Catullus (84–54 B.C.), Roman poet.
17. *with Bergsonian trimmings:* Henri Bergson (1859–1941), French philosopher. His lectures on "Creative Evolution" before World War I were popular with American visitors in Paris.
18. *"The Bohemian Girl":* 1843 opera by Irish composer Michael Balfe (1808–70).
19. *Hammerstein:* Oscar Hammerstein (1895–1960), American composer. He wrote "Home James!" (*see note 4 above*). Hammerstein's father and brother also had careers in musical theater.
20. *shimmy:* shoulder-shaking dance. (*See note 5 to "Benediction."*)
21. *Carlyle's:* Thomas Carlyle (1795–1881), Scottish essayist and historian.
22. *St. Vitus dance:* A form of chorea occurring usually in children. Patients have involuntary, jerky muscular spasms.
23. *Kipling:* Rudyard Kipling (1865–1936), English writer, author of *Kim, The Jungle Book,* and *Captains Courageous.*
24. *O. Henry:* pseudonym of William Sydney Porter (1862–1910), popular short-story writer known for surprise endings.
25. *Herb Spencer:* Herbert Spencer (1820–1903), English philosopher.
26. *"Pepys' Diary":* Samuel Pepys (1633–1703), English diarist and naval historian. His diary, written between 1660 and 1669, gives a vivid account of life in seventeenth-century England.
27. "Mens sana in corpore sano": Latin for "A healthy mind in a healthy body."
28. *fourth proposition of Euclid:* Euclid, Greek mathematician, circa 300 B.C. In the thirteen books of the *Elements* he set forth geometric postulates and proofs. In the *Data* he made ninety-four propositions proving that if certain elements in a figure are given, the other elements can be determined.
29. quod erat demonstrandum: Latin for "which was to be demonstrated."
30. *Prometheus:* In Greek mythology Prometheus defended men from Zeus and gave them fire from heaven. Zeus punished him by chaining him to a rock where eagles ate his liver. Each night the liver grew back and it was eaten again by the eagles. He was rescued generations later by Hercules.
31. *Isaac Newton:* Isaac Newton (1642–1727), English scientist known for setting forth the laws of gravity.
32. *Hippodrome:* Manhattan theater at Sixth Avenue and 43rd Street featuring circuses and other spectacles.
33. *Schopenhauer:* Arthur Schopenhauer (1788–1860), German philosopher.
34. *William James pragmatism:* William James (1842–1910), American philosopher.

The Ice Palace

Fitzgerald wrote "The Ice Palace" in December 1919, shortly after a return visit to Montgomery, Alabama, where he had been stationed during the war and where, in July 1918, he had first met Zelda Sayre at a country club dance. In an article that appeared in a 1920 issue of *The Editor,* he describes the story as having been prompted by a recent visit with a girl to a Confederate graveyard in Montgomery: "She told me I could never understand how she felt about the Confederate graves, and I told her I understood so well that I could put it on paper." Back in Minnesota, the image of the graveyard was paired in Fitzgerald's mind by way of contrast with images of the St. Paul ice palaces of the 1880s that his mother had described to him earlier. The two images came together, as Fitzgerald put it, "as all one story—the contrast between Alabama and Minnesota," which embodies the North-South conflict at the heart of "The Ice Palace." The story is the first of what has come to be known as Fitzgerald's Tarleton Trilogy—three stories, "The Ice Palace," "The Jelly-Bean," and "The Last of the Belles," all reflecting Fitzgerald's complex and ambiguous feelings about the South—set in "a little city of forty thousand," clearly a thinly veiled Montgomery. The story of Sally Carrol Happer's relationship with Harry Bellamy in "The Ice Palace" is an autobiographical version with an alternate ending of Scott Fitzgerald's courtship with Zelda Sayre. Sally Carrol Happer's legacy in the story is, first, that of the Southern belle, embodied in the character of Margery Lee, whom Sally Carrol so admires; but she is also a free, independent spirit with the glitter and sparkle of Fitzgerald's most memorable flappers before and after her. Fitzgerald included "The Ice Palace" as the second story in *Flappers and Philosophers.*

1. *"Then blow, ye winds, heigho! A-roving I will go":* These lines are from "A Capital Ship," by Charles E. Carryl (1841–1920). Carryl's popular song incorporates the old sea song "Ten Thousand Miles Away."
2. *Carmen from the South . . . Dangerous Dan McGrew:* Roger lightheartedly compares Sally Carrol to the free-spirited and ill-fated heroine of Georges Bizet's last and most famous opera, *Carmen* (1875), set in the south of Spain; Dangerous Dan McGrew, from the ballad "The Shooting of Dan McGrew" by Robert William Service (1874–1958).
3. *Ever read any Ibsen?:* referring to Henrik Ibsen (1828–1906), the great Norwegian playwright, whose work often deals with individuals, both women and men, struggling against society. Later in the story Roger finds Sally Carrol, who had read no Ibsen when he earlier asked the question, reading Ibsen's verse drama about the Norwegian folk hero Peer Gynt (*Peer Gynt,* 1867).
4. *the Serbia in the case:* The incident that sparked World War I was the assassination in 1914 of Archduke Ferdinand in Sarajevo by Serbian nationalists, an act which ultimately led to Austria-Hungary's declaration of war on Serbia.

5. *the ice palace:* Ice palaces have a long history, dating back to eighteenth-century Russia. The first ice palace in St. Paul was built for the Winter Carnival of 1886, an event postponed because of an outbreak of smallpox. Ice palaces were then built again in 1887 and 1888, though those planned for 1889 and 1890 were not built because the weather did not cooperate. In 1896, the year of Fitzgerald's birth, ice structures on a smaller scale, called ice forts, were constructed, as they were in 1916 and 1917. The next ice palace to be built after the magnificent one of 1888 was in 1937, and it consisted of enormous screens, forts, and backdrops. Fitzgerald reports that he drew on a sketch of an ice palace of the 1880s, found in a newspaper of the period, for his conception of the ice palace in the story.
6. *"Kubla Khan"... "caves of ice!":* the famous poem fragment by Samuel Taylor Coleridge (1772–1834) and its first two lines.
7. *Wacouta Club:* One of a number of winter sports clubs in St. Paul, the Wacouta Club was established in 1885.

Bernice Bobs Her Hair

The idea for "Bernice Bobs Her Hair" originated in a ten-page letter (circa 1916) that Fitzgerald wrote to his sister Annabel when he was nineteen and she fourteen. He instructed her in great detail in the areas of "Conversation," "Poise," and "Dress and Personality" as to how she could become a social success. The story that grew out of this letter was written in January 1920, and it was originally a ten-thousand-word story called "Barbara Bobs Her Hair." After four magazines rejected it, Fitzgerald shortened it to seven thousand words, altered its climax (making it in his words "snappy"), and Ober sold it for $500 to *The Saturday Evening Post* with its new title, "Bernice Bobs Her Hair." Written in the same month as "The Camel's Back," the story was published in the May 1, 1920, issue and was Fitzgerald's fourth contribution to the magazine. Bernice fits in to the category of what Fitzgerald called the "wonderful kid," a young woman of about sixteen who is on her way toward free-spiritedness and liberation, the variety of flapper that Bernice has become by the time of the story's unexpected turn. With her last gesture in the story Bernice signals her independence from the social hypocrisy of her cousin's world, though ironically it is the precise world into which Fitzgerald had earlier given his sister the rules of entry. Fitzgerald included "Bernice Bobs Her Hair" in *Flappers and Philosophers.*

1. *Hill School:* boys' prep school in Pottstown, Pennsylvania.
2. *Hiram Johnson:* A founder of the Progressive Party, Hiram Johnson served as governor of California (1911–17), then as a U.S. senator until his death

in 1945. He opposed America's entry into World War I, as well as its joining the League of Nations and the World Court.

3. *Ty Cobb:* outstanding baseball player who played for the Detroit Tigers (1905–26) and then the Philadelphia Athletics, retiring in 1928. He led the league in batting from 1907 to 1915 and 1917 to 1919. His lifetime batting average was .367.
4. *red penny:* Pennies from 1787 were made from copper or, beginning in 1856, an alloy of copper with nickel or zinc. Fresh from the mint, the coins were red, though they would later turn reddish brown or brown. From 1859 to 1909 pennies featured the head of an American Indian.
5. *Annie Fellows Johnston:* Johnston (1863–1931) was a children's author, best known for the Little Colonel books, a series of thirteen novels dating from 1896. The sentimental, nostalgic novels dealt with the aristocracy of Old Kentucky.
6. *"Little Women":* Louisa May Alcott's successful novel (1868–69) depicting family life in nineteenth-century New England.
7. *League of Nations:* The League of Nations was formed after World War I to promote world peace and diplomacy.
8. *amuse people or feed 'em or shock 'em:* from the third act of Irish dramatist Oscar Wilde's 1893 play *A Woman of No Importance.* Lord Illingworth: "To get into the best society, nowadays, one has to either feed people, amuse people, or shock people—that is all."
9. *Marie Antoinette:* Marie Antoinette (1755–93), Queen of France, wife of Louis XVI.

The Offshore Pirate

Fitzgerald began writing "The Offshore Pirate," originally entitled "The Proud Piracy," in late January 1920, during which time he lived in a New Orleans boardinghouse and made frequent trips to Montgomery, Alabama, finally convincing Zelda to resume their engagement. When he returned to New York he continued work on the story while awaiting publication of his first novel, *This Side of Paradise.* He mailed a version of the piece to Ober in late January, describing it as "a very odd story" and suggesting that Ober cut the ending if he thought it lacked "pep." Ober, likely in consultation with *Post* editor George Horace Lorimer, asked Fitzgerald to change the ending, which he did, sending the revised story back to Ober with the comment that "the required Jazz ending" contained "one of the best lines I've ever written." The *Post* bought the new story for $500 and published it in the May 29, 1920, issue, less than two months after Scott and Zelda were married in the rectory of St. Patrick's Cathedral in New York and began their honeymoon at the Biltmore

Hotel. In an odd twist, the *Post* had cut Fitzgerald's "Jazz ending" in the magazine version, perhaps because they thought that it might be confusing to their readers, and substituted what was, in effect, a third one. But whatever its ending, "The Offshore Pirate" is one of Fitzgerald's most beautifully dreamy and delightful stories; and Ardita Farnam is perhaps his most exemplary flapper. In her exchanges with the pirate, she spells out the details of the flapper creed based on faith in herself, freedom from family and social expectations, and courage: "courage as a rule of life," she says, and "[a] sort of insistence on the value of life and the worth of transient things"—a creed that could have been spelled out in words and actions close to Ardita's (as it likely was in those months of the story's composition) by his fiancée Zelda, the living embodiment of the Fitzgerald flapper. Fitzgerald included "The Offshore Pirate" as the first story in *Flappers and Philosophers* with its "Jazz ending" restored, and this is the version reprinted here.

1. *The Revolt of the Angels, by Anatole France:* Jacques-Anatole-François Thibault (1844–1924), winner of the Nobel Prize for Literature in 1921 and better known under the pseudonym Anatole France, was a witty French critic, historian, novelist, and poet. *The Revolt of the Angels* (1914) is a satire on Christianity. A skeptic like Voltaire, France mocked both church and state, attacking ignorance and superstition.
2. *statue of France Aroused:* monument to French heroism in World War I erected on Marne battlefield by American sculptor Frederick MacMonnies.
3. *"Narcissus ahoy!":* In Greek mythology Narcissus, son of the river god Cephissus, rejected the advances of the nymph Echo, who then pined away until nothing was left but her voice. As punishment Narcissus was compelled to fall in love with his own image, and he too pined away until he was transformed into the flower narcissus.
4. *Stonewall Jackson:* Thomas Jonathan Jackson (1826–63) was a Confederate general and Civil War hero regarded as a great tactical genius. Richard Taylor in *Destruction and Reconstruction: Personal Experiences of the Late War* (1879) noted that Jackson liked to suck on lemons. Historian James I. Robertson says that this is a myth and that Jackson just ate whatever fruit was available.
5. *Sing Sing:* New York state penitentiary at Ossining, New York.
6. *Winter Garden and the Midnight Frolic:* The Winter Garden at Broadway and 50th Street was one of the Great White Broadway Theaters. The *Midnight Frolic* shows were performed on the roof garden of the New Amsterdam Theater, 214 West 42nd Street. Florenz Ziegfeld staged the *Ziegfeld Follies* at New Amsterdam (1913–27), and showgirls from the *Follies* performed in the *Midnight Frolic* shows, which started at midnight and featured dance

music between acts. The *Frolic* shows depended on drink sales after the performances. After Prohibition the *Frolic* shows became the *Nine O'Clock Revue,* shows that were sustained instead by admission charges.

7. *Orpheum circuit:* a chain of theaters making up a major vaudeville circuit in the Midwest and on the West Coast. Vaudeville was family entertainment in contrast to burlesque, which was characterized by bawdy style. Entertainers sought jobs on the Orpheum circuit, where they were assured of a long run going from theater to theater.
8. *Plattsburg:* World War I training center in Plattsburg, New York.
9. *Booker T. Washington:* Booker T. Washington (1856–1915), the founder of Tuskegee Institute in 1881, was a black leader and educator. His autobiography is entitled *Up from Slavery* (1901).
10. *Callao:* port in Peru near Lima.
11. *rajah:* prince from India.
12. *Catharine of Russia:* Catherine the Great (1729–96) was born Sophie Augusta Fredericka. Empress of Russia (1762–96), she was regarded as an enlightened despot.
13. *Biddeford Pool to St. Augustine:* popular East Coast resorts. Biddeford Pool was in Maine, St. Augustine in Florida.
14. *Pollyanna:* from the novel *Pollyanna* (1913) by Eleanor H. Porter. The main character, Pollyanna, is a child who always looks for something to be glad about despite troubles. The name has come to refer to foolish cheerfulness.
15. *"Oh, blessed are the simple rich, for they inherit the earth!":* A reference to the Beatitudes, Matthew 5:1–2; Luke 6:20–26. From Matthew: "Blessed are the poor in spirit: for theirs is the kingdom of heaven." From Luke: "Blessed be ye poor: for yours is the kingdom of heaven."

May Day

"May Day" was composed in March 1920 on the threshold of "The happiest year since I was 18," as Fitzgerald put it in his *Ledger.* His first novel, *This Side of Paradise,* was to be published on March 26, and Zelda Sayre would become his bride on April 3. But this long, intricately woven story that Fitzgerald thought of as a novelette originated in the dark spring of 1919, when everything he wrote was rejected, his job writing copy for an advertising agency was disheartening, and his only escape was to throw himself into drunken parties with former college friends and just-met acquaintances who were, like him, living and wandering aimlessly in New York, their prewar idealism quickly fading to disenchantment. As the now-famous May Day riots of 1919, described vividly in the story, were taking place in New York and all over the country, Fitzgerald scarcely seemed to have taken notice of things beyond his own personal tribulations. Less than a year later, however, he brought his recollections of the spring and early summer of 1919—of the May Day riots, of his drunken escapades, and of his personal despair—together in the story of his partially autobiographical persona, Gordon Sterrett, in "May Day." In the table of contents of *Tales of the Jazz Age,* he describes the three central episodes of the story, which appeared in the July 1920 issue of *The Smart Set,* as having taken place "in the spring of the previous year." The events were "unrelated, except by the general hysteria of that spring which inaugurated the Age of Jazz," but he wove them together into "a pattern which would give the effect of those months in New York as they appeared to at least one member of what was then the younger generation." When Fitzgerald collected "May Day" in *Tales of the Jazz Age* he included it, for no obvious reason other than its general sense of finality, in the section entitled "My Last Flappers," and he changed the ending of the *Smart Set* version to the much less ambiguous one that we have in the *Tales of the Jazz Age* version reprinted here.

1. *Biltmore Hotel:* large, elegant hotel at Madison and 43rd Street in New York City. It was gutted and rebuilt as the Bank of America Building.
2. *Delmonico's:* elegant restaurant at Fifth Avenue and 44th Street. It opened at that location in 1898 and closed in 1923.
3. *Welsh Margotson collars . . . the "Covington":* Welch Margetson was a London haberdashery. The "Covington" was a detachable shirt collar.
4. *J. P. Morgan:* J. P. Morgan (1837–1913) was an American banker, influential in the financing and management of most of the U.S. railroads in the late nineteenth century. With Andrew Carnegie he organized and financed the United States Steel Corporation.
5. *John D. Rockerfeller:* John D. Rockefeller (1839–1937) was an American oil financier. He and his brother William formed the Standard Oil Company. He was one of the richest men in the world, with a fortune estimated at a billion dollars.
6. *Bolsheviki:* the most radical of the Russian Marxist groups led by Nikolai Lenin. The Bolsheviks advocated war against the bourgeoisie and dictatorship of the proletariat. After the Revolution in 1917, the party was referred to as the Communist Party.
7. *Shell hole:* slang for coward.
8. *Key:* In *Tales of the Jazz Age* Rose is the speaker. Since this response is to Rose's earlier remark, Fitzgerald likely intended the speaker here to be Key.
9. inconnu: unknown person, stranger.
10. *Boche-lovers:* Boche is a slang term for German.
11. *Childs':* Childs' Quick Lunch restaurants introduced the self-service cafeteria concept in 1889 with a chain of restaurants catering to downtown businesses.

12. *Columbus Circle:* Intersection of Broadway, Eighth Avenue, and 59th Street at the southwest corner of Central Park. A statue of Christopher Columbus was erected in the center of the circle in 1892.
13. *Maxfield Parrish moonlight:* Parrish (1870–1966) was a popular American painter and illustrator. He illustrated books and magazines, and his prints and calendars gave him wide exposure to the public. He used pure, transparent, thin oil glazes in combination with thin layers of varnish, giving his colors a great luminosity. His brilliant, cobalt-blue skies were known as "Maxfield Parrish blue."
14. *Commodore:* The Commodore Hotel was on the northwest corner of 42nd Street and Lexington. It was gutted and rebuilt as the New York Grand Hyatt.
15. *It... Hudson:* This sentence in *Tales of the Jazz Age* reads, "It must have been thirty seconds after he perceived the sunbeam with the dust on it and the rip on the large leather chair that he had the sense of life close beside him, and it was another thirty seconds after that before that he realized that he was irrevocably married to Jewel Hudson."

THE JELLY-BEAN

Though Fitzgerald records in his *Ledger* the composition date of "The Jelly-Bean" as May 1920, he likely began writing it in late January or February while he was awaiting the publication of *This Side of Paradise.* He wrote Ober that he was sending along a story that was the second in a series of "Jellybean stories (small southern town stuff) of which The Ice Palace was the first." The *Post* rejected the story, as did several other magazines, but after the publication of *This Side of Paradise* in March, Fitzgerald revised and returned the story to Ober in June with the setting changed from Tarleton, Georgia, to "a little city... in southern Mississippi," so that it would not be considered "a series with The Ice Palace." *Metropolitan* bought "The Jelly-Bean" for $900 in June 1920 and published it in the October issue. Fitzgerald included it as the lead story in his second story collection, *Tales of the Jazz Age,* changing its setting back to Tarleton and including it in the category of "My Last Flappers." Nancy Lamar, the Southern belle–flapper in "The Jelly-Bean," is undeniably in the line of descent of Sally Carrol Happer in "The Ice Palace" (years later Fitzgerald would describe "The Jelly-Bean" as "the first story to really recreate the modern southern belle"); but Nancy's extraordinary impulsiveness points to a self-destructive streak just below the surface of the free-spirited, fun-loving Fitzgerald heroine, a quality that had not been evident before in his earlier flappers or belles. *Metropolitan* commented in a headnote to the story that Fitzgerald was known for writing about "the young American flapper"; but as it also pointed out, "Here is a new story which shows another side of Fitzgerald's realistic gift."

1. *gob:* slang for sailor in the U.S. Navy.
2. *"Back Home in Tennessee":* "Just Try to Picture Me (Back Down Home in Tennessee)," 1915 song with lyrics by William Jerome and music by Walter Donaldson.
3. *Sally Carrol Hopper:* In "The Ice Palace" her name was "Happer."
4. *Liberty bonds:* bonds issued by the United States to pay for World War I.
5. *Dresden figures:* The ceramic industry of Dresden, Germany, was known for elegant, hand-painted porcelain. Real lace was dipped in liquid porcelain and then applied to ceramic figurines. Dresden figures were thus delicate and fragile.
6. *dope:* Coca-Cola.
7. *Lady Diana Manners:* Diana Cooper (1892–1986), British actress and socialite known for unconventional behavior.
8. *"Slow Train thru Arkansas":* Thomas William Jackson's 1903 book *On a Slow Train Through Arkansas* convinced many readers that people in Arkansas didn't wear shoes. The book cover depicts a train being held up by cattle on the tracks.
9. *"Lucille": Lucille, or, A Story of the Heart: A Pathetic Domestic Drama in Three Acts,* 1836 play by William B. Bernard (1807–75).
10. *"The Eyes of the World," by Harold Bell Wright:* Harold Bell Wright (1872–1944). During the first quarter of the twentieth century his novels outsold every other American writer. *The Eyes of the World,* published in 1914, is critical of the realism and naturalism in literature and art during this time. Dale B. J. Randall in "The 'Seer' and 'Seen' Themes in Gatsby and Some of Their Parallels in Eliot and Wright," published in *Twentieth Century Literature,* 10 (1964), 61, notes similarities between *The Eyes of the World* and *The Great Gatsby.* Both books deal with "the relationship between falseness and fame." Randall also notes that the dust cover of *The Eyes of the World* may have inspired the billboard of Dr. T. J. Eckleburg looking over the wasteland of ashes.

The Diamond as Big as the Ritz

In the summer of 1915 Fitzgerald paid a visit to the Montana ranch of his Princeton classmate and lifelong friend Charles W. (Sap) Donahoe, and this visit inspired the setting for what would become his most extravagant fantasy, "The Diamond as Big as the Ritz." The story provides a powerful foreshadowing of themes that Fitzgerald would develop more fully in *The Great Gatsby,* themes related to the emptiness of the American Dream and the carelessness and immorality of the very rich, who, like the Washingtons, care only about preserving the personal wealth that their diamond mountain represents. Fitzgerald began "The Diamond as Big as the Ritz" (originally entitled "The

Diamond in the Sky") in the fall of 1921 at White Bear Lake, Minnesota, and mailed the twenty-thousand-word manuscript to Ober on October 16, ten days before the birth of the Fitzgeralds' daughter, Scottie, calling it "a wild sort of extravaganza partly on the order of The Off-shore Pirate + partly like The Russet Witch." Though Fitzgerald had hopes that the conservative *Saturday Evening Post* would buy the story, he was not surprised when they declined to publish his scathing indictment of the American middle-class obsession with wealth. When *McCall's* and *Harper's Bazaar* also declined the story, Fitzgerald trimmed it to fifteen thousand words; and Ober eventually sold it for $300 to *The Smart Set,* which published it in their June 1922 issue. Fitzgerald selected "The Diamond as Big as the Ritz" for inclusion in the "Fantasy" section of *Tales of the Jazz Age,* maintaining in the table of contents that he had written it "utterly for my own amusement." Earlier he had lamented to Ober the fact that "a genuinely imaginative thing like The Diamond in the Sky brings not a thing," while "a cheap story like The Popular Girl written in one week while the baby was being born brings $1500."

1. *St. Midas' School:* fictional school, the naming of which references the legend of King Midas, who turned everything he touched to gold.
2. *Ritz-Carlton Hotel:* luxurious hotel at Madison and 46th Street in New York City.
3. *duvetyn:* good-quality wool with a smooth, plush appearance like velvet.
4. *Tartar Khan:* The Mongolian Tatar tribe (often misspelled as Tartar) under Genghis Khan overran Asia and Russia during the thirteenth century.
5. *Crœsus:* Greek king of Lydia (560–546 B.C.) known for his wealth.
6. *acciaccare:* an embellishing musical note.
7. *Titania:* queen of the fairies in Shakespeare's *A Midsummer Night's Dream.*
8. *Gargantua:* fictional giant in stories by the French writer François Rabelais (1494–1553). Gargantua was voracious and vulgar but intelligent and educated in humanist ideas of the Renaissance.
9. *George Washington:* George Washington (1732–99), first president of the United States. Washington had no children.
10. *Lord Baltimore:* Lord George Calvert Baltimore (circa 1580–1632), English statesman. He was refused permission to settle in Virginia. His son Cecil founded the colony of Maryland on land granted to him after his father's death.
11. *El Dorado:* mythical kingdom in South America rich with gold.
12. *General Forrest:* Nathan Bedford Forrest (1821–77), Confederate cavalry leader. He is believed to be one of the founders of the Ku Klux Klan.
13. *first Babylonian Empire:* circa 1850–1600 B.C.
14. *to peach on you:* to betray.

15. Pro deo et patria et St. Mida: Latin for "For God and country and St. Midas."
16. *canteen expert:* The Red Cross, YMCA, and other charities set up hospitality centers for soldiers. Young women hosted the coffee and hot chocolate bars and entertained the soldiers.
17. *Empress Eugénie:* Eugénie Marie de Montigo (1826–1920), empress of France as wife of Napoleon III. Noted for extravagance, she lived in exile after 1870.
18. *Nemesis:* Greek goddess that dealt out divine justice and avenged wrongdoing.
19. *Prometheus Enriched:* reference to Aeschylus' drama *Prometheus Bound* and Percy Bysshe Shelley's poem "Prometheus Unbound." (*See note 30 to "Head and Shoulders."*)
20. *God was made in man's image:* Genesis 1:27: "So God created man in his own image, in the image of God created he him; male and female created he them."
21. *cut me off with a hot coal:* Rather than waiting for blisters to heal, a hot coal might be applied to them, popping the blister and cauterizing the wound. Scar tissue formed.

Winter Dreams

In his scrapbook beneath a quarter-page photograph of his first serious love, Ginevra King, and an announcement of her coming wedding in September 1919, Fitzgerald penned this handwritten line: "THE END OF A ONCE POIGNANT STORY." The love story of Fitzgerald's relationship with Ginevra King, which began during the Christmas holidays of 1914 and ended when she threw him over "with the most supreme boredom and indifference," is at the heart of "Winter Dreams," the most important of the stories that anticipate the subjects and themes of *The Great Gatsby.* The writing of "Winter Dreams" was begun while the Fitzgeralds lived with their ten-month-old daughter, Scottie, at the White Bear Yacht Club outside St. Paul, Minnesota, during late August 1922; he finished it in mid-September in St. Paul's Commodore Hotel, shortly before the Fitzgeralds returned to New York for the publication of *Tales of the Jazz Age.* In the version of "Winter Dreams" bought by *Metropolitan* for $900 and then published in the December 1922 issue (the version reprinted in this volume), Fitzgerald's full-paragraph description of Judy Jones's house at the beginning of section three is used with only slight alteration to describe Daisy Fay's house in chapter eight of *The Great Gatsby.* In the version of "Winter Dreams" that Fitzgerald revised for inclusion in his third story collection, *All the Sad Young Men* (1926), he removed virtually the entire paragraph of description of the house. This is but one of many substantive changes Fitzgerald would make when he revised the story; but this one is particularly interesting since it suggests that Fitzgerald did not wish to draw attention to the fact that he had taken descriptions from his "popular" fiction and put them in *The Great Gatsby,* which had appeared less than a year before *All the Sad Young Men.* The most important connections between "Winter Dreams" and *The Great Gatsby,* of course, lie in the parallels between Dexter Green and Jay Gatsby, between Judy Jones and Daisy Fay, and between the relationships in two of Fitzgerald's most beautiful love stories.

1. *bloomers:* full, loose trousers gathered at the knee.
2. *knickerbockers:* pants that rolled up just below the knee. The style came from Dutch settlers in New York in the 1600s.
3. *"The Pink Lady" and "The Chocolate Soldier" and "Mlle. Modiste":* Broadway musicals.
4. *coupé:* two-door automobile.
5. *the war came to America:* Congress voted to enter World War I on April 6, 1917. The war ended with the armistice on November 11, 1918. The battles were all fought in Europe.

ABSOLUTION

In his *Ledger,* Fitzgerald recounted an episode in his life when, at the age of eleven, he lied in confession by saying to a priest, "Oh, no, I never tell a lie." This event is the origin of his brilliant story "Absolution," which, like "The Ordeal" and then "Benediction," centers on a moral dilemma associated with a sacred rite in the Roman Catholic Church. In April 1924, just before leaving Great Neck, New York, to live on the French Riviera, where Fitzgerald would complete *The Great Gatsby,* he wrote about "Absolution" and his novel-in-progress to Maxwell Perkins: "Much of what I wrote last summer was good but it was so interrupted that it was ragged & in approaching it from a new angle, I've discarded a lot of it—in one case 18,000 words (part of which will appear in the Mercury as a short story)." Then in late June, after writing the draft of the novel that would be published in April 1925, he wrote Perkins that "Absolution" was to have been "the prologue of the novel." Years later Fitzgerald would write in a letter that the story "was intended to be a picture of [Gatsby's] early life." Understandably Fitzgerald's comments have prompted speculation about the circumstance of the story's composition and its relationship to *The Great Gatsby.* "Absolution" may indeed have been a prologue to a very early draft of the novel that Fitzgerald began while he and Zelda lived in Great Neck between mid-October 1922 and April 1924. This draft of the novel, however, does not survive. The manuscript that Fitzgerald wrote on the Riviera during the summer and fall of 1924, in essence the version of *The Great Gatsby* that was finally published, does not, of course, contain "Absolution" as a prologue. After its publication in the June issue of *American Mercury*, Fitzgerald selected "Absolution" for inclusion in his beautifully haunting 1926 collection *All the Sad Young Men*, which also contained his Gatsby-related "The Rich Boy," "Winter Dreams," and " 'The Sensible Thing,' " as well as what was perhaps truly his last flapper story, "Rags Martin-Jones and the Pr-nce of W-les."

1. *the valley of the Red River:* the Red River Valley in northwestern Minnesota has broad, flat prairies.
2. *"Blatchford Sarnemington, Blatchford Sarnemington!":* perhaps a reference to Samuel Blatchford (1820–93), who was a justice of the U.S. Supreme Court (1882–93).
3. *second wave of German and Irish stock:* German immigration to Minnesota peaked in the 1860s and '70s. Germans left because of overcrowded cities, lack of jobs, and inheritance laws leaving land only to the eldest son. The Minnesota Territory and Northern Pacific Railway advertised in Germany for immigrants. In 1878 there was a second wave of Irish immigrants escaping famine. Swedes left Sweden because of religious persecution, the lack of land, and mandatory military service, and were attracted to Minnesota because of the farmland and jobs available in the timber industry and iron mining. Railroad transportation sped settlement of the territory. The immigrants took advantage of the Homestead Act to become landowners.
4. *James J. Hill:* James J. Hill (1838–1916), wealthy railroad magnate of the Gilded Age. After acquiring railroad properties, he formed the Great Northern Railway Company in 1889. He and J. P. Morgan won a fight with Edward Harriman and Jacob Schiff for control of the Northern Pacific. Known as "the Empire Builder," he started with nothing but a vision of the future.
5. *Alger books:* Horatio Alger, Jr. (1832–99), popular American writer of boys' adventures. He wrote 118 novels in book form, another 280 in magazines, and more than 500 short stories. Most of his stories had a "rags to riches" theme, with young protagonists who found success through pluck and luck.
6. *collection of cigar-bands:* Collecting cigar bands and labels was a popular hobby in the first decades of the twentieth century. The chromolithographed labels produced from 1860 to 1920 were beautiful works of art.
7. reform *school:* perhaps the Minnesota State Training School in Red Wing.
8. "Domini, non sum dignus . . . anima mea": part of the Latin Mass. Translation: "Lord, I am not worthy that Thou shouldst enter under my roof, but only say the word, and my soul shall be healed."

9. "Corpus Domini... æternam": "May the Body of our Lord Jesus Christ keep my soul unto life everlasting."
10. "Sagitta Volante in Dei": Psalm 91:5, "Thou shalt not be afraid for the terror by night; nor for the arrow that flieth by day."
11. *things go glimmering: Childe Harold's Pilgrimage,* canto 2, stanza 2, by Lord Byron: "Ancient of days! august Athena! where, / Where are thy men of might? thy grand in soul? / Gone—glimmering through the dream of things that were."
12. *pennon:* flag, ensign of a knight.
13. *German cuirassiers at Sedan:* The Battle of Sedan on September 1, 1870, was the decisive battle of the Franco-Prussian War. Napeoleon surrendered. Cuirassiers are mounted soldiers wearing body armor.

Selected Bibliography

Allen, Joan M. *Candles and Carnival Lights: The Catholic Sensibility of F. Scott Fitzgerald.* New York: New York University Press, 1978.

Bruccoli, Matthew J. *F. Scott Fitzgerald: A Descriptive Bibliography.* Revised edition. Pittsburgh: University of Pittsburgh Press, 1987.

———. *Some Sort of Epic Grandeur: The Life of F. Scott Fitzgerald.* New York: Harcourt Brace Jovanovich, 1981.

———, ed., with the assistance of Jennifer McCabe Atkinson. *As Ever, Scott Fitz—: Letters Between F. Scott Fitzgerald and His Literary Agent, Harold Ober, 1919–1940.* Philadelphia: Lippincott, 1972.

——— and Jackson R. Bryer, eds. *F. Scott Fitzgerald in His Own Time: A Miscellany.* Kent, OH: Kent State University Press, 1971.

——— and Margaret M. Duggan, eds., with the assistance of Susan Walker. *Correspondence of F. Scott Fitzgerald.* New York: Random House, 1980.

———, Scottie Fitzgerald Smith, and Joan P. Kerr, eds. *The Romantic Egoists: A Pictorial Autobiography from the Scrapbooks and Albums of Scott and Zelda Fitzgerald.* New York: Charles Scribner's Sons, 1974.

Bryer, Jackson R. *The Critical Reputation of F. Scott Fitzgerald: A Bibliographical Study.* Hamden, CT: Archon, 1967.

———. *F. Scott Fitzgerald: The Critical Reception.* New York: Burt Franklin, 1978.

———, ed. *New Essays on F. Scott Fitzgerald's Neglected Stories.* Columbia: University of Missouri Press, 1996.

———, ed. *The Short Stories of F. Scott Fitzgerald: New Approaches to Criticism.* Madison: University of Wisconsin Press, 1982.

———, Alan Margolies, and Ruth Prigozy, eds. *F. Scott Fitzgerald: New Perspectives.* Athens: University of Georgia Press, 2000.

Fitzgerald, F. Scott. *F. Scott Fitzgerald's Ledger: A Facsimile.* Washington, D.C.: NCR/Microcard Editions, 1972.

———. *All the Sad Young Men.* New York: Charles Scribner's Sons, 1926.

———. *The Crack-Up.* Ed. Edmund Wilson. New York: New Directions, 1945.

———. *Flappers and Philosophers.* New York: Charles Scribner's Sons, 1920.

———. *The Great Gatsby.* New York: Charles Scribner's Sons, 1925.

———. *Tales of the Jazz Age.* New York: Charles Scribner's Sons, 1922.

———. *This Side of Paradise.* New York: Charles Scribner's Sons, 1920.

Fryer, Sarah Beebe. *Fitzgerald's New Women: Harbingers of Change.* Ann Arbor, MI: UMI Research Press, 1988.

Higgins, John A. *F. Scott Fitzgerald: A Study of the Stories.* Jamaica, NY: St. John's University Press, 1971.

Kuehl, John. *F. Scott Fitzgerald: A Study of the Short Fiction.* Boston: Twayne, 1991.

———, ed. *The Apprentice Fiction of F. Scott Fitzgerald: 1909–1917.* New Brunswick, NJ: Rutgers University Press, 1965.

———, and Jackson R. Bryer, eds. *Dear Scott/Dear Max: The Fitzgerald-Perkins Correspondence.* New York: Charles Scribner's Sons, 1971.

Mangum, Bryant. *A Fortune Yet: Money in the Art of F. Scott Fitzgerald's Short Stories.* New York: Garland, 1991.

Milford, Nancy. *Zelda: A Biography.* New York: Harper and Row, 1970.

Mizener, Arthur. *The Far Side of Paradise: A Biography of F. Scott Fitzgerald.* Boston: Houghton Mifflin, 1951.

Petry, Alice Hall. *Fitzgerald's Craft of Short Fiction: The Collected Stories—1920–1935.* Ann Arbor: University of Michigan Press, 1989.

Piper, Henry Dan. *F. Scott Fitzgerald: A Critical Portrait.* New York: Holt, Rinehart and Winston, 1965.

Prigozy, Ruth, ed. *The Cambridge Companion to F. Scott Fitzgerald.* Cambridge: Cambridge University Press, 2002.

West, James L. W., III. *The Perfect Hour: The Romance of F. Scott Fitzgerald and Ginevra King, His First Love.* New York: Random House, 2005.

———, ed. *Flappers and Philosophers.* Cambridge: Cambridge University Press, 2000.

———, ed. *Tales of the Jazz Age.* Cambridge: Cambridge University Press, 2002.

Wilson, Edmund, ed. *The Crack-Up.* New York: New Directions, 1945.

Acknowledgments

I wish to thank Judy Sternlight at Random House, who first suggested this project to me and who has guided it from beginning to end. I am also grateful to Vincent La Scala for his extraordinary vigilance, to Gabrielle Bordwin for a cover design that catches so many of the words in these stories in a single image, and to Allison Merrill for her sharp reader's eye. My graduate and undergraduate Fitzgerald seminar members at Virginia Commonwealth University have provided useful suggestions during the preparation of this volume, and I am grateful to them. Thanks also to Matthew J. Bruccoli of the University of South Carolina for his ongoing support; to Rebecca M. Dale for her research assistance; and to James L. W. West III of Pennsylvania State University for his helpful advice to me on this project. Finally, thanks to Rebecca Angus Mangum for her patience and her support during the preparation of this volume.

Reading Group Guide

1. In *This Side of Paradise*, written before any of the stories in this volume, Amory Blaine describes the generation coming of age in the early 1920s as a generation "grown up to find all Gods dead, all wars fought, all faiths in man shaken." The main characters in these early Fitzgerald stories are part of this generation. To what degree are their actions and their codes of behavior—from the early flappers to the later sad young men—dictated by the moral complexity that comes with growing up in an age when the conventional wisdom of their elders no longer prevails? To what degree does gender play a role in their development of a system of values to live by?

2. The young women in these stories all seem to value individual freedom and independence, from the youngest like Bernice and Marjorie in "Bernice Bobs Her Hair" to the most seasoned like Ardita Farnam in "The Offshore Pirate." But as Zelda Fitzgerald remarked in "Eulogy on the Flapper," the flapper eventually "comes home, none the worse for wear, to marry, years later, and live happily ever afterwards." In light of the fact that most of the young women in these stories either wind up married or headed in the direction of matrimony, do their professed beliefs

in individual freedom seem illusionary or, at worst, disingenuous? For the young women in these stories, what is the relationship between individual liberty and economic freedom?

3. When Anton Laurier comes to the home of Horace and Marcia in "Head and Shoulders," Horace makes this remark to him: "About raps. Don't answer them! Let them alone—have a padded door." Do you think Fitzgerald wrote this clever line for Horace simply to end the story on a light note? Or could it have deeper implications that reflect Horace's true feelings about the course his life has taken after meeting Marcia? Could there be deeper biographical implications of this remark in light of the fact that Fitzgerald was about to embark on a life with Zelda? Discuss.

4. There is wide disagreement over the artistic value of "Benediction"—more so than any other story in this collection—particularly over whether it earns what some consider its "O. Henry" ending. There is also considerable debate among critics as to what Lois plans to do in the future. What do you think the torn up and discarded telegram left in the wastebasket suggests that Lois plans to do next? And do you think the story "earns" its ending? What is the connection between the story's conclusion and what happens to Lois during the Benediction ceremony earlier in the story?

5. Fitzgerald maintained that "the test of a first-rate intelligence is the ability to hold two opposed ideas in the mind at the same time, and still retain the ability to function." Throughout his fiction, he does seem able to appreciate the superficial attractiveness of the world he is also criticizing. "Bernice Bobs Her Hair" originated in a detailed letter Fitzgerald wrote to his sister advising her as to how she could make herself more acceptable to a society that is very much like the society Marjorie is grooming Bernice to enter. Does Fitzgerald appear to value, even to glorify, the exclusive society depicted in the story? If so, how do you reconcile this with Bernice's dramatic act at the conclusion of the narrative? What could account for what might

be called Fitzgerald's "double vision," not only in this story, but also in many of the stories in this collection? How are his themes strengthened or weakened by his double vision?

6. "The Diamond as Big as the Ritz" seems like an indictment of the capitalistic system that has produced individuals like Braddock Washington, who would rather blow up his diamond mountain and kill himself in the process than have the diamond market ruined through its discovery by the government. To what degree is the story, with its references to Hades and the twelve men of Fish, allegorical? How do you reconcile your ideas about its allegorical meaning with Fitzgerald's contention that he wrote the story "utterly for my own amusement"?

7. Dexter Green is one of Fitzgerald's saddest young men at the end of "Winter Dreams." The catalyst for his sadness is Devlin's revelation about what has become of Judy Jones. Is it finally Dexter's loss of Judy Jones herself that brings him to the edge of despair, causing him to contemplate "the gray beauty of steel that withstands all time," or is it some deeper thing she symbolizes? In either case, why do you think Dexter is devastated to learn what he learns from Devlin about Judy?

8. In the story "Absolution," Carl Miller's "two bonds with the colorful life were his faith in the Roman Catholic Church and his mystical worship of the Empire Builder, James J. Hill." Given what lies "[o]utside the window" in the last paragraph of the story, what is Rudolph's bond with the "colorful life" likely to be? Is it easy or difficult to imagine Rudolph, like Jay in *The Great Gatsby,* earning a fortune and wedding his visions to the "perishable breath" of a spoiled rich girl like Daisy Fay Buchanan?

About the Editor

Bryant Mangum is professor of English at Virginia Commonwealth University and is the author of *A Fortune Yet: Money in the Art of F. Scott Fitzgerald's Short Stories.* His essays have appeared in *The Cambridge Companion to F. Scott Fitzgerald*, the *Fitzgerald/Hemingway Annual*, *New Essays on F. Scott Fitzgerald's Neglected Stories*, and *American Literary Realism*, among others. He lives in Richmond, Virginia.